HOPE

Between

US

A. M. KUSI

Published by A. M. Kusi 2022

amkusinovels@gmail.com

Visit our website at www.amkusi.com

Editor: Kelly Golland of CREATING ink

Sensitivity Edit: Renita McKinney of A Book A Day

Proofreader: Judy's Proofreading

Cover Design: Regina Wamba of ReginaWamba.com

OTHER BOOKS BY A. M. KUSI

<u>A Fallen Star (eBook FREE on all retailers)</u>

(Book 1 in The Shattered Cove Series)

<u>Glass Secrets</u>

(Book 2 in The Shattered Cove Series)

<u>Defying Gravity</u>

(Book 3 in The Shattered Cove Series)

<u>The Lighthouse Inn</u>

(Book 4 in The Shattered Cove series)

<u>His True North</u>

(Book 5 in The Shattered Cove series)

<u>In The Grey</u>

(Book 6 in The Shattered Cove series)

<u>Brave Love</u>

(Book 7 in The Shattered Cove series)

<u>Beautiful Collision</u>

(A Shattered Cove Novel)

<u>One Holiday Kiss (eBook FREE on all retailers)</u>

(A Shattered Cove Short Story)

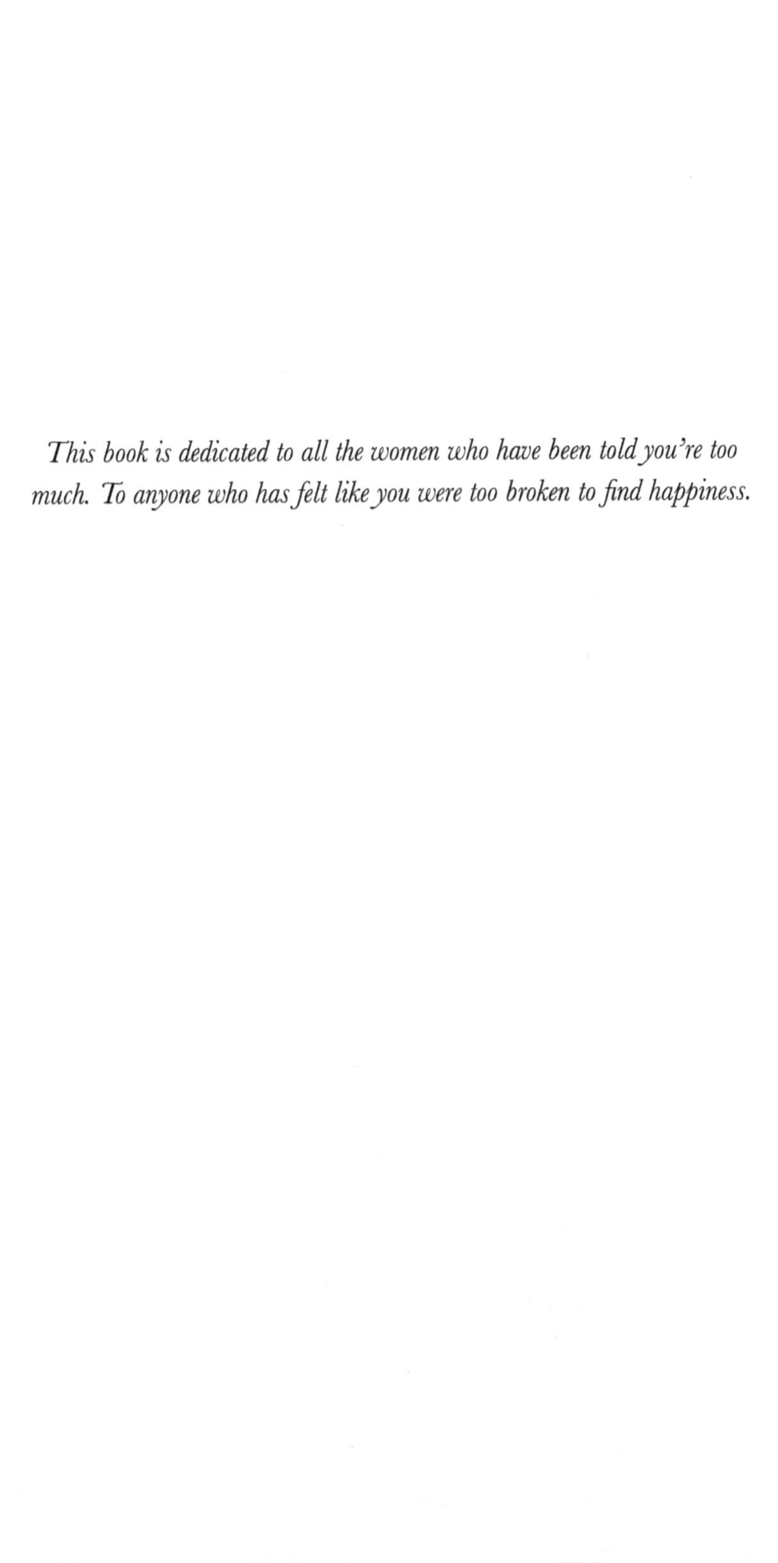

This book is dedicated to all the women who have been told you're too much. To anyone who has felt like you were too broken to find happiness.

"You aren't the things that haunt you. You aren't the pain you feel. You aren't defective or broken. You're human, you're doing the best you can, and you have so much more to offer the world than the demons you're fighting."
— Daniell Koepke

"Standing up for yourself doesn't make you argumentative. Sharing your feelings doesn't make you oversensitive. And saying no doesn't make you uncaring or selfish. If someone won't respect your feelings, needs and boundaries, the problem isn't you; it's them."
— Lori Deschene

GET A FREE SHORT NOVEL

Join our newsletter to get a FREE short novel that's not available on any retailer. Plus updates about new releases, giveaways, pre-orders, sneak peeks, and more.

Visit the website below to join now.

WWW.AMKUSI.COM/NEWSLETTER

TABLE OF CONTENTS

1

———

AARON

Aaron Ridley scrubbed a hand over his face as he sat back in the chair behind his gleaming cherry desk. The old photo of his brother, Emmanuel, with his arm around Aaron smiling at the camera caught his eye. Heaviness descended onto his shoulders as it did every year on the same day—the anniversary of Emmanuel's death.

Aaron closed his eyes, trying to conjure a memory of his brother laughing and smiling, but it was faded and warped. Much like a real photograph would be after overuse.

More than a decade had passed, but Aaron still felt the loss. *I wish I could have saved you, E.*

His gaze circled his office, skimming over the certificates of philanthropy and his two degrees attached to the rainbow accent wall opposite his desk. The hundreds of overlapping handprints brought a little relief to the tightness in his chest. They belonged to kids he'd been able to help. But for each one he'd taken into his center, there were ten more sleeping under a bridge or trading their bodies for food in their belly or poison in their veins.

Emmanuel's face popped into his mind again, cold and lifeless, no trace of the horror his brother had faced before he'd taken his last breath. Aaron let out a deep exhale and shook his head, as if he could rid himself of the tragic thoughts.

Knock. Knock.

Aaron cleared his throat and sat straighter in his chair. "Come in."

David shyly peeked his blond head around the door before he walked in, tucking his shaggy locks behind his ear. The kid reminded him so much of a young Emmanuel it was eerie.

"H-hey, Mr. Ridley. I, um, my therapist said you wanted to see me?"

Aaron motioned to the chair across from him. He forced a smile that he hoped was warm instead of mirroring the sadness that crept in, more so with the stark reminder of the boy who could be Emmanuel's twin sitting in front of him, except for his skin tone. "Yes, I just wanted to check in with you and see how you were doing. Ms. Silver said you'd had a rough session yesterday."

David took the seat, crossing his legs neatly and staring at his hands.

"You know anything you share with her is private, unless she fears for your safety." Aaron waited a beat. He'd learned a lot in his years working with homeless LGBTQ youth. Sometimes these teens needed your silence, and other times they needed a push. David, much like his mother, had seemed scared of his own shadow when he'd arrived in town. But during the last several months in regular visits at Hope Facility, he had come out of his shell.

"Yeah. I just . . ." David's shoulders slumped. "I wasn't going to hurt myself. I just had a bad week. Sometimes these thoughts come up in my head—but I'd never act on them."

David shook his head vehemently. "I'd never do that to my mom."

Aaron leaned in, resting his elbows on his desk. "It's important that you feel safe here. And it's my job and Ms. Silver's job to make sure you get the help you need to thrive. What is it that drives those thoughts? Did something happen this week in particular that made it extra hard?"

David gulped, his attention darting to the small hole in his jeans on his knee. He pressed his finger over it. "I just get tired of pretending sometimes."

"Pretending what?"

David bit his lip. "I think . . . I need . . . need your help." He let out a breath and looked up at Aaron. His blue eyes shone with unshed tears and determination.

This was the part Aaron lived for—when he was presented with a problem and had the power to fix it, helping make these youths' lives just a little easier.

"I'm listening."

David's voice broke. "Where I come from, people like the youth here . . . people like me, are punished."

Aaron's mind raced. He didn't have much on the kid in his file. Something told him that Smith wasn't David's legal last name. His mother, Brynn, had signed a permission slip, and he wasn't a live-in boarder like most of the others were. Legally, Aaron didn't require more details from them. But wanting it was another story. Their mutual friends didn't seem to know too much either, or what they did know they hadn't shared with him.

Aaron leaned in, listening intently to any morsels of information David was willing to share. Were he and his mother, Brynn, in trouble?

"When my mom brought me here, it was the first time I'd

felt like I could be me." David blinked, as if trying to clear the tears.

"That's what we're here for. You should be able to be you and not worry about your safety."

David nodded. "This place is so different. Even Shattered Cove is different from where I grew up."

"Where was that?" Aaron tried to sound as casual as possible.

David's back straightened, his eyes nervously darting around the room. "Uh, well, out west."

Aaron nodded. "How can I help you? Are you in danger?"

David shook his head, his blond hair falling across his face. "Not anymore."

Aaron's chest tightened. The thought of anyone trying to hurt David or Brynn made his guts twist. *What had happened to them?*

"Tell me what you need." Aaron focused on the fourteen-year-old in front of him.

David smoothed his hair back, his chin lifting and shoulders squaring. "I thought there was something wrong with me my whole life. After we got away—"

"What do you mean, got away?" Alerts blared in Aaron's mind at the word the young man used.

David opened, then closed his mouth before he looked down. His shoulders carried a tightness that wasn't there before. He eyed the door.

Aaron lifted his hand. "It's okay if you don't want to talk about it, but I'm here to help you any way I can."

David nodded and relaxed back into the seat. "Anyways, my mom brought me here because we both thought I was gay. I didn't know there were so many people like me."

"Sometimes it can take a while to figure out your sexuality. You're still young; it may take a little experimenting."

David shook his head. "This isn't about my sexuality. It's about my gender."

Aaron tipped his head to the side, waiting to hear how he could help. "Go on."

"After doing some research, and reading some of the books you have here in the library, and talking to some of the other kids, I realized . . . I'm transgender."

Aaron sat back in his chair, his face softening as he gave the young *girl* what he hoped was a comforting smile. "I'm sure that's a lot to grapple with. But I'm proud of you for telling me, and for taking a step towards living your truest life. Do you need some resources?"

David shook his head. "Not exactly. I wondered if you'd help me tell my mom?"

It wasn't uncommon for teens at the center to ask Aaron to mediate conversations with family, and he was happy to lend them that support.

"Sure, no problem. And I have a packet of information about what it means to be transgender—resources, the names of doctors . . ." Aaron stood and opened one of the file cabinets against the back wall, then found a packet of what he was looking for. He set the manila folder on the desk in front of David.

"What should we call you now? Or do you still want to go by David for the time being?"

She shifted in her chair, smiling. "I thought maybe Danielle."

Aaron nodded. "Alright, Danielle. You can have your mom stop by anytime and—"

A knock interrupted his speech.

Danielle jumped to her feet. "That should be her."

No time like the present, I guess. Aaron's gaze flicked to the door as Danielle opened it. Brynn, roughly the same height as

Danielle, glanced up at him with those brilliant green eyes that were always searching her surroundings.

Aaron reached out. "Come on in and have a seat." He motioned towards the chairs across from his desk.

Brynn crossed her arms over her body, bowing her head as she timidly walked in. She seemed to take as little space as possible in the room, tucking her body into the seat, just like every other time he'd seen her at some of their mutual friends' gatherings.

Aaron sat, hoping the position would make him seem a little less threatening than his six-foot-eight stature allowed.

"Is something wrong?" Brynn asked, looking to Danielle instead of him, her short brown hair falling over the side of her face. Brynn made no move to fix it, as if she was most comfortable hiding behind the curtain. She reached out a slender hand to Danielle's knee, the oversized threadbare T-shirt drooping low enough for Aaron to make out her delicate and pronounced collarbone. The woman was tiny with barely any meat on her bones. *Do they have enough to eat?*

"No, nothing is wrong," Aaron assured her.

Brynn's magnetic gaze flicked to his before dropping to his broad chest.

"I wanted to tell you something, and I wanted Mr. Ridley here while I did it," Danielle offered.

Brynn focused back on her child.

"Mom, I'm transgender." Danielle's eyes lit as she stared back at her mother.

Brynn's eyebrows drew together, her green orbs growing watery. "That means you . . . you're not a boy, right? It means you are really my daughter?"

Danielle nodded.

Brynn stayed silent for a moment, as if digesting the news.

When in similar situations, some parents had suspicions, but for others, they could be in total shock.

Brynn lifted her hand to Danielle's cheek, softly caressing her skin. "I love you."

Danielle jumped from her seat, then wrapped her arms around her mother, and Aaron breathed a sigh of relief.

"What does this mean for me? What do we need to do?" Brynn asked, pulling back, then turning to him.

He pointed to the manila folder. "In here are some pamphlets and resources. There are names of some doctors in Boston who specialize in this. They will be able to talk you through your options of possible puberty blockers, hormone therapy, and everything like that."

Brynn's eyes widened as her face fell. Her shoulders turned in again before she grew so still, he wasn't sure she was breathing. She looked terrified.

"What's wrong?" Aaron asked.

Danielle turned to her mother, then back to him. "We can't go to the doctor."

"Why?"

Brynn's attention focused on her daughter, brushing the blond hair from her face with a smile full of sorrow. "I don't have health insurance."

"Oh, there are a lot of programs available. Maybe the state—"

Brynn shook her head, tears swimming in her eyes.

"We can't have our names on record," Danielle offered. "They might find us."

"David," Brynn chastised.

Danielle faced her mother. "I trust Mr. Ridley, Mom. If anyone can help us, it's him."

So they were hiding from something—some*one*. Aaron's

heart thudded. He hated to think of someone hurting either of them.

"Are you in danger?" he asked Brynn.

Getting to her feet, she shook her head. "No, I, uh, I don't . . . We better go. Thank you for your time."

"Brynn."

She stopped, looking at him.

He stood, reaching out and holding his hands open at his sides. "I just want to help. Whatever you tell me doesn't leave this room. I promise."

"Just tell him, Mom," Danielle pressed.

Brynn searched his eyes, as if struggling with the decision. "We're safe now. But if our names were put into any legal database, we might not be. I'll figure something out."

She picked up the manila folder and wrapped her arm around Danielle. "Thank you for your time, Mr. Ridley."

Aaron's heart raced. *I must make her see reason.* His gaze flicked to Danielle—the teen who reminded him of Emmanuel now more than ever in his mannerisms and his expressions. His brother had tried to end his life before he came out as trans. And then once Emmanuel told their parents, his mental health spiraled from their reaction. *Because he didn't get the help he needed.* Aaron couldn't let Danielle become a statistic—not when he could help her.

"Queer youth who don't get the support and resources they need are at higher risk for homelessness, drug abuse—"

Brynn shook her head and tightened her grip around Danielle, ushering her out the door.

"And suicide," Aaron finished.

Brynn froze, her shoulders ratcheting up to her ears.

Aaron seized his opportunity and stepped forward. "The statistics for people in her situation are staggering. Trans women of color only have a life expectancy of thirty-five years."

Brynn gasped, letting go of Danielle to face him. Yes, Dani was white, which meant she had some privilege. But life was going to be harder for her regardless.

"Your child needs assistance. Let me help you find a way. I can protect you." *Let me save her.* This was why he'd started Hope Facility—so other kids didn't have to end up like his brother.

Brynn turned, her guarded gaze locked on him. "I appreciate everything you have done for my so—my daughter, Mr. Ridley. But I can't . . . It's just not possible."

"This is your daughter's future—her life!"

"You don't think I want what's best for my child?" Brynn snapped, her eyes shining with unshed tears.

"Of course you do. I just—"

"Just what?"

"I just don't want Danielle to get hurt," Aaron blurted.

Brynn turned to leave once more, and Emmanuel's face flashed in his mind. His bruised and broken body. The horror he could never remove from his mind's eye. Panic coursed through his body like a tidal wave—Danielle couldn't end up like that. *Do something!*

"Marry me."

The words fell from his mouth before his brain could catch up. Brynn gasped, turning to him, eyes wide.

Danielle's mouth dropped open.

He stepped out from behind his desk, his hands up, as if to explain his sudden onset of insanity. "Marry me, and I can get you on my insurance. You can change your name, and we can help change Danielle's name from David. She can go to the best doctors, and I'll take care of everything."

Brynn opened her mouth, as if she wanted to say something, but then closed it instead. Fear flashed in her wide eyes before they darted to the door, as if she needed an escape.

"I'm sorry. I know it sounds crazy. I just . . . I've seen what happens to kids like Danielle and I just—" He squeezed his nape, sweat beading on his forehead. "I can't let that happen to her—not when I have the ability to help her. I want to help." Aaron swallowed. "It wouldn't be real. Just for show, only so you can get Danielle the help she needs."

Brynn tugged Danielle into the safe confines of her side and shook her head. She opened the door, then turned back to him. "No."

The finality of her word sucked the remaining air from the room.

"I'll find another way." Brynn disappeared, closing the door behind her and her daughter.

Aaron paced the office, raking his hand through his hair. "What the fuck? Did I really just propose?"

What is wrong with me? I can't just propose to clients. He slumped into his seat and practically slammed his head against the desk. *I'm such an idiot. Did I really just ask Brynn to marry me? Did I just ruin the one place her daughter had to feel welcome and safe?*

"What have I done?"

The marriage wouldn't have even been real. So why was he so disappointed?

2

BRYNN

B rynn set the plate with a club sandwich in front of the older man at the counter. "Here you go."

He gave her a grateful smile. "Thank you, ma'am."

Brynn nodded and walked to the coffee machine behind her. Her feet ached, as they always did after a ten-hour shift at the High Tide diner. She picked up a cloth and wiped the drips from the blue Formica counter, then glanced at the clock on the wall. *Almost done.*

The door opened, letting a rush of cool fall air into the establishment. Several tall men with leather cuts walked in, and Brynn tensed as they took a booth in her side of the restaurant. She swallowed, lifting the coffee pot with one hand and tucking menus under her arm. Grabbing four mugs with the other hand, Brynn dangled them off her fingers, straightened her shoulders, then took a fortifying breath before she walked over and set the cups on the table between them. "Would you like some coffee?"

"Yes, please," the roughest-looking man with a scar down the side of his face answered.

She handed out the menus and poured them each a cup of java. "I'll give you a minute." She returned the pot to the coffee machine and went to the kitchen.

Betty-Lou, one of the owners of the diner, looked up from the pastry table in front of her and smiled. "I think I made one too many apple pies. You might need to take one home to David. Oops, I mean Danielle."

Brynn's mouth tilted up briefly in gratitude. Betty-Lou was one of two people she'd told this week. The woman was a saint who'd saved her when she and her child were on the verge of starving, so Brynn shouldn't have been surprised that she was so accepting about Danielle.

"She'll love it," Brynn answered.

Fred, Betty-Lou's husband, walked in from the doorway to the diner. "Hey, sweetie-pie." He smacked his lips on Betty-Lou's cheek.

She blushed and shooed him away. "You old flirt."

"That's why you married me. We both know it wasn't because of my good looks." He chuckled and turned to Brynn, giving her a playful wink. "I believe the boys out there are ready to order."

Brynn nervously looked to Betty-Lou. Betty-Lou's face softened, as if the woman could read Brynn's emotions. "Who is it?"

"The Pirates," Fred answered, pulling out an apron for himself.

Betty-Lou turned to Brynn. "The Pirates are a biker gang from the seacoast. They help women and children involved in domestic violence situations. You know those ones you see on the internet that surround kids or women on their way to court? Or leaving their abusive partner? That's what they do," Betty-Lou filled her in.

Those rough-looking men out there did that?

"That isn't all they do." Fred gave his wife a knowing look.

Betty-Lou straightened. "There's never been any proof they take it further."

"So they're . . ." Brynn wasn't sure she wanted to finish the sentence.

Betty-Lou smiled. "They're a little rough around the edges, but they're good men."

Brynn nodded, plucking her order pad from her apron as she turned and left the kitchen. She scanned the room, making sure no one else had slipped in while she was in the back. The old man at the counter was half finished with his sandwich, a newspaper in his hands. All that was left were the four men in black in the corner, their heads leaning in, as if they were discussing something private.

The hair on the back of her neck stood on end, her skin prickling, as if she was being watched. She searched the room again. No one was paying her any attention. Her gaze flicked to The Oyster Bookstore across the road. Danielle was there, no doubt poring over her books. *I wish she could go to school like her friend Aspen.* Education was important. And Brynn wanted more for her daughter than she'd ever had.

She squared her shoulders and walked over to the bikers. "Are you ready to order?"

"I'll take the biggest, greasiest burger you got with a side of fries," the one closest to her said, placing his menu on the table in front of her.

"Sounds good to me." The man with dirty-blond hair and piercing blue eyes next to him agreed, passing his menu down.

"Make that three," the gruff, bearded man in the corner said.

She scribbled on her pad, looking to the man with the scar. "Should I make it four?"

He shook his head. "Nah, I'll have the cobb salad with extra grilled chicken."

Her eyebrows rose. "Okay, it will be out shortly."

She reached for the stack of menus at the same time he did, their fingers brushing. Brynn flinched and tore her hands away.

Four sets of eyes locked on to her as heat crept up her neck.

"S-sorry." She scooped up the menus and darted to the kitchen.

Turning her back on the cooking area, she then braced her hand on the stainless-steel salad counter and forced deep breaths into her lungs.

A clanging sound made her jump.

"Sorry, just me being a klutz." Fred picked up the metal ladle he'd dropped and put it into the sink to be washed.

Brynn pressed a hand to her racing heart. She hated how her body overreacted to noises or touches. She was always on alert, her body searching for danger around every turn. *Because danger was there for so long.*

"Why don't you get your things? I can finish this order up. You've been here since five and your shift is just about over." Betty-Lou plucked the paper pad from her hands, tearing off the bikers' orders.

Brynn nodded and went to the back room. Trailing her hands over the row of grey metal lockers, she stopped at hers. After twisting the knob on the lock into the right combination, she opened it and exchanged her apron for a worn sweatshirt she'd found at the free clothing drive the local church put on. Brynn stretched her neck from side to side, letting go of a deep lungful of air. She'd managed to stay busy enough this week, forcing thoughts of a tall, dark-eyed man from her mind.

Marry me.

Was he absurd?

His facility had been a lifesaver for Danielle. In the last few days, Brynn had switched pronouns and started the process of trying to remember to call her child Danielle instead of David. Her daughter's bright smile flashed in her mind, as if she'd gotten her child back. *Had I been blind to her sadness before? Was I too busy?*

Working two jobs was arduous, but it kept a roof over their heads and food in their bellies. Danielle now needed a whole new wardrobe, and Brynn was barely making ends meet as it was.

Marry me. Aaron's words kept repeating in her mind. No, she would never be under a man's control again.

Betty-Lou walked into the small room, not much bigger than a closet. She straightened, her lips pursed.

"What is it?" Brynn asked, getting to her swollen sore feet.

"Someone was asking about you—a man."

The blood drained from Brynn's face as her heart raced. *Is it him?* "Is he still here?"

Betty-Lou nodded.

Brynn grabbed her purse, slinging it over her shoulder, and followed Betty-Lou to the door leading to the diner. She paused in front of it, standing on tiptoes to peek outside the tiny diamond-shaped window while placing her hand on the stainless-steel salad counter for balance.

"Left side by the window. He showed me a picture of a much younger and blonder you but asked for Miriam McKerman."

Lightning bolted through her body, terror seizing her chest. *He's here. He's found us.*

"It's okay. I told him I'd never seen you before. Told him I know everyone in this town and I'd never laid eyes on you," Betty-Lou assured her, pressing her hands to Brynn's shoulders.

She had to know.

Brynn sucked in a deep breath and peeked out the doorway. A man she didn't recognize sat with his back to her, peering out the window. His button-up shirt and khaki pants fit in with what most of the disciples wore from the cult. He had to be from the Livingston clan.

Brynn pulled back, pressing against the wall. "They've found me."

"Is that him?" Betty-Lou clarified.

Brynn shook her head. She'd never told Betty-Lou about her past, but the woman was observant.

"No, but he could work for him."

Betty-Lou nodded. "You stay here and I'll take care of it."

"I have to check on Dav—Danielle."

"Call Pippa. She has a secret room in the back of her bookstore. She can safely hide in there until we sort this out."

Brynn reached for her cell phone as Betty-Lou disappeared into the diner. It rang twice before the bookstore owner picked up.

"Hi, Pippa. Is Danielle there?"

"Yes, he—I mean *she's* helping me put away a new order that just came in. It's like a beaming light has been switched on behind her eyes, Brynn. She's effervescent. Thank you for trusting me and telling me about this important moment in your lives."

Relief flooded her veins, but she didn't have time to discuss this. "Can you take her to that secret room Mason built? And if anyone comes in asking for me, please don't tell them anything."

"What's going on? Are you okay?" Pippa's tone turned worried.

Brynn swallowed the panic stuck in her throat. "Just keep my daughter safe, please. I'll be there as soon as I can."

"Okay, done. Anything you need, let me know."

"Thank you." Brynn hung up as Betty-Lou came back in.

"The Pirates are going to escort the man out of town."

Brynn's eyes widened. "They are?"

Betty-Lou nodded. "I don't think he'll be coming back anytime soon when they're done with him."

"I . . . I need to leave." *Leave Shattered Cove. Run from New Hampshire all together.*

Betty-Lou grasped her hand and led her to the locker room once again. "I know from experience that, sometimes, it's better to take a stand. You must be careful, of course. Be smart about it. In Shattered Cove, you have friends and resources. If you leave, you'll be starting over again."

How did Betty-Lou know she was thinking of leaving town and not just the diner?

But if she did leave, Danielle would lose all her friends and the Hope Facility. Without that support system, she might crawl back into her shell and become depressed. What would become of them if they left? What kind of future would they have if they continued to run?

"But what if he finds us?"

"Sweetheart, you've got a whole town who'll band around you. A sheriff who takes violence against women and children more seriously than anyone I know, friends with their own special talents, and four new biker acquaintances who have just put the fear of God into that little snake that slithered in here."

Brynn nodded, her mind reeling. Betty-Lou was right. Brynn was done running. She wouldn't let Paul take anything else from her. And she would do whatever it took to keep Danielle safe.

But she couldn't do this alone. Danielle needed real help, and Brynn couldn't give that to her without health insurance and an official ID. If she used her own name, that would put them in more danger. Danielle needed a support system, people who understood what she was going through on a personal level that Dani could lean on. As hard as Brynn would try—and she'd do whatever it took—it just wouldn't be enough. *I need help.*

Aaron had offered her a solution. A crazy, ridiculous idea that, right now, was her best shot at keeping herself and Danielle protected. She'd trade her soul to the devil himself if it meant keeping her baby safe.

Hopefully, Brynn wasn't running from one nightmare into the reality of another.

3

───────────

BRYNN

Brynn zipped up the back of Danielle's pink dress. It was secondhand, but you'd never know looking at it. Danielle's eyes lit up, sparkling with happiness as she studied herself in the spotted old mirror. It wasn't the best, but it was all they had in the room they rented month to month above the garage of a kind older woman, Mrs. Giddeon, who mostly kept to herself.

Brynn held her breath as her daughter gazed at her own reflection. Mirrors had been tough, but Dani smiled, and Brynn sighed in relief. Today was a good day. The dress and makeup probably had something to do with it.

"You look beautiful." Brynn clipped a sparkly barrette on the side of Danielle's hair so that the grown-out bangs were out of her face.

Her daughter's grin grew. "I can't wait to show my friends my new dress."

A pang of pride flitted in Brynn's chest. Danielle's friends from the center and Aspen would be more than welcoming, but it was the rest of the world she was concerned about. How much would her daughter have to struggle out there? If someone used the wrong pronoun, would Dani slip back into her depression? Would someone want to hurt her?

Brynn's gaze darted to the scuffed flats by her mattress. There wasn't much room in the small space with two twin beds, a few pieces of old rickety furniture, and mini appliances. A tiny bathroom with a stand-up shower was the only addition to the modest space. It wasn't much, but it was the first thing she'd ever had to herself. A roof over her daughter's head, food in their bellies, and clothes on their bodies was something she was thankful for every day. She never took it for granted.

Brynn sat on the edge of the bed, her dark-blue floral summer dress rising just above her knee. She instinctively pulled it down.

"Are you going to tell Mr. Ridley tonight?" Dani asked.

Brynn slipped the grey sweater over her shoulders. "I'm going to talk to him. But, sweetheart, you do know it wouldn't be real, right?"

Danielle slipped her coat on and rolled her eyes. "Yes, Mom. You've told me like a hundred times."

"But you're comfortable with this? We could pack up and leave, find somewhere else—"

"No. Please, Mom? I don't want to move. I have friends here. Please don't make me go." Whatever happiness had lit her daughter's eyes moments ago now dimmed.

"Alright. I just want you to know that's why we're doing this. I don't want to make any more trouble for Mr. Ridley, and I'm not even sure if he was serious, but I'll talk to him."

"Yes!" Dani smiled.

Brynn slipped the silver flats onto her feet and stood. "Let's go. We don't want to miss the bus."

Nerves twisted her belly, skating up her spine, her hands trembling as she locked the small apartment behind her.

Crisp autumn air cut through her thin sweater, but it was all she had. This or the hoodie full of holes she usually wore, but that wouldn't be appropriate for the quinceañera the Hope Facility was putting on. She drew the front closed tighter and adjusted her purse across her body as they trudged down the driveway, then the quarter of a mile to the bus stop. She looked up at the sky, taking in a long pull of crisp air that smelled like dead leaves with the hint of woodsmoke from a neighbor's chimney. *Am I doing the right thing? Can I trust Aaron? Why would he help us?*

Brynn needed answers, and she intended to get them.

After the bus pulled up outside the Hope Facility, Brynn walked into the giant recreation room, usually reserved for sporting games and leisure activities for the kids. Gone was the lounge furniture—except the pool table in the back corner. Instead, dozens of circular tables decorated with white linen and red rose centerpieces surrounded a makeshift dance floor. Couples in suits and ballgowns moved together to the upbeat music, blasting through the speakers. Gold, black, and white balloons and streamers decorated the space, making it the most elaborate party Brynn had ever witnessed.

"There's Mr. Ridley," Danielle pointed out.

Brynn searched where her daughter had gestured, finding him talking to the drag queen Miss Marsha Divine. Aaron's bright, white teeth contrasted with his coppery brown skin. The top two buttons on his salmon-colored dress shirt were undone, giving a peek to the hollow below his throat. The grey suit fit his muscular frame like it was tailored to him. His head tipped back as he laughed at something Miss Divine said, the disco light reflection moving across his strong jaw and sharp lines of his face. The same unfamiliar feeling she got whenever she was around him swirled in Brynn's belly before moving south to her most secret places. *What is that?*

Jarred by the foreign sensation, she cast her gaze around the room, already filling with people for the quinceañera fundraiser. A rainbow of color all in one place. Every race and creed, gender and sexual orientation sharing food and drink, laughs and conversation. This place was the epitome of acceptance and love. There was no way she could take Danielle from here, from her new home. *I'll do whatever it takes to protect her.* Even if it meant marrying a stranger.

"Stay in this room, okay?" Brynn stipulated.

"I see Kate and Will. I'm gonna go say hi. I'll see you later." Dani left her, heading over to her friends by the drink table.

Brynn sucked in a big breath and let it out. It was now or never. She tugged her sweater tighter around herself and made her way to Aaron. His brown eyes caught on her as she moved closer, a cautious smile turning the edge of his pink- and brown-tinged lips up. He focused back on Miss Divine before patting her shoulder and meeting Brynn the rest of the way.

"Good evening. I wasn't sure you'd show up after . . ." He rubbed the back of his head.

Brynn's gaze dropped down to his broad chest, to his expensive-looking grey suit. "I-I wondered if we could talk?"

He turned his head and leaned closer, as if he couldn't hear her over the loud music. "I'm sorry, what?"

"Could we talk?" she repeated, her body uneasy being so close to a man. His clean scent drifted over her—lime and coconuts with a hint of vanilla.

He met her gaze, his eyebrows quirking up in surprise. "Sure. Uh, here? Or my office?"

This conversation needed to remain private. "Can we go to your office?"

He blinked, as if surprised, then nodded. Aaron held out his hand for her to lead the way. He stayed close behind but didn't touch her as they maneuvered through the room towards the hall. A few people said hello to him, and he offered them a friendly greeting with promises to catch up with them later.

The fact he had made her his priority in this moment brought a rush of emotion she hadn't expected.

She waited outside his office as he pulled out a key from his pocket.

He unlocked the door and waved towards the room. "After you."

She inhaled a shaky breath, adrenaline coursing through her veins. Her heart raced in her chest like a thousand galloping horses. She was alone with a man, vulnerable and scared to death.

Aaron left the door cracked open before he made his way to the seat behind his desk. She breathed a little easier with nothing between her and escape.

"How can I help you?" he asked, resting his elbows on his desk.

Brynn sat across from him in one of the empty chairs and squeezed her trembling hands together. "Were you serious? About your offer?"

"You mean to marry you?"

She nodded.

"I wouldn't have offered otherwise. I know you don't know me that well, Brynn, but I'm an honest man. What you see is what you get. It means I'm blunt and to the point. There's no sense in dancing around issues or sugarcoating things."

His confession scared her while another part of her found

it refreshing. How amazing to be absolutely honest with another person without games or masks?

"I'd like to understand why a man like you, Mr. Ridley, would tie up his whole life for a woman and child like us."

He sat back and released a breath. "You want to know what my ulterior motives are?"

"Yes."

He cleared his throat and tugged the pink shirt away from his neck. "I was a teenager when my younger sibling, Amber, came out and told me she was trans. Amber told me *he* was, in fact, Emmanuel."

Brynn's shoulders relaxed a fraction. *That makes sense—why this is a cause he's so passionate about—but it doesn't explain why he wants to help me.*

"My parents are from the South and are heavily involved in their church. They were not as accepting of Emmanuel as I was. He eventually got kicked out at seventeen. He ended up homeless, drug-addicted, and then he . . ." Aaron looked down at his desk, his voice filled with emotion. "He took his own life."

Brynn covered her mouth as tears blurred her vision. Her heart ached for what Aaron and his brother had gone through. How was it that this man and her shared something in common? She understood what it was like to lose a sibling to suicide. "I'm sorry."

Aaron's glassy eyes met hers, his expression soft. "So, you see, all this—" He waved to the office around him. "—is for my brother, Emmanuel Hope Ridley."

He wiped the emotion from his eyes.

Brynn sat in stunned silence. She'd never witnessed a man cry before. Where she came from, showing emotion of any kind was forbidden and even punished. "I'm sure he would be proud to know all you've done in his memory."

Pain reflected in his gaze, one Brynn knew all too well—regret, for not having done more to help the one you loved most.

"The reason I proposed marriage was because I promised my brother I would dedicate my life and do whatever it took to save kids like him."

"And that's the only reason?" Her belly twisted. She wanted to know, and she needed all the facts.

His eyebrows pulled together. "Yes."

She nodded. "If we do this, no one can know it isn't real for Dani's and my safety."

"Can you tell me more about who you're running from?"

She inhaled a shaky breath. He was risking a lot to help her and her child. Brynn owed him at least this.

"Everyone."

More lines appeared between his brows, but he didn't press for further information.

She looked down to her clasped hands in her lap. "The marriage, of course, wouldn't be real. It would never be . . . consummated."

"Brynn? Look at me." Aaron's voice was soft, but the command was clear.

She obeyed, locking eyes with him once more.

"You set the boundaries here, and I'll respect them. I won't ask you for anything you aren't willing to give freely. You're in control of this arrangement."

She blinked, unsure if she'd heard him right. Did men like this really exist? Was he being honest with her? Would it change after she said the vows?

Her eyes dropped to his unbuttoned collar. His umber throat bobbed as he swallowed. Aaron's large hands rested on the desk, palms down. She was going to have to let those hands touch her at some point—occasionally—just to make their union believable. Would he be gentle? Or rough? And what if this wasn't pretend? Would having sex with someone as attractive as Aaron feel different? *Would I enjoy it?*

She shook her head, ridding the ridiculous thoughts, then stood abruptly. "One year, and then we can separate. We'll say it just didn't work out."

Aaron nodded, his gaze a mix of emotions she couldn't read.

"And if you . . . need to . . . um, have female company . . . you can be discreet?"

Aaron frowned. "I won't be having any . . . company."

"Y-you're going to remain celibate?"

"Yes. I wouldn't disrespect you like that. Real or not, we'll be married."

"I . . . I don't know what to say to that."

"Do we have a deal?" He tipped his head to the side.

She drew in a deep breath and let it out before responding. "Yes. Thank you, Mr. Ridley."

"Please, call me Aaron."

"Right. When should we, uh, take the next steps?"

"Let me get some things in order, then I'll reach out."

"Okay. I better go." She turned and walked out of the office, her heart thundering in her ears.

Oh my God. I'm getting married.

Hopefully, her husband wouldn't find out.

4

AARON

Aaron opened the door for The Oyster Bookstore, breathing in the scent of paper and fresh greenery. *Mm.*

A few giggles drew his attention to the back. He walked through the rows and rows of books, past the plants and striking sculpture made entirely from folded book pages, towards the rainbow rug where story time was held every week.

Brynn's soft voice lifted over the children's laughter as she acted out the different voices while reading from a book. Three kids sitting on the floor around her feet lapped up the attention while two adults in the corner scrolled through their phones.

"And they all lived happily ever after. The end." Brynn closed the book and gave the children an actual smile. It was the first time he'd witnessed the full action on her face, and he almost stumbled back a step. She was gorgeous. She tried to hide it, wearing plain baggy clothes, as if trying to draw the least amount of attention to herself. Her shoulders perpetually hunched in like she was always trying to disappear, but that goddamned smile lit up the whole room.

"Can you read another one?" a young boy asked.

"Oh." Her gaze flicked over to Aaron before her eyes widened. She turned back to the boy. "Sorry, guys. My shift is over. I've got to get home. But we can read one next time you come in." She stood as the kids opened the book she just read and huddled around it.

"Can we talk for a few minutes?" Aaron asked.

She nodded and led him towards the side of the store. Aaron paused next to the new addition to the shop, and motioned towards the shelf. "Brynn?"

She turned around. "Yes?"

"How about in here?" He pulled the copy of Beauty and the Beast forward. The secret door behind the shelf opened with a click, so he pulled it wider and ushered her through.

"Troy's at the front desk, but I shouldn't be long," Brynn reminded him.

They walked into the space. Twinkling lights hung above by the punched tin ceiling. Every wall was also covered with built-in bookshelves, and one of those ladders that moved along them. Brynn walked past the hanging chairs and over to the window seat. Sunlight shone over her, casting her in a halo. She was beautiful.

He stepped forward as she nervously tucked her short brown hair behind her ear, her eyes darting between him and the door.

He dropped down to his knee and reached into his pocket for the box there.

Brynn's eyes widened as he opened the blue velvet box with the gold trident shining on it.

"What are you doing?" she asked, resting her hand over her heart. Was it beating as wild as his?

"Just because it isn't real, doesn't mean you don't deserve an authentic proposal and a ring." Aaron offered the jewelry to her.

Color rose to Brynn's cheeks as she looked to him and then to the ring and back again. "I-I don't know what to say."

"Do you like it?"

Her gaze zeroed in on the rose cut emerald ring set in a delicate gold band. "It's beautiful. Too beautiful. I can't accept this."

He slipped the ring from the box and held out his hand for hers. "Do you know why I chose an emerald?"

She shook her head.

His hand remained open, patiently waiting for hers as he explained. "According to legend, emerald was one of the stones given to King Solomon with the belief the stone held power to help him rule over all of creation. Other cultures believed using the green stone would help someone see their future, protect them from evil spirits, and more importantly, give the person wearing it the ability to reveal the truth or falseness of their lover's vows."

She inhaled a quick breath. Like everything else with this woman, even her gasps were muted.

He offered her what he hoped was his most charming smile. "I picked it out because it reminded me of your eyes."

She swallowed, emotion filling her gaze as she lifted a trembling hand to his. The moment her palm slid into his, energy buzzed, spreading down his arm like liquid fire.

Brynn flinched, her eyes growing wide, her attention darting back to him, as if she had felt it, too, and wanted an explanation.

He lifted his hand again, silently asking for her trust. She hesitated before her soft fingertips grazed his palm once more.

Aaron gently closed his long fingers around hers and slipped the ring onto her finger.

"Is it too loose?" he asked.

She pulled her hand away, and he immediately missed the connection. She twisted the ring around her finger and shook her head. "No, it's perfect. Thank you. I'll give it back to you after."

He stood back up and sat in the open space next to her on the window seat, leaning back against the wall and stretching his long legs out. "No. It's a gift for you to keep."

"I don't know how I'm going to repay you for this." Her voice grew quieter, shifting into a whisper.

"You don't owe me anything. Everything I give is free of strings. That's what a gift truly is. You can pay it forward to someone else in the future when they need help and when you have the means to do so."

"Wow! I'm speechless." She pressed her hand to her chest. "Thank you. Truly."

"Now that you've accepted my ring, I wondered if you had any idea of which venue to use for the wedding?"

She shifted in her seat, turning to him so that her face was lit in sunshine, making her eyes sparkle like the gem on her finger. "Couldn't we just go to city hall?"

He shook his head. "If you want people in our very gossipy small town to believe this is real, we'll need to make an event of it. You and Danielle will need dresses."

"I can't afford all this."

He held up his hand. "I'm going to pay for it, just like I would if this were different and we were really in love."

"I can't let you do that. It's not even real."

"You will legally be my wife, and that means I will treat you as such. You'll get all the perks of being Mrs. Ridley without conceding on your boundaries. How does that sound?"

"Like it's too good to be true," she answered bluntly.

"I know it's gonna take time to earn your trust. But I'm a patient man."

She shook her head. "I'm buying the dresses. I can't let you pay for everything."

"Fine. You get the dresses, I'll take care of everything else." He'd let her keep her pride, and made a note to call the boutique in town and have them give her a sale price while he covered the rest. "Is there anything special you want for the wedding?"

"I'd just like Betty-Lou and Fred Moore from the diner invited, along with Pippa and Mason."

He nodded. "Any preference on where?"

"It doesn't matter to me. Somewhere small and affordable. We don't need to go crazy."

She was so sweet and grateful, and all he was doing was helping her out. "Would you like to go over everything with me, or should I take care of the details?"

"If you need help, I can do it, but I'd prefer to just get this over with."

"Got it. I'll take care of all the details and you can just show up. And after the wedding, you and Danielle are fine to move into my house?"

Brynn's eyes widened.

"I just figured for this to look real, you'd be coming to my home. I have three bedrooms, so there will be plenty of space for all of us."

She fidgeted with the sleeve of her grey sweater, the same one she'd worn to the quinceañera. "I-I hadn't thought that far. I guess . . . it makes sense." She sighed. "This is a lot more than I realized."

"You don't have to do anything you're not comfortable with. We can wait." Even though Aaron didn't want to. The sooner he married Brynn, the sooner he could feel confident Danielle was going to be okay.

She was silent a moment and then shook her head. "No. This is for Danielle. She needs to see a doctor before she gets any further into puberty. I can't watch her go into a depression again. Not when I just got my kid back . . . I'll do it."

He nodded and tried to come up with a way to lighten the mood. "What's your favorite kind of cake?"

"Chocolate."

"I like vanilla, so maybe we'll go half and half on the cake." He chuckled.

The tips of her mouth lifted slightly in a ghost of a smile, but he'd take it.

"What's your favorite flower?"

Brynn stilled, her smile turning into a frown, her gaze seeming to drift far away as she stared at his chest.

"Brynn?" Aaron reached out his hand to cover hers in an attempt to bring her back from wherever she'd gone to.

She startled, her body pressing as close to the wall and as far from him as possible without falling off the window seat.

He held up his hands. "I'm sorry. I didn't mean to scare you." *What kind of hell has this woman been through?* Aaron had never been prone to violence, but the malice that churned in his gut at the thought of anyone hurting this waif of a woman burned like acid in his veins.

"I-I'm sorry. I don't like to be touched."

He nodded. "Okay. We can start slow. We're gonna have to kiss on the wedding day, at least once." Probably more if people happily tap their cutlery against champagne glasses.

She swallowed, the color in her face draining as she looked down at her hands, her shoulders going rigid.

"Everyone who knows me knows I'm an affectionate guy. If we do this, you're going to have to get used to me touching you from time to time."

Her wide eyes shot to his, fear shining bright.

"Touching you like holding your hand, or resting my palm on your waist, kissing your cheek, or your lips when the occasion calls for it," he clarified.

She looked sick. Was she disgusted by him? Or the thought of him touching her? Or was it any man?

"We can go as slow as you need. Would it help if I warned you beforehand?"

"I don't know."

"Do you want to practice here, while we're alone?"

She waited a beat, looking down and then back to him. "We can try."

"Okay. First, I'd like to hold your hand."

He reached out his palm to her.

She hesitated and then slipped her small hand in his. Aaron gently closed his fingers around her, giving her a moment to adjust before he rubbed his thumb in slow soft circles over the back of her hand.

Her shoulders lowered from her ears.

"You doing okay?" he asked.

"Yes."

"Good. Do you want to dance?"

Her brows drew together. "But there's no music."

Aaron pulled out his phone and tapped his John Legend playlist, pressing play on a song. A slow, romantic melody bled from the tiny speaker of his cell. He stood without letting go of her hand and tugged her gently to her feet. Their height difference was stark, the top of her head came to just below his chest.

"I'm going to wrap my arm around your waist, is that

okay?"

Her nod was curt, as if she wasn't sure but was pushing herself past her comfort zone.

His large palm reached the length of her waist. He could feel her rib bones. Was she skipping meals?

He led her in slow purposeful steps around the room, and slowly, she relaxed into his hold.

"I'm going to move a little closer now, so we can dance like we would at the wedding. Is that alright?" he asked.

"Okay." Her voice was all breath.

He tugged her closer, wrapping both his arms around her waist, and she did the same. Leaning down, he inhaled her lavender scent. Her body was still tense in his arms, so he carefully moved to the music as it changed to a jazzier ensemble, the music still slow and deliberate. It took two turns around the room, before Brynn's head relaxed against his upper stomach.

Pride swelled in his rib cage that she'd trusted him enough to let him touch her, a gift he wouldn't take for granted from a woman like Brynn. This was huge.

"Okay. Now's the time for our final hurdle . . . Can I kiss you?"

Brynn tensed against him, this time holding him tighter. But after a moment, she tilted her head up and showcased her long delicate neck. His eyes dropped to her pink full lips, waiting for her verbal consent.

"Yes," she whispered.

He dragged a knuckle across her porcelain cheek, and she shivered. Or was she trembling? He searched her eyes, apprehension mingled with fear shining back. But it was the first glimpse of arousal in those emerald orbs that urged him on.

Ever so slowly, he leaned in until he could taste her exhale on his lips. He held her face reverently as he lowered his mouth to capture hers.

Brynn reared back. "I'm sorry, I can't."

He nodded, letting the disappointment roll off him. "That's alright."

"I'll do it for the wedding, to make it believable. But only when needed. And yes, thank you, a warning would be nice before you touch me otherwise." She stepped back again, putting even more space between them, and focused on her fidgeting hands.

"Whatever you need."

"I appreciate your patience and understanding. I hope you know that." She lifted her chin.

He nodded.

"I better go." Brynn turned and left the room.

Aaron let out a sigh and raked a hand over his face. They'd made progress today—a lot in fact. That was nothing to be taken lightly. He'd entered this agreement to help Danielle—to ensure she didn't end up like his own brother had. But maybe he'd be able to help Brynn too.

5

BRYNN

Brynn pressed a hand to her racing heart as she leaned against the bookcase. *Did I really just let a man touch me? Hold me? Oh, God! I almost kissed him.*

She placed her trembling fingers over her lips. Why did her body turn to liquid heat when he touched her? Was she getting sick? Was something wrong with her? Confusion spun, making her dizzy.

"Oh, Brynn, I'm glad I caught you." Pippa stepped in front of her, her trusted service dog, Lady, by her side.

Brynn straightened and forced a neutral expression. "Oh? Was there something I could help you with?" She started walking to the front of the store. Aaron would be coming out of that room any second, and Brynn needed to make her escape now. Could Pippa hear her heart thudding?

"Dav-Danielle said you were getting married. Is that true?"

Brynn stopped by the desk, gathering her things. "Yes."

Pippa's eyebrows rose, and what seemed like a hundred

questions flashed in her eyes. One of the things Brynn loved about Pippa was that she respected people's privacy. "I didn't know you two were dating."

Brynn remained quiet. Her eyes darted to the secret library door—she needed to get out of here.

"Does this have to do with me needing to hide Danielle the other day?"

Brynn gave a swift nod. "Partly. Aaron's offered us a solution, and protection." She hoped Pippa understood what she was saying. But Brynn needed someone to talk to. Someone needed to know what was going on in case things did go badly, even though it seemed like they wouldn't.

Brynn needed a witness. And a big part of her missed being able to talk about the things on her heart with another woman—even if she couldn't talk it over with her sister. *I wish it could be my Brynna.*

Pippa's expression softened. "Aaron is a good man. Everyone in this town respects him. He's been a huge help in the community. You couldn't have picked a better guy."

"I hope so," Brynn admitted as the secret door opened. "Come have coffee with me? I'd really love a listening ear if you have time?"

"Okay. I guess Troy can handle the shop for a little while by himself."

Eyes focused forward, Brynn rushed to the front door, hoping Pippa was close behind. She couldn't speak to Aaron again today—could barely think when he got so close.

As Pippa and Brynn crossed the street, Lady walked a few steps ahead of them. Sprinkles of rain fell from the overcast sky, the damp air charged with energy, as if a storm was about to hit. Hopefully it wouldn't do too much damage.

The bell above the door to The Stardust Café jingled as

they entered. A few people working on computers sat at small square tables around the room. The cozy café was warm and smelled of cinnamon and roasted coffee beans.

They stood in line behind an older couple.

"Oh," Pippa said with excitement. "Remy has the mermaid cookies I like. Maybe I'll get two since breastfeeding helps me burn the extra calories." She laughed.

"How are the twins?" Brynn asked.

"Camilla has clearly let us know she's the boss. She can be a little dictator. God forbid she isn't fed the moment she gets hungry or changed as soon as she's done peeing."

Brynn smiled, memories of David as a baby playing flitting through her mind. "Those days are tough, but the moments in between make it all worth it."

"Oh, yes. And Andrew is such an easygoing baby, so they balance each other out. And Aspen is a big help."

"I bet."

Remy, the owner of the café, smiled at them as the elderly couple moved on. "Hello, ladies. What can I get for you today?"

"I'll take some of your mulled cider and two mermaid cookies, please." Pippa reached into her coat pocket.

Remy grabbed a cup and marked it with a Sharpie before looking to Brynn.

"The cider sounds nice." Brynn unzipped her purse and handed over a five-dollar bill.

Remy worked on collecting their drinks and the cookies.

"I just can't believe you're really getting married." Pippa tucked her change back into her pocket.

"You're getting married?" Remy asked, setting their drinks on the counter.

Pippa bit her lip and looked over to Brynn apologetically.

Brynn shrugged. "It's no secret. Aaron Ridley and I are going to be married soon."

Remy's eyes widened a fraction before she smiled. "Oh, I'm so happy to hear. Aaron deserves a good woman like you."

"Do you know him well?" Brynn asked.

Remy laughed and pushed her micro braids over her shoulder. "We dated years ago, before Mikel came back."

Brynn must not have hidden her shock well because Remy's brows drew together, and her smile disappeared. "Oh, nothing like what you're thinking. We went on a few dates, but it never moved past being platonic really. I was still in love with Mikel, and Aaron and I were better off as friends. He was the perfect gentleman the whole time. He was the one to bring up that we probably weren't a good fit and there was no use beating around the bush. I always loved his honesty."

A sliver of comfort lit inside Brynn with the confirmation Aaron had been consistent throughout the years, and she offered what she hoped was a reassuring smile. "Thank you for sharing that with me."

"Of course. You two enjoy your treats." Remy pushed the bag of cookies towards them.

The women took their items and walked to a table by the window as the rain turned into more of a drizzle, the lights on Main Street reflecting in the puddles on the road. A few people under umbrellas walked past, hurrying along their way.

"This is so good." Pippa set her cider on the table and licked her lips, and Lady settled on her belly by their feet.

Brynn lifted her own cup to her mouth and took a sip. Cinnamon and tart apple mixed with cloves and just the right sweetness met her taste buds. It was warm and comforting, perfect for such a dreary day and the difficult conversation ahead.

"I won't press you for any details you don't want to give, but I'd like you to know that I'm here for you, whatever you need." Pippa met her eyes, her expression soft and understanding.

Brynn nodded. Danielle had told Aaron some of it. And no matter how many meetings she'd gone to, her story always got stuck in her throat. But maybe it was time to be brave and break down the secrecy that had been forced upon her over a lifetime. "I grew up in a cult. At least, I know that's what it is now."

Pippa nodded, sympathy filling her attentive gaze.

Brynn wrapped her cold fingers around the warm cup of cider, staring at the steam rising as she recounted her tale. "Life on the compound was . . . horrible. There were good memories, don't get me wrong. That's what made it so hard to leave. But I knew if we didn't run, we'd be next."

"Next?" Pippa asked.

Brynn swallowed the lump of emotion in her throat. "My sister didn't make it out. And after I'd received a particularly bad beating, I took my child and ran in the dead of night."

Pain throbbed, slicing through every breath as Miriam limped towards the room where David was sleeping. The door creaked as she opened it, and she held her breath, hoping neither her husband, nor one of his other wives or one of the dozens of children nearby, would hear. Moonlight filtered into the dark boys' room. She cast her gaze over the several angelic faces lost to their slumber, wishing they could all get out.

She blinked the tears from her swollen and bruised eyes. She couldn't save them, but she could get David out.

She stepped gingerly towards his bed, laying her good hand firmly over his mouth. His eyes flew open, hands shooting up in defense. She bit back the whimper of pain that wanted to leave her mouth from the impact of his hand on her shoulder. Her other arm was tucked carefully against her body, unusable. It was most likely broken, along with a rib or two. Paul hadn't been very forgiving this time.

"Shh. Grab whatever clothing you can carry and come with me," she whispered.

He stood, his cot creaking under his movements. His eyes must have adjusted to the light, because they widened and filled with tears as he looked at her. Guilt shone in her son's eyes, tearing her apart like a flash of lightning.

"We're leaving." She limped towards the door.

He followed obediently, his hand reaching out to steady her as they took the stairs down, one at a time. They needed to move fast once they were out of the house. Escaping the compound and then walking miles to the nearest bus station before the sun came up and everyone found out they were missing.

Her family members' voices melded with their leaders' in her head. "If you leave, you'll burn in hell," they'd said. Well, she couldn't stay anymore, because living on the compound was hell. And if their god would punish her for trying to stay alive, protecting her only child, then so be it. She'd pay the price with her eternal soul. She'd venture out to a world unknown to live with the gentiles.

Anything was better than the constant fear of her child or her getting hurt.

"Wow. That must have been so difficult." Pippa's voice brought her back to the present.

Brynn nodded. "It was. I left behind my family, and everyone I'd ever known."

"And after all these years, your safety is still in jeopardy?"

Brynn sucked in a long breath tainted with cinnamon. "Yes. My ex is a prominent leader in the group, and by leaving I know I've caused shame and disgrace to his whole household. The religion I was raised in doesn't leave much room for forgiveness without punishment. He will blame me. I thought maybe we were safe, but a man came in the diner asking for me last week."

Pippa's hand covered her mouth. "Oh my God!"

"I have been trying to live under the radar, so that means no health insurance for Danielle. She obviously needs to see a doctor now. Aaron offered me a solution to solve my problems. I'd get to legally change my name and get health insurance for my daughter. We could begin the process of changing her name too. Her biological father isn't on her birth certificate." *It would have raised too many red flags if Paul Livingston had his name on the record of all the children he'd fathered with his many wives.*

"Wow. I know I keep saying that word, but I'm just astonished. I can't believe you've been through so much."

You don't know the half of it.

"Are you sure that's all this is with Aaron?" Pippa asked.

"What do you mean?"

Pippa broke a piece of her cookie off and slipped it into her mouth, chewing and swallowing before continuing, "I always thought there was a spark of chemistry between you two."

What? No. "I'm sure Aaron sees me as a pitiful woman who needs rescuing. It's not really me he's doing this for anyways. It's for Dani." Brynn wasn't sure Aaron's brother's story was public knowledge, so she didn't want to betray his confidence by giving Pippa that extra bit of information.

The corner of Pippa's lips turned up as she nodded, mischief flashing in her eyes. "I think he sees you as a little more than that."

Anxiety flit in her belly, taking off like a flock of birds. That was definitely nerves. There was no way the flutters were the first rays of hope and excitement. No way at all.

People like her didn't get happily ever afters like the heroines did in the books she stocked the shelves with at Pippa's store. People like Brynn were broken beyond repair. There was no hope for someone like her who had been so thoroughly used and abused. The only reason she kept going was for Danielle and Brynna. She's made a promise and she had every reason to keep it.

6

BRYNN

Brynn's eyes fell over the room. Pastel pink walls with shimmery champagne accents housed rows and rows of white wedding gowns. Off to the side were other formal dresses in every color she could imagine. She was as out of place, especially so when a glass of champagne was thrust into her hand upon entering by the store owner.

Brynn had never drunk alcohol, and she certainly wasn't going to start now. She'd probably spill it all over one of the very expensive dresses.

"Oh, Mom, look at this one." Danielle gripped the tulle fabric excitedly. The dress was something out of a dream, lace three-quarter-length sleeves and topped with a solid piece of shimmering fabric beginning above the breast of the manikin. A strip of white ribbon cinched the waist before the dress puffed out with a yard of tulle like a real-life princess gown.

"Oh, it's lovely," Charli said. She was one of the owners of The Shipwreck bar who Brynn had met at the sexual assault meetings the bartender used to attend. They'd grown almost as close as her and Pippa.

"Definitely." Pippa lifted it off the rail. "You should try it on."

"Shall I add it to the dressing room?" the boutique owner, Sybil, a beautiful Black woman, asked.

Brynn lifted the price tag and gasped. *Three thousand dollars? I can't afford this store.*

"Didn't you mention you had a sale going to the future Mrs. Ridley?" Charli's eyebrows rose as she turned to the owner.

I must have said that out loud.

"Oh, Mrs. Ridley?" Sybil asked, as if confirming something.

"Soon to be," Brynn answered for her.

Sybil smiled and nodded excitedly. "Oh yes. Everything in the store is on sale. Eighty—"

Charli cast her a look.

"I mean, ninety percent off," Sybil finished.

Brynn crossed her arms over her chest. "But there are no signs." She turned in a circle. "And that's one heck of a deal." There was no way that was true. Something suspicious was going on.

"How cool is that, Mom?" Dani beamed.

"Very," she replied. It did seem very odd, but she may as well take advantage of the discount.

"Now, I have just the gowns for you, young lady. What color were you thinking?" Sybil asked Danielle.

Her daughter's eyes glittered with happiness at being called young lady no doubt. "Pink."

Sybil held out her hand for Dani's. "I'll take you to the endless options."

"What kind of style are you looking for?" Pippa led Lady to a rack of silk gowns. The dog obediently sat while her owner began rifling through the dresses, always at her side in case she had a seizure.

"Something simple," Brynn answered.

"But elegant," Charli suggested.

"Oh, how about this one?" Pippa held up a strapless plain silk dress with a bow in the front, but it would only reach to her knees.

Brynn shook her head.

"That's too plain," Charli agreed. She pulled out a spaghetti-strapped chiffon dress. "How about this?"

"I think I'd feel too self-conscious showing all that skin." Brynn turned back to the dress on the manikin. "I like this style. Maybe something like this."

Sybil returned. "How is it coming along, ladies?"

"Where's Dani?"

"She is all set up in the changing room." Sybil motioned to the row of rooms, one of which had a curtain drawn closed.

"The bride would like to try this one on. Do you have any more like it?" Pippa asked.

"Oh, yes. I have something I think will be perfect. I just got it in, uh, in off the display, I mean." Sybil disappeared into the back room.

Brynn's brows drew together suspiciously. She set her glass of champagne down on the coffee table by the lounge sofa and made her way to the changing room to check on Dani.

"How is it coming, sweetheart?"

Dani opened the curtain and walked out. She'd chosen a pale pink dress with a sweetheart neckline and a poufy skirt much like the one Brynn was interested in.

Brynn covered her mouth as tears sprang to her eyes at the beaming smile lighting up her child's face. "Gorgeous."

"You look like a princess," Pippa added, sitting in the over-stuffed chair beside the dressing rooms.

"All she needs is a crown. I think I saw some by the front, let's go choose one." Charli reached out her hand to Dani as Sybil returned with a mass of white in her hands.

"Here you go. Why don't you try this on and we can go from there?" Sybil hung it in the dressing room next to the one Dani had exited.

Brynn entered the cubicle and closed the curtain. She slipped off her clothes, her eyes staying glued to the wedding gown before her. She pulled it off the hanger and stepped into it, dragging the lace sleeves over her arms. They reached all the way to her wrist, and the detail was different than the one at the front of the store. The solid material that covered her breasts and stomach had the same heart shape as her daughter's dress, though it, too, was covered by the lace and fitted to her body. The waist had a sparkly belt of crystals wrapping around to the back, and the chiffon skirt pooled out like the one Cinderella wore to the ball.

"Do you need help doing up the back?" Sybil asked from outside the curtain.

Brynn jumped and released a deep breath to ease her racing heart. "Can you send Pippa in?"

A moment later the material door swished aside as Pippa walked in.

"Can you do up the buttons in the back? I don't want . . . any questions," Brynn confessed.

Pippa blinked. "Of course."

Brynn spun around and closed her eyes so she didn't have to see Pippa's reaction to the scars on her back in the reflection of the mirror.

After a small gasp and a momentary pause, Pippa began fastening the buttons. "Looks like it's exactly your size, too, just a little long."

After the last button was done up, Brynn turned around, emotion welling in her eyes. "Thank you."

Her gratitude was for far more than doing up her dress. Pippa had given her a job under the table, she'd been a listening ear, a protector of Dani, and a friend when Brynn had needed one most.

"Always. Let's go show everyone how stunning you look. I think this might just be the one." Pippa smiled affectionately before leading her out of the room.

Charli and Dani had returned, and even Sybil waited nearby.

"Oh my God! That's perfect," Charli squealed.

"Mom, you have to pick that one," Dani agreed.

"There's a full-length mirror over here." Sybil directed her to a circular stage with a step in the middle.

Brynn lifted the dress and got herself situated in the center before smoothing it out. She looked up for the first time into the reflection and gasped. The dress was gorgeous. And was that her in the mirror? She ran a hand over her face, then down her bottle-dyed brown hair that she'd sheared off to sit just above her shoulders after they'd escaped.

"I'm beautiful." Tears blurred the image before memories of the first time she'd put on a wedding dress ran through her mind.

Miriam pressed her hand over the scratchy white fabric, smoothing it over her waist. Her mother tightened the last button, cinching it around her neck like a noose. Miriam swallowed as her mind raced and her heart thudded in her ears. Nerves and fear twisted her belly, making her want to throw up. She cast a glance at her younger sister, Brynna, who watched on with wide scared eyes. It would be her next.

"Can't we wait a little longer, Mother?" Brynna asked.

"Hush, before your father hears you. You know it's a woman's duty to

marry and provide her husband with children. It's our only calling besides serving our husband," their mother sternly reminded them.

"But Mr. Livingston is so old," Brynna pointed out, as if this would make any difference to their mother.

"He's younger than your father was when we married, and I was thirteen. Miriam is already fifteen. It's time she did what she was put on earth for."

"But, Mother—"

"Enough! Miriam will marry the son of our most holy leader and bring honor to our family. She will serve him in her wifely duties and bear his children so that we may continue the kingdom of heaven. And she will obey him in all things as we are commanded by the holy prophet to do. A woman's place is to be silent and serving, for this will bring honor and blessings upon her and her husband's household." Their mother quoted the same declaration that she'd repeated their whole life.

Brynna cast Miriam a sympathetic look as her eyes filled with tears.

Miriam placed her hand over her sister's. "I'll be okay. We'll still be able to see each other. And soon we'll have a little baby to play with too."

"Mom?" Danielle's voice brought her back to the present.

Brynn's stomach twisted as bile rose in her throat. The horror that followed that same evening was the first time she'd questioned anything she'd been taught.

"Brynn? Are you okay, honey?" Pippa asked, taking her hand.

She flinched.

"You're shaking." Charli moved to her front, blocking her reflection in the mirror.

Brynn forced a smile. "Sorry, just overwhelmed with everything for a moment. It's just hit me all at once that I'm getting married."

She turned to Dani, smoothing her blond hair out of her face, and staring into the blue eyes that reminded her so much of Paul's. She would do whatever it took to make sure her daughter never experienced the kind of pain and degradation Brynn had endured. She escaped a prison of hell on earth, and would take the necessary actions so that her child could live as who she was, out and proud in the sunshine.

But what if Aaron changed after the vows were said? What if he demanded more from her? Would she do what she had to in order to keep Dani safe? Even if that meant Brynn had to sell her body to the devil himself?

Not that Aaron was a devil. He'd managed to earn a scrap of her trust. Maybe a little more seeing as she'd agreed to marry the man. Only time would tell.

Brynn reached out and pulled Danielle into her arms, hugging her tight and breathing in the cotton candy smell of her daughter's new perfume. Strength filled her bones from the contact. Paul, her family, and everyone else back at the compound had tried to break Brynn and control her by using her love for her child.

In her experience, love was used to control.

So, she certainly wouldn't be falling in love with her new husband.

7

AARON

Aaron walked out of The Stardust Café with one less thing on his to-do list for the wedding that was now less than two weeks away. It was time for the one task he'd put off until as late as possible. He sat on one of the benches on the sidewalk and switched the bouquet of flowers from his right hand to his left before pulling out his phone. He scrolled to his parents' contact information and pressed the call button, sliding the cell up to his ear. It rang three times before his mother picked up.

"Hello? Aaron, is that really you?" His mother's voice lilted with cautious hope.

"Yeah, Mom, it's me."

"It's so good to hear from you. How are you doing?" she asked, her voice gaining confidence.

Things had been strained between them after they'd kicked Emmanuel out, but since his death, their communication had turned to birthdays and Christmas calls. If his mother found out he'd gotten married without inviting her, she'd be heartbroken. And he couldn't explain to his parents this wasn't real, not with the way those two worshipped the sanctity of marriage.

"I'm good, Mom. I'm actually calling because I'm getting married two Saturdays from now, and I wanted to know if I should include you and Dad in the guest list?"

The other end of the line was silent a moment. "My baby is getting married?" His mother's voice broke as if she was starting to cry.

Aaron's stomach churned uncomfortably. "Her name is Brynn, and she has a daughter."

"I'm getting a grandbaby too?" His mother almost sounded excited, her Southern twang more evident now.

"Well, she's fourteen, so not much of a baby anymore."

"We'll be there. What time? Oh, it doesn't matter. We'll come into town on Friday. Maybe we could meet for dinner? Never mind that, you'll probably be having your bachelor party then. We'll figure something out."

"I'll send you an invitation and include The Lighthouse Inn's information for you and Dad. Jasmine's already put a room on hold for you. I guess I'll see you then." Aaron got to his feet.

"Thank you, sweetheart. I can't wait to see you."

"Bye, Mom." He pulled the phone away and ended the call before sliding it into his pocket and releasing a long exhale. That had been a little easier than he'd expected.

Aaron lifted the bouquet of wildflowers to his nose, inhaling the mix of sweet scents blending with the crisp fall air. He straightened his shoulders as he walked down the street to the diner where a little birdie had told him Brynn was getting off work shortly.

He reached for the handle as a few leather-clad men approached from the inside—the members of The Pirates

Motorcycle Club. Aaron held the door open for them as they exited, giving him a nod.

He walked into the diner, the smell of greasy food and warm fruit pies melded together with fresh coffee, making his stomach rumble. His gaze met Brynn's across the room. Her eyes widened, flicking to the flowers in his hand, then back to his face before her cheeks reddened. Her attention darted around the room, as if she was looking for an escape before they landed on her daughter, hunched over a textbook at a booth. Brynn's expression softened before determination lit her emerald gaze. Her chin lifted and she met his eyes once again when he stopped in front of her.

He held out the flowers and offered her what he hoped was a friendly smile.

"Good afternoon, beautiful. These are for you."

Brynn slid her dainty hand around the long stems, staring at the colorful flowers with wonderment before she lifted them to her nose. The corners of her mouth tipped into the briefest smile as her eyes drooped closed for a second. The evident, though muted, joy on her face brought a spark of happiness zinging through him. *God, I like doing things to make her smile.*

He leaned a little closer and whispered, "May I kiss your cheek for our audience?"

Brynn's gaze shot to the few people around the diner whose attention was now on them. She swallowed audibly, lowering the flowers, and gave him the tiniest nod. He moved slow, so as not to spook her, gently pressing his lips to her flushed cheek. She trembled at his touch. *Do I scare her that much?*

Aaron backed a step away, giving her space as he turned to Dani. "Hey, sweetheart, how are you?"

Dani beamed up at him. "Hey, Mr. Ridley. I'm just working on school stuff."

"I think you can call me Aaron now." He winked.

Dani's smile grew. "Cool."

"What are you doing here?" Brynn asked, still seeming a bit stunned as she eyed the flowers in her hand like they were a bomb.

"I heard you might be getting off work, and I thought I'd give you both a ride home." He didn't want them having to take the bus, and he wanted to know where they lived.

"I'm still here for another hour." Brynn smoothed one hand over her apron.

"I think we're set. You can head out early, honey," Betty-Lou said from behind the counter before she gave him a knowing smile.

"Are you sure? I haven't rolled the silverware for tomorrow." Brynn fidgeted with the bouquet in her hands.

"I'm positive. Fred and I have everything under control. We have a new girl starting in an hour anyways. It will give her something to do when we get slow after the dinner rush." Betty-Lou waved before heading to one of the tables with customers.

"I'll be right back." Brynn turned and left through the double doors that Aaron assumed led to the kitchen.

He sat across from Dani as she packed her books into a backpack. "What's your favorite subject?"

"Math."

Aaron's eyes widened. "Not too many kids would say that, I think. It's good. Math will take you far."

"Yeah. Hey, do you think you could help me with it sometime?"

"Sure, if your mom doesn't mind."

Dani's attention darted to her foot toeing the ground nervously before she focused back on Aaron. "Well, she doesn't really know how to do what I'm working on now. She looked it up online, but I don't understand it the way she tried to teach me. I think she feels bad."

"A lot of people forget what they learned in school when they don't use it every day."

Dani blinked up at him. "Yeah, but it's probably because she didn't go to school after she turned thirteen. Even then, it wasn't like my schoolwork. The stuff we learned back at the compound was mostly spiritual stuff. I was on the building crew, so I learned some basic geometry. But they don't let girls do that stuff."

"Compound?" Aaron repeated, warning bells ringing in his head. Where the hell had these two come from? It sounded like a cult.

"Yeah, it's where we lived with my dad and all his—"

"Ready?" Brynn stopped by the table, cutting her daughter a look.

Aaron got to his feet. He would get to the bottom of this and find out more, but it was just another thing he'd have to do in Brynn's time as he earned her trust.

"My car is just down the street." Aaron led the way, holding the front door for them while gently pressing his hand to Brynn's lower back.

She tensed and turned her face to him.

Shit. I forgot to ask. But touching her felt so natural—almost right.

He shook the thought away. That was ridiculous. "Is this okay?" he whispered.

She gave him a curt nod, her pace increasing, as if she wanted to get this over with as soon as possible. She crossed her arms over the worn hoodie with frayed edges and a few holes. Did she not have a proper jacket? He'd have to fix that.

"It's right down here." He motioned across the street.

They walked to one side, Dani trailing slightly behind

them as they passed a few people on the street who sent them friendly smiles and nods. Aaron returned them, but Brynn kept her focus on the ground.

Nancy Plotts—the town gossip—and a few of her older friends who were heading into the café stopped and pointed at them before whispering to each other.

"Seems we've got the bitties' tongues a waggin'." Aaron chuckled as they passed them.

Brynn's cheeks turned rosy, from the chill in the air or from the extra attention he wasn't sure.

"It's just here." Aaron pointed to his white Range Rover.

Brynn stopped, her shoulders deflating a tiny bit before an emotionless mask slipped over her features. He pulled out the key fob and unlocked the door.

"This is your car? Cool!" Dani reached for the back door and let herself in.

Brynn walked to the passenger side, Aaron following, and reached for the door handle. Her hand grabbed his instead, and she jerked it back, as if she'd been burned.

A twinge of rejection lit Aaron's rib cage. He flexed his jaw. *This isn't personal.* He opened the door and cleared his throat. "Here you go."

She ignored the hand he held out for her and grabbed the car door instead, climbing inside with effort. She set the bouquet on her lap and her bag on the floor before she buckled. He shut the door.

Inhaling a deep breath, he returned to the driver's side and got in. The engine rumbled as he started the SUV.

"Ready to go?" he asked.

"Yup," Dani answered, seemingly unfazed by her mother's stone wall of silence.

Aaron shifted the car into gear and pulled out onto the road. "Where to?"

"Straight down here and make a right. Do you know where Pine Street is?"

He nodded. "On the outskirts of town?"

"Yeah, we live on that road."

He followed her directions. Dani filled the silence, talking about her friends and when she planned to go to Hope again. She asked Aaron lots of questions about the center, and he answered each one when he could fit a word in. Brynn focused out her window as a light fall rain drizzled down.

"It's the next house on the right." Brynn's soft voice spoke for the first time in twenty minutes.

Aaron flicked his blinker on and pulled in. It was a cute white house with forest-green shutters. "This is a nice place."

"Oh, that's not where we live." Dani leaned over to the front seat and pointed to the one-car garage that had seen better days. "We live up there."

Aaron's stomach hardened. Was that place even safe? He exited the truck.

"You don't have to get out," Brynn protested.

"I'll just walk you ladies to the door." He stepped out from the car.

Brynn was quick to follow, Dani rushing ahead of them into the garage to get out of the rain. Aaron retrieved his umbrella before he walked to Brynn's side of the car. He held it above her, staying by her side as they made their way to the dilapidated building.

Brynn stopped in front of the dirty door with a loose handle. She turned and looked up at him. Rain pitter-pattered on the umbrella above them. The smell of wet earth surrounded them, carrying with it a few notes of her floral scent, or maybe that was the flowers in her hand.

"This isn't real. You don't have to buy me flowers or drive

me home." Brynn's gaze was vulnerable as her eyes roamed over his face.

"If you want people to believe this is real, I have to treat you as I would my actual girlfriend, or in this case, fiancée. Otherwise, people will talk, and that's the last thing I'm sure you want."

She swallowed and nodded. "Thank you for all of this. I promise I'll pay you back eventually."

He shook his head. "There is no running tab. I told you, what I give comes with no strings. You'll see that eventually."

She blinked, her big doe eyes seeming skeptical and untrusting. The thought angered him, not at Brynn—no, she was a victim. But for whoever had done this to her, caused such a deep wound of trauma that she couldn't even trust there were good men out there. Was he doing the right thing? He glanced at Dani. Yes. Of course he was.

"I reserved the Emerson family barn for the wedding and reception. Do you want to meet with me and Mrs. Emerson and Nova? We can tell them how you want everything deco- rated, go over the finer details?"

"I . . . I really don't want to sound ungrateful, or make more work for you, but I don't care. It's not real. We can just keep it simple. You don't need to put up too much of a fuss for me."

His chest squeezed tight, and he couldn't help himself. He slowly lifted his hand, in plain view so she could see what he was doing before he brushed his thumb over her jawline to her cheek until he was cupping the side of her face.

Aaron locked eyes with her, hoping his truth would show in his gaze. "You deserve the world, Brynn. And I aim to keep reminding you until you believe it yourself."

She shivered, her eyes volleying between his, as if she didn't know what to think.

He let his hand fall to his side once more. "I'll take care of everything. You just show up at Pippa's. She and Charli promised me to help get you and Dani ready. They'll pick you both up Friday evening."

"Okay. Our dresses are supposed to be delivered this week. They had to shorten mine." She slammed her mouth closed, as if she thought she'd said too much.

"Does this door lock?" He motioned to the weak-looking handle hanging on the door.

She shook her head. "No, but the one upstairs does."

He'd have to fix it for her and Dani's added protection. "Make sure to lock up behind you."

She nodded.

He waited until she went in before he returned to his car. The windshield wipers swished across, clearing the rain long enough for him to make out the dim light glowing from one of the windows above the garage.

He sighed. This was going to be a lot more complicated than he originally thought. But if he could help one kid from ending up like his brother, it was worth it.

8

BRYNN

Brynn closed her eyes, trying to take in a deep breath, but her chest was tight with anxiety. Today was her wedding day. Pippa brought her stepdaughter, Aspen, and Charli when they showed up Friday night to take her and Dani to dinner at Atlantis. From there, they headed to the loft apartment above the bookstore that Pippa used to live in before she moved in with Mason. They'd played games, had non-alcoholic drinks, and eaten snacks while watching movies and sharing laughs. It was one of the best experiences of Brynn's life. She'd never had a sleepover with friends before. She was so glad that Dani was getting to experience this. It was exactly what Brynn needed before the big day.

But morning had come and with it the nerves and anxiety as she got ready to walk down the aisle for the second time and pledge her life to another man. Aaron must have known how hard today would be for her because he sent an entire crew to assist her with her hair and makeup. She'd never been so primped and spoiled in her life. It was like she was one of the women in the romance movies they'd watched the night before.

She stared into the mirror, hardly recognizing herself. Her short hair was pulled up into a fancy elegant updo. A veil cascaded down the back of her head to the middle of her back. The dress fit like a glove and felt like butter on her skin. The tailor had fixed the hem so that it was the perfect length for her five-foot frame. Brynn touched her pink cheek. Her eyes had a smoky shadow effect to them with shimmery glitter that made her green eyes sparkle like the ring on her finger. Her lips were bright bloodred. She'd never in her life worn makeup. Dressing up like royalty was new to her.

Dani wrapped her arm around Brynn's waist and smiled at her own reflection. Dani, too, had been primped and doted on. But unlike her mother, Dani had lapped up the attention.

Dani beamed. "You look like a queen, Mom."

"And you, my beautiful princess." Brynn leaned down and kissed her daughter's cheek.

"Mom, you're going to get lipstick on me." Dani swiped at her face.

Pippa came up beside them. "This is no-smudge, long-lasting lip stain. So no worries there."

"You ladies ready?" Charli smiled. "Your chariot awaits."

Brynn licked her lips and forced herself to inhale as her head grew dizzy. She turned to her daughter, her reason for everything, and exhaled.

She was doing this.

Brynn carefully made her way down the stairs, Pippa and Charli helping to hold her dress up so as not to get it dirty. A long white limo parked at the curb, and a driver in a suit and hat held the door open. Brynn's eyes widened. She followed Dani's lead and climbed in. Mixed feelings of not wanting to be a drain on Aaron and a thrill of excitement that this was for her tumbled in her belly.

Pippa, Charli, and Aspen joined them, each of them dressed in satin knee-length slips of various gemstone colors. The limo pulled out onto the road, starting towards their destination.

"Are you ready for this?" Pippa whispered beside her, reaching out her hand to envelop Brynn's. Usually, she didn't like physical touch from anyone besides her daughter, but Pippa had become a close friend.

"I hope so."

"You're in safe hands. As your friend and someone who cares a lot about you and Dani, I wouldn't let you do something like this unless I thought it safe."

Brynn turned to face her. "Thank you, for being here for me. For all you've done for us. I don't know how I'll ever repay you." Her debt with people was racking up.

Pippa gave her a kind smile. "Repay me by doing whatever it takes to find your happiness."

"Look, Mom, a sign for the wedding!" Dani pointed excitedly out the window.

Right past the sign for Emerson Farm was another surrounded by white balloons. *Congratulations, Mr. and Mrs. Ridley.*

This was it. It was too late to turn back now. She inhaled a shaky breath, focusing on bringing fresh oxygen into her lungs, the only thing she could control in this moment as the limo pulled to the front.

"Wait here, I'll make sure everything is ready." Charli slipped out and disappeared into the barn.

Dani squealed. "I'm so excited."

Aspen gave her a hug and asked, "Do you have the flowers?"

"Don't worry, they were delivered here this morning. Charli will bring them back," Pippa assured them.

A moment later, Charli returned, bouquet and basket in hand. The driver opened the door, and she leaned in. "Everyone is ready, the music has just started. You're on, sweetheart." Charli handed the basket of pink rose petals to Dani.

Aspen and Pippa got out first. "We're gonna go find our seats. Good luck."

Pippa kissed Brynn's cheek, then brought her into a warm hug.

"Here you go." Charli held out the bouquet of pink and white roses mixed with ruscus greenery.

Brynn accepted the gorgeous bouquet and walked hand in hand with her friend over the white cloth aisle that led from the limo to the barn. When Aaron mentioned getting married in a barn, this beautiful glossy wooden structure was the last thing she expected. Soft slow music filtered out through the door before the first chords of "Be My Melody" by Burwell started. Butterflies fluttered in Brynn's stomach as the lyrics danced through her. Had Aaron chosen this song to tell her something? She shook her head; that was stupid. This was just pretend.

Dani looked up at her. "Do I go now?"

Mikel, Remy's husband, walked towards them in a black suit, a pink rose pinned to his pocket. "You ladies ready?"

"Yes," Dani answered for her.

"Go ahead, then." He waved his hand inside.

Dani gave her mother one more hug. Brynn wrapped her arms around her, holding until Dani let go. She swallowed back the rush of tears that wanted to fall. Her mind dizzied as breathing became difficult. Her skin flushed hot, then cold. Mikel held out his arm, and she hesitated in taking it. It would be rude not to, but she hated how Paul had ruined her that she couldn't even accept a friendly gesture from someone without cringing away.

Forcing a smile on her face, she brushed past him, then gasped upon entering the barn. Feet thudded as people stood, rivaling her racing heartbeat drumming in her ears. Thousands of fairy lights and hanging flowers strung from the ceiling had the room looking like a secret alcove from a fairy tale. Firelight danced from candles on the walls, the only other light in the room besides the strings above. She put one shaky foot in front of the other, stepping on pink petals Dani had dropped for her.

Everyone's attention turned to her as she rounded the corner. Heat rose in her neck to her cheeks. Her chest cinched tight, her eyes growing blurry.

Aaron stood at the makeshift altar, decked out in a grey three-piece suit and matching boutonniere to Mikel's. Aaron's flowers had the same bit of greenery as Brynn's bouquet. His soft brown eyes widened, dropping down the length of her dress and back up as a beaming smile split his face. The tension left her body as his gaze locked with hers. Everyone in the room disappeared until it was just the two of them, and she floated the rest of the way down the aisle.

He reached out his hand, and she took it without hesitation. Relief and comfort washed over her, calming the nerves in her gut and replacing them with warm butterflies. He leaned in, his clean citrus and wood scent drifting over her, grounding her further into the moment.

"You look beyond beautiful." When he pulled back, his eyes swirled with an emotion she hadn't seen from him before.

"Friends and family, we are gathered here today to join together this man and this woman in the bonds of love and marriage," the officiant announced.

Brynn tuned her out as she focused on the man in front of her—the man who was about to become her husband. After escaping Paul, she vowed never to marry again unless it was for love. But here she was, this time marrying for protection.

Aaron lifted a ring from his pocket, holding the band up to her left ring finger. "I, Aaron Ridley, vow to care for you, Brynn. To put your needs first, and always be a listening ear."

Chills raced down Brynn's skin. Emotion clogged her throat. A selfish part of her pretended this was real, that he really meant every word he said. Why not give in to the fantasy for this one private moment in time?

"I'll be your best friend, treating you with the honor and respect you deserve. I vow to never betray your trust and to do my best to make you smile every day for as long as we're together."

Her chest rose and fell as he slipped the cold metal onto her finger.

A tap at her elbow had her turning toward Dani who was offering her Aaron's ring. Brynn's gaze raked over the intimate crowd of familiar faces from Shattered Cove and Hope Facility. Betty-Lou smiled at her from the front row, dabbing tears from her eyes. It didn't feel right to deceive these people who'd been nothing but kind to her, but this is what she had to do to keep her daughter safe and cared for. Brynn collected the ring, turned back to Aaron, and lined the gold band up to his finger.

"Repeat after me," the officiant directed.

Aaron must have written his own vows and known Brynn wouldn't want the pressure. But now that she was here, she didn't want to add any more lies to this arrangement.

"Actually, I have my own."

"Oh." The officiant's eyebrows rose as she smiled. "Go ahead, then."

"I, Brynn, vow to give my all to the time we will share together. I will be your partner, support you, and be the best friend that I can."

Hope flashed in Aaron's watery gaze as he smoothed his thumb over the soft flesh on the top of her hand affectionately.

"I promise to try my best to give you what you need." Brynn slipped the ring over his knuckle.

He didn't let her hand go, his eyes peering into her, as if he wanted to say a million more things.

"By the power vested in me by the state of New Hampshire, I now pronounce you husband and wife. You may kiss the bride," the officiant announced.

Aaron dropped her hands and slowly cupped her face, his attention locked on her, as if trying to read her reaction.

Anxiety swarmed in her veins like hundreds of buzzing bees. Warm liquid sloshed in her belly, making her feel out of control and heady.

Aaron leaned in, his sweet breath tickling her lips a moment before his mouth collided with hers.

Fireworks exploded in Brynn's body.

She gasped as his lips tangled with hers, that warmth inside her now turning to liquid fire, stirring her up, and fueling a pulse between her thighs.

She gripped his suit, holding on for dear life as applause and cheers reminded her they were not alone. Aaron pulled back, a dreamy smile playing on his lips. He wrapped his arm around her waist, then led her down the aisle, past the guests throwing handfuls of pink and white petals.

Once they exited the barn, he pulled her against his firm body, wrapping her in a hug. "You won't regret this, Mrs. Ridley."

He backed off, his grin widening as his finger traced the

upward curve of her lips. She hadn't even realized she was smiling, too, until that moment. She looked up at the sharp angle of his jaw, to the handsome face of her husband, her heart thundering.

Not falling for her husband might be harder than she thought.

9

———————

AARON

Aaron's mind was still reeling from their explosive kiss as he tried to focus on the legal paperwork the officiant slid in front of them. Brynn's dainty hand shook as she pressed ink to the document. She peeked up at him, her cheeks rosy and flushed. She was absolutely stunning. *And she's my wife.*

Her eyelashes fluttered as she handed him the pen. He scanned the paper. Instead of finding Brynn, she'd signed as Miriam McKerman. A cold chill shot through his body. Here he was, believing they'd made progress, that she was letting him in, and he didn't even know her real name until right now.

He took a deep breath and scribbled his signature on the line.

The officiant took the paper back and signed herself. "Congratulations. It's official."

Aaron nodded. "Thank you."

"They should have the tables set up in the barn now for

your guests, but I believe the photographer wanted to see you first."

"Right. Enjoy the rest of dinner." Aaron pressed his hand to Brynn's back. She didn't flinch this time, which was something.

Brynn—or Miriam?—walked out into the crisp evening. The sky had turned a burnt orange as the sun began to set—it would be perfect for the photos.

"Aaron?" she whispered.

"Hmm?" He guided her towards the photographer. Dani was already standing there with her best friend Aspen.

"No one can know my identity. I hope you understand. I'll legally change it to Brynn once I submit the married name change."

He stopped, then faced her. She looked up at him, shivering in the cool fall air.

Shrugging out of his jacket, he then wrapped it around her shoulders. "I won't lie and tell you I'm not disappointed finding out this way. But I understand you must have a really good reason to keep the secrets you do. I hope you know I meant my vows. For as long as we're married, I plan to protect you and work on becoming your friend. That means I hope you eventually see I'm trustworthy."

Her expression softened before she nodded. "I meant what I said too."

He smiled. "I'd say this marriage is off to a good start, then."

Her lashes fluttered as she shivered again.

"We'll get this over with and get you in the barn near the fireplace soon." His palm stretched over her back, rubbing up and down to warm her.

She tucked her head as he ushered her to the waiting photographer.

They posed with Dani, and then it was time for just the two of them.

"Come together a little closer and move sideways so I can get your profiles with the sun setting over the mountains in the background," the photographer, Ryan, instructed them.

Brynn tensed as a few guests milled out of the barn, their attention falling on her.

Aaron leaned in to her ear and whispered, "Trust me?"

Her brows drew together, unsure, as she gazed into his eyes, gratitude flickering in the flecks of gold sparkling in her green orbs. She nodded once.

Aaron slid his hands onto her hips, turning them sideways. He lifted his finger to her chin, forcing her to meet his eyes.

"That's perfect." Ryan snapped the photos. "Let's take the jacket off her and put it back on you, Aaron." Clicks from the camera became background noise as Aaron took the lead, moving through the poses. He took the liberty to skim his hands over her neck, down her shoulders, trailing her spine. His mouth gently rested on her forehead, and then centimeters away from her lips.

Her emerald eyes clouded with what looked like lust, her lids half closed, chest rising and falling more rapidly as he cupped her face and stared at her. Everything else fell away around them, and a rush filled his veins at the power in her faith in him.

"Now kiss." Ryan stepped closer and got down on his knee to capture a different angle.

Aaron didn't hesitate. His lips met hers, infusing everything he couldn't say but wanted her to know. How he'd not been able to take his eyes off her since she walked down that aisle. How he'd been knocked off his axis at the altar when she stood across from him like a dream come true.

Her skin was hot to the touch. Was she burning with the same fever?

"Now how about one with you behind her?" Ryan asked, drawing him out of the trance her lips captured him in.

Her focus hazed, as if she was as undone by his touch as he was hers. Another surge of pride puffed out his chest, and he walked behind her, wrapping his arms around her waist—there was no way she wouldn't feel his hard cock in this position.

A small gasp left her kiss swollen lips.

"Perfect. Now, Brynn, tip your head up and look at Aaron," Ryan directed.

Brynn hesitantly obeyed. She sucked in her bottom lip the tiniest bit and he fought the urge to pull it from her teeth with his thumb. *Whoa. Calm down.*

"Got it. I think that's everything unless you wanted something else?" Ryan stood.

Aaron shook his head and took a step away from Brynn. "Nope, that's good."

"Those will turn out beautifully," his mother said from behind.

He turned to face her, and reality came crashing down on him. He gave his parents a curt smile and removed his jacket once more to wrap around Brynn's shoulders before putting his arm around her. She instinctively leaned into him. Did she even realize she'd done that?

"Hey, Mom, Dad. This is my wife, Brynn." Wow, that would take a bit of getting used to; he had a wife. "Brynn, this is my parents, Samuel and Iris Ridley.

Lines appeared in the corner of his mother's eyes as she smiled at Brynn and held out her hand to shake. "Oh, you are beautiful. It's so nice to meet you."

Brynn returned the gesture, a flicker of a smile turning her lips upwards before it was gone. His father extended his hand next, and Brynn repeated the gesture.

"Son, you look like you've been well," his father remarked.

Aaron nodded. "Thanks for coming. Brynn's daughter, Dani, is around here somewhere." *And hopefully you keep your comments to yourself.*

Maybe inviting them had been a mistake. But they wouldn't know Dani was trans, just like Emmanuel, unless someone told them.

"I was just telling Samuel, we haven't had a vacation in forever. Maybe we can get together this Thanksgiving? It's been so long since we celebrated a holiday as a family." His mother's hopeful gaze volleyed between him and his wife.

Brynn turned to him.

He nodded. "That might be nice."

"I'll call you next week and make plans, or are you both going away longer for the honeymoon?"

"No," Brynn said, her first words to his parents. "I mean we'll be here next week."

His mother cast a questioning glance his way, then smiled again at Brynn. "Alright, then, I'll call you. I'd love to meet our new granddaughter."

Aaron's hand dropped to the small of Brynn's back. "Let's head in. I'm sure the tables are set up for dinner."

He led them all back into the barn, and gone were the rows of chairs, now replaced with long family-style tables decorated in white linen with greenery and flowers woven down the center of each one. He had Nova Emerson to thank for all her input. He'd given them vague instructions, the overall goal of what he wanted to achieve, and the Emersons had blown it out of the water. Everything was perfect. And by the awe in Brynn's eyes, she thought so too.

Dani was sitting with Aspen, Pippa, and Mason.

"Are the twins with Grandpa tonight?" Aaron asked Mason.

He smiled, only half his scarred face turning up. "They sure are."

"And we have the treehouse all set up and winterized so the girls will be cozy for their sleepover," Pippa added.

Brynn tensed next to him. They had to keep up appearances. Everyone would be expecting them to end their night in wedded bliss.

"Sounds fun. Hey, Dani, my parents wanted to meet you." Aaron motioned to his mom and dad.

Dani stood and smiled. "Hello."

His mother's eyes widened, her mouth dropping open. No doubt she, too, noted the similarities between Dani and Emmanuel.

She recovered quickly with a smile. "You are just as beautiful as your mother. So nice to meet you, sweetheart. You can call me Yaya, and Samuel here, Papa, if you like."

Dani cast a quick glance at her mother before she nodded. "Okay."

"Well, we better get to our table. The speeches will start soon," Aaron announced.

His parents said their goodbyes and went to their table as Aaron slipped his hand in Brynn's and led her past the dance floor and up onto the small stage to their table, which sat below a banner that read, *Just married. Mr. and Mrs. Ridley.*

"Speeches?" Brynn asked as she settled into the seat next to him. She didn't pull her hand away, and that brought a spiral of happiness through him.

"I know we didn't really have anyone else in the wedding party, but since it's tradition, I asked a few people to say a little something." He gave her a wink and motioned to her champagne flute. "Drink?"

She shook her head. "I don't drink."

"Oh." He waved to Nova from the corner who for all intents and purposes was as close to a wedding planner as he'd gotten.

She came over, brushing her dark hair from her face, and gave them a warm smile. "How is it going?"

"Great. Everything is beautiful. Is there a chance we could get a bottle of sparkling cider brought over, and another glass for Brynn?"

"Sure thing." Nova disappeared through the crowd, coming back a moment later with what he'd requested.

"Thank you."

"No problem. Let me know if you need anything else." She gave them another smile, then left them alone as he poured Brynn's drink.

"You didn't have to go to all that trouble," Brynn said, taking a sip of the cider. Her nose wrinkled, as if she wasn't expecting the bubbles, and it was the cutest thing he'd seen.

He chuckled.

"What?" she questioned, putting the drink down.

"You're cute when you do that."

Her eyes widened before she swallowed and looked towards Mikel who'd gotten a microphone and moved to the dance floor.

"Testing one, two. Can everyone hear me?"

"Yes," the guests answered unanimously.

Mikel stood sideways, looking between Aaron and the tables full of people. "I don't like to give speeches, so it figures this asshole would ask me."

The crowd laughed, and Aaron smiled.

"But who better to speak to the character of Aaron than the man who once wanted to hate him?"

Everyone drew quiet.

"Even though I really tried to dislike him, because he was dating the love of my life at the time—the woman that is now my wife—I couldn't." Mikel turned to Aaron. "Because Aaron Ridley is one of the best men I've come to know. And, Brynn —" Mikel turned to her. "—you're one lucky woman to have captured this guy's heart. He's the kind of person that will give you the shirt off his back. And fight by your side for a just cause."

Aaron shifted in his seat. *This is uncomfortable. I just do what any decent human does. I don't deserve this level of gratitude.*

Mikel lifted his glass of sparkling cider and winked at them. "To Aaron and Brynn. May your marriage be filled will laughter, joy, friendship, and lots of passion."

Aaron laughed as his body warmed with joy. He sipped his champagne in cheers.

Mikel handed the microphone off to Pippa. She smiled, and Lady sat by her side.

"I've known Brynn for a few years now. We work together and we've become friends. She likes to keep to herself, so a lot of you may not know her as well as you'd like. But she is one amazing strong woman." Pippa and Brynn shared a look as Brynn's eyes teared up.

"I know Aaron through the lifesaving work of the Hope Facility. And let me tell you, I couldn't have picked a better match for Brynn." Pippa raised her glass. "To Brynn and Aaron, may your marriage be all that you hope and more."

Tinkling of glasses followed the collective cheer.

Brynn turned to him. "Why are they doing that?"

Had she never been to a wedding before? "They want us to kiss."

Her eyes dropped to his lips as she licked her own.

He leaned in. "Ready?"

"Okay."

His lips danced over hers, slow and reverent. He took his time before parting his mouth and tracing the seam of hers with his tongue. She opened for him. Lust fire rushed through his veins, as if they were filled with gasoline. Her sweet floral scent wafted over him as her taste enveloped him in a cascading avalanche of sensations, a low growl rumbling in his chest. Brynn gasped and pulled away, her eyes wide. Cheers and clapping came back into focus.

Aaron pressed his palms onto his legs and let out a deep breath. He needed to get his body in check and remember this wasn't real. This was for show. And this might be his wedding night, but they would not be consummating it. *This is just pretend—all to help Dani.* His gaze caught on his bride, his stomach flipping. Why does it feel so real with Brynn?

10

——————

BRYNN

rynn's feet ached and the nerves in her belly twisted as Shattered Cove passed outside the window of the limo. It was just her and Aaron now. His long legs stretched wide, his thigh pressing against hers in the back seat. She sat straight as a board, her body still tingling from all the touching they'd done. Her mind spun as she focused on her breathing. Inhale. Exhale. Aaron's citrusy, sweet scent wafted into her senses, and she resisted the urge to dip her nose into his jacket still snugly pulled around her.

The ceremony had been beautiful, something pulled from the pages of a fairy tale. She'd never expected so much. Her first wedding had been a solemn affair.

Miriam walked down the aisle on her father's arm. It was the first time she'd gotten to be near her father in so long. The pride in his eyes brought a flutter of excitement to her. She just wanted to do what was right. Maybe he'd spend more time with her now that she was the reason for her family being connected to the prophet's. It was an honor, and her father would be the one to reap the benefits the most.

Miriam's eyes remained lowered as they were supposed to do, her head

77

meekly bowed. She stole a quick glance at her soon-to-be husband with his five other wives lined up behind him. All but one gave her a cold, unwelcome frown. The last, a girl not much older than Miriam's fifteen years, took the last spot in line, her expression one of sympathy before her gaze darted once more to the floor.

The prophet himself stood by Paul Livingston, his son. Miriam had trouble focusing as she stood across from the man old enough to be her father. Most of the ceremony passed without a word from her, both her father and her future husband speaking for her. That was how it had always been. Miriam learned long ago a woman's place was to be silent and obedient. And that's just what she'd do to please God and follow her life's mission to serve and submit to her husband and birth the next generation. This is what she'd been raised to do after all, and she'd known no different.

"Brynn?" Aaron's voice ripped her back to the present.

"Hmm?" She tried to shake off the ominous feeling sinking in her gut. Paul had seemed nice at first, until the wedding night. Everything changed then. Would it be the same with Aaron?

"We're here." Aaron slid out of the vehicle and held his hand for her to take.

She slipped her fingers into his, surprising even herself how easy that had become throughout the night. He waved to the driver, then led her down a gravel road with lamps lighting their way. She turned her head from side to side, nothing but a canopy of trees on either side.

"Where are we?" she asked, slowing. Her feet ached from the heels, but she wasn't in a hurry to be alone with her husband.

"My house is right down here. There isn't really a place for the limo to turn around, so it's easier if we walk. Do your feet hurt?"

She nodded. "I'll be okay."

He stopped, then bent his knee to the dirt. Her eyebrows rose as he held out his hand for her foot.

"Give me your shoes."

Her eyes darted around them.

His expression softened. "You're in pain. Let me help?"

She swallowed and nodded, placing her hands on his shoulders and lifting her foot.

Aaron slid his hand to her ankle, sending a tremor up her limbs. He removed the heel and did the same to the other one. Even outside and alone this felt far too intimate.

He stood, holding her shoes in one hand. "Now, you have two choices, Mrs. Ridley. You can let your groom carry you across the threshold, or you can walk in the grass where it's softer on your feet."

The idea of being in Aaron's arms was all too enticing, and that scared her. She wasn't supposed to want to be close to him. But for the first time since she was fifteen, she wanted to be near a man. That was progress.

Still, she dipped her head and took the grassy route. Aaron slipped by her side, guiding her down the driveway.

They turned a corner, and she froze. A large wooden house stood in front of them, with several lanterns hanging outside. The moonlight shone down on it, reflecting off the large panes of glass that seemed to make up the whole bottom floor. This was the type of home Brynn had only ever seen in magazines. It was gorgeous.

"There's a boathouse over there, where that little light is coming from." Aaron pointed towards the right of the house. "Inside are canoes and kayaks you and Dani are welcome to use. Just make sure you each wear a life jacket."

"Boathouse?" She turned, confused, and then her eyes widened. Gone were the trees from her right, replaced with glittering dark water. The man owned a lake.

"Come on inside, I had your bags delivered earlier. But we can get the rest of your stuff tomorrow if you wish." Aaron walked towards the house, up the stone steps, and Brynn followed, peeking back at the lake.

Is this all real? A sliver of fear wound up her spine and around her throat, cinching tighter. Paul was rich, too, and Brynn had learned fast that with money came power, enough to control the lives of those less fortunate.

Lights flicked on, and Brynn took it all in as Aaron placed her shoes by a few of his own in what he called a mudroom. He led her up a couple steps into a giant kitchen with exposed dark beams and a high A-frame ceiling. The walls were a warm, coffee ice cream color, and the cupboards all matched the dark ceiling.

Aaron passed the large square island and the four barstools along the side of it. He motioned towards the stainless-steel refrigerator with a screen much like an iPad on the front. "Please help yourself to anything in the house. If you want something special, you can just add it to the list on the smart screen. My home is your and Dani's home for however long you wish. I want you to be comfortable here."

She nodded. Appreciation bubbled up that he included Danielle in his welcome.

"Hungry? You didn't each much at dinner."

He certainly was observant. She hadn't eaten much because of her nerves, and they were still very much present. "No, thank you."

Aaron walked into the next room. A long table surrounded by ten or more chairs solely occupied the room. Three low-hanging chandeliers that seemed more like pieces of modern art hung over the table.

"This is the formal dining room, but I never really use it unless I have guests. I usually eat at the bar in the kitchen. But through here is the living room." He walked through the arched doorway.

Brynn followed, her gaze sweeping over the opulent room. An L-shaped light-grey almost-white couch filled with colorful pillows sat on a white rug. The dark coffee-colored floors matched the beams on the vaulted ceilings much the same as the kitchen. She tipped her head up to the stairs that led to a second story in the house.

He pointed to two doors off to the side. "The one on the right leads to the bathroom down here with an adjoining laundry room, and the other leads to the basement where I have a TV set up along with games and couches, and a wet bar as well as a gym."

Brynn searched the room once more, realizing there wasn't a TV, unless it was hiding in some fancy system. Instead, there were three bookshelves filled with an array of novels in genres from non-fiction to romance.

"I'll show you the upstairs." Aaron gripped the iron banister as he climbed.

Brynn followed a few feet behind, her heart racing. *Is this when everything changes? Sure, he said he wouldn't expect me to consummate the marriage, but maybe he lied? Maybe he read more into me letting him get close today. I felt his erection while we were taking photos. I didn't mean to arouse him. But what if he blames me like Paul did and forces me to take care of it? Was my dress too revealing?*

"Brynn?" Aaron stood in front of her, his kind brown eyes studying, as if he could tell she was spiraling. But that couldn't be because she'd learned long ago how to steel her features and not show any emotion. It had been a survival skill she'd honed.

"Are you sure you don't want a drink to relax a little?" Aaron asked.

She shook her head. "No."

"May I ask why you don't drink?"

"I was never allowed." *And I'm afraid it will make me feel out of control, which is the last thing I need in your presence.*

He nodded. "Just so we're clear, there are no rules in this house from me except basic respect, which I don't expect to be a problem anyway."

That depends what your definition of respect is.

Paul had a long list of demands in how his wives should respect him.

"I keep trying to set you at ease, but the tension in your shoulders tells me I'm doing a piss-poor job of it." Aaron sighed.

She blinked up at him, still stunned by his honesty. A sliver of calm relaxed her shoulders just a bit.

He pointed to the first door. "I figured Dani could stay here."

Brynn opened the door and gasped. It had pink walls and a four-poster bed with curtains tied to each post and string lights surrounding the top. Posters of Dani's favorite comic, *Selfie,* adorned the walls. A big wooden dresser with a matching vanity lined one wall, and a spacious closet opened to the side. There was also a bookshelf with a few titles already on the shelves. This room was designed for a teenage girl.

Brynn turned to Aaron. "Did you do this for Dani?"

He stuck his hands in his pockets in a self-conscious gesture as he looked away. The movement only endeared him to her. *He's really trying.*

"I wanted her to be comfortable and feel welcome."

Brynn's lips turned up into a smile. "She'll love it."

Aaron's gaze fell to her lips before his own grin appeared. He nodded towards the hall. "Come on, still a few rooms to go. That's the bathroom." He walked to the second-to-last door and opened it.

Brynn peeked in. It was a little bigger than Dani's room, simple and clean. A bed with a soft green comforter took up most of the space. There was a dresser and matching side tables. A desk sat in the corner by a window overlooking the lake with a bouquet of sunflowers. There was a closed door which she imagined led to another spacious closet. And her suitcases were stacked neatly by it. A few paintings adorned the walls, soothing pastel colors, making the room cheery and bright. The space seemed a little feminine for his tastes.

"Whose room is this?"

"It's yours." He backed into the hallway before opening the final door to the master suite. The walls were a similar blue to his office, his comforter a deep navy color. Black-and-white photographs of nature spread out onto his walls in black frames. His dressers were black, as were his side tables.

The rug underneath his bed was a light grey, contrasting with the dark wood floors.

"Your house is lovely," Brynn mused.

"The bathroom in here has a tub, unlike the other down the hall. It's equipped with jets too. If you ever want to use it, feel free."

She stepped back into the hallway and nodded. A bath sounded divine. She reached up and scratched the back of her neck, and then tugged at one of what seemed like a hundred hair pins stuck in her hair-sprayed hair.

"Do you need help taking your hair down?" Aaron asked, always the observant one.

She blushed. Her body ached from all the activity. She was drained from the anxiety and action of the last week. What she wanted most was to fall into bed and sleep for three days straight. The sooner she could get out of this dress and hairdo, the sooner she could do that. "Yes, please."

Aaron's shock showed in his widened eyes and the slight part of his full lips. "Come on in here."

He opened the bathroom door, though it was larger than her whole apartment, so it could hardly be called that. There was a glassed-in shower as well as a large whirlpool-style tub. Slate floors, and a double sink. Brynn stepped in front of the mirror, taking the opportunity to study her new husband as he focused intently on his task.

Aaron pulled pins out and set them in a growing pile on the sink. Her veil followed. His hand brushed against the curve of her neck, and she closed her eyes. Goose bumps erupted on her sensitive flesh. Why did his touch affect her so?

He ran his fingers through her scalp, massaging as he did so. A tiny moan escaped her mouth before her eyes shot open. A flush of embarrassment heated her cheeks as he smiled and continued his ministrations.

"Do you need help with the buttons on the back of the dress?" Aaron asked, biting back a smile.

She froze, all the warm fuzziness gone, replaced with icy fear.

His eyes met hers in the mirror. "Brynn, I meant it when I said I would respect your boundaries. This looks like a complicated task to do with help, let alone by yourself. I just didn't think you could reach it. I only meant to be of assistance. I'll undo it just enough so you can go back to your room alone and get it off for bed."

Her chest tightened, his calm voice and kind promise bringing a wave of guilt crashing down on her. If Aaron was as good as everyone said, and she hoped so, it was unfair to be so suspicious of him. But she couldn't help it. So much reminded her of her past—of Paul.

She nodded and looked down at the sink. "I would appreciate it."

Aaron moved slowly, undoing the top button, his knuckles grazing her spine and sending bolts of lightning buzzing through her. Her head was fuzzy, and her heart raced. Everything was warm and tingly as he moved down her spine, the dress loosening with each undone button.

"That should be enough for you to slip it off." His voice was raw, as if he, too, was affected by her closeness.

She turned around, facing him. His eyes dropped to her lips.

She licked them instinctively. "I know I keep saying it, but I'm so grateful for everything you've done."

His swallow was audible. Some unseen energy surged between them, thickening the air and making it hard to draw in a full breath. Tingles raced up her body, as if tiny threads were winding them together, cinching tighter and tighter, drawing her to him like a magnet. Her focus fell to his lips, so soft and sweet.

Brynn blinked and shook her head, as if it would rid her of the spell. She muttered goodnight and escaped to her bedroom, locking the door behind her before she could do something stupid like kiss her husband.

11

AARON

Aaron hefted the last box up the stairs. Brynn and Dani didn't own much, so it had only taken one trip from their apartment to his home. Dani was fluttering around her new room with what seemed like a permanent smile on her face.

"This is the best room ever, Aaron. I feel like a princess!" Dani squealed.

He chuckled. "I'm glad you like it. I already told your mom, but I want you to know nothing is off-limits in the house. You're welcome to anything. Just make sure you wear a life vest when you take a boat out onto the lake."

"Okay!" Dani bounced onto her bed, then spread out like a starfish.

"Did you check the closet?" Aaron asked.

Dani sat up. "Yes. Oh, the clothes are perfect. Thank you so much."

He nodded. "Of course."

"Is that the last of it?" Brynn asked, coming up behind

him. She was back to wearing a pair of worn jeans and a threadbare T-shirt.

"Yup. I was thinking we could order out for dinner and have it delivered. Sound good?"

"Yes," Dani readily agreed.

"I can cook," Brynn offered.

"Nonsense. I'm sure you're as tired as I am. Let's just order out and relax tonight. Pizza, Indian, Chinese, Ethiopian food, or we could order from Atlantis."

"I've never had most of those," Dani mused. "How about Chinese?"

Aaron blinked. *They've never had Chinese food?*

Brynn must have read the question in his expression because she explained, "We don't get the chance to eat out much."

Aaron clapped his hands.

Brynn jumped and took a step back, making him immediately regret the quick movement.

"Sounds like I have my work cut out for me. We'll have to order one of everything so we can figure out what your favorite is."

"That's too much," Brynn protested. "I'm sure we'll love whatever you pick."

"But it's more fun my way. Besides, leftovers are the best." Aaron gave her what he hoped was a reassuring smile.

Brynn nodded, her expression unreadable.

"I'll go put the order in." Aaron left them alone and walked downstairs to the kitchen, where he pulled a menu from the drawer.

Brynn walked in as he turned around. "Oh, I meant to tell you. Just make a list of everything we need to do like getting you and Dani on my insurance and—"

"You don't have to put me on there. Just Danielle would be perfect." She crossed her arms over her chest.

"You need insurance too. Besides, I get a deal with a family plan." *Maybe. Probably it was true.* She was his wife now, and he'd be damned if she went without even the most basic needs. When was the last time she'd had a general checkup?

She sighed. "Okay, if you're sure."

"Absolutely. And once we get a copy of the marriage license, you can get your name change done. What then? Driver's license?"

Brynn rubbed her thumb on an invisible spot on the counter. "I hadn't thought of that. But I guess I could use it." She hesitated and then shook her head more confidently before she looked at him. "Yes, that would help me be more independent."

He smiled. "Great. Anything else?"

She licked her lips and her gaze darted to the floor. "No, you've already done enough."

"Come on. We're together for a year. If money wasn't an object, what would you buy?" A dress? Some sparkling jewelry? He'd love to buy it all for her. Gifting things was quickly becoming his favorite thing to do.

"I'd like to get my GED."

Wow. It wasn't something he could buy, but he'd still love to help her. "I have some study books at Hope. I'll bring them home for you."

"I would appreciate that." She gave him a small smile, and a burst of warmth socked him in the chest. Earning one of her smiles was like winning the goddamned lottery.

"To get Danielle's name and gender change on her birth certificate, we'll need a doctor to fill out some paperwork. Should we expect any problems from her biological father?"

The ghost of a smile immediately disappeared. Aaron

hated to bring it up, but he needed to be prepared for the battle that lay ahead.

Brynn shook her head, her gaze darting up to him and then down to his chest, as if she was too ashamed to look him in the eyes.

"No, he's not on her birth certificate. Only the first wife gets that honor." Her mouth clamped closed, and her eyes widened as she looked up at him, as if she was horrified the truth had passed her lips.

Other wives? What the fuck did that mean? The more pieces to the puzzle of Brynn he found, the more questions it raised, and none of them were comforting.

But he wouldn't press. The wedding and the move had clearly taken a toll on her. And she was at least able to be in the same room as him without looking like she wanted to flee. And now she was giving pieces of herself to him, bit by bit. A change of subject was in order.

"Do you like spicy food?" He motioned to the Chinese restaurant menu on the island in front of him.

Her shoulders relaxed, gratitude shining in her eyes. "I like the hot wings from the diner that Fred makes."

"Great. I'll order dinner. Why don't you go take a bath and relax. There are some Epsom salts under the sink. You put a cup in the water and it helps relax your muscles. By the time you're done, the food should be here." He pulled his phone from his pocket as she squinted at him, as if she couldn't believe he was real, and then she nodded.

Whoever she'd been with before had done a number on her. And Aaron was going to enjoy undoing the damage one fractured piece at a time, until Brynn could hold her head up high with confidence and see the fucking fantastic, beautiful woman she was.

12

—————

BRYNN

Brynn slid her purse over her shoulder and walked down the stairs. Aaron was stretched out on the couch with a novel in his hands. Something about the image brought a flutter to her belly. She swallowed and waited at the edge of the room.

Whatever Aaron was reading must have been riveting because he didn't look up. She peeked at the side and recognized the title from the bookstore. He was reading romance? Sure, she'd seen a few novels on his shelves at a quick glance, but she'd assumed maybe someone else had left them, maybe an old girlfriend or something.

She cleared her throat.

He lowered the book and gave her a bashful smile. "Oh, hey."

"Hello. Uh, can you point me in the direction of the nearest bus stop?"

His brows drew together before he flicked his wrist to the side and checked his watch. "Do you have a late shift at the diner?"

She shook her head. "No. I, uh, attend a meeting in town."

"Oh, well, I'd be happy to drive you." He closed his book and set it on the coffee table in front of him before he got to his feet.

"I don't want to be any trouble. I'm really okay to take the bus."

His attention turned to her. "The closest bus stop is probably three miles away. I don't mind, really. We'll figure things out until we get you your license. Is Dani coming?"

Three miles? That was too far to walk. She'd be late. Maybe next week she could plan ahead, or stay in town after her shift. With all the excitement of the wedding and moving all her things, she hadn't thought to research it beforehand.

"Yes, she'll be right down."

He nodded. "It's no problem. I'll go get my wallet."

Aaron bypassed her and jogged up the steps just as Dani walked down them, a backpack hung on her shoulder most likely filled with activities to keep her occupied while Brynn was in her meeting.

She made her way to the garage, then climbed into the car, her daughter following. Aaron was a moment behind them, pressing the button to open the bay door. He started the Rover and buckled before backing out. Soft jazz music hummed through the speakers as he turned around and drove them down his long driveway towards town.

"What time do you need me to pick you up?" Aaron asked, turning the music down a notch.

"I don't want to trouble you. I can catch the bus at least to the stop closest to you."

He tapped his fingers on the wheel to the beat of the music. "It's really not any trouble. In fact, I don't mind hanging around town while you're busy. Does Dani go with you, or does she want to join me for some milkshakes and arcade time?"

"Can I go with Aaron, Mom? Pleeease?"

I don't have money to waste on games and eight-dollar milkshakes. "I don't want us to be any more trouble."

Aaron reached out his arm, as if to squeeze her knee, but then seemed to think better of it, returning his hand to his own lap. "Brynn, I promise I won't offer something unless I'm willing to do it. We'll have fun. And it's my treat."

"I can't let you pay for her. You've already done too much for us."

"There's no keeping score. I told you. If you'd rather send her with some spending cash, that's fine. But I did invite her, and my mama taught me that a gentleman always pays for his guests," he said, his Southern drawl enunciating "mama."

After she'd found out his brother's story, she was surprised to see his parents at the wedding. The introductions seemed strained, yet they were apparently going to be sharing Thanksgiving with them. Had they changed?

"Are you okay with that?" Aaron asked.

Brynn blinked. "Hmm?"

"The arcade?"

"Oh, yes. I guess so. But I prefer to pay for her." She dug out her worn wallet and pulled fifteen dollars out before handing it over to Dani.

"Thanks, Mom."

"You're welcome." She sat back in her seat and peered through the car window as the bare trees made way to open fields with hay bales wrapped in white so they looked like giant marshmallows. They passed a row of houses.

"Where exactly am I taking you?" Aaron asked.

"The Methodist church on Ocean Spray Avenue."

If he wondered why she was attending a church meeting

at seven in the evening on a weeknight, he didn't voice it. Maybe he knew about the meetings for sexual assault survivors. Shame squeezed her throat tight, making it hard to swallow.

He pulled the car in front and parked it, opening his door, as if he was going to get hers for her, but she beat him to it.

"I'll see you in an hour. Thank you." Brynn rushed out of the car, not even looking behind her as she closed the door and ran up the uneven steps to the church entrance.

Walking inside, she sucked in a breath of cool air that smelled like old books and dust. She turned down the steps leading to the basement, where the temperature dropped another few degrees, and tugged her grey sweater tighter before opening the door with shaky hands. Several chairs formed a circle, a few of them occupied by familiar faces: Jasmine who owned The Lighthouse Inn and part of Atlantis; and Belle, the sexual assault nurse examiner who'd taken care of Brynn when she'd first arrived in Shattered Cove hospital battered and bruised with a broken arm and ribs. Of course, Cassidy Clark, the group therapist, was there, refilling her coffee by the refreshments table.

Nerves twisted in Brynn's gut. She'd gone faithfully to these meetings for a while, but she'd never spoken up. She hadn't been ready. But maybe now she might be able to.

She walked towards the therapist, nodding as Cassidy gave her a warm smile.

"It's nice to see you again," Cassidy remarked.

Brynn grabbed a mug and tea bag before pouring hot water into the cup. "I'm . . . I think I need to talk to someone."

Cassidy stepped closer, as if to give them a little more privacy. "Do you need to speak with me privately? Or are you okay with sharing in the group?"

Brynn lifted the tea bag before dunking it in the hot water again, turning towards the small group. She'd heard Jasmine's story and figured she might be the one to give her the best advice in this situation. "I'd like to try in the group if that's okay?"

"Of course. We're just about to start." Cassidy grabbed her coffee and headed to the group where Charli was already sitting. Another two women Brynn didn't recognize filtered into the room as Brynn squeezed her hand around the hot mug, grateful for its warmth. She walked to an empty chair and took a seat.

Belle smiled at her. "It's nice to see you again."

"Thank you."

"Alright, I think we can get started if everyone wants to grab a seat. Most of you know the drill. Feel free to help your-self at any time to refreshments at the table over there." Cassidy pointed behind Brynn. "Now, I like to begin every meeting with some affirmations. Would you all like to repeat after me . . . I am strong."

"I am strong," the women spoke in unison.

"I am brave. I am worthy." Cassidy's sharp gaze circled the room, taking in every face with her welcoming smile. "This is a safe space. Anything you say here will remain private. You all know I'm Cassidy Clark, the facilitator of this meeting, and Belle, my co facilitator and a certified SANE nurse. Did you want to start us off, Brynn?"

Panic crawled over Brynn's skin like a thousand fire ants, terror clamping her mouth shut. Her sister's face flashed in her mind. Her sister deserved justice, and at the very least to have her story told. It was one way Brynn could honor her, and it was a stepping-stone. Maybe if she shared about her sister, it would get easier to talk about her own past trauma.

"My sister and I grew up in what I now know was a cult."

Brynn searched the faces in the room. Some eyes widened with shock, and others with sympathy. "My sister and I were total opposites. She was so strong and stood up for me and herself." Brynn's throat clogged with emotion, making it hard to speak as her eyes stung. "The prophet and his disciples didn't like that. Women weren't allowed to do very much. Being obedient and submissive were absolute musts. From the time we were children, we were not given any room to express ourselves. We were to be obedient robots, there to serve and care for the other children and the men." Brynn closed her eyes, trying to stave off the tears. "We were brainwashed with their dogma. We really believed this was our true calling, that this was the way to eternal salvation. We followed the prophet's commands, as if they were straight from God, and didn't question anything . . . but my sister did."

Brynn opened her eyes, locking gazes with Cassidy. "And they punished her for it. They blamed a possessive spirit for overtaking her body because she asked questions and wasn't satisfied with their answers. She spoke out when they married me off at fifteen to an almost forty-year-old man as his sixth wife."

Jasmine gasped.

Brynn shook her head, anger rising. "And when it came time for her to marry, she downright refused. By then I was . . . falling apart. But I was too scared to run away. She stayed, for me." Hot tears fell down Brynn's cheeks. "I was scared I would burn in hell if I left. I was terrified of the world beyond the compound. We'd been told horror stories that made it seem like the rest of the planet was evil. By then, I had my son, uh, daughter, and I thought of this innocent little baby that needed me to protect them. Could I risk it all for my selfishness to not want to serve my wifely duties whenever my husband demanded?" Brynn gave a mirthless laugh and shook her head. "Rape was a word I learned much later . . . My sister finally had enough. She ran one night, but they caught her. And they punished her so severely . . ." Brynna's swollen and bruised face flicked through her mind's eye like a reel from a horror movie. Her dress torn from the lashes, her back bleeding.

Everyone in the compound had been summoned to witness the punishment that the prophet and Paul doled out.

"That was the first time I spoke up." *And I have the matching scars to prove it.* With each truth stuffed down for so long that bled from her lips, Brynn gained a little more of her power back. "But it was too late."

A sob tore out of her. The more she spoke, the faster it all came. A riot of emotions gurgled in her gut, spreading out through her veins until she was more manic than anything.

Belle handed her a tissue and moved to sit closer, Jasmine took up the spot next to her, and Charli scooched closer— their warm steady hands on her back giving her the strength to tell the rest of the story.

"Being told almost every day how inherently evil you are, that you're bad, stupid, not good enough . . . eventually, you believe it."

"They knew how to break you down so they could control you," Cassidy said.

Brynn nodded. "And it worked for a long time."

Belle rubbed her hand in a circle on Brynn's back. *Could she feel the raised scars?* "When you find out who and what you are capable of, that's when you start climbing out. I've known you since you first came to this town." Belle gave her a knowing look. "And I can tell you, you are miles from that scared and lost girl. Healing takes time, and lots of effort."

"Trauma doesn't ever leave us. I know that isn't what you all want to hear." Cassidy sighed. "But the truth is you can heal from it, just like all wounds heal. Trauma leaves lasting scars. You won't be the same as you were, but you can still find happiness."

Brynn shook her head. "I don't think I deserve it. Not after—"

"Shame is an ugly monster. The most devious because it tricks you into believing you're not worthy when, in fact, you are. You deserve everything good." Cassidy lightly touched her knee. "Brynn?"

She met her eyes.

"It was not your fault."

Brynn shook her head. "But—"

"You were a child. Your sister was a child. You were a victim of your environment. You are not to blame for the actions of others."

"I should have left with her," she argued.

"And then you both would have been terrorized."

Brynn gasped.

Cassidy's expression softened. "You will drive yourself mad with the maybes of life. We can't go back. All we can do is move forward. Take it one day at a time, one minute when even that is too much."

"I feel so guilty that I'm living life and she's dead."

"There are no words to take that shame from you. That is something you will have to work through. And it will be a grieving process," Cassidy finished.

Jasmine cleared her throat and turned towards Brynn. "I had already started my journey of healing when Atlas came along. But he presented a lot of new struggles for me, as well as a safe place for me to land. He didn't heal me; I did that on my own. But my relationship with him provided the opportunity for growth. I'm sure you know what I mean. Being a newlywed might be stirring up some of this stuff and opening the wound again, so it all feels fresh. Just give it some time to settle."

Right. They think my marriage is real. "Was it hard for you to be with a man after . . . ?"

Jasmine nodded. "There are some things we can't do sexually because it triggers me. But Atlas is so patient and gentle. It's how I knew he was different, that he was worth the extra work I had to do internally, and the risk involved with being vulnerable."

Is there any hope for me? Aaron was both patient and gentle and about a million other things.

"Sometimes Aaron seems too good to be true," Brynn confessed.

"Maybe that's because all you've ever known was the wrong kind of people. Your intuition must be telling you deep down that he truly is someone to be trusted if you married the man." Jasmine gave her a tender smile.

"Right." Brynn nodded. It didn't seem right to deceive these people about her sham of a marriage, but it was what she had to do for Dani. And a part of her would feel like she betrayed Aaron by telling them too.

"Trust that voice inside." Charli echoed the same words Brynn had once shared with her.

Brynn nodded. She had a lot of work ahead of her. But if she didn't deal with it, she knew in her heart that Dani would be the one to suffer. And Brynn wouldn't put her child through any more.

Guilt crashed over her. *I wasn't strong enough to leave earlier. That horrible place left a lasting mark on Danielle. But it ends here, with me.*

13

AARON

Aaron shot up in bed. His blurry eyes blinking as he tried to make sense of what had woken him. He turned to the clock. It was three-thirty in the morning.

A strangled cry came from the next room and he was on his feet and to the door as fast as he could make it. *Had someone broken in?*

Aaron stepped into the hallway, his body on alert.

"No, please don't!" Brynn shouted from her room.

Aaron gripped the knob and whipped the door open, switching on the light.

He blinked at the brightness as he scanned the room for an intruder. Brynn was tangled in the sheets, her face wet with tears as she cried out.

He debated what to do: if she woke and found him here, she might freak the fuck out, but leaving her so traumatized seemed heartless.

"Please stop, you're hurting me!" Brynn's pleading tore a

hole straight through his heart. He wanted to comfort her—needed to. But how?

He kneeled on the bed to reach out to her shoulder and gently shake her. "Brynn? Sweetheart? You're dreaming."

Brynn's eyes flashed open.

Aaron held up his hands in surrender. "You were having a bad dream. I just wanted to make sure you were okay."

Brynn sat up, eyes wildly searching the room. She inched towards him as she swung her head to the dark window.

"You're safe here. Nothing is gonna hurt you on my watch," he assured her.

He hesitated, unsure if he should stay or go. What did she need?

Brynn turned to him, her body trembling and her attention darting wildly around the room as if searching for an intruder. She reached out to him. Stunned, he opened his arms right before she fell into them. She sobbed against his chest, clinging to him, as if her life depended on it.

"I'm sorry. I'm so sorry," she kept repeating, over and over.

"Shh. It's alright. There isn't anything to be sorry about." Aaron moved to sit against her padded headboard, cradling her against him. He leaned his mouth down to her sweaty forehead and pressed a tender kiss to her crown. "I've got you, sunshine. You're safe with me."

Her sobs quieted, but she remained in his arms. A few minutes later, her tearstained face slackened, and her breathing evened out. Ropes of affection mingled with protective instincts and weaved around his chest, cinching tight. Peering down at her angelic face, he cursed the son of a bitch who made this beautiful creature afraid in her dreams. It was killing him that he couldn't fix this. Invisible dragons were harder to slay than flesh and blood—but not impossible. He had to believe that. He would do everything in his power to protect Brynn and Danielle from their past.

Aaron brushed a stray strand of hair from her face with his finger. Her skin was silky soft, so delicate like the woman in his arms. This was the first time he had the opportunity to study her so close for so long. And it was the first time he noticed the roots of her hair had begun to grow out. It seemed Brynn was a natural blonde. Was her hair one more thing she'd had to change to escape her ex?

She wouldn't have to give anything else up for anyone; Aaron would make sure of it. It was time someone gave to her instead of taking. And he was just the man for the job.

Aaron gently slid her onto the bed, then reached over her to pull the covers up. When he tried to pull away, Brynn clung tighter to his chest. He'd stay for a little while longer. Hopefully, she wouldn't regret this in the morning and freak out that he was in her bed. *Only one way to find out.*

BRYNN

Brynn slipped into consciousness, her body cloaked in warmth, reveling in the heady peaceful feeling of being safe. Tears formed behind her closed eyes. She'd never experienced this. She didn't want to open them and leave this dream. Instead, she snuggled closer into the warmth at her back.

A strong arm slipped around her waist, tucking her closer. She froze. Brynn's eyes shot open, her body going rigid. She held her breath as she took in her surroundings. Sage-green comforter. Flowery pictures on the wall. Her room. So why wasn't she alone?

My nightmare. Memories of last night came crashing over her, removing any trace of comfort left. The meeting must have stirred things up. Last night, she'd been terrified that Paul had found her. And then Aaron had come in, still keeping his distance, yet checking on her. She was only half awake when she'd asked him to stay. *Why did I do that?*

Well, he'd listened, if his soft breath on her neck was any indication. This wasn't a dream. And now . . . what did this mean? Would he expect something physical from her? Would he require her to deal with the erection pressing against her thigh? Would he blame her too? And why did his possessive hold of her bring a flutter to her most secret places?

Warmth bloomed in her core despite the uncertainty that lingered. Being held so tightly released something inside. She didn't have a choice but to be locked in his embrace—and somehow, it freed her from the shame of enjoying it. *I'm so fucked up.* Her mind spun. *What does this all mean?*

Aaron's chest rose before he released a long exhale. His body stiffened, as if he'd woken and just realized he was wrapped around her. She closed her eyes, trying to even out her breathing. Could he feel her heart racing? Numbness settled into her bones as she separated herself from her body like she had so many times when Paul visited her room.

Aaron's hold relaxed as he slowly slipped his arm from under her while she pretended to be asleep. *What is he going to do?* Chills raced over her skin, and she held her breath. Aaron paused, his gaze burning the side of her face as she worked hard not to react. The soft comforter dragged up her arm, all the way to her neck. His warm calloused palm smoothed the hair that had fallen onto her face out of the way. His thumb took one last tender swipe on her cheekbone before he quietly left the room, the door snicking shut behind him.

She freed the gulp of oxygen from her lungs. Tears dripped out of the corner of her eyes; she'd never experienced such gentleness. Brynn breathed out a sigh in part relief, part confusion. Why did she feel so cold without him in bed? She should be grateful he kept his word and didn't try anything—and she was. But he'd left this . . . this *other* feeling behind. Brynn didn't have a name for it, but it was uncomfortable. Like a deep wanting.

She opened her eyes and wiped them before she checked

the clock. She needed to get up and get ready for work. And face Aaron. Would he bring up the nightmare? Would he mention he'd stayed the whole night in her bed? The heat of humiliation rose in her cheeks. *Oh, God. Things are going to be so awkward. What if he asks me about it?*

Nevertheless, she had to get going. Her bills wouldn't pay themselves. Danielle needed her. Brynn couldn't afford to fall apart when she was all her daughter had.

She sat, rubbing her eyes as the blanket lowered to her waist. She reached out her hand to the side of the bed Aaron had slept on. It was still warm. She leaned forward, the urge rising unbidden as she inhaled the pillow beside hers. The faint notes of his scent filled her senses, bringing with it a tease of the same floaty sensation she'd experienced while in his arms.

Brynn shook her head and got out of bed. Confusion swirled in her mind and body. Hot and cold. Scared and excited. Nervous butterflies danced in her belly.

She grabbed her things for the day, then crept out the door, breathing out a sigh of relief at the empty hallway. She scurried to the bathroom, locking the door behind her. Her hands trembled as she set her things on the counter, her eyes purposely avoiding the mirror, as always. She couldn't look into the face she couldn't recognize. Instead, she turned the shower on and stripped naked. She held her hands over her breasts, as if her nakedness was something she, too, should be ashamed of. She climbed in the shower once the water was warm enough and scrubbed her body that never felt clean enough. She'd read that every seven years your body is totally regenerated with new cells. Only four more to go before she'd have the pleasure of the knowledge Paul had never touched this one. Maybe then she'd be able to *feel.*

Sometimes it was like she was in a costume, the outward

layers numb with Novocain. It was easier to shut that part of her off after she married Paul. Then it didn't hurt so bad. But even now, years later, she couldn't turn it off completely. The only time she experienced physical sensations was with Aaron for some reason. The fact that he could bring these sensations back terrified her. Did it mean he had some sort of control over her? Or was it her intuition telling her he was safe? Only time would tell.

* * *

Brynn finished getting dressed, then made her way down to the kitchen where the savory smell of bacon and pancakes wafted through the air. Aaron stood in front of the stove, a spatula in his hand as he flipped a pancake in the pan. A light-blue button-up dress shirt stretched across his wide shoulders, making her mouth go dry. It tapered in at his waist, tucking into a royal-blue pair of slacks that fit his butt like a glove. Brynn's cheeks flamed as she snapped her attention away, towards her daughter who was eagerly attacking her breakfast plate.

"Hey, Mom. Aaron made chocolate chip pancakes. They're so good. You have to try." Dani smiled before taking a sip of her orange juice.

Aaron turned, giving her a welcoming grin. Her belly flipped.

"Hungry?" he asked, turning back to pick a plate off the counter. He added the latest pancake from the pan and threw on a couple strips of bacon before he handed her the plate.

Guilt crashed over her. She should have been the one to get up and cook for them. Aaron was letting them live here without paying rent, and she hadn't even contributed to groceries yet. Not to mention she'd been raised to believe it was the woman's job to cook and clean. *I'm even failing at being a fake wife.*

"Thank you. I'm sorry. I should have been up to make breakfast. I'll do it tomorrow." Brynn sat on the stool next to Dani.

Aaron shrugged and opened a drawer, taking out a fork before setting it in front of her. "No need to apologize. Pancakes happen to be my specialty. Chocolate chip, banana, blueberry, birthday cake—the possibilities are endless."

"Birthday cake pancakes?" Dani asked, her eyes widening.

Aaron chuckled. "Absolutely. They even have sprinkles. You'll have to let me know your birthdays so I can make it special for you that day."

Brynn swallowed the lump of emotion that rose. He was being too nice. He had to want something from her.

His warm brown gaze switched to her. "I'm heading to Hope today for a few meetings. Did you want Dani to come with me and hang out at the center while you work?"

"Can I, Mom?" Dani asked, scraping the last bite of pancake from her plate before she stuffed it into her mouth.

Brynn handed her a napkin. "What about your homework?"

"I can do it there," Dani promised.

"Well, then, I guess so."

"You know, I'm hiring at the center." Aaron's focus slid to the left before returning to her. "I need another personal assistant. And Marge could use some help in the kitchen. Or even just an extra chaperone. That way you could spend your day close by and not have to work so many other places. And—"

"No."

Aaron snapped his mouth shut.

"I'm sorry. Thank you, but I . . . I'm good where I am."

Sweat beaded on her forehead. She wasn't used to standing up for herself, especially to a man. But she wasn't the weak Miriam anymore. Now she was Brynn. And Brynn asserted herself and fought for her needs. Brynn knew how to set boundaries.

It was clear Aaron was just trying to be nice, but she couldn't let him control so many aspects of her life. As it was, she lived with him and relied on him for transportation. She couldn't allow him having anything to do with her income, her one source of independence.

"Okay." He nodded, a flash of disappointment in his gaze.

She let out a breath and relaxed her body. She hadn't even realized she'd tensed. Was it really that easy? He just accepted her declining the offer?

Aaron picked up his own plate and leaned against the counter as he shoveled a bite in his mouth, seemingly relaxed. "Once Danielle's paperwork is finished, are you planning on enrolling her in school?"

Brynn's heart swelled with joy and she nodded. "Yes."

"That's exciting. You'll be in Aspen's grade, won't you?" Aaron asked Dani.

Her daughter beamed. "Yup! I can't wait. She's been showing me her homework so I can keep up with what they're learning."

"Once we get the name changes official, it will make the paperwork easier." Aaron took another bite.

Brynn nodded. Her daughter going to school was a dream come true. Almost no one back on the compound went to school. Instead, they did their own version of classes. Girls were taught cooking, childrearing, sewing, and religious studies. The boys were also taught the religious text, but their other teachings were specific to the job they'd been assigned by the prophet. Most were laborers, woodworkers, what most in Shattered Cove would call handymen. Some of the favorites were sent to college to earn degrees to be lawyers, bank managers, and even police officers so they could integrate into the society around the compound. That way, the Livingstons could control everything. No one could stop them if they owned the law, and the money.

"Not hungry?" Aaron motioned to her untouched plate, concern marring his brow.

Brynn snapped back into the present, quickly grabbing the fork and cutting into her pancake. "Sorry."

Aaron walked over to her side and set the maple syrup jug beside her plate. His hand gently rested over hers, sending a warm buzz up her arm. He leaned in as she turned to face him.

He focused on her so intently, she couldn't look away. He held her captive with his amber orbs as everything faded from around them.

Mouth parted, his voice low and soft yet firm at the same time, he said, "You have nothing to be sorry about. Don't ever apologize for speaking your truth."

Her breath caught in her throat. His words were like a battering ram against the walls around her heart. No one had ever seen through her like this nor encouraged her to stand up for herself, except for her therapist. The contrast between Aaron and the man in Brynn's past was night and day. Still, a big part of her held back. If her experience had taught her anything, it was that men were not safe. They were not to be trusted. They always wanted more than you were willing to give.

So, why did that small voice inside her disagree? Why did her gut tell her that, this time, she was wrong? And why did she want to believe it so badly?

15

BRYNN

Letting out a sigh, Brynn set her bag by the door and toed off her shoes. Her feet ached from being on them all day. First, she'd worked the shift at the diner before heading over to the bookstore to lock up. She pinched the space between her neck and shoulder, attempting to massage out some of the tension as Dani zoomed by towards the stairs to her room.

A sliver of disappointment sunk in her belly. She hadn't seen her daughter all day. Brynn had gotten used to being able to check in with Dani anytime she wanted. It was the best way to make sure she was safe. *But she's safe with Aaron too.* Brynn had finally gotten comfortable dropping Dani off at the Hope Facility. The staff there was so welcoming and kind.

Aaron came into the mudroom, prompting Brynn to quicken her pace to the kitchen. They hadn't spoken about the previous night, but she couldn't help but think his words this morning encompassed that too. *You have nothing to be sorry about.*

Brynn grabbed a glass from the cupboard and filled it

halfway with water before drinking it down, trying to calm her ever-present nerves. She just wanted to lie in bed and sleep for two days, but her tasks weren't done yet. She needed to make dinner.

Aaron set his refillable coffee mug by the sink. "How was your day?"

She blinked up at him. "Uh, busy . . . How was yours?"

He crossed his arms and turned around to lean back against the counter. His forearms stretched against the crisp blue fabric of his dress shirt, which he'd unbuttoned a little more, showing off a few dark curls on his chest. Brynn swallowed as his rumbly voice stopped. *Shoot. I missed what he said.*

"I'm sorry, what did you say?"

A small smile played on his lips. "What did I tell you about apologizing?"

Heat crept up her neck, and something warm settled below her belly at his teasing tone. "I'm sorry—I, I mean, can you repeat that?"

"My day was pretty good. We're almost at capacity again and I hate to turn kids in need away. I've been talking with a few other directors and I'm not sure another addition is feasible because of zoning laws unless I buy the property next to it."

"Isn't that a department store?"

He nodded. "Yeah, but they are going out of business, and the lot will be available. I was thinking of getting it and then having Mikel and Andre at Seacoast Construction to oversee the project and turn it into more dorms."

"Can you do that?" she asked.

He tipped his head to the side. "It would mean cashing out some of my investments."

She studied him more closely. "You mean you'd pay for it? Not the center?"

"I guess now that we're married, we should talk about this. I usually like to keep my finances private."

"Oh, you don't have to. It was rude of me to ask. I'm so —" She stopped herself, that time earning an even bigger grin from him.

Aaron shook his head. "No, really it's fine. Like I said, you're my wife now."

"Only in name," she reminded him.

His eyes met hers, something that looked a lot like determination flashing in them. "In every way that counts."

She swallowed.

"I funded Hope Facility myself. We do fundraisers and get some government grants, but it's never enough. So, I supplement everything with my own savings. While I played professional ball, I invested most of my earnings, and I picked the right ones for my portfolio. I'm a multimillionaire."

Brynn blinked and swallowed as she looked away. "You played pro ball?"

"I don't say that to . . . Hell, I don't even want anyone knowing."

"I won't say anything," Brynn promised. How many secrets had she kept? So many. But this one felt different. She was honored he trusted her enough to share these very personal details with her.

He nodded. "Thank you."

"It's the least I can do." She flicked her attention back to his soft gaze. Tension rose, some invisible force tugging her towards him. She reached for the handle on the fridge just to have something to ground her. "What do you want for dinner? There is some chicken in here, and leftover rice. I could make a stir-fry?" She shifted her weight to one achy foot, trying to give the other a break.

Aaron's arm reached out in front of Brynn, his citrus scent

wafting over her. "How about I cook us all dinner while you go take a bath and get off those feet?"

Her attention darted to him once more. "Oh, no. I'm fine. I need to pull my weight around here. It's my job to cook."

"Who says?" He shut the fridge.

Brynn nervously twisted her fingers in front of her. "Uh, I'm not sure what you mean?"

"Who said cooking dinner was your job? I don't remember us talking about that."

"I . . . I'm sorry." The apology slipped from her lips. "I just figured that . . ."

He stepped closer, towering over her. She sucked in a quick breath, a mixture of fear and curiosity swirling inside her.

"I think it's time we talked about our expectations and roles." He motioned to the barstools. "Want to join me?" He walked over and took a seat without waiting for her answer.

Brynn followed, careful not to sit too close, anxiety spiking as she turned towards him. *Is this where he changes? What expectations? Is this because of last night?*

"We really rushed into this. Usually, I'd imagine things like this are already handled when someone gets married." Aaron chuckled, his easygoing manner helping to set her at ease some. But a part of her was still waiting for something bad to happen.

"I guess I always viewed a marriage as something unique to each couple. What works for one, doesn't for another. And I think if we talk about our needs and what we expect from each other, we can create a plan that serves us best. How does that sound?" he asked.

Aaron wanted her to tell him her needs? They would come up with a plan together like equals?

She nodded, still too stunned for words. Here was a man

that held so much power in name, money, and status, and even over her situation, and he was offering her a seat at the proverbial table as an equal.

Aaron tapped the counter with his finger. "I'll start. I see my role as taking care of you and Dani. I mean that as in putting a roof over your heads, making sure you're comfortable, and have everything you need. Your safety is my top priority. And I hope we can ease into a friendship and continue to communicate honestly like this."

"What do you need from me?"

"Friendship. Communication. And I hope to earn your trust."

He was silent a beat, so Brynn took her cue. "That's it? What about chores around the house?"

He shrugged. "I mean, of course you can pitch in, but don't think I expect you to do everything. We can take turns. Even include Dani if you want. Maybe a chore chart, and we can take turns drawing out what we'll do to make it fair. And as far as cooking dinner goes, we can switch off. And when you're driving, if I get home first, I'll start dinner, and you can if you feel up to it."

She nodded. "You cook and clean?"

He chuckled. "You can thank my mama for that. She always told me she wasn't raising no little boy, but a man. And men pick up after themselves."

The corners of her mouth tugged up. She liked the way his eyes lit when he spoke.

"Now, it's your turn. What are your expectations and needs for me and this marriage?" Aaron prompted.

Brynn stared at the wood countertop. *What do I need?* "I think how things have been going is beyond amazing."

He slapped a hand over his heart. "Amazing? Pulling out

the big praise for this already?" He leaned in and winked. "Honey, I'm just getting started."

Her stomach flipped as more of those flighty creatures woke and fluttered in her gut. "I need your honesty, and for you to continue respecting my boundaries. And I need to feel like I'm contributing somehow. I'd like to pay for the groceries at least."

Aaron inhaled and let it out slowly before he spoke. "How about we go fifty-fifty with the food?"

"But there's two of us and only one of you," she pointed out.

"I'm a six-foot-eight man; I eat more than you two combined and then some. Besides, I want you to keep your money for Dani's and your future."

Brynn's chest tightened. Right, for when she and Dani left a year or so from now. It would be nice to have a safety net. Gratitude swelled in her rib cage as she nodded. "Okay, fifty-fifty."

His grin grew and her heart stuttered. Tingles raced through her, gathering low in her womb. That wanting feeling was back, making her entertain the idea of wrapping her arms around him for a hug, or even to kiss him on the cheek. Her face heated at the scandalous forward thought.

"Sounds like we have a plan." Aaron nodded. "But remember, we can always modify it as needed. Just let me know if you want to talk."

"Okay."

"How about I get dinner going and you go on up and enjoy a bath? Use those Epsom salts under the sink. I got a couple new scents. And this weekend we can go get groceries together when you're off work."

Another bath sounded heavenly. "Are you sure you don't need help? I could—"

Aaron waved his hand. "I'm positive. You enjoy."

"Alright. I think I will." Brynn slid off the stool. "Being your fake wife definitely has its perks," she teased, which was a first for her.

His eyes widened and then darkened. Aaron reached out and crooked his finger under her chin, tilting her head towards him ever so slightly as his focus remained locked on her. Her body buzzed with frantic energy at his touch. Tension thickened the air, making it impossible to draw a full breath.

"You asked me to be honest?" he said.

"Y-yes?"

"I'd love to give you a full-body massage after your bath until you're so relaxed you fall asleep." His voice was rough and low. "But I don't want to make you uncomfortable."

Why was there a sudden surge of wetness between her thighs at his words?

He dropped his hand and got up, heading over to the fridge presumably to start dinner. Brynn was still reeling, trying to get her bearings. The man knocked her off her axis constantly until she wasn't sure which was up or down anymore. Until she was floating somewhere in the unknown.

She gathered her wits and headed towards the stairs, halting at the entrance to the living room before turning back, Aaron's gaze locked on Brynn. A thrill shot through her that she couldn't explain at having captured his attention.

"Aaron?"

"Hmm?"

"You really are the best fake husband. I hope you know that. You're going to make some woman very happy one day."

Surprise reflected in his gaze before it turned to determination. "That means a lot coming from you."

Brynn spun round and made her way upstairs, trying not to think of his big strong hands rubbing all over her body. But it was no use. The image festered until—while surrounded in hot water in a steam-filled bathroom with a locked door—Brynn's hands wandered from her neck, then down her chest. She lifted one heavy breast, closing her eyes and imagining it was Aaron's palms instead. Heat a thousand times hotter than the bathwater ignited in her core, and she squeezed her thighs together as her fingertips gently grazed over her torso. Pinching her nipple, a small moan drifted into the room.

Brynn froze, eyes snapping open as embarrassment burned her cheeks. *What am I doing?* Shame crashed over her. *Is this lust? Does this make me wicked? Is something wrong with me?* Had she just betrayed Aaron by thinking those thoughts of him?

Paul's words repeated in her mind: *You're a filthy whore of the world who will bring eternal damnation down on your own head.*

Brynn shook her head. No. He couldn't control her anymore.

I'm a good person.

But what was going on with her body lately? Who could she talk to? Pippa? Her stomach dropped at the thought. Too embarrassing. In the compound, no one ever talked about such things. Perhaps there was something wrong with her. Maybe she was a deviant.

There was one way she could find out.

16

AARON

Aaron pressed his hand to Brynn's lower back as she pushed the cart through the grocery store.

"Do we need more orange juice?" he asked.

Brynn nodded. "And oat milk."

He grabbed a bottle of each. "Do you and Dani want regular milk?"

She shook her head and focused ahead, towards the eggs. She hadn't looked him in the eye since he walked into the living room and found her so engrossed in one of his romance novels that he had to call her name three times for attention. She'd flushed the reddest he'd seen her yet and had avoided his eyes ever since.

"We can get both," he offered again, pointing towards the dairy case.

"Honestly, I've gotten used to your oat milk. It's rather good."

He smiled. "Glad to hear it. What's next on the list, honey?" He took the opportunity to lean in closer, inhaling her sweet scent as she pulled up the grocery list on his phone that he'd handed her.

Her hand trembled slightly. Was she uncomfortable with this? "Are you okay? Or is playing the newlyweds too much today?"

She turned to him for the first time since that morning, gratitude shining in her eyes as she blinked twice in sucession. "I'm okay."

"Good." He smiled, hoping to set her at ease. "So, if I told you I was going to lean in and kiss you right now while nosy Miss Nancy Plotts in aisle two was watching, you'd be okay with that?"

Her breath hitched. "I mean if you think it's necessary."

"Oh, it's necessary." *Because it's taking everything in me to keep my hands off you.*

He leaned in slowly before he gently pressed his lips to hers. She melted against him, a soft gasp leaving her parted mouth. He slid his lips around her bottom one, tugging ever so slightly. A tiny mewl left her throat and shot straight to his cock. No matter how much she fought it, there was no doubt Brynn felt this chemistry too.

"Goodness me, you two are gonna melt the whole refrigerator section," Mrs. Patterson teased as she passed by Nancy, her cart loaded with canned cat food.

Brynn pulled away, hiding her face against his chest.

Aaron laughed and gave the old woman a smirk. "Good morning, Mrs. Patterson. How's Jake?"

Her eyes lit up. "Better than ever. He's loving his classes." The woman's gaze dropped to Brynn. "I hope you're not embarrassed, dear."

Brynn lifted her head hesitantly, her cheeks still slightly flushed.

"Oh to be young and in love again. Savor every moment

you have. And don't ever take chemistry like that for granted." Mrs. Patterson winked, then waved to them. "I better be off. I'm going to get the fixings for my famous shepherd's pie for Jake's dinner tonight."

"You'll have to come help Marge make a big batch for the kids again someday soon. They loved it last time," Aaron added.

"Oh, I'd love that. Just let me know when. Have a great day." She left them and swerved down the next aisle.

Brynn pushed the cart forward, and Aaron's hand returned to her waist. "I think it's safe to say we pulled it off, Mrs. Ridley."

A small chuckle came from Brynn. God, he wanted to see how a full belly laugh sounded from her. What would it take?

"I have a joke for you." He picked up a box of crackers and set them in the cart.

"A joke?"

"Yeah. Did you hear about the first restaurant to open on the moon?" Aaron asked.

Brynn wrinkled her nose and looked at him.

"It had great food but no atmosphere."

She shook her head, the corners of her mouth turning up. It wasn't a laugh, but it was something.

As she put things in the cart, he kept going. "What did the ocean say to the other ocean?"

She shrugged. "I don't know, what?"

"Nothing, it just waved."

This time she chuckled.

"You heard the rumor going around about butter?"

Brynn smiled. "No, but I'm sure you're going to tell me."

"Ah, never mind. I shouldn't spread it."

Brynn's shoulders shook up and down as she stifled a giggle and placed the last item they needed in the cart. She steered it towards the checkout. He emptied the contents onto the belt while they waited their turn.

Aaron leaned in towards her ear, resting his hands on either side of her hips. "What do you get from a pampered cow?"

"What?"

"Spoiled milk."

She bit her lip as the checkout woman greeted them. Aaron slid his card through the reader. He'd accept her cash for half later. He didn't like having to split groceries like this, but if it was what she needed, he'd do it.

He pushed the cart to the car and unloaded the grocery bags in the trunk before joining Brynn in the front. He turned the ignition on. Brynn shivered and placed her hand over the vent. He turned the heat up a little—she seemed to run much colder than he did.

Aaron tried again. "You know, it was so cold in D.C. the other day, I saw a politician with his hands in his own pockets."

Brynn was silent for a moment before she turned towards him, then burst into laughter.

He beamed as her light rapture tumbled out of her. His breath caught at the full smile lighting up her face. "So you like political jokes?"

She shook her head, clutching her belly as she took a deep breath and let it out. "No, but of all the things I've learned about you, silly jokes were not something I expected."

"That's what's so funny? My take at humor? Should I be insulted?" he teased.

She met his gaze. "This whole thing is so crazy it's hilarious. I married a stranger who treats me better than I ever expected. The same man that kisses me in public to convince old ladies we married for love and are not conning the insurance agency so I can get my transgender daughter the basic care she needs. And now, you try and distract me from my embarrassment over said kiss with silly jokes. I don't know whether to laugh or cry, but I think I've cried enough in my life, so laughter it is." She sniffed. "I'm sorry. I think I'm losing it."

He reached out his hand, taking hers and rubbing his thumb across her soft flesh. "Hey. This has been a lot. It's completely normal to be overwhelmed."

"This is what I mean. You're too perfect."

His eyebrow rose. "Is there such a thing as too perfect?"

She blinked up at him, her eyes watery. "I didn't think so until I met you."

His heart lurched. "I have a confession to make."

Her brows drew together. "Oh?"

"I didn't tell you the jokes to distract you from embarrassment, though that would have been the honorable thing to do. My reasons were purely selfish."

"How so?" She turned towards him.

"I wondered what it would take to make you laugh like you just did. I wanted to hear the sound of pure joy as it tumbled from your mouth." He reached out and pressed his thumb to her lips as they parted on a gasp. "And I wanted to see how much more beautiful a full-blown smile on your face made you."

Her elegant neck bobbed as she swallowed, her green eyes wide like a baby fawn.

"See? Purely selfish reasons. I'm nowhere close to perfect."

"I think you and I have very different definitions of the word 'selfish.'" Her voice was all breath, her pupils dilated.

Every molecule inside him pulled toward her like a magnet. He cupped the side of her face, and she didn't flinch this time. Her eyes glazed over with want.

He leaned in. "I'm going to kiss you again."

"Is someone watching us?" she asked.

"Probably," he mumbled before locking his lips with hers. He slid his tongue inside her mouth, tempting his patience. God, she tasted so good. Like fucking heaven.

He pulled her lower lip between his teeth, gently raking it, testing her. She let out a whimper and clutched his shoulder. It was the encouragement he needed to deepen the kiss. He slid his fingers through her hair at the back of her neck, anchoring her to him. Tongues and lips tangled. Brynn melted into his kiss. Her confidence seemingly growing as she sucked his tongue and nipped at his lip.

It took everything inside him not to wrap his arms around her and tug her into his lap. He wanted to touch her, everywhere. His self-control was hanging on by a thread. His cock was hard as a rock and pressing into the zipper of his jeans. Aaron pulled back, chest heaving as he stared at Brynn. Her eyes were hazy with lust, her hair a mess from him running his fingers through it. Lips swollen from his kiss. She was breathtaking.

She blinked, as if just coming back to reality, then turned in her seat, facing the front and placing her hands together neatly in her lap. "Are we going home now?" she asked, her voice wobbling a little.

"Yeah, I just need a minute." He pressed his hand to his cock, willing it to go down.

Brynn's eyes darted to the movement, the familiar blush returning as her gaze widened. "Oh, I'm so sorry."

"Sweetheart, this is the last thing in the world you should ever apologize for."

"But it's my fault I've caused you pain."

He shook his head. Who the fuck told her that? "First off, I'm not in pain. Second, you're not responsible for anyone's body but your own. That kiss was the hottest one I've ever had in my life. I just need a minute to cool down."

"It was?" she asked, her surprise written all over her expression.

"It definitely was."

"And don't you need to, uh, well, you know, um . . ." She motioned to his lap.

"Don't know what anyone told you, but it will go away on its own. Especially if we ignore it."

"Oh. I thought . . . never mind." She turned towards the window.

What did she think? If she didn't already have a kid, he might have guessed she was a virgin by how she spoke about bodies and sex. A part of him was curious about exactly what she did know, and the devil on his shoulder wanted to find out the fun way.

He smiled and shifted the car into gear. That kiss was proof. He was winning his wife over, bit by bit. All he needed now was a very cold shower and to keep moving slowly, onwards and upwards. Each time they unpacked something, a million more questions would pop up. But he had time to win her over. Eleven more months and a couple weeks was plenty, surely. He flicked his gaze over to her as she looked out the window. Slow and steady was the way to go with Brynn.

If only his heart could get the memo.

17

BRYNN

Brynn turned the page in the romance novel she was reading, her eyes glued to the book. In the last three weeks she'd gone through half of Aaron's collection. She'd learned so many new things. And as hard as she wanted to deny it, she now had a name for those feelings Aaron stirred within her. Arousal. Lust. Desire. Her vocabulary list had grown as much as her sexual education.

"This came for you." Aaron's deep voice made her jump and slam the book closed, embarrassment rising to her cheeks. Had he seen what she was reading? Well, it didn't matter; these were his books. He'd probably already read them.

Brynn accepted the letter from his hands, addressed to Brynn Ridley. "Thank you."

A flutter flipped through her belly every time she saw her name in print like that, or when someone referred to her as Mrs. Ridley. It wasn't real, but these last few weeks had gone much smoother than she thought possible. Aaron was steady, his emotions didn't get the better of him. He said something and then he did it. And he was always checking in with her and Dani.

Aaron walked over to the espresso machine and got busy making himself a drink while Brynn ripped open the envelope. It was her official name change document with her new social security card. Relief washed over her as tears of joy pricked her eyes. This was the last document she needed to really start living out her independence. Now she could work for an actual paycheck instead of under the table. She could get an education. She could—she could do *anything*. And all of this was possible because of Aaron.

Her attention darted to the man with his back to her, his bulky biceps highlighted in the black muscle shirt he wore. Aaron's muscles flexed as he wiped the foam from the steamer before turning and handing her a latte.

"Thank you." She picked it up and sipped as he did. A bit of foam stuck to the top of his full brown lips, and the urge to press her own mouth there rose.

Whoa! Too many romance novels for me.

He licked his lips, and it stirred that familiar lust in her core, so she shifted on her seat, averting her gaze to her cup.

"Coffee is delicious. Would you believe the first cup I ever had was from working at the diner?" She couldn't look at him. This was such a tiny piece of her past, but it was huge for her to share something so personal with a man. Would he judge her if he really knew what had happened?

"Did they not have coffee where you were from?" His voice was gentle as always, as if he was careful about what he asked.

She took another sip of the warm rich liquid and shook her head. "Coffee was not allowed. Nor other caffeinated drinks. Sugar either." She turned to him as he took the seat next to her at the bar in the kitchen.

"I bet everyone there had great teeth." He winced. "Sorry, I'm trying to think of a positive to that, but what I mean is was it a choice, or was it forced on everyone?"

"There weren't many choices there. Even less if you were a woman."

"Thank you for sharing that with me." Aaron met her gaze as his finger gently skimmed the back of her wrist. Such a small gesture, but it set a swirl of emotions skittering through her.

"Now that you've got your name change done, what's the next step?" he asked, pulling his hand back to take another sip of his latte.

"I'll make an appointment to enroll Dani in school, then I'll sign up to take the GED test." Her eyes darted back to the foam in her cup as her shoulders tensed.

Aaron's gaze bore into the side of her face. "Why don't you have a high school diploma, or a general education degree?"

She shook her head, digging her nails into her palms as her body heated, this time with more embarrassment. Did he think she was stupid?

"I bet that made things really difficult for you leaving home." Aaron was using his careful tone again, as if she was a scared animal he might spook. She hated it and loved it at the same time. She didn't want to be treated like she was made of glass, but if he wasn't careful, she would definitely bolt.

She turned to him, tipping her chin up. "They told me I'd never make it. Told me I needed them to survive. But I proved them wrong. And now I'm going to get this GED and maybe even take some college courses someday." Her confession was lit with defiance and soaked in vulnerability.

Aaron smiled and nodded. "I'm proud of you."

Her mouth dropped open before she clamped it shut. Of

all the things she expected him to say, it wasn't that. And the pride shining in his eyes seemed so genuine.

"You can do anything. Don't let anyone ever tell you different," Aaron continued.

"Why are you so nice to me?"

Aaron squinted as he studied her before a determined flame lit his gaze. He turned to face her fully, slowly reaching towards her chin, as if giving her time to stop him. The man had super-fast reflexes, but everything he did with her was slow and controlled. The contrast only made that feeling in her chest grow. His knuckle grazed her cheek and then he cupped the side of her face. His dark-brown gaze was intent, and he focused on her like nothing else existed.

"Brynn, this should be the default in how you're treated. You deserve the world . . . and I aim to show you just how big and beautiful it can be."

Her pounding heart melted to hot liquid honey, filling her chest with a mixture of awe and hope.

"What else?" he asked, dropping his hand to his side as he sat back in his seat.

Cool air brushed over where he'd touched, sending an acute sense of loss barreling over her. "What do you mean?" she asked, confused.

"Get Dani in school, get your GED, and what else? How about that driver's license?"

Her eyes widened. "Oh, well, I don't know how to drive, actually."

"You've never gotten behind the wheel before?" Aaron took another drink of his coffee.

Brynn shook her head. Women were not allowed to ride a bike, much less drive a car at the compound.

"Grab your coffee and follow me." He stood, draining his cup.

"Uh, okay, where are we going?" She slipped her hands around the mug and followed as he walked towards the entryway.

"To show you how to drive, of course." Aaron slipped on a pair of sandals with his socks still on. It was the one fault she could find with the man. Who wore socks with slides?

"Let's go," Aaron urged her.

"But I, I can't—"

He spun round, his gaze soft, his mouth turned up in an encouraging smile. "You haven't tried it yet, so how would you know? It takes practice, but you'll get the hang of it in no time. Promise." He lifted the keys from the hook and winked before opening the door and heading out towards the garage.

She stood there, nerves melding with excitement in her belly. Affection blossomed, igniting every cell like fireworks. A piece of her armor broke off, slipping into oblivion as Aaron offered her another big step towards her total independence.

"You coming?" he called.

Brynn slipped on a pair of flip-flops and stepped outside into the sunshine. To her left was a gorgeous blue lake fed from a mountain spring, and to her right was the man who had earned more trust than she'd thought possible in such a short amount of time, holding the keys to her ultimate freedom.

If only this was real.

18

BRYNN

Brynn paid the cabby and climbed out of the car after Dani. They'd had her first appointment with a doctor to get a referral to a specialist who dealt with transgender children. Aaron had offered to go, but Brynn wanted to do this on her own. As usual, Aaron respected her boundary.

"I can't wait to see if Aaron got the new copy of *Selfie* for me from Pippa's store." Dani skipped ahead towards the house.

"Dani, you shouldn't be asking him for anything. He's doing so much for us already," Brynn chastised.

Dani slowed her pace, turning towards her mom. "I know, Mom. I already paid Pippa off for the episode by helping around the bookstore. Aaron just offered to pick it up for me."

"Oh." Well, now she felt like an asshole. She reached out to tuck her daughter into a hug. "I'm sorry. I shouldn't have assumed. I just don't want you to get too used to this life with Aaron because it's temporary."

"I know. I won't." Dani nodded, pulling away and walking into the house.

Brynn took her time to get to the door, her gaze raking over the now mostly bare trees. She pulled her sweater closer to ward off the crisp fall chill and stopped by the entrance to the house, taking a deep inhale of the fresh air with notes of woodsmoke. This place was absolutely beautiful. *I wish I could stay here forever.*

She shook her head. This was temporary. Aaron had been beyond kind to help her and Dani out. But he'd eventually get tired of playing house and want his own future, free of Brynn's baggage.

Brynn opened the door and entered the house as Dani came running down the stairs holding a dress that Brynn hadn't seen before, her smile beaming.

"Mom! Look what I found on my bed. Aaron must have got it for me. There's one for you too." Dani thrust the dress out to her.

Brynn blinked. "There's one for me too?"

Dani nodded and turned towards the stairs. "I'm gonna go try it on."

"Is Aaron up there?"

"I think he's in the gym."

Brynn hung up her purse and slid her shoes off before climbing the stairs. She opened her bedroom door. Just as Dani had said, there was a dress unlike any that Brynn had ever seen. It was gorgeous—too beautiful. She stepped in, taking a closer look. Her hands slid over the silky dark-green fabric, the softest she'd ever felt. It must have cost him a fortune. Next to it was a black blazer, and a shoebox. *This is too much.* She turned around and headed downstairs towards the basement.

The steady thumping sound from the gym only increased

the drumming of her racing heart. She opened the door and froze, her mouth running dry at the sight of Aaron, shirtless. Sweat ran down his chest, highlighting each dip and hard edge to his defined eight-pack—or was a ten-pack a thing? *Of all things holy.*

His strong arms pounded into the punching bag hanging from the ceiling, his calf muscles clenched as he darted from side to side. Brynn struggled to suck in a breath—the temperature had gone up at least twenty degrees in here. Her inner walls clenched, a riot of lust sloshing over in a boiling frenzy. Why did every cell in her body crave this man? He was the best-looking person she'd ever seen, hands down, but he was also incredibly patient and thoughtful. He respected her, which made everything so jumbled in her head.

"Did you need something?" Aaron asked, his back still to her.

He knew she was there this entire time? She stumbled forward. Quickly gripping the edge of the doorframe, she righted herself as heat flamed her cheeks. "I, uh, I, there's a dress on my bed." *Of course he knows that, stupid.*

He stopped, his arms falling to his sides as he turned around to face her, his expansive chest heaving with heavy breaths.

"How did the appointment go?" he asked while biting the Velcro strap to his glove and pulling it open with his teeth before he pulled it off. He removed the other and set them on a bench before retrieving his water.

"Good. We're being referred to a doctor in Boston."

Aaron guzzled down half the water in the bottle before nodding. "If you let me know the dates, I can arrange to take you. I can keep busy while you guys are in the appointment, unless you change your mind and want me to be there."

"You've already done so much for us. I hate to take more time from you."

He took a step closer, his umber skin glistening with sweat. "I don't mind. In fact, I'd love to be there in whatever capacity you're comfortable with."

"I appreciate it . . . So, about the dress?"

He smirked. "I figured we should celebrate with dinner out tonight. Dani had her first doctor appointment to begin this new journey for her. You signed up for the GED test, and you're killing it on the driving lessons."

"I backed your car into a tree," she reminded him. God, that had been scary. But Aaron had remained as calm as a cucumber, telling her it was just a car and it happens to everyone at least once.

"I already had Link fix the dent." He waved his hand, as if it was no big deal.

"Do I have to ask again why there is new clothing on my bed?"

He exhaled and shook his head. "No. I just wanted to do something special for my girls."

The endearment was like a sucker punch to her chest. *His girls?*

"I know this past month hasn't been easy for you. There's been a lot of transitions. I thought it would be nice to go out together and relax."

She opened her mouth to tell him this was too much, but he lifted his hand.

"Gifts are a part of being my wife. Maybe we should have put that in the prenup." He chuckled, his smile easy and relaxed, even a bit amused.

"I'll be sure to give it all back to you when we . . ."

His smile dissolved as he shook his head. "That isn't necessary."

"But—"

"A gift doesn't come with strings." Aaron walked over to the other side of the room where a gym bag sat on the floor. He unzipped the pocket and pulled out a velvet blue box with a golden trident on it. He walked back to her and held it out.

With trembling hands, she accepted the box. It was the same type her engagement ring had come in. One of the finest jewelry craftsmen in the whole East Coast owned this company, Poseidon's Treasure, and he lived right here in Shattered Cove. Brynn had passed his table at the farmer's market and the local festivals a time or two, her gaze lingering on the exquisite handmade pieces, far out of her price range. "Aaron, I, this is too much."

He lifted her hand to his lips and pressed a kiss to her knuckles. Deep brown eyes locked on hers. "Wear it or don't. It's yours. But know this—nothing is too much for my wife."

"But I'm a fake wife," she reminded him. This was beginning to feel too real. She needed to keep the walls up between them. She couldn't risk believing in more.

He sighed, and was that disappointment in his eyes? "But no one else knows that. I've made good money in my life and the right investments. As my legal wife, you're entitled to reap those rewards too. And when we're in public, people will expect me to spoil you like my life-long partner deserves." He took a deep breath. "I like to give gifts, especially to the people who deserve them the most. If it makes you uncomfortable, I'll stop." His hands dropped from her face as he backed away, his shoulders slumping.

Giving gifts brought him joy? How could she take that from him after everything he'd done for her? Was his happiness worth her pride?

Brynn's gaze dropped to the box in her hands. She opened it. The silver chain sparkled in the lighting. A silver pendant with pieces cut out in the shape of the continents adorned the center. Her breath caught as she looked up to him. "I'd be honored to wear it."

The corner of his mouth turned up. "May I?"

She handed him the box, then turned her back to him, lifting her short hair off her neck. He stepped closer, and though he wasn't touching her, she could still sense his heat at her back. His musk was stronger, but if anything, he smelled better. He lowered the necklace in front of her face, his fingers brushing the back of her neck as he attached the clasp, making a tremble rock through her at the intimate contact.

She turned around, grasping the pendant between her fingers. "It's beautiful."

He licked his lips. "You are."

She swallowed, searching his eyes. Her, beautiful? No. She was plain, and if he only knew just how ugly inside, he'd go running the other way.

"Do you know why I chose this?" He fingered the chain from her neck to her collarbone, making a fresh bout of heat ignite within her.

She shook her head, afraid her voice would fail her.

"To remind you, whenever you forget." He wrapped his big strong hand around hers that held the Earth pendant. "That you deserve the world, and you should never settle for less."

He'd stolen her breath. His heated eyes locked on hers. Tension rose between them. Her body burned for him. Her mind raced, but one thought screamed louder than all others. This man was a whole other kind of dangerous than she was used to. *Because he makes me want to know what it would be like to have everything . . . with him.*

19

AARON

Aaron's gaze roamed over the busy dining room of Atlantis as he rested his arm over the back of Brynn's chair. The fire from the candle in the mason jar at the center of the table danced, casting her in a warm glow. His hand pressed onto her silk-covered shoulder of the green dress he'd picked out for her, slowly running it up and down the soft material. She shivered.

"Are you cold? Do you need your jacket?" he asked.

She shook her head before she leaned back in her seat. The enormity of her trust in him, to be this close and let him touch her wasn't lost on him. He might have been taking them out in public as often as possible just for the excuse to get closer to her.

"I love my necklace, Aaron. Thank you so much for the dress too," Dani repeated for the second time that night from her seat across from them. Her cheeks were rosy, and her eyes glittered with excitement as she plucked the pink gemstone heart pendant from her chest.

"You're very welcome. A young girl deserves to have something special every now and then."

He got so much joy from taking care of them. The more he learned they'd been deprived of, the more he wanted to give. He so badly wanted to erase the pain in Brynn's eyes and tempt her to give in to the connection between them.

"Did you always live here?" Danielle asked, filling her fork with a bite of mashed potatoes.

"No, I actually grew up down south in Georgia."

"Is that why your parents sound different to us?" Dani asked.

"Danielle," Brynn scolded.

Aaron chuckled and continued his lazy circles up and down her arm. "It's fine, really." He focused on Dani across from him. "Yes, my parents have strong Southern accents."

"Why isn't your accent as strong?" She took a drink of her iced tea.

"I kinda lost it when I moved away. It comes back if I spend some time in the South for a little while."

"That's cool. We used to have to say a bunch of things where we lived before, but we don't say them here."

Brynn stiffened beside him.

"Sometimes it's good to leave things behind and move on into a better future." Aaron wanted to press, but using her child for information was wrong. "Are you excited about seeing the doctor in Boston?"

Brynn tilted her head to gaze at him, so he offered her a reassuring smile.

"Yes. I can't wait." Dani bit her lip while swirling her fork around the mash potatoes on her plate.

"Are you nervous?" he pushed.

She swallowed and nodded.

"That's normal. I'm sure your emotions will fluctuate

throughout this process," Aaron assured her before returning to look at Brynn. "What is it?"

She swallowed and jerked her attention away. "N-nothing."

"I have to go to the bathroom." Dani placed her napkin on the table and stood. "If they ask, I would like their peanut butter chocolate cheesecake for dessert, please."

Aaron waited until Dani slipped into the women's restroom across the busy restaurant before he leaned in towards Brynn, inhaling her sweet scent. "Have I told you how beautiful you look tonight?"

A small smile turned her mouth upwards before she tipped her face to him again. "Yes."

"Do you believe me?"

Her eyes widened before she blinked, as if caught off guard. "I . . . I feel special in this dress."

"That isn't an answer." He dragged his knuckle over her cheek because he loved the way she responded to his touch. And there was so much more of her he wanted to explore. Each inch she gave him felt like a treasure.

"I don't know what you want me to say."

Their gazes locked.

His throat tightened. "I only want your truths. Do. You. Believe. You. Look. Beautiful. Tonight?"

Her lips parted on a breath before her gaze dropped to the table. "I don't know. I haven't been able to truly look at myself in a mirror in a long time."

He moved his finger below her chin to tilt her face towards him. "Then I'll just have to keep reminding you until you see for yourself how stunning and radiant you are, inside and out."

Pain flickered in her expression before it was overrun with astonishment.

"I'm going to kiss you now." He waited until her attention flicked to his lips before he leaned in, gently gliding his mouth against hers before he deepened the kiss.

A tiny whimper escaped her, turning his cock to steel. He wove his fingers through her hair to the back of her neck, guiding her closer, then he sucked her bottom lip into his mouth, needing more. The smallest of moans left her as he pressed his thumb to the side of her throat. She shuddered before she pulled away, heat-filled eyes wide. She wanted him just as bad as he wanted her.

She tucked her hair behind her ear as her attention darted to the room, where Dani exited the bathroom and walked towards them.

"Are you okay?" Aaron slipped his hand from Brynn's shoulders to her palm.

She nodded tightly, focusing on her half-eaten plate as Dani rejoined them.

He leaned in and whispered, "Do you not want me to touch you?"

She turned to him, emotion welling in her eyes as she bit her lip and shook her head. "I'm fine."

"Only your truths, remember?" His voice was gentle but firm.

"I . . . could use a break," she admitted.

He smiled and pulled his hand back to his own lap. "Anything you need. You just have to tell me, and I'll do everything in my power to make it happen, or stop it from happening as the case may be."

Admiration glowed in her gaze before she nodded. "I appreciate that more than you know."

Dani curiously looked between them.

Aaron lifted his fork and knife before cutting into the spicy Italian sausage. "How do you like your food?"

"It's so good. Do you think we can make this at home?" Dani asked, taking another bite of her salmon.

"Sure. We can get some from Nash Emerson. He's a friend and local fisherman. He gets all sorts of fish."

"Do you like your dinner, Mom?" Dani asked.

Brynn smiled at her daughter. "The pasta is delicious."

"Atlas makes it himself. I think it would be fun to take a pasta-making lesson from him sometime. Would you both like that?" Aaron asked.

"Yes!" Dani agreed.

"Brynn?"

"Actually, that does sound fun." Her eyes lit with an emotion he hadn't seen on her face yet.

"What do you do for fun? Like hobbies?" he asked.

Brynn touched her chest. "Me?"

He nodded.

"I don't really . . . I've never . . ." Her eyes darted back and forth over the table.

"You seem to like to read," he offered.

She'd been going through his romance collection faster than he'd thought possible with her work schedule.

Her cheeks stained crimson as she reached for her water glass. "Is that considered a hobby?"

"Definitely. It's one of mine."

"Me too. I love reading," Dani added.

"What do you want to study in college?" he pressed, before taking another bite of his meal.

Brynn's attention focused back on him. "I-I don't really know. I haven't actually thought about it yet."

Because you've been too busy trying to survive. His heart broke for her. "What brings you joy? What's something you'd want to do even if you wouldn't get paid to do it?"

She licked her lips and set down her fork. "Help people

coming from tough situations like others have helped us. I'd like to pay it forward."

And just like that, another piece of his soul fell for Brynn.

"Then you should do it." His voice came out gruff, so he cleared his throat as her eyes met his. "I have a degree in social work and psychology. Those help me run the Hope Facility. But you don't need all that, unless you want to. I have some books at home to help you get started if you want to look at them. Maybe they can help you narrow down your interest?"

A grateful smile split her lips. "I would love that."

"If you ever want to come to the center and hang out with some of our counselors, you're more than welcome," he added.

"Let's start with the books."

"Sounds like a plan." Excitement spun inside him at the idea of sharing something in common with Brynn. If only he could be certain she felt the same way.

Aaron's phone rang from his pocket, so he pulled it out. "Sorry, let me put this on silent." His gaze froze on the screen, the message from his assistant confirming what he'd feared.

"Is everything okay?" Brynn asked.

Aaron blinked up at her, sliding the phone back into his pocket as he sighed.

"Was it your parents?" Concern marred her forehead.

He shook his head. "No, I haven't heard from them. It was a situation at the center."

"Oh?"

He nodded before grabbing his glass and taking a sip. He set the drink back on the table, his finger tracing the rim as he focused back on her. "We've had an influx of teens needing a place to stay. They meet all the requirements for Hope Facility, but we just don't have the room. I can hire staff, but we've run out of the space to build. I hate to turn anyone away. And some of these kids have nowhere else to go but remain on the streets. I hate that I can't save them all. And I just wish there was a quicker solution. I'm looking into buying some more buildings and converting them, but it will take time."

"The way you care about these kids, people you've never even met, is touching," Brynn added.

Because I see Emmanuel in every one of them. He cleared his throat. He didn't deserve any special praise for helping someone in need when he had the means.

"Did you know that forty percent of all homeless youth are part of the LGBTQ+ community? And queer youth are one hundred and twenty percent more likely to become homeless than their heterosexual counterparts?" Aaron asked, quietly.

Brynn shook her head, her eyes widening, as if putting the pieces together that Dani could have ended up that way.

"Nothing will be ready until the spring. That's a lot of youth from the surrounding states who won't have a place to go." Aaron sighed.

"Have you ever considered host families? I mean ones who have been vetted and checked out? Or what about renting out hotel rooms?"

Aaron was struck silent, her idea sinking in and taking form. Would it be possible? He'd have to have Leslie figure out the logistics. Maybe move some teens already well established into locals' homes so the new ones would have a chance to settle and get acclimated before going through some initial therapy first.

Brynn sank back in her seat. "Sorry, that was probably a stupid idea."

"No." He placed his hand on hers, brushing his thumb over the top. "That's a brilliant idea. It won't help everyone, but background checks and classes won't take as long as building new dorms. We could create a whole system of host families. That's genius."

"Genius? No." She shook her head. "But do you think the kids will be safe?"

"We'll come up with a rigorous vetting process, references, and constant check-ins with the kids." He lifted her hand to his lips and kissed her knuckles. "Thank you, Brynn."

She nodded shakily, her throat bobbing as she swallowed before she went back to her meal.

Maybe if Aaron consistently showed her he was trustworthy, and that he respected her, she'd open up a little more. Because every time she shared something with him, Aaron couldn't help but be blown away. The fact that she might have saved dozens of teens from freezing to death this winter, or risking the unthinkable for a warm bed, only made him even more grateful to her.

20

BRYNN

Brynn handed over the paper bag to the customer across from her. "Thank you, and enjoy the new books."

"Oh, I think I will." The older woman gave her a wink and turned towards The Oyster Bookstore front door.

Brynn cast a quick glance around the front desk, making sure no one else was waiting for her help. So many little ones and their parents or grandparents had gathered inside today for the drag queen story hour that Pippa hosted every Friday afternoon.

Brynn slipped out from behind the desk and took the opportunity to re-shelve some of the novels in the growing pile beside her. She emptied her hands quick enough and diverted to the correct row of books in the store. Pippa had given her a list of books like the one she'd liked from Aaron's collection.

Brynn moved to the dark romance section, peeking over her shoulder to make sure no one was around before she lifted the desired book off the shelf and read the description. The heroine was a woman like her, wounded and scared of the world. *Though I'm not as scared as I once was.* The heroine was taken captive by the hero in the book, made to submit. And something about that pricked at Brynn's consciousness and made her belly flip. The last thing she should find arousing is submission. *Is there something wrong with me? Surely not if other women find this type of book interesting.*

"Excuse me?" a soft voice from behind Brynn spoke.

Brynn jumped, shoving the book back on the shelf as the heat of embarrassment flooded her veins. She spun around, tucking her hair behind her ear, hoping she didn't look as discombobulated as she felt. "Yes? How can I help you?"

The woman smiled and adjusted the huge bouquet of yellow and orange flowers with a few pieces of greenery sticking out. "I'm looking for Brynn. Would you happen to be her?"

Brynn blinked slowly as her brows drew together and a sliver of panic coiled in her belly. "Yes, I am."

The lady's eyes sparkled as she handed over the flowers in the clear glass vase. "Then these are for you."

Brynn held her hands out, accepting the gift.

The woman must have misunderstood her confusion because she started naming flowers. "Delphiniums, some striking lisianthuses if I do say so myself. These are free spirit roses, and of course starry asters. Your husband certainly picked out a gorgeous melody of flowers for you. These blooms showcase individuality and uniqueness, like a one-of-a-kind relationship." The woman waved her hand. "Do you know anything about flowers?"

Brynn shook her head.

"Well, these capture the essence of boundless love and the fresh hope of springtime."

Brynn swallowed. "Oh, thank you."

"My pleasure." She dug into her pocket and handed

Brynn a business card with Lily's Flower Shop emblazoned in feminine script. "I'm Lily, by the way. I just bought the florist shop this spring. Do you think it would be okay to add mine to the collection of local business cards by the register?"

Brynn gave her a smile and motioned down the aisle of bookshelves towards the front. "I'm sure that wouldn't be a problem."

Lily followed her to the register before she deposited a handful of colorful cards into one of the empty cardholders. "Thank you so much."

Brynn nodded. "Absolutely. Thank you for the flowers."

Lily beamed and gave her a wink. "My pleasure." She left through the front door as a few giggles came from the small crowd at the back of the store. Marsha Divine's voice acted out all the characters' voices in the books she read to the children.

Brynn eyed the gorgeous bouquet beside her on the desk. She reached for the small note tucked in the center.

To my wife,

Just a little beauty to brighten your day.

Though it pales in comparison to you.

-A

Brynn pressed a hand to her chest as emotion welled in her throat. Her heart soared.

Pippa walked in the front door, a smile splitting her face. "Those are gorgeous."

Brynn beamed. "They are, aren't they?"

"How is everything going?" Pippa asked as Brynn tucked the note into her pocket.

Brynn cast a quick glance around them, but everyone was seemingly occupied with story time or far enough away they wouldn't hear. Just in case, she lowered her voice. "Good. I started weekly therapy. And Aaron has been great, better than, actually. I don't even have a name for how he's been. Too perfect almost."

Pippa's brow creased. "Like you're waiting for the other shoe to drop?"

Brynn scrunched her nose. "Why would a shoe drop?"

Pippa shook her head. "It's a saying that means you are always waiting for something bad to happen."

Was that what Brynn was doing? "I just . . . you and Mason love each other, but . . ."

"But we still had plenty of ups and downs of our own," Pippa finished for her.

Brynn nodded. "It hasn't really been like that for us. It's been easy . . . it's felt like a fairy tale, and I just don't know how to handle it because sometimes . . ."

"Sometimes?"

Brynn let out a sigh and closed her eyes as she confessed, "Sometimes it feels too real. Like this isn't pretend." She focused back on Pippa's sympathetic gaze. "I think I'm starting to develop feelings for him that I have no business having."

"Have you talked to Aaron about this?"

"No. I-I don't even know . . ." Brynn's voice quieted. "I think he might have feelings for me . . . But what if it's all in my head?"

Pippa reached out her hand to cover Brynn's. "The only way you'll know is to talk to him. It's better to communicate that now and know you're both on the same page. If not, you can set some boundaries so your heart doesn't get more involved. But I have a hunch you're not the only one catching feelings."

Brynn's eyes widened. "Really?"

"The way that man looked at you at the wedding, either

he's in the wrong business and should have been an actor, or .
. ."

"Or he feels the connection too," Brynn finished for her. "But he's so blunt most of the time. Why wouldn't he say something?"

"Maybe because he's worried he'll scare you away," Pippa suggested.

Brynn nodded. "Perhaps you're right."

Pippa shrugged. "Only one way to find out, ask him."

Brynn took a deep breath, then exhaled. Communicating with people always intimidated her. She'd been silenced most of her life after all. However, Aaron was approachable. But what if she spoke up and it ruined the perfect dynamic they had now? She couldn't risk disrupting their arrangement for Dani's benefit.

"I'll think about it," Brynn promised.

Pippa nodded. "Sounds good. You're off the clock now. Any fun plans for the night?"

Brynn bit her lip. "I think I'll make a nice dinner for Aaron to thank him for the flowers and . . . everything."

Pippa smirked. "You do that."

"I just need to grab a book before I go." Brynn walked around her friend and employer, returning to the dark romance shelf. She picked up the book, running her hand over the acronym BDSM. She'd have to look that one up later. She paid for her book, taking advantage of her employee discount and gathered her things before she headed out, juggling her flowers. When she reached the edge of the bookstore window, her stainless-steel water bottle dropped to the ground with a loud clank.

She bent down carefully and grabbed it, freezing as her gaze snagged on the cherry cough drop wrappers piled on the ground. Brynn stood, searching her surroundings, a chill weaving through her soul like an omen. Paul sucked on that exact brand, as if they were candy. He'd reeked of artificial cherry.

A few people milled about the street. Nothing seemed amiss. She shook her head. Paul didn't know where she was. She was safe in Shattered Cove—at least for now.

* * *

Brynn slid the cheesy lasagna from the oven and set it on the stove to cool before she slid the tray of brownies in and shut the door. Dani was busy sketching in her notebook at the bar with headphones on. Brynn leaned against the counter and took a minute to study her daughter. Dani had blossomed since living with Aaron this past month. Her daughter had been both terrified and excited to start school at Shattered Cove middle school. Thankfully, she had Aspen by her side. Some days were tough—like today when someone misgendered her and used the wrong pronouns. Those days were difficult. Brynn wished she could take the pain away from her daughter. Her chest ached knowing Dani's life would always be filled with struggles because of transphobia.

The front door opened, then shut.

"Honey, I'm home," Aaron called from the mudroom. The jangle of keys being hung on the key hook preceded his entrance to the kitchen. He smiled, his gaze flicking to the bouquet in the middle of the kitchen island before landing back on her.

"You got the flowers." He stopped beside her, leaning in to give her a kiss on the cheek before waving to Dani. "Hey, sweetheart. How was school?"

"Fine," Dani answered, her shoulders hunched.

She'd had a difficult day at school and withdrew into her

sketchbook and music. The school was having her use the nurse's bathroom rather than the girls' restroom, and though it may seem inconsequential, it was one more thing making Dani different from the other kids at her school. Brynn's stomach churned with concern. How much more challenging would days like this be for Dani if they hadn't gotten her into the right doctors to start her transition? *I made the right decision for her in marrying Aaron.*

It was things he did like that which had her spun topsy-turvy inside. No one was here to witness this except them. Was he this way with his other female friends? She tried to think of a time she'd seen him kiss anyone else's cheek. *Marge from the center.* Yes, he did greet her that way. And he'd told her he was a touchy-feely guy.

"You okay?" he asked, backing away.

"Yes. I—thank you. They're beautiful. But you didn't have to."

He shrugged. "I wanted to . . . Something smells delicious. Is that lasagna?" He picked up a few pieces of shredded mozzarella that had escaped the package and dropped them into his mouth.

Her focus fell to the bob of his throat before he licked his lips. "Yes, it is. You said you like Italian food, right?"

He grinned, his eyes lighting up. "Absolutely. Lasagna is one of my favorites."

Brynn smiled in relief. "Good. I made some brownies too."

He clapped a hand over his heart. "Damn it, woman, if you weren't already married to me, I'd propose right now."

He was in an interesting mood today. Calm, cool, and collected Aaron was full of energy and flirtation it seemed.

"Why don't you get a drink and take a seat, and I'll bring it over."

"I can help." He reached into the cupboard and took down three plates.

The way he was always ready to serve others was just one of the reasons she admired him. But today was her opportunity to pay him back in some small way. Which meant she needed to speak up. "Yes, but you're always helping—that's the point. I wanted to do something special for you to say thank you."

He set the plates on the counter by the stove and turned to her. "I appreciate the gratitude. Why don't we use the dining room tonight? Make it extra special."

She nodded. "That would be nice."

Aaron turned to the fridge, then grabbed a couple bottles of water and an iced tea before nudging Dani's shoulder. Dani looked up at him, pulling her earbuds from her ears.

"Come on, let's get set up for dinner in the dining room. You can tell me all about your day." Aaron handed her the iced tea.

Dani left her things on the counter and followed him into the dining room. Brynn got to work serving the pasta casserole onto plates and checked the timer for the brownies.

This was why things with Aaron were so easy. Because he listened to her and respected any boundary she set. *Because he's a good man.* Maybe she could let down her guard and trust in this powerful feeling growing inside her with each promise kept, and gentle care given. And for however long this fake marriage lasted, he was hers. If only she didn't want . . . *more.*

21

BRYNN

Brynn's back ached from being hunched over the pile of books in front of her. Her test appointment for her GED was right after the holiday. And Thanksgiving was in two days, which meant Aaron's family was coming. She had so much to do, but studying for this test was her priority.

"Brynn?"

She jumped out of her seat, her pen clattering to the table, the book she'd been studying thumping closed.

Aaron held up his palms, eyes flaring like her reaction had scared him. "Sorry. I didn't mean to startle you."

She shook her head, breathing out a sigh of relief. "No, I'm sorry. I didn't even hear you come in. You're home early."

He paused. "No, I'm not."

Brynn flicked her gaze to the clock, panic shooting through her veins. "Oh my God. I didn't even realize how late it was. I haven't started dinner." Like she was supposed to do. *Oh no. The man gives up so much for me and I can't even hold up my end of the agreement.*

She left the books and scrambled over to the fridge,

151

searching for the ingredients she took out to defrost this morning. She grabbed the package of ground turkey and blinked at the sting in her eyes when her focus landed on the half-frozen meat. *Damn.*

"Brynn?" Aaron's voice was close behind her as she collected the veggies she'd need.

I can defrost it in the microwave and then hurry up and get the asparagus going while that's in there. She walked her loaded arms to the counter next to the stove, then emptied them and searched for the pan to boil the veggies, but it wasn't there. She needed to hurry. "Where's the pot?"

"It's still in the dish drainer," Aaron answered.

Of course. Because he did the dishes last night. She stood, grabbing it by the sink. *He's been cooking and cleaning and I'm not even pulling my own weight like we agreed.*

She placed the pot in the sink and turned the water on.

"Brynn?" Aaron repeated her name, his big hands resting on her shoulders.

She tensed and reached to shut the tap off, but he beat her to it. "Stop."

"Sorry." She whipped her hand back.

He tugged her shoulder towards him. "Turn around and look at me."

Reluctantly, she obeyed, her gaze focusing on his chest. "I'm sorry."

His chest deflated on a sigh. "You have nothing to be sorry for."

She shook her head, denying his words. "I didn't have dinner ready. I'm not being useful—"

"Look at me." His voice was firm with a hard edge like she'd never witnessed before.

She met his dark eyes. A spark of something ignited in her core at his tone.

"Whoever convinced you that you only exist to be useful is an idiot. You don't have to apologize for existing. You're allowed to take up space."

Her heart lurched as tears blurred her vision. "But we agreed that I'd have dinner ready if I got home first. You do so much for us, and I failed to—"

"No. This isn't about dinner."

She blinked up at him, confused. "It isn't?"

He rested his hands on her shoulders. "Your value isn't equated with these archetype roles that the patriarchal world has deemed the height of a woman's success."

Brynn digested what he said as he continued, "I don't know much about your past, but I'm not *him*, Brynn. I don't care if you ever cook again. I care about your happiness. I want you to live your best life. If we have to order out every night that I don't cook, I can deal with that. If you want to make a meal, great. If not, I'm a grown man who can fend for myself."

His words hit her like tiny arrows, loosening something inside her. A weight lifted from her shoulders. He really didn't care?

"I do like to cook," she admitted.

He smiled. "Then cook when you want to. But not if it's gonna cause you stress. Not if it takes you back there."

She gasped. How had Aaron known?

"My ideal marriage is a team effort. We both lean on each other when we need to."

There he went again, speaking, as if this was a real marriage. Hope bubbled inside her, rising and expanding with each lingering moment he stared into her eyes, as if she was the only thing that mattered in this world.

He brushed his thumb over her cheek, tucking a piece of hair behind her ear. "And while we're at it, you should know you can be as fucking loud as you want to. To voice your own thoughts, opinions—especially if they're different from mine. You don't need anyone else's permission—least of all mine—but if you want it, it's yours. My greatest desire for you is that you find your voice and that inner confidence. Just know that having you in my space is a gift unlike any other."

How could she not fall for this man when he said things like that?

"What if I don't know who I am?" Tears blurred her vision.

He cupped her jaw, tilting her face towards his as he leaned in. "Then you're allowed to take the time to figure that out." His sweet cinnamon breath coasted over her lips. "But what I see is the most kind, beautiful, brave, and strongest woman I've ever known."

She blinked, causing the tears to drip down her cheeks as she shook her head. "I'm so weak. If you only knew how much. In the moments where it really mattered, I failed."

"We all fail sometimes. But it meant you tried. Neither of us can go back and change the past. We have to learn from it and try better in the future. You've got to learn to let that go. You're the only one with the keys to the prison of your regrets." He swiped her tears with his thumbs, and she closed her eyes, relishing how his touch grounded her amid the swell of emotions clamoring inside.

"I'm going to kiss you now unless you say no," Aaron said, making her eyes shoot open.

He wanted to kiss her? "But no one is here to see."

"This one's for us." He melded his mouth to hers, sending a firestorm rocketing through her, incinerating all other emotions and igniting a deep want inside Brynn's body.

He traced the seam of her lips before she opened for him. He tasted like freedom and risk. Of second chances and hope.

She clutched his shirt over the hard ridges of his abs, sending lust thrumming through her with every rapid heartbeat.

The scratch of his five o'clock shadow brushed her sensitive jaw as he deepened the kiss, twirling her higher and higher in a whirlwind of sensations she'd never experienced.

He pulled back, resting his forehead to hers, their shared panting breaths between them. For the first time in a long time, she let herself hope for more. Because for the first time in her life, she felt safe in a man's arms.

And after that kiss, it was clear she wasn't the only one falling in this relationship.

22

———

AARON

Aaron checked his phone one last time, counting down the minutes until Thanksgiving dinner would be over and he could wave goodbye to his parents. He loved them, of course, but he couldn't help the anger that arose whenever he thought of how they had treated his brother. It was great they'd welcomed Brynn and Dani into their life, but why hadn't they been more welcoming of their own son?

"The place looks great, son. You've done well for yourself." His father brought a glass of spiced cider to his lips as he stared out the window towards the blue lake beyond.

"Thanks." Aaron peeked towards the kitchen his mother had shooed him out of an hour ago. Laughter from Dani and his mom filtered through the room. Brynn's eyes lit with cautious joy as she added pie crust to a pan for his mother's sweet potato pie recipe. His mother had insisted on helping to cook the meal.

"What do you catch in the lake?" his dad asked.

"Trout, bass, and a few northern pike." Aaron turned back to the view.

Blue skies with a few crisp white clouds blew overhead. Brown leafless trees surrounded both sides of the lake, with a few evergreens mixed in. The view was most beautiful during peak foliage season with the bright reds, oranges, and yellows.

His dad nodded. "Want to watch the game? Where's your television?"

"Downstairs in the game room."

His father's forehead wrinkled. "You don't have one up here?"

"I don't watch a lot of it." He motioned to the bookshelf, ignoring the reminder of just how little his father really knew about him. "Come on, I'll show you."

Aaron led his father downstairs, getting him settled on the sofa in front of the large screen. His mind kept wandering to Brynn. Would his mother say something to hurt her or Dani's feelings?

He stood. "I'm gonna go check on dinner."

"Sure." His father kept his gaze to the TV.

Aaron jogged back upstairs, his mother's voice halting him.

"You are such a pretty young lady, just like your mom. I love that dress."

"Thank you. Aaron picked it out for me," Dani answered, the smile in her voice evident.

"My son always had a great eye for beauty." His mother stared at Dani, her eyes taking on a sad sheen. "You remind me so much of my daughter . . ."

"What's next?" Brynn asked.

His mother shook her head and turned towards Brynn. "Now, Danielle can help set the table. You can slip that pie into the oven and set a timer. Dinner should be ready in about thirty minutes."

"I'll grab the plates." The sound of the stool skidding over the floor preceded the clank of plates being stacked.

Aaron should move, but a part of him wanted to see how his mother would treat Brynn when she thought he wasn't around.

"Brynn?" His mother's voice lowered, and Aaron's senses turned to alert.

"Yes?"

"I just wanted to thank you for having us."

"This is Aaron's home, and you're his family. Of course, we'd have you."

"I'm sure he's told you things haven't been so easy between us in a long time . . . But receiving that phone call about him getting married, it made me realize how much I've missed out on. I hope we can move forward from here. And I think I have you to thank for that chance." His mother sniffed.

Aaron's heart lurched, a mix of emotions roiling in his chest.

"Oh, I . . . I'm glad you came too. Cooking, this afternoon, has been fun," Brynn answered, her voice strained, as if she didn't know what to say.

Aaron probably should have prepared her with more backstory first. He backed up and made a point of making noise as he approached the kitchen this time. Brynn turned as he entered, but his mother's back remained towards him.

"How's it going in here?"

His mother turned, blinking away the wetness in her eyes with a glowing smile. "Great. We're having fun. Where's your dad?"

"Watching the game." He stepped forward and picked a warm roll from the basket.

His mother walked over and slapped his hand away. "Dinner will be ready in twenty minutes. Don't fill up on bread." She turned to Brynn. "He and his sister were always sneaking rolls before every holiday meal, and by the time we sat down for supper, they'd be too full. Until it was time for dessert, of course."

Aaron pulled in a deep breath. He should correct his mother that his *sister* was his *brother.* But he didn't want to ruin dinner. Brynn and Dani deserved a holiday without his family drama. They all just needed to get through the next couple of hours.

* * *

An hour later they were all sitting around his dining table finishing up their dinner. Brynn had wanted to do something special and picked up some flowers from Lily's Flower Shop for the center of the table. He'd offered to take her shopping for decorations, but she refused. The woman hated him spending his money on her. Hopefully, she'd come around some day.

"Aaron, you should bring Brynn and Dani to see your hometown in Georgia sometime," his mother said before turning to lean in towards Brynn who was across the table next to him. "There are some marvelous restaurants in Atlanta. Have you ever been to a basketball game in an arena?"

Brynn shook her head. "No."

"Then it's settled. You'll have to come for one of the games. We could get box seats and cater the whole thing," Mother finished, as if it was already decided.

Brynn just smiled politely and turned her attention to Aaron, as if gauging his reaction.

"Do you have any plans for Christmas?" his mother asked, her gaze volleying between Brynn and Aaron.

"Iris," his father warned.

His mother spun to look at her husband by her side. "What?"

His dad's eyes pinned her to the spot.

She turned back to Aaron. "I'd love to see you for the holidays." Her attention darted to Dani at the table's end. "You'll have to tell Yaya Ridley what you want for Christmas."

Dani's eyes widened. "You mean a gift?"

His mother clasped her hands together. "Why, of course a gift. Maybe two if you're extra good for your mama until then."

Dani beamed.

"So, are you planning on taking some time off from your little project now that you're married?" his father asked him.

Aaron's brows drew together. "Project?"

"That place you run for those confused people," his dad clarified.

Aaron's body went rigid as he cast a quick glance at Dani and then to Brynn who placed her hand on his thigh, bringing him a wave of comfort while her attention remained glued to his parents. It was the first time she'd initiated physical contact, and that small gesture spoke volumes.

Aaron sighed. "You mean my multimillion-dollar nonprofit? No, I have no plans on stopping my work there. I'm helping teenagers have a safe place to go when their small-minded parents kick them out." *Like Emmanuel should have had.*

His father's hands balled into fists on the table.

His mother winced. "Surely, your father only meant that being around people like that might make things uncomfortable for your new wife and daughter. What might people say about your reputation? What if they think you're spending time with so many people that are . . . well . . ."

"Gay?"

His mother's eyes widened in horror, as if he'd cursed the Lord himself to his face. "Look, I don't think we should be discussing business at the dinner table, it's improper. Does anyone want dessert?"

"You don't like gay people?" Dani asked, the earlier joy drained from her expression as a wariness marred her young features.

"We love everybody, honey, just as the Lord commands. But some people are confused. We love the sinner but hate the sin."

Dani's watery eyes flicked to her mother's. Brynn stood, and Aaron was right behind her. He held his hand out for Dani. She got up and walked over to him, shoulders hunched.

Aaron looked down at his parents' confused expressions, bracing himself before he spoke. This might be the last time he ever saw them because he wouldn't tolerate their ignorance. "You will not disrespect my family, especially in our home."

His mother's mouth opened, then closed. His father remained stoic; his mouth set in a grim line.

His mother shifted in her seat. "How is this disrespecting your family? Your job, sure, I see that. Like I said, it's best to avoid business at the table, right, Samuel?" his mother pressed.

Dani tugged at the hem of her dress nervously. "I didn't ask to be born in the wrong body."

Brynn left his side and pulled Dani into her arms.

His parents' attention focused on her. His mother's forehead pinched together before she covered her mouth, tears welling in her eyes. "You mean . . . ?"

"Dani is just like Emmanuel. My *brother*. And if you can't accept her and love her for who she is, then you should leave."

"Aaron, don't be like this. We were having a good dinner. Let's just avoid the topic. I think that's best for everyone."

"I can't do that," Aaron said.

Brynn turned to him. "We can go."

He strengthened his hold on her waist, keeping her in place. "No. They can leave."

"Let's go, Iris." His father threw his napkin on the table and stood. When his wife didn't move, he tugged her hand. "Iris."

She shook her head, getting to her feet. "I just got him back."

"We're not wanted here." His father's voice was firm.

His mother wiped away the tears freely falling down her face and turned to Brynn. "It was lovely to meet you and be a part of this day." And to Dani she said, "You were so helpful, and you set the table beautifully." Finally, she focused on Aaron, pain lancing over her features. "Despite what you must think, I love you. But I can't go against my beliefs."

"If you can worship a god that would send people you claim to love to a place of everlasting torture and you're okay with that, then you don't really love me."

His mother gasped before his father wrapped his arm around her and ushered her out of the dining room. Her tears ripped a hole in his chest. The last thing he wanted to do was hurt his mother. He was being torn in two, but he had to remember they were the ones choosing this.

Brynn and Dani stayed silent. The door opened, then shut. He watched from the window as they passed by towards their car.

"Dani," Brynn said, "why don't you take a plate of dessert into the kitchen?"

After a moment of hesitation, Dani agreed.

Brynn stepped towards him. "Aaron—"

He held up his hand. "I just need a minute."

Aaron walked by, heading to his office where he shut the door and uncorked his bottle of whiskey. He grabbed a glass, poured in three fingers, then took a gulp. Alcohol burned down his throat. He sat in his chair, his shoulders heavy with defeat. Emotions pricked the back of his eyes. He grasped the glass tighter, as if that would give him an ounce of control of the riot of emotions clamoring through him. He'd just lost his parents. And for what? Why did they put so much faith into one verse and not another? How about the one that commanded them to love everyone as they would love themselves? How about the judge not lest ye be judged?

Aaron drained the rest of his glass, then set it on the table before leaning his head against the chair. *And I just walked away from Brynn when she tried to talk to me, probably ruining any progress we've made.* But he couldn't support her until he'd processed his own emotions.

He turned to gaze out the window as a few snow flurries fell. *What can I do to fix this?*

23

BRYNN

Brynn kissed Dani's forehead, then pulled the covers up to her chin.

"Aaron said he was going to take me holiday shopping tomorrow. Do you think he still will? Or . . . do you think he's mad at me?" Dani asked.

Brynn's heart lurched. She shook her head. "No, sweetie, I don't think Aaron is upset with you. You didn't do anything wrong."

"Then why hasn't he left his office?"

Brynn sighed and rubbed the hair from her daughter's forehead. "I think he's disappointed in his family."

Dani nodded. "Oh, that makes sense . . . Aspen's family isn't like that."

Brynn's lips parted in a soft smile. "No, I think most families out there aren't like Aaron's or ours. But we get to create our own family now, right?"

Dani smiled and parroted the words Brynn had hammered into her since they left. "Right. With friends who really care about us and love us for who we are, not who they want us to be. Love with control isn't really love at all."

"Exactly. Now you sleep tight. I'll see you in the morning." Brynn placed one more kiss on her forehead, then stood.

"Mom?"

"Yeah?"

"Thank you for loving me like you do."

Brynn's heart swelled with affection tainted with regret for how long she'd let Dani endure life on the compound. *If only I'd been braver.*

"You never have to thank me, sweetheart. Unconditional love is what you deserve." Wow. Wasn't that what Aaron had been trying to tell Brynn? She walked out into the hall, switching off Dani's light and closing the door before she swiped the tears from her cheeks.

She looked right, towards her bedroom where her book and comfortable bed were calling. Instead, she turned left and headed downstairs. She hesitated at his office door. She would have never approached her previous husband, or father like this. But Aaron was different. He wanted her to use her voice. And the wary part of her needed to see him when he was at his worst, needed to know if he had a temper and what that would look like. Another part of her was still reeling that he'd stood up for Dani to his own parents. She knew from experience how hard that was on a child, even if they were an adult. Above all, she wanted to make sure he was okay.

Inhaling a deep breath, she straightened her spine and knocked.

"Come in," Aaron's voice called through the door.

Brynn walked into the room, leaving the door cracked open behind her. The only light in the room came from the green lamp on his desk. A glass of amber liquid rested on the oak tabletop next to a half-full bottle. *Is he drunk?*

Fear snaked up her spine as she flicked her attention from the drink to his face partially hidden in shadows.

Aaron stood to his full height, making it seem like the room was closing in. Her scalp tingled, a small warning in the back of her mind telling her to run. Would he disappoint her? Would he hurt her?

She held her ground as he walked forward, then stood in front of her, leaning closer with a faint hint of alcohol drifting from his hot breath. Her stomach twisted with anxiety as his arm reached out beside her, making her flinch.

The room flooded with light before he drew his arm back to his side. He'd only turned the switch on.

His brown gaze swept over her, pain reflecting in his eyes. "I'm sorry."

Her forehead wrinkled as she blinked, stunned. He was apologizing to her?

"I'm sorry for my parents, and I'm sorry I shut you out when you tried to talk to me."

She shook her head. "No, Aaron, *I'm* sorry. I came to check on you . . . I know what it's like to go against what your family wants for you."

His eyebrows rose. "Oh yeah?"

Here he was, leaving the door open for her to continue without pressing her for more than she was willing to give.

"It sucks when the people who are supposed to love and protect you thrust their own bigotry on you, hidden under the guise of religion . . . I left everyone I'd ever known behind when I snuck out with Dani one night with nothing but the clothes on our backs and a small bag of food I'd stolen from the kitchen."

Aaron's eyes glistened with unexpected emotion. "I wish I knew you before, then I could've been there to help."

Something slid into place inside her. It was the first time a man had truly wanted to protect her without using it as an excuse for control. She searched his handsome face, trying to memorize the way he was looking at her, as if he actually loved her. But that was impossible. No one could truly love someone so broken. *It's because he doesn't know the worst of it.*

"I never want to come between you and your family. Dani and I can go if we're causing you problems. We aren't even in love."

Aaron gently cupped her jaw. "Things have always been strained and difficult with my parents, ever since Emmanuel came out to them. But you make the hurt better. And I'll choose you every time."

His eyes burned into hers, her world spinning until she wasn't sure which way was up or down, east or west anymore.

She inhaled a shaky breath, gathering all her courage to speak. "Be careful. That sounds an awful lot like something a *real* husband would say to his *real* wife."

He leaned in. "I already told you, this is genuine for me. That's my truth."

Tears pricked her eyes as she searched the depths of his amber orbs for some hint that he was lying. His thumb stroked her jaw, stirring up the hot arousal in her core. It was like someone had taken all the best qualities from the heroes in the romance novels she'd read and put them all into one man.

You're not worthy.

You're nothing but my slave.

Stupid whore.

Dirty slut.

"Sunshine?"

She blinked away the memories, focusing on his full lips instead. "Hmm?"

"I'm going to kiss you unless you tell me no." He hesitated a moment, giving her the chance to object.

Brynn wanted his lips on hers, as if she needed her next breath. But she yearned to know this was special, just like before. "It's just me and you here."

The corner of his mouth turned up. "This one's for us." He crashed his mouth onto hers, tasting sweet and smoky with a hint of vanilla. Her tongue darted into his mouth, and he groaned. A rush of excitement and the heady feeling of power enveloped her that she was the one to illicit such a reaction from him. His hand gripped the back of her neck, the other sliding down her spine, leaving spirals of lust shooting from the contact like tiny explosions.

She clutched his shoulders, digging her fingers into his shirt, needing more for the first time in her life. She was held. She was protected. She was safe. She pressed her body against his, igniting her skin in liquid fire like she'd never experienced. His erection pressed into her belly and a new wave of intoxicating control hammered inside her.

Aaron pulled away, tipping his forehead to hers, his chest heaving, his arms trembling. "You better go to bed."

She blinked, trying to digest his words in the smoky fog of lust that addled her brain.

He must have read the question on her expression because he backed away and said, "You're not ready for this—and that's okay. We move at your pace."

Something inside her chest snapped as her heart warmed, as if it was glowing within her. She gave one quick nod and turned from the room, still trying to catch her breath. The man wanted her so much he was shaking, yet still he sent her away because he knew it was the best thing for *her*.

Brynn's feelings were all jumbled in a mix of emotions. Disappointment for not being ready. Gratitude that he'd known and respected her enough to sacrifice his own pleasure. Fear that she was exactly what Paul had called her—a whore.

Why did she love the gentle protective side of Aaron in real life and fantasize about him taking away her control? That went against everything she'd fought for these last few years.

I'm broken.

But some of the women in the books she read fantasized about that, too, so maybe it wasn't just her who felt this way?

If Aaron did break into her room and try anything, despite her saying no, she would feel violated. She didn't really want that to happen.

So why do I keep imagining it?

I need to talk to my therapist.

Brynn walked into the bathroom and turned the shower on. She waited until it was warm enough to step inside, hot water cascading down her sensitive skin. She pumped a handful of soap in her palm before rubbing it over her neck, down her breasts, lingering on her nipples. She closed her eyes, imagining it was Aaron's hands instead of her own. She squeezed the soft flesh harder as heat gathered in her pussy. Next, she pinched her nipples. Why did pain feel so good? Her breaths came harder as she slid her middle finger between her slick folds, still manhandling one breast.

Aaron's chest would be hot against her back, his hard cock pressing against her waist. "You know you want this, you dirty little slut. That pussy is mine and you're going to give it to me whenever I want."

Her eyes flew open as hot red shame filled her cheeks. "Oh, God." She whipped her hands away from her body and covered her face as she slumped to the ground in the shower, tears pouring from her eyes.

How was she supposed to look Aaron in the eye tomorrow, knowing she imagined him like that?

And why did she want to do it again?

She rocked back and forth, grateful for the shower to muffle her quiet sobs. It didn't matter if a piece of her was falling in love with her husband because she would never be who he needed. She clutched the silver pendant around her neck. He thought she deserved the world, which was one more reminder that he didn't know her at all. She was fucked up beyond repair, and no man could deal with her demons. Not when she couldn't even fight them herself.

24

———

BRYNN

Brynn shifted uneasily in her seat as her trauma therapist sat across from her in a red chair that matched the sofa Brynn was on.

"What did you want to talk about today?" Cassidy Clark asked.

Brynn opened her mouth, then closed it, looking down. "I . . . I wanted to talk about . . . this book I read."

Cassidy tipped her head to the side. "Oh?"

Brynn nodded. It wasn't a complete lie; she read a few books with this theme. "The heroine has been through sexual trauma, like me. But this heroine, in the book, she fantasizes about non-consensual experiences with men that are . . . rough." Cassidy's expression didn't change, so Brynn continued, "Then there is a scene with the hero, and he ties her up and calls her names. But then he also sort of praises her at the same time. He acts like he owns her body, but when it's over he takes care of her."

"And you want to understand why this is so appealing to . .

. some women?" Cassidy asked, as if she was carefully wording her question.

"Yes. As someone who's been through that trauma, I never want to experience it again. It was horrific." Brynn crossed her arms around herself. "But it got me wondering why some women might, uh, fantasize about it."

Cassidy nodded. "There are a lot of women who have rape fantasies, or bondage kinks who have had sexual trauma, just as there are women who haven't been abused. Some sources say around sixty percent of women have had these types of fantasies. But let's take some guesses why that might be." She crossed one leg over the other. "A fantasy is just that —it's not real. No one really wants to be raped. In a fantasy, who holds the control?"

Brynn leaned back on the couch. "The one having the fantasy."

"Right. And in a healthy BDSM relationship, like the scene with bondage from your book, the person submitting is the one that has the true control. The whole point of the power exchange in a dominant and submissive relationship is so that the submissive is freely and consensually giving up their control to the dominant within the boundaries they set. This means the submissive person in this scenario makes the rules of how far the dominant can take the scene. How hard they're flogged. How long they're bound. It can give them the freedom to relax and enjoy the present moment, to get out of their head." Cassidy paused, keeping eye contact. "The dominant person has to agree to them and respect those boundaries. Of course, the dominant person may have boundaries they are not willing to cross themselves, but that's where the negotiations come into play. Communication is a huge part of this lifestyle as well as the absolute need to trust your partner. This requires constant honest and frank back-and-forth discussions. However, the submissive in these relationships has the power to stop things with their safe word—always."

"Oh," Brynn commented. That did seem appealing. And when Cassidy broke it down, Brynn didn't feel like such a deviant for being aroused by the fantasy.

Cassidy nodded. "The power exchange can help some to get out of their head long enough to reconnect with parts of themselves they wouldn't have otherwise."

"So, it can be healing?"

"I would say it is less about trauma and more about healing one's relationship with intimacy and trust. It can be liberating and lead to a fantastic sex life."

Would that be possible for Brynn? The thought of having Aaron do these things to her like the hero in the novel, to have him treat her like he cherished and loved her, would be a dream come true.

"And what about the part where the hero in the book was tending to the heroine after being tied up?" she asked.

"That's called aftercare. Submission takes a huge emotional toll because you're giving your whole self in a complete exchange of power. It can be intense and exhausting. Some even cry from the emotional release after a scene, which is what they call these encounters."

"This is normal?" Brynn asked shyly.

"Every person on this planet has their own kinks. It's all relative if it's between two consenting adults." Cassidy cleared her throat. "But I highly urge my clients who've been through any type of abuse to really examine their reasons for wanting to indulge in these types of fantasy and lifestyles. It can retraumatize in some cases, and in others it can help you heal. The partner you choose must be one you can trust to be attentive to your cues, if you're triggered and go non-verbal, and be willing to stop at any time and disregard their own pleasure."

Like Aaron did.

Cassidy continued, "Someone who has not identified their triggers could be retraumatized by BDSM. And someone who cannot confidently set and enforce boundaries, or has trouble recognizing when someone is manipulating them, is at high risk for being abused again." Cassidy took a breath. "The only clients I would advise to explore this lifestyle are those who have learned to manage their PTSD symptoms, to be able to define and enforce their boundaries, recognize red flags such as manipulation, and have a partner they can fully trust who also has an interest in it."

Brynn interlaced her fingers in front of her lap, digesting all that Cassidy had explained. "I see. That makes sense."

Cassidy leaned forward. "Intimacy is one of the strongest ways an adult can experience attachment. It's a place we feel most vulnerable. And for some, love can be almost inseparable from humiliation and pain. Those desires are nothing to be ashamed of."

Brynn took a deep breath, relief pouring over her. *So, there's nothing wrong with me?*

"Communication, empathy, trust, and patience are a must for any relationship, but especially with these types." Cassidy's gaze narrowed slightly before she sat back in her chair. "Are you thinking about entering into this type of arrangement?"

Brynn's face flooded with embarrassment as she fixed her gaze on a yellow spot on the beige carpet. "I was curious about the book."

"Right, well, when you engage in any sexual activity, you should ask yourself: Am I doing this because it brings me pleasure, or because I'm trying to replay my trauma and punish myself?"

Brynn nodded, taking this all in. She just needed to clarify this one more time. "And people with these types of fantasies .

. . they aren't . . . I mean, it doesn't mean something is wrong with them?"

Cassidy shook her head. "No, Brynn, it absolutely doesn't."

Brynn nodded. "Sometimes I think I might be ready to have sex with Aaron, but I still don't quite feel ready. What if I freeze? What if I go back to that room and Paul—" She shook her head. "I'm so scared."

"It seems like your husband has been patient thus far. He married you knowing this was a struggle for you, correct? Or do you feel pressured by him?"

Brynn shook her head. "No, not at all. Aaron is gentle and patient and kind."

Cassidy relaxed into her chair. "That's great news. When you get to that point, start slow and speak up when something bothers you. Let him know your triggers as you discover them."

Brynn took a deep breath. "Is it possible for someone like me to have a normal intimate life someday?"

Cassidy waited a beat and then said, "Healing is different for everyone. There may be some situations where you can't do certain acts, positions, or what have you. There may be times when you are fine, and other times where you can't even be touched by the person you love, whom you know will never hurt you. Just remember we're all a work in progress, and tomorrow is a new day. Healing isn't linear, it's up and down, but you are always moving forward—even when it doesn't feel like you are."

Brynn swallowed the lump of emotion in her throat. "Thank you."

"And, Brynn?"

"Yes?"

"Just because you were violated in the worst ways doesn't make you any less worthy."

Tears blurred Brynn's vision with her admission. "But I'm so broken." Her shoulders caved in as she bowed her head in her hands. Wet tears dripped down her arms, soaking into her pants.

The couch sunk beside her as Cassidy's citrus perfume wafted over. "Can I place my hand on your shoulder, Brynn?"

Brynn nodded.

Cassidy's palm was warm and brought a little comfort to the emotional storm raging within Brynn as she spoke her truth out loud for the first time.

Cassidy waited until her sobs had subsided before she spoke, "Honestly, we're all a little broken. We all have things in our past that have hurt us. Some more than others. I wish I could tell you there was a reason for all the suffering you've endured. But what I do know is everything you've been through in your life has brought you to where you are today. It's shaped you into who you are. Think of where Dani would be right now if you hadn't have gotten the courage to leave."

"But I should have left sooner. My sister would still be alive if I'd gone too."

Cassidy's expression softened. "If you had gone, you and Dani would have been punished as well."

Brynn wiped the tears from her eyes as more sprung in their place. "But maybe, if I'd done something more . . ."

"You were a child, brainwashed and abused. You were a victim of your circumstance." Cassidy leaned forward and pointed at Brynn. "You defied everything that had been ingrained in you to escape to a better life and bring your child out of that hell. You stopped the cycle from repeating for Dani. You saved your daughter's life. That's no small feat, Brynn."

"But I failed my sister."

"You couldn't have saved her."

Brynn gasped, her hand clasping her shirt and pulling it away from her chest as she tried to breathe, but a crushing invisible weight pressed against it. Her breaths became shorter, but it wasn't enough oxygen. She was suffocating.

Cassidy stood and went to her desk as Brynn's heart raced. *I'm having a heart attack. Something's wrong and I can't even call out for help.*

"Here." Cassidy returned with a brown paper bag and placed it over Brynn's mouth. "You're having a panic attack. And I need you to take deep breaths. Breathe with me." Cassidy sat on the coffee table and moved into Brynn's line of vision, her nostrils flaring as she inhaled.

Brynn tried to copy her, though her mind was woozy. The bag over her lips deflated until she breathed out, filling it back out again.

"Good, keep going," Cassidy encouraged.

After what felt like an eternity passed, Brynn's breathing had evened out, and her heart rate was back to normal. Her stomach was nauseous and all her energy drained. She just wanted to close her eyes and escape into sleep.

"Do those happen often?" Cassidy asked.

Brynn shook her head. "Not like that."

"We've talked about a lot today and it probably stirred up several different and even confusing emotions for you. If you feel like you need some medication to help—I mean if you have more panic attacks—please call me and I'll get you something prescribed right away."

Brynn nodded.

Cassidy placed her hand over Brynn's. "You are stronger than you feel. And if your sister was here, she'd tell you how proud of you she was."

Brynn sniffled, grabbing the tissue Cassidy handed her and wiping her eyes and nose.

"Your homework is to write her a letter. Write everything out that you feel in your heart to her. And then I want you to imagine what she would say back to you. Do you think you can do that?" Cassidy asked.

Brynn nodded numbly. "I'll try." She stood, then headed out the door, closing it behind her before she turned and bumped into someone. "Oh, I'm so sorry."

Belle smiled back at her. "No, I'm sorry, I had my head buried in my phone." Her gaze flicked to Cassidy's office door and then back to Brynn. "Appointment go well?"

Brynn nodded, trying to hold it together a little longer. "Yeah."

Belle's expression softened. "If you ever need anything, I'm here."

"Thanks." Brynn stuck her hands into the pockets of the warm expensive wool coat that just happened to appear in her room after work one day with a note from Aaron about it being an early Christmas gift.

"Brynn?" Belle asked.

"Yeah?"

"I just wanted to say that I know sometimes it can seem like we're back at square one with our healing. I know what it's like to want to move past things and feel like you're getting nowhere. But I want to remind you that you're so far from the person you were when you arrived three years ago. I've been so proud to see you come more and more out of your shell and take the steps you have every meeting."

Brynn blinked in surprise, warmth filling her chest. She had come a long way, hadn't she? "Do you . . ."

Belle leaned a little closer. "Do I what?"

"Do you think you still have the photos of me you took at the hospital?"

Belle nodded. "They would still be in your digital files."

"How would I get access to those?" Maybe it would help Brynn to have a physical reminder of how far she'd come. Or maybe it would bring it all back. She'd still like to have them, even if she never looked at them.

Belle's brows drew together in concern. "Are you thinking of pressing charges?"

Brynn shook her head vehemently. "No. I just . . . I'd like to have a copy for myself."

Belle nodded, studying her more closely. "I can get them to you. I'll just need you to sign a request form."

"Okay." Brynn let out the breath she'd been holding.

"You're a lot stronger than you realize, Brynn," Belle said.

She swallowed the ball of emotion that rose in her throat. "Thank you, Belle. That means a lot."

Belle laid her hand gently on Brynn's arm and whispered, "If you ever need any legal help, please let me know. I can help even without telling my husband all the details and keep you anonymous. Bently really does want to help women in your situation because he's lived it too."

"Is that why you were able to trust him? Because you have that in common?" Brynn asked.

Belle had shared her dark past with their weekly group in bits and pieces as it was relevant.

"I think it made it easier to relate to each other." Belle smiled sympathetically.

Brynn nodded. "Do you think someone who hasn't come from that life would be able to understand?"

Belle cocked her head to the side. "I think if they have empathy and any amount of human decency, they will love you even more for having survived. They'd see how strong you really are." She paused before she continued, "You've been through hell, Brynn. You've overcome more than most people can imagine. It's normal for you to be hesitant to trust and move forward. You have scars that will be with you for the rest of your life, as all warriors do. The struggle is to not let them define you. We all have good days and bad, but we keep moving forward. Just try not to let your past taint your future, because that's giving the ones who hurt you power. Fight for your happiness. If anyone in the world deserves it, it's you."

Brynn swiped the tears that dripped from her eyes. "Thank you, Belle."

"I'm here anytime you need me. You have my number; don't be afraid to use it." She winked and pulled Brynn into a hug.

Brynn was overwhelmed with everything. She had so much to process. But Belle was right. Brynn wouldn't let Paul or her family steal her future. And it was time she took a risk for her.

Walking out of the building, she squinted at the sunlight. She probably looked a mess, but she didn't have it in her to care.

She made her way down the salted steps of the office building to where Aaron's SUV was parked by a tree right in front. It was the little things like this that he did for her, like pulling up so she didn't need to stay in the cold longer than needed. Or that he kept the heat on hotter than he liked, judging by the fine mist of perspiration below his hairline. Or how he'd asked or warned her when he was about to kiss her so she could make the choice.

She couldn't have asked for a better man. He was almost too good to be true. And that didn't scare her as much as it used to because her intuition told her Aaron was worth the risk.

He climbed out of the car and headed to her side to open the door like he usually did, his smile fading as she got closer, worry pinching his expression tight.

Right now, despite everything, she needed to feel safe. "I—"

He wrapped his strong arms around her without letting her finish, as if he read her mind. Aaron pulled her close, shutting out the rest of the world for this one perfect moment where everything made sense, and she was cared for.

I don't think I deserve you, but I'm falling in love with you anyways.

25

AARON

Aaron pressed his arms around Brynn, caging her against the counter as they kneaded pasta dough together, the buzz of her touch blocking out the sounds of the other couples in his kitchen. She leaned her head towards his, her cheek grazing his. A rush of electricity zipped through his body. His palms cocooned hers as they worked, turning an everyday task into something much more sensual.

"I think you've kneaded the pasta enough, don't want to overwork it." Atlas winked at Aaron. "Go ahead and wrap it in Saran wrap and let it sit for fifteen minutes to let the gluten work while we prepare your space to roll out the pasta dough," Atlas instructed them.

Jasmine, his wife, stood by his side and handed them the plastic wrap.

Their pasta lesson had turned into more of a triple date after Aaron had suggested they hire Atlas for a private lesson in pasta making, and Brynn had told him to invite Jasmine too.

Aaron backed up from the counter, immediately missing the feel of Brynn's body pressed against his. Wiping his hands on the towel to remove most of the sticky dough remnants, his eyes wandered over his wife. She was stunning the first time she'd worn the emerald silk dress he'd bought her, but tonight she'd forgone the leggings, and he got an eyeful of her bare legs for the very first time ever.

He leaned in to her ear. "You look gorgeous."

A slight pink tinged her cheeks. *How far down her body does that blush spread when she comes undone?*

The corners of her lips turned up, her eyes sparkling with something akin to excitement. "Thank you."

He ran his nose up the shell of her ear. "Should I stop?" He pulled away a fraction as her eyes darted to him.

She shook her head. "No. I like hearing it far too much."

"Good." He smiled triumphantly.

Atlas handed them a silver pasta attachment for the cream-colored KitchenAid mixer Aaron had barely used.

Brynn grabbed a paper towel and wiped the counter off. The scent of savory tomato sauce, garlic, and fresh basil wafted through the kitchen. Mason stirred the sauce at the stove, sprinkling in a little salt.

"Oh, I want to do this part too." Pippa joined them on the other side of Brynn.

Atlas winked. "Everyone will get to do the fun part."

"Does anyone want some wine while we wait? I brought a red and white from the local Fates Winery." Jasmine placed six glasses on the counter.

"Ooh, I can't drink alcohol because of my epilepsy," Pippa reminded them, patting her faithful service pet, Lady, on the head.

"We brought some sparkling cider too." Atlas opened the fridge and pulled out the bottle.

Pippa selected an empty glass and scooted it toward Atlas. "I'll take some of that."

"Red for me," Mason added.

Jasmine poured for them, and they each took their glass.

"Would you like some cider, Brynn?" Aaron asked, collecting an empty cup.

"Actually, I'd love to try a little wine."

He looked up, trying to hide his surprise. "Sure. Which kind?"

She tugged her bottom lip into her mouth nervously. "I'm not sure."

"Then you can try a little of both." Jasmine extended her own glass of white to Brynn.

Brynn tentatively took it, inhaling the glass before her chest rose and fell, determination sparking in her gaze. She tipped it to her lips and nodded before licking her lips. "It's not bad. It's sweet."

Aaron poured a tiny bit of red in another glass and handed it to Brynn. Her dainty fingers wrapped around the stem before she brought it to her lips, the corners of her eyes creasing as she swallowed. "That one is . . . a little . . ." She swallowed again.

"Dry?" Jasmine supplied.

"Yes."

Jasmine smiled. "I like the sweet wines the best too."

Aaron poured her a glass of white wine. "Thank you."

"My pleasure." First, the legs, and now wine. Brynn was surprising him at every turn tonight. What had changed?

"The meatballs can go in the oven now," Atlas instructed.

Pippa set her drink on the island. "That's me."

Brynn slowly sipped her wine, as if savoring every note.

"Okay, Mason, you can shut the sauce off and everyone can gather round the island here. I'll show you how to make bow tie pasta, or as we Italians call it, *farfalle*." Atlas waved them over to the mixer, picked up the silver attachment, then placed it on the KitchenAid.

Aaron moved behind Brynn, wrapping his arm around her waist, and she relaxed against him. They'd come so far from the woman who flinched away and couldn't even be in the same room as him.

Atlas walked them through how to feed the dough into the machine, starting at level one and turning the knob to get the pasta as thin as a three or four on the dial, depending on what type they were making. But Aaron couldn't look away from the beauty in his arms. He treasured this gift. Brynn's long eyelashes almost touched her cheeks each time she blinked. And she had a smattering of light freckles on either side of her button nose. His palm skidded over her stomach, electric heat unfurling inside him.

Her breathing hitched.

Aaron leaned in, taking a lungful of her sweet floral scent.

She sipped her wine as Pippa took the first turn making pasta. Aaron swirled his thumb back and forth over Brynn's belly, not moving his hand. She pressed closer to him, as if they were magnets drawn together, two unstoppable forces. He had no control over his cock. The moment she'd come down the stairs with those bare legs, he'd been half hard.

With her pressing against him, there was no way she wouldn't feel what she was doing to him. *So why isn't she moving away? Unless* . . . Did she like knowing she had this reaction from him? Was this her way of telling him she was ready for more?

She took another sip of her wine, then placed it on the counter as she took her turn with the pasta.

The front of his body tingled where she'd been. He curved

forward, as if every cell in his body couldn't resist the pull towards her.

I need to get myself under control. I can't scare her away. Slow and steady.

If only his cock would get that memo.

* * *

Dinner was full of laughs and fun stories. Brynn didn't share much, but she listened and joined in the merriment. She'd drained her glass and had another. Her hands roamed up and down Aaron's thigh. It must be the alcohol, though, because Brynn had never been so forward with him before. He'd kissed her temple, and her cheek tonight, but he didn't dare go for more, afraid of losing himself in her honey-tinged lips.

"This was a lot of fun. We'll have to do it again," Mason said, looking between Atlas and Aaron.

"Absolutely." Atlas pulled on his coat, then grabbed Jasmine's.

"Maybe I could pay you to come to the center some time and teach a culinary arts class to the kids who are interested?" Aaron asked Atlas.

"Sure. We're closed Mondays and Tuesdays, so one of those days would be good. I'd be happy to volunteer an afternoon."

They all turned towards the women who were laughing and hugging goodbye. Jasmine leaned in to whisper something to Brynn who turned her back to the men as she spoke into Jasmine's ear.

"I'm glad we had an excuse to get away for a few hours. Pippa needed this," Mason noted.

"Brynn too," Aaron agreed. It was wonderful to see her eyes lighting up throughout the night.

Mason zipped his coat. "I can bring Dani back in the afternoon. I have a feeling they'll be up all night and will then need a sleep-in."

"I appreciate it. Dani has therapy at two, so any time before one is good. Next time they can come here," Aaron suggested.

"Sounds like a plan."

Pippa and Lady were the first to join them in the mudroom with Jasmine and Brynn not far behind.

"Thank you for coming." Aaron waved.

"Thank you for having us. This was so fun," Jasmine agreed. "Bye, guys."

"Bye." Brynn smiled, leaning against him again.

He wrapped his arm behind her as their guests left, then released her to lock the door behind them. Turning back to the woman who filled his mind and heart, he asked, "Did you enjoy yourself?"

She nodded, and the corner of her lips turned up as her glazed eyes slowly blinked. God, he would never get tired of her joy.

He walked up to her, and she slipped her hand in his, leading him past the clean kitchen towards the couch in the den. She tripped, but he caught her as she swayed and righted herself again. He sat beside her, and she curled into his side with his arm snug around her. The roaring gas fireplace added a comfortable warmth to the room, flames sending flickering light over her glowing skin, making her eyes sparkle.

He stroked his thumb over her cheek. "You feeling okay?"

She nodded lazily, a contented smile on her expression as she leaned on his arm, her face tilted towards his. "I feel very good. The best I've ever felt actually."

"Really?" He chuckled. "That must be some good wine."

Her nose wrinkled. "Much better than the red."

"On our wedding, you told me you didn't drink."

"I don't. Not usually. I mean this was my first time."

"Ever?"

She nodded. "Back on the compound, alcohol was forbidden. So were a lot of things. If anyone broke the rules, they were punished. But now I can do whatever I want."

So, was the wine a part of rebellion against the people who had hurt her? The skin on the back of his neck prickled. "Punished how?"

"Depends on the crime. The very least was a public beating. The worst was . . ." Pain replaced the happiness in her glazed eyes, and he hated he was the one to bring up the past that hurt her so much. But he wanted to know all there was about her. How could he help her heal if he didn't know? *But I'm not her therapist.*

"I'm so sorry you had to go through that. Is there a chance you want to talk to Bently and see if there is anything that can be done? There is a statute of limitations for most crimes, but—"

Brynn sat up, shaking her head vehemently. "No. No cops. No one can know. My husband will know, he'll find me and then—"

Aaron's blood grew cold. "Your husband?"

Brynn's eyes widened before she slammed a hand over her mouth, as if she could take the confession back.

"Brynn? Are you legally married to someone else?"

Tears welled in her eyes as she shook her head. "His father is the leader at the compound. They have people who work for them in the police force there, government, their own lawyers and bank. He can't ever know where to find me and Dani."

Aaron pulled her into his arms, tucking her against his

body, her legs hanging off his lap. "I won't let that happen, sunshine. I'll keep you and Dani safe."

She trembled in his arms, clinging to him, as if he was her only safety. His hand rubbed her back in what he hoped were soothing circles, and her breath evened out.

"Brynn?"

"Yeah?"

"Is our marriage legal?" He had to know.

She pulled away, her green gaze locked on his. "Yes. I wasn't . . . my marriage to Paul was only before God. Only the first wife gets the honors of a legal marriage. That's why he isn't on Dani's birth certificate." She gulped. "I was his sixth wife."

"Christ." Aaron cupped her jaw in his hand. What had this woman been through?

He held his breath, a sinking suspicion making him sick. "How old were you when you were married?"

She looked down. "Fifteen."

Everything in him wanted to roar in anger and wrap her into a protective shell, then go after the monster who took advantage of Brynn as a child like that. Where were her parents?

He pulled away from her, his fists clenching at his forehead as he ground his teeth so hard, he thought they might snap.

Brynn's gentle touch settled on his cheek. "Do you hate me?"

His brows drew together as he dropped his hands and turned towards her again. "What? Never. Why would I . . ." *I think I love you.* But she wasn't ready to hear that.

"I didn't tell you about my marriage. And I . . . I have so many issues."

He pressed his thumb to her lips, silencing her. Her green eyes widened and then heated.

"None of that was your fault, you hear me? Whatever you did in your past was to survive and it brought you to me. I don't even care if you had literal blood on your hands. You're here with me now. No one will ever hurt you again. I'll protect you. You hear me, sunshine?" He moved his finger away from her mouth.

She hesitated, eyes lighting with a hundred emotions at once before her lips crashed over his. Fire and want. Hope and promises weaved between their mouths with each glide of her lips against his.

His hand slid up her ribs, stopping right under the swell of her breast. A tiny mewl escaped her, shooting straight to his cock. Brynn deepened the kiss, her tongue darting into his mouth as she rocked against him, much bolder than she'd ever been before.

His body tensed, lust burning his veins. He hadn't known what wanting truly was until this moment. It took everything in him to pull away.

Her dazed eyes stared back at him, confusion swirling in the emerald depths.

"You're tipsy."

"But it's not just the wine. This happens other times too. My body . . . it's like whenever you're near me I burn hotter than that fireplace." She waved to the flickering flames. "I've never felt that way before, like I need . . . you to touch me or I might burst."

Her cheeks were rosy either from the wine, or from her confession, maybe a mixture of both. Her kiss-swollen lips glistened in the firelight.

This was the most she'd ever opened to him, and Aaron wished it wasn't because of the alcohol. But he wouldn't take advantage of her like this. No, he had to protect her—even from herself.

He stood. Her arms tightened around his neck as he carried her upstairs to her room. Her body trembled against his before he set her on the bed. He moved to her feet, taking off her shoes and placing them neatly on the floor. He skimmed his hand up her leg, past her thigh, and over the silk on her belly. Her inhale was quick as he wove his hand between her breasts, resting on the pulse points on her neck as he leaned his face to hers. Her heart raced faster than even his.

"You're not ready, beautiful. But when you are, I'll touch every inch of you and worship your body as it should be worshipped." Aaron placed a chaste kiss on her lips.

He straightened and turned, then walked out of the room before the last thread of his self-control snapped. Because Brynn deserved someone who would put her needs above his own. And he wouldn't be a one-night drunken regret for her.

Aaron wanted forever.

26

___

BRYNN

Brynn nervously tucked her hair behind her ear, taking a deep breath as she stood at the base of the stairs. The clank of dishes came from the kitchen. Brynn's head ached, a slight pulse in the front of her forehead. She'd drunk too much last night and had made a fool of herself in the process. *I can't believe the things I said to Aaron. Or the promise he made me.* Heat rushed to her core.

Nevertheless, she had to face him in the light of day, and she wasn't sure how to act. Should she pretend nothing happened last night? Her belly churned anxiously. *I just need to get this over with.*

Brynn walked to the kitchen, her gaze settling on Aaron's shirtless form, his muscles bunching and flexing as he cooked over the stove. Her mouth went dry, more so than when she'd woken up. His basketball shorts hung low on his waist, showing off two back dimples. She'd only ever seen one other man so naked, and Paul was older and out of shape. Aaron was . . . perfection.

He turned, and smiled. "Good morning, beautiful." He set

down his spatula and flicked off the gas before walking around the kitchen island.

But her attention focused on those defined abs that had haunted her dreams since the day she'd found him boxing. His arms wrapped around her, pulling her against him in a warm embrace that smelled like the fruity vanilla delight that he was.

His lips pressed to hers in a chaste kiss, much like the one he'd given her before he left her room. Aaron let go and backed up a step. "I was going to bring you breakfast in bed. I figured you might want to sleep in a little more. How's your head?"

She pressed two fingers to her temple, then dropped her hand to her waist. "It's not so bad. How'd you know?"

He grinned. "Headaches are typical of hangovers. You didn't drink a lot, but for someone so tiny who doesn't usually partake, it wouldn't take much."

"Oh."

"I put some Advil on your bathroom counter. Take two with some water. And this breakfast should help make you feel a little better too." Aaron spun around and used the spatula to scoop scrambled eggs onto a plate with toast, bacon, and some sausage.

"This is all for me?" Her stomach rumbled in hunger.

He chuckled. "Sure is, sunshine."

Her gaze locked with his. He'd called her that last night too. "I'm sorry about . . . what I said, I didn't mean to . . ."

He set the plate on the counter and stepped closer, taking both her hands in his as she looked up at him. "Hey, listen, there is nothing to be embarrassed about. Alcohol tends to lower people's inhibitions. I'm glad you told me. Now we both know we're extremely attracted to each other."

"You . . . I mean, you're attracted to me?"

He nodded, his dark eyes flashing. "I thought I made that clear in your bedroom?"

"But . . . never mind." She shook her head.

Aaron threaded his fingers through hers. "No, tell me."

"You stopped."

He sighed and brushed a lock of hair from her face, his knuckles skimming her cheekbone. "You'd been drinking, and that means that you couldn't consent. When we take that step, I want you fully present and able to enjoy everything you let me do to you. When we are together, it won't be just one night, but when I know there is a possibility for a future with you."

Warm wetness seeped into her panties. His words were almost as intoxicating as his touch.

"Do you understand, sunshine?" His hot breath tickled her lips.

"Yes," she said on a sigh.

His mouth slanted over hers, gentle yet determined. Aaron wanted her. And he'd mentioned a future. But was she capable of that? She'd never imagined getting married again—of letting a man have so much control over her. But things with Aaron had been different.

He pulled away, licking his lips, his biceps flexing. "I'm gonna go shower." His chest rose and fell as his gaze lingered on her.

She nodded, and then he was off, back up the stairs. Brynn reached out to the counter to steady herself, her mind and body reeling. A swarm of joyous butterflies burst in her belly, thudding against the walls of her rib cage, as if trying their best to escape.

Aaron wants me.

And I . . . oh, God! I want him too.

Her gaze fell to the plate he'd made for her. She picked up

a piece of toast and took a bite as the buzzer rang for the dryer. *The laundry!* She'd thrown it in last night, and Aaron must have switched it on this morning. *He won't have any towels.*

She set her food back down and walked to the laundry room, quickly pulling out a warm towel and folding it before heading upstairs.

"Aaron?" she called through his open bedroom door.

He didn't answer, but the shower was running in the bathroom to her left, that door, too, open a crack. Steam rose to the ceiling.

"Aaron? I've got a towel for you."

"Brynn." Her name on his lips was like a plea. *Was he hurt?*

"Yes?" She opened the door a little more, determined to leave the towel on the sink when she froze.

"Fuck, Brynn." Aaron's back was against the tiles, nothing but a thin wall of glass separating them. His eyes were closed, water trickling down his torso, over his abs, below the deep V of his hips to the . . . Brynn's eyes widened. That was a cock. A thick, long, uncut cock that made her heart race and her inner walls clench.

His hand moved up and down the shaft as he stroked himself. Her knees wobbled. An invisible string tugged her closer, but fear locked her in place. She should leave, but she couldn't look away. His face grimaced, her name falling from his lips once more as his breathing grew ragged.

Brynn spun around and raced from the room, taking the towel with her in her haste, but not before his ragged muffled cry met her ears. She raced to her own bathroom, out of breath. Her skin heated, and not from embarrassment, but lust. That had been one of the hottest things she'd ever witnessed. *I wish I could have seen him come.* Brynn covered her mouth. "Oh my God."

Sure, she'd read about scenes like that in her romance

novels. But seeing it in real life was a thousand times better than her imagination could conjure up.

Would sex feel different with him? Everything else did. Could she really do this? Have sex with a man again? And what would it be like to choose to be intimate with a man for once? Never in a million years did Brynn think she'd want to, but she'd never expected someone like Aaron. The chemistry between them was unlike anything she even knew existed.

I think I'm ready.

27

BRYNN

Brynn stared out the window at a row of houses as Aaron drove towards home. It had been a long afternoon of driving to Boston and meeting with Dani's doctor.

She caught Dani's reflection in the mirror and turned towards her daughter. "How do you feel about what the doctor said?"

Dani shrugged, then adjusted the several dangly bracelets on her wrist. "I wish we didn't have to wait for the bloodwork before I start the hormones. I mean, I thought the whole point of getting the insurance and going to the specialist is so I can start this transition."

Brynn bit her lip. She didn't know the right answer. She was learning right alongside her daughter in this. "The doctor said the hormone blockers will help stop male puberty from happening. And then once they know your blood levels, we can start you on a low dose of estrogen. You're almost in high school and it might be best to deal with one big thing at a time. There are so many adjustments and hormone changes anyways at this stage in your life, like the doctor said."

Dani's shoulders hunched.

Brynn reached out and placed her hand on Dani's knee. "But we have time to think about your options. I want to do what's best for you, okay? We're in this together."

Dani smiled.

Brynn settled back in her seat, wishing to uplift her daughter's spirit after an emotionally challenging afternoon. "Are you excited to get your ears pierced?"

"Yes!" Dani squealed.

If anyone back at the compound knew, to say they would be livid was an understatement. It only made Brynn want to give that to Dani even more. A rush of defiance soared through her. God, it felt good to rebel against the Livingston clan in this way. *What else have I been holding back on because of their teachings? Maybe I can push the limits a little more.*

"Do you guys mind if I stop by Hope for a few minutes? I have something I'd like to show you," Aaron asked.

"Oh, no, that's fine," Brynn said.

Aaron flicked his blinker on and turned into the parking lot of Hope Facility. There were way more cars than usual in the parking lot, so they'd had to park further away. They climbed out of the car and Dani hooked her arm in Brynn's.

"Is there something going on today?" Brynn asked.

Aaron smirked. "It's a surprise." He opened the first set of doors, and she walked in, Dani skipping ahead through the foyer.

The sound of upbeat music vibrated through the entryway. She followed Dani into the main room. Possibly a hundred people took up the space in between colorful red and yellow stations. It was an indoor carnival of sorts. The smell of buttery popcorn and fried dough filled the space. Upbeat pop music filtered in from the live band performing on the stage.

"What do you think?" Aaron moved closer and shouted over the crowd and live music.

Brynn's eyes widened, taking it all in. Laughter rose from her right. A group of teens played a game of darts to win one of the stuffed animals from one of the half a dozen games lined up.

"What is this?"

"This is your idea come to life. The first step anyways."

Her brows drew together in question. "What do you mean?"

"This is a chance for potential host families to meet and get to know the displaced youth here. A chance to draw in those interested and answer their questions so that we can match them with youth who need a home and a host family. And over there—" He pointed to a table at the far end with a dozen or so people she recognized as Shattered Cove residents from the diner. "—are where they sign up and make an appointment with Bently and the Shattered Cove PD to get fingerprinted for their background checks. The table next to that—" His hand moved to the one with the pretty woman with dark hair who was smiling and laughing with the person across from her. "—is where my assistant, Leslie, is signing people up for classes and volunteering positions."

"But we just talked about this like last week."

He shrugged, leaning in. "When I know what I want, I go after it. You had a brilliant idea to help us find rooms for some kids who would've had to wait until the new dorms were ready in the spring. Now, at least some of them will have a place. And I've spoken with the other centers like mine in the surrounding states and they're arranging similar events."

There was so much to unpack in what he was saying, but her mind was still spinning.

"Oh my God!" Dani squealed and pointed, jumping up and down. "That's Violet Sanders! Ohmygodohmygod! I have to go over there."

"Who?" Brynn asked, searching the crowd where her daughter pointed.

"The author of *Selfie*! How did you . . ." Dani jumped into Aaron's space and hugged him around the waist. "Thank you, thank you, thank you!"

He smiled and patted her back. "I thought you'd like that. I told her I had someone special who wanted to meet her."

Danielle's eyes grew glassy as she pulled away. "You brought her here for me?"

He nodded. "Go on and introduce yourself."

Dani turned towards Brynn, as if asking permission. Brynn smiled, her chest pulling tight with love and gratitude at the utter joy shining in her daughter's eyes.

She sped off, weaving through the crowd towards one of her idols.

"Aspen should be here shortly. Mason said they were running a little late. Something about a diaper blowout," Aaron informed her.

Brynn tore her eyes away from Dani and the gorgeous Black woman in the wheelchair embracing her to focus on the man who'd just made more than one of her daughter's dreams come true. How could she ever repay him? She'd start by trusting him, by taking the leap and believing he'd catch her. Tonight, she'd tell him she was ready to take those next steps they spoke about days ago.

"Thank you, Aaron."

He leaned forward and brushed his mouth to hers. "Don't think I forgot about celebrating that you passed your GED."

Her belly flipped. "We haven't gotten the results yet."

He shrugged. "We both know you nailed it."

"How can you be so sure?"

His eyes locked with hers. "Because I believe in you, sunshine."

Her breath hitched. "When we get home, I want—"

"Aaron!"

Brynn's gaze turned towards the beautiful Leslie, making her way towards them.

"Leslie, this is my wife, Brynn," Aaron introduced.

Leslie turned her smile to Brynn, her eyes widening a fraction before she gave a seemingly practiced smile. "Oh, yes, we've met. It's so nice to see you again." She turned to Aaron. "I have some people with questions, and I think you'd be the best one to answer them." Leslie focused back on Brynn. "Would you mind terribly if I stole him for a moment?"

Brynn bit her tongue and shook her head. "No, of course not."

Aaron leaned over and kissed her cheek. "I'll be right back."

Leslie hooked her arm through Aaron's and led him across the room.

Something sour burned in Brynn's belly as she stared after them. Leslie made a point to touch Aaron's arm as she laughed and smiled at the couple across from them. Aaron smiled at something she said, and Brynn's stomach threatened to revolt. Her skin was hot and clammy all at once. *I think I'm going to be sick.*

Had she and Aaron dated? They seemed so at ease with touching one another, something that took Brynn so much effort. Monogamy wasn't something Brynn was used to. So why did the thought of anyone else close to Aaron make her sick? *Is it because I care about him more than I have for any* man before? The thought was a blow to her chest, sucking the air from her lungs. *But what if I never get there?* Aaron was a patient man but, surely, he'd have a breaking point.

A man is a man, Miriam. They have needs. It takes several women working together to please a man. We must all do our part as the holy prophet commands.

Her mother's words rang in her mind, making the room tilt.

Aaron turned, as if he felt her eyes on him, giving her a small wave.

Brynn turned away, heading towards her daughter. If not for Dani, she'd give in to the voices screaming inside her head to run.

How could I be so stupid to think I was enough?

Fairy tales and happily ever afters weren't for people like Brynn, and she'd do well to remember that.

28

AARON

Aaron waited as Brynn hugged Dani goodbye. Dani wasn't ready to leave the carnival and her favorite comic book author yet, so Mason had offered to drop her home later. Aaron should have stayed until the event was over, but Brynn had withdrawn and seemed stiff and uneasy. The last thing he wanted to do was put her in an uncomfortable situation. Maybe the crowd was too much?

Either way, his wife came before even his business. Besides, Leslie was capable of filling in for him when needed.

Aaron pressed his hand to Brynn's lower back to guide her to the car, but she flinched away. He frowned and dropped his hand to his side, fisting it. *Maybe I pushed her too far tonight.*

When they got to the car, she opened the door before he could, and rushed in, shutting herself inside. He leaned back on his heels, then rounded to the driver's side, climbing in. Aaron started the engine and pulled out of the parking lot, waiting a few minutes in silence to see if she would talk to him of her own accord, but Brynn sat stiffly by the door, as if she was trying to get as far away from him as she could.

"What's wrong?" There was no use dancing around the issue; that had never been his style.

"Nothing."

"Bullshit."

She flinched, turning her face a fraction towards him before she gazed back out the window.

"Was the party too much? The crowd?"

"No."

"Did you feel unsafe?"

She shook her head.

He sighed, his grip tightening on the steering wheel as he turned off the main road, heading towards his house. A light, wet snow had started falling from the grey skies. He turned his windshield wipers on, the only noise in the otherwise silent car except the heat blowing through the vents. He kept it a little warmer than he liked for Brynn's sake.

"If you don't talk to me, I can't fix it."

Brynn's shoulders rose and fell with a deep breath before she shook her head.

Aaron's patience was thinning. This woman drove him mad. He wanted her with every fiber in his body, and it was a daily test of strength not to act on one of the millions of fantasies he'd played through his mind since he'd gotten to know her.

He pulled onto the gravel shoulder of the road, then slipped the car in park before he faced her. She spun around, her gaze alert and unsure. He hated that she still doubted him after everything.

"You're going to tell me what's bothering you so I can make it better." He kept his voice even and controlled.

Brynn's eyes darkened before hurt flashed. She looked down at her hands. "I just . . . I know you're a man and you have needs. I don't know if I can . . ." She sighed. "I know we agreed you would remain celibate, but I understand if it's too much. But—"

Aaron unbuckled his seat belt and left the car, slamming the door a little harder than he meant to as he stepped into the icy cold. He walked to the back of the Rover, taking in deep breaths to calm himself. *She thinks I want to cheat on her? Why would she think that?* He raced through the afternoon in his mind, going over everything that happened. *Leslie.* It had to be her that Brynn was worried about. *But I introduced her as my wife to Leslie.* Did she really think he was that kind of guy?

She's projecting her past onto me. Anger and frustration swelled as he tipped his head to the sky, chunky wet snow falling on his head and sliding down his skin, cooling him. A car whizzed by, splashing some of the slush near his feet.

Aaron took one more calming breath before climbing back into the car. Brynn sat straight as a board, her shoulders hunched, as if she was trying to be as small as she could, as if she wanted to disappear.

He turned to her, gentling his voice. "Don't hide from me, sunshine."

Brynn peeked over at him.

"Can I hold your hand?"

Her palms fisted in her lap as she hesitated, then she tentatively placed her hand in his open palm. The small act of trust brought a frisson of comfort to him.

"Brynn, can you look at me?"

She shook her head.

"Okay, well, I'm going to say some things, and I really want you to listen. Can you do that?"

"Okay."

"It hurts me that you think I'm the kind of man who would want to cheat on my wife."

She winced.

"I'm not your ex, Brynn. And whoever told you that infidelity is part of being with a man, lied to you. It's unfair for you to project your past experiences with your abuser onto me. But I also understand how hard that is for you. You've been hurt, deeply, and traumatized, and that takes a lot of time to work through."

Brynn met his gaze, tears welling in her watery green spheres.

Aaron cleared his throat. The urge to take away her pain roared within him. "I have not, nor will I have intimate relations with a woman that isn't you while we're married. You are my wife in every sense of the word. The ring on my finger means I am yours. And this—" He pressed the band on her left hand. "—means you're mine. Mine to protect. Mine to cherish. Mine to love." His voice caught on the last word.

Brynn's eyes widened, but he continued. "I'm a patient man, but even I'm human. I can't tell you how many times I've thought about you and me together."

Her face bloomed crimson and her eyes dropped down to her lap once again.

"I've thought about tracing every inch of your body with my mouth, finding all the spots that make you sigh and whimper like you did when I kissed you. Discovering all the ways I can make you come."

Her swallow was audible as she met his eyes once again, lust shining through.

"But I don't want to scare you or move faster than you're ready for. You call the shots, remember? So, if you want more, I need you to tell me. And if it's too much, I need you to tell me that too. This is only going to work with clear communication. And I don't want to fuck this up. I want your body, yes. I also want your friendship, and above all your heart and soul. But that won't work without the gift of your trust."

"Why would you go through all this for me? There are so many other women who wouldn't be this much trouble."

He brought her hand to his mouth and kissed her knuckles. "Because you're my sunshine." And like the earth, he was powerless to her and her gravity. "From the moment I laid eyes on you, you consumed my thoughts." He'd been caught in her pull and never wanted to be freed.

Brynn blinked, as if in disbelief, her gaze hazy and unfocused. That was okay, because if it was the last thing Aaron did, it was to convince this woman that, like the sun, she deserved the world that revolved around it.

29

AARON

Aaron lifted the string lights onto the evergreen as he balanced on the ladder.

"A little to the left," Marge, the resident mother hen and main chef for Hope Facility, instructed.

Aaron moved the lights accordingly. "Here?"

"Perfect."

He twisted the rest of the tiny bulbs around the corner and plugged the end into the star at the top. "Okay, Tommy, plug it in and we'll see if it all works."

The young boy at the base of the ladder walked to the outlet and plugged the end of the cord into the wall. The lights blinked on, lighting the whole tree.

Marge clapped first and then several of the teens around the rec room whooped and joined her. Aaron carefully climbed down before he stepped back to review his handiwork.

"Not bad." He motioned to the plastic storage bins stacked off to the side by the pool table. "Alright, guys, those bins are full of ornaments for you to decorate the tree."

Tommy smiled. "We can put them anywhere?"

"Anywhere on the tree, or heck, even the greenery around the room." Aaron motioned to the boughs hanging along the walls.

"This is so cool," one of the other kids said, lifting the lid from a bin.

Aaron's gaze swept the large festive space. Most of the teens wandered closer, peeking at the ornaments, some of them grabbing armfuls.

Crash!

Two of the kids closest to Aaron flinched before their gazes dropped to the broken glass ball on the ground.

"I'll grab the broom," Marge offered, heading out of the room.

The redheaded boy looked up to him, his eyes wide. "I'm sorry, Mr. Ridley."

"Me too." Kent shuffled nervously.

Aaron lifted his hands up. "Hey, no worries, guys. It happens. Just be careful so you don't get cut. I'll clean this up; you guys go decorate the tree."

"O-okay." Kent backed away, going around the other side of the bin, but his cautious gaze remained on Aaron.

Marge returned, broom in hand. Aaron grabbed it from her and swept up the mess.

"It looks fantastic as always. I'm sure it will be even better once the kids get the ornaments up." Marge smiled at the scene in front of them. Twenty or so teens surrounded the tree, decorating it while laughing and joking around. A small crowd had gathered at the table of hot cocoa and cookies Marge had laid out for everyone. More young men and women scattered about the giant room, on couches or at tables, some playing games, others with their headphones on, scribbling away at their notebooks. A few of the volunteers had tables set up with ornament-making crafts, or other activities. It was just another day at Hope Facility during the holidays. This was the hardest time of year for most of the kids, especially since they didn't or couldn't be around their families. Every year Aaron did his best to make it a joyful occasion. And on Christmas morning, they'd each have a gift with their name on it under the tree before they all enjoyed a giant holiday brunch.

I need to talk to Brynn about that. Now that he was a married man, he had to include her and Dani's traditions in his day. Would they want to come with him to the center? Maybe they could celebrate together early on Christmas Eve instead.

Aaron walked the dustpan to the nearest garbage, and Marge grabbed the broom from him.

"I got it," he argued.

She shook her head, her grey locks swaying with the motion. "No, no. I got another batch of cookies coming out of the oven, so I'm going that way anyways."

"Alright, thank you."

"Wow. This place looks fantastic," Bently said as he walked through the entrance of the facility, his arm around his wife.

"Just wait until the tree is all decorated." Aaron chuckled, stepping towards them.

"Hey, Aaron," Belle greeted him.

"Mrs. Evans, thanks for agreeing to drop by."

She shook her head, her red lips curving into a smile. "I'll never get tired of being called Mrs. Evans."

Bently leaned over and kissed her temple. "Good thing, because you're stuck with me for life, angel."

"I think I can live with that," Belle teased before facing Aaron. "Is Brynn here by chance?"

Aaron shook his head. "No, she's having a rare day off at home today."

"Aww, I hope she gets some rest." Belle tucked a strand of loose hair behind her ear.

"Me too."

"I'm gonna go nab one of those cookies. You want one, Belle?" Bently asked.

She shook her head. "No, but is that cocoa I smell?"

"Sure is," Aaron answered.

"I'll have one of those."

"Coming right up." Bently kissed her cheek and then headed towards the table of goodies.

Belle picked a piece of lint from her sweater. "What did you want to chat about?"

Aaron surveyed the room. "Actually, do you mind stepping into my office?"

Lines formed between Belle's eyebrows. "Sure. Is everything okay?"

He nodded and motioned towards the hall leading to his office. "Yeah. I just need your advice."

She followed him into his office, setting down the bag she was holding on the floor beside the chair before she undid her coat and sat. Aaron took the seat across from her behind his desk.

"How can I help?" she asked.

"What we talk about—can it be in confidence?"

She nodded. "Do you want me to keep it from Bently too?"

He hesitated. "No, I mean, it's nothing like . . ." He took a deep breath and let it out. "I wanted to know, from your experience being a SANE nurse, if you had any advice on how to help a partner who's gone through sexual trauma. Is there anything I can do to make her feel safer? Or maybe something I shouldn't do?"

Belle relaxed into her chair, her gaze wandering to the rainbow handprints before landing on him. "I'm not saying this is the case, but for some people it will take a lot for them to be able to be intimate with someone again. We have good days, and bad days."

We? So, Belle was talking from experience. Aaron's chest twinged. *Why weren't people doing more to help end this epidemic of sexual assault?*

"It's a lot of work to be with someone who has been through any trauma. Someone who has complex PTSD like Brynn will need a lot of support and therapy, but ultimately, she has to do the work. As her partner, you can help her by giving her patience, validation, empathy, and don't be afraid to encourage her to push past some of the areas that are more difficult for her, to go out of her comfort zone. But don't push too much."

He nodded. He'd been doing all of that, as far as he knew.

Belle leaned forward. "I think she's trying as hard as she can to overcome her demons. All you can do is keep loving her like you do and be patient."

His throat bobbed. *I do love her.* But Brynn would be the first one to hear him say the words aloud. "She's one amazing woman."

"Brynn has come a long way since she arrived in Shattered Cove." Belle's gaze clouded over as her forehead marred, as if in concentration.

Had Belle treated Brynn when she arrived?

"She's trying. And I can see you are too. You both have what it takes to make this work."

Aaron swallowed the lump of emotion in his throat. "Thank you. I'd do anything for her."

"I can see that."

"Should we go see if Bently ever got that cocoa?" Aaron stood.

"Absolutely. But first, I need to use the restroom." Belle got to her feet.

"Right around the corner. First door on your right."

His phone rang in his pocket.

"Thanks." Belle grabbed her coat and disappeared out the door as he pulled his phone up, glancing at the caller.

Wifey.

He swiped to answer. "Hey, sunshine, how's your day going?"

"Good. How about you?" Brynn asked.

"Awesome. The tree is being decorated as we speak. I saved a few ornaments for Dani to add on after she gets out of school. You sent her with a note so she can be dropped off here, right?"

"Yes. I'm sure she'll love that." The gratitude was evident in her voice.

"We'll be home by five thirty."

"I was going to make some steak for dinner, then I realized I don't know how you like yours cooked."

"Medium-well, but I'm not picky."

"You're the most easygoing person I think I've ever met." She chuckled, the sound but a tease of her joyous laughter that warmed his soul.

"I just don't see the point in stressing over things that won't matter a year from now. Hell, even a couple hours."

She hesitated. "I like that about you."

"There's a lot that I like about you too. Maybe after dinner we can talk about it?"

Her breath was shaky on the other end of the line.

"Thank you, Aaron, for everything you've done and keep on doing for us."

"It's been my pleasure." When she remained silent, he asked, "What did the stamp say to the Christmas card?"

"I don't have the slightest idea." He could hear the smile in her voice.

"Stick with me and we'll go places."

Brynn's light laughter chimed like the tinkling of bells, stirring him up and bringing a flash of warmth to his heart.

"I'll see you at five thirty," she said.

"See you then, sunshine."

He waited until she ended the call before he pulled the phone away from his ear, his gaze catching on his reflection in the glass. Had he ever smiled this big? He tucked the cell back into his pocket and moved around the desk, his foot caught on something making him stumble. He reached out an arm to steady himself and focused on the ground to Belle's bag that she'd left. He picked it up but managed to only grab one handle, some of the contents tumbling out, including a folder. He reached for the items, his hand freezing as his attention focused on Brynn's name scrawled on the top by the Shattered Cove hospital records sticker. So, Brynn had visited the hospital here. And Belle must have treated her which meant . .
.

Anger heated his veins as his grip tightened on the paper. Inside might be proof of what the monster of her past had done to her. His fingers itched to open the envelope. He wanted to know.

Aaron's thumb brushed the flap of the folder. Just one peek and he'd get a glimpse into what happened to his wife. Wouldn't that make him understand how to help her better? God, he wanted to help her so badly. And she was the farthest thing from an open book. Temptation wound around him. He grit his teeth.

No. Not like this. To open this folder would be betraying Brynn and all the trust they'd built, even if she never found out. If she wanted him to know, she'd tell him. And if she wanted to keep what happened a secret from him forever—as hard as that would be for him—that was her choice too.

He stuffed the envelope back into the bag and carried it out of the room to find Belle.

Tonight, he'd have dinner with his wife, and take another baby step towards building a future that would last.

30

BRYNN

Brynn walked out of the department of motor vehicles holding the plastic card in her trembling hand. She'd done it. She'd passed the tests and gotten her driver's license. She blinked at the name in disbelief. *Brynn Ridley.*

Aaron looked up from his phone, his mouth splitting into a huge smile. He ran up to her, arms wide. She couldn't help the grin that tugged the corners of her mouth. She opened her arms as his body thudded against hers. He picked her up and spun her around, making the world spin almost as fast as her racing heart. She wrapped her legs around him, holding on as he twirled her a second time while squeezing her tighter.

"I knew you could do it, sunshine!" He pulled back enough to kiss her hard on the mouth. Her mind was dizzy from all the excitement and twirling.

He stared at her with so much affection and pride glowing from his brown eyes that it stole her breath.

"We have to celebrate." He lowered her to her feet. Her knees wobbled from the sudden loss of his touch.

Aaron opened the passenger door, then stopped short. "Do you want to drive?"

Her stomach flipped. *He's so thoughtful.* "I think I'm too excited."

"Alright. I've got a surprise for you anyways. Hop in." He motioned to the front seat.

She climbed in, buckling herself as he shut the door and jogged to the driver's side. Fat snowflakes fell from the grey sky, dusting over the frosted grass.

He shifted the warm car into reverse and backed them out of their spot, heading into town instead of towards home.

"Where are we going?" she asked.

He turned to her and flashed a smile, showing off his white teeth before focusing back on the road ahead. "That's the point of a surprise. You don't know until you get there." He reached out, clasping her hand in his as he drove past a row of houses and turned right onto a road she hadn't traveled before.

The curiosity was almost too much for her frayed nerves. She'd thought she was going to throw up before her driving test. She hadn't even been able to sleep much last night, she'd been so worried about failing. But she trusted Aaron. And if he had a surprise for her, she knew it was going to be good— better than she probably imagined.

Brynn gazed at him out of the corner of her eye, her mind replaying the things Aaron had said to her after their argument just like they had every day since. He'd pushed her to talk, which wasn't comfortable. It was hard to voice her thoughts, feelings, and needs. It made her feel too exposed and vulnerable. But then he'd listened. Then, he'd admitted his feelings for her, and her belly had somersaulted. A million fluttery sensations spiraled through her at his confession. And even in her disbelief he'd stolen her breath. *Because you're my sunshine.* Had sweeter words ever been spoken to her? She'd never been cherished by anyone except her sister, and even that was so long ago.

And then he'd claimed her. *This means you're mine. Mine to protect. Mine to cherish. Mine to love.* Being told she was someone else's should have made her afraid. But Aaron's possessiveness felt different than Paul's because it went both ways. *And he's mine.* She'd been told to be quiet and obedient her whole life. Her mouth soured at the memory. Why did she crave Aaron to take control, then? The way his usually gentle voice had gone firm and unyielding in the car had her body igniting with lust. *Because I trust him.* She didn't even know if she could have sex with a man, much less let him do the things that she read about in her novels. Aaron had made it clear she was the one in control of their next steps. For her to make a move seemed too forward. But now she had to make a choice. *Am I ready to take the next step with Aaron? I want to, but what if I'm a disappointment? What if it's not as good as I hoped?*

There was only one way to find out.

Aaron pulled into a car dealership, and her brows rose. She turned to him as he parked in front.

"Ready to pick out your new wheels, Mrs. Ridley?" He unbuckled his belt.

"W-what? Today? I—I don't think—"

"Come on, we'll just look. No harm in that, is there?" The corner of his mouth lifted in a suspicious smile.

"I suppose not." She climbed out of the car, Aaron closing her door as an older Black man exited the main entrance, a steaming cup of coffee in his hand.

"Good afternoon. Aaron, long time no see." He shook Aaron's hand.

"It's been too long. Toby, I'd like you to meet my wife,

Brynn. Sunshine, this is Toby Brown of Brown's Dealership." Aaron wrapped his arm around Brynn's shoulders.

She leaned into his side and accepted Toby's hand and shook it. "Nice to meet you."

"How's your son?" Aaron asked.

"Keith is around back getting everything ready. He'll be out here in a second. Can I offer you two coffee, or tea? Maybe some water?" Toby looked between Aaron and Brynn.

"I'm fine, thank you," she answered.

"Me too."

The purr of an engine drew Brynn's attention to a shiny black, small SUV. It parked beside them, and a young man climbed out with a smile.

"Hey, Aaron." He clapped hands with her husband and pounded his fist.

"Keith. Damn, you look healthy." Aaron laughed.

Keith patted his belly. "Mom's cooking will do that to ya." His gaze wandered to her.

"This is my wife, Brynn," Aaron said.

"What did this guy do to trick you into marrying his ugly mug?" Keith teased.

Brynn bit back her smile.

"Asshole." Aaron playfully shoved Keith's shoulder.

Keith snickered.

"Alright, my old bones can only take so much of this cold weather. I'm gonna head inside and get the paperwork ready. As hard as it is to believe, you're in capable hands." Toby motioned to his son.

"Gee, thanks for the vote of confidence, Dad." Keith waved him off.

Toby chuckled and went back inside.

"Paperwork?" Brynn asked, turning to Aaron.

"For your new car—if you choose to get one. They are having a sale, right, Keith?" Aaron turned to the young man.

"Right." Keith nodded so fast he looked like a bobblehead.

Funny how when she'd gone shopping for wedding dresses, the same thing had happened. But Brynn had never been a lucky person. She narrowed her eyes on Aaron. *No. He wasn't even at the dress shop.*

She was being paranoid. "I thought we were just looking?"

"Can you give us a minute, Keith?" Aaron asked.

"Sure, take your time." Keith walked into the main building.

Aaron turned to Brynn, taking her cold cheeks in his warm hands. His breaths came out in a puff of smoke in the cold air. She pulled her coat tighter across her chest.

"I want you to have the ability to be more independent and not need to rely on me or the bus to go where you want. To do that you need some wheels."

He wanted this for her? Her heart squeezed. "I don't think I can afford something as nice as these. And you're not buying me a car, so don't even think of asking."

"I figured you'd say that. So that's what Toby is in there doing. I'll have to cosign the loan, since you don't have any credit, but it will be in both our names. And he'll work out a payment that's affordable."

She blinked. When would this man stop surprising her at every turn? Gratitude welled inside, sloshing over the edge and spilling into her chest. "Kiss me."

His lips quirked up. "For Keith?"

"No. For me."

He leaned in, capturing her mouth much like he'd done to her heart. She stood on tiptoes, clutching his wool jacket in her hands as his fingers threaded through her loose short hair.

When he pulled back, his lips were shiny, and the happiness that reflected in his eyes mirrored her own. Never in a million years would she have expected someone like Aaron to exist. And now that she'd found him, she wasn't sure she wanted to let him go. No, she wanted more perfect moments like this, where he looked at her, as if she was his whole world —and she believed it.

31

AARON

Aaron slipped his hand from his coat pocket to wave towards Mikel who was carrying a bag of takeout across the street before he disappeared into Remy's café. Seems like he wasn't the only husband who wanted to surprise his wife for lunch today. Though Aaron had ulterior motives. Brynn's birthday was coming up in a few days and he was still wracking his brain with what to do for her.

He paused in front of the bookstore, taking in the festive lights in the shop windows on either side of the main road of town. Silver and red candy canes crisscrossed on streetlamps. Snow-dusted wreaths hung on the wall between storefronts. Holidays in Shattered Cove never got old. Maybe he, Brynn, and Dani could take a stroll to Green Park tonight, get some cocoa, and see the tree all lit up.

His gaze caught on a man turning abruptly from the edge of the bookstore window, a small piece of paper dropping from his hands to the sidewalk.

Aaron shook his head. "The trash is two steps away, asshole."

The man didn't even turn around; he just kept walking. Aaron plucked the wrapper from the ground and threw it in the trash. He turned and grabbed the handle on the door before pulling it open and heading inside. The warmth hit him first with the smell of books second. His gaze darted to the empty front desk. *Where is she?*

He strolled down one row of books, noting the few other customers milling around the store. Her giggle in the far-left corner dragged his attention that way, bringing a smile to his face. Aaron froze, his grin disappearing. Brynn was standing by the children's shelf, her open palm in Ricky Emerson's. Ricky traced his finger over the lines on her hand, his voice low. Aaron's shoulders tensed. His hands fisting at his side. He wanted to wipe the smirk off Rick's face. Aaron grit his teeth and took in a deep breath. Normally, he was the peacemaker, the one who kept his cool under the most stressful situations. But not when his wife let another man touch her, especially when he understood just how much trust it took for her to let a man get close. This fucking crossed the line.

Aaron puffed out his chest and strode forward. Ricky turned to him first, his eyes widening a fraction before his smile grew.

Motherfucker.

Brynn spun around as Aaron grabbed her hand and pulled her into his chest. "Hey, sunshine."

She let out a surprised squeak as he slipped his fingers through the hair at the base of her neck and tugged with enough pressure to tip her head up to meet his mouth. His other hand grabbed a handful of her ass and squeezed her body tighter against his.

Her lips were tense at first, but a moment later she relaxed against him. His kiss wasn't asking; it was telling, possessive, as if each swipe of his lips against hers would brand her. Did it mark her heart as much as it did his?

Ricky cleared his throat, then chuckled. Brynn tensed, as if just realizing they were not alone. It brought a thrill to him that she was just as lost in his touch as he hers.

He pulled back, grazing his teeth on her lower lip and tugging just a little. She stared up at him, her hazy green eyes dark with want.

"I'll just . . . uh, leave you to it. Nice to see you again, Aaron. Have a good afternoon, Brynn," Ricky announced before his footfalls moved farther away from them.

Brynn shook her head, as if trying to rid herself of his trance as she straightened, her gaze darting around the room. Her cheeks reddened. "Aaron, I'm at work. I don't think that was appropriate here."

"He needed a reminder that you're a married woman."

Brynn blinked, her brows drawing closer together. "Ricky?" She shook her head. "He's a regular at the diner. He was reading my palm. He was just being nice. He's like that with everyone."

He stepped forward, bending so his mouth was by her ear. His hand moved to her lower back, his other hand brushing over the sensitive spot between her ear and shoulder. "I don't like to see another man touching you."

She shivered in his arms—or was she trembling? Was he going too far? Images of Ricky's smirk flashed in his mind and a fresh rush of jealousy filled his veins.

"Why does it bother you so much?" Brynn asked, her voice all breath.

He pulled back enough to face her, his thumb wiping over her throat. Her pupils were black as midnight with only a small sage ring around them, the flecks of gold catching the light in the room, much like this woman had captured him.

"You want my truth?"

She nodded once.

"Because I feel like you're mine . . ."

Her eyes shuttered and her throat bobbed as she swallowed.

No one else came near them in the store, as if the customers could sense the tension between them. He was crossing all sorts of lines he'd set for himself, but he couldn't take it for one more goddamned second. His self-control had snapped the moment she'd let another man touch her.

"Does that scare you?" he asked.

She licked her lips, her eyes searching his. "It should make me terrified . . ."

"But?" God, he hoped there was one.

"With you, for some reason, it has an entirely different effect on me."

Those green flames turned into lust fire, and blood rushed to his cock. His control was hanging on by a thread. Aaron just needed her to give him the go-ahead. "What kind of effect?"

The blush on her cheeks deepened, spreading down to her neck as her eyes dropped to his chest. "I . . . I—" She slammed her mouth closed before taking his hand and dragging him towards the romance section.

What the hell is she doing?

Brynn picked up a book and flipped to the middle, her eyes raking wildly over the text. She turned the page twice before she handed it to him, pointing to a paragraph.

Bethany's panties were soaked. Ruined, much like her, and all it had taken was for Jamie to look at her like that.

It didn't hurt that he was shirtless. Those defined abs on display leading to the V that dirty dreams and her wildest fantasies were made of.

Bethany's pussy ached for his cock. And when his deep voice ordered her to get on her knees, she didn't hesitate.

Aaron looked up from the novel to Brynn. She was biting her lower lip and looking anywhere but at him.

He closed the book and put it back on the shelf, his hand shaking as he tried to rein in his frayed control.

"Come with me." His voice came out rough, as if he'd swallowed gravel. He took her hand and guided her to the front desk where Troy was waiting. Aaron turned to Brynn. "Grab your coat, sunshine."

"Why?" she asked.

"Because you're taking the rest of the afternoon off. Troy can handle the store alone. Can't you?" His hard gaze turned to the man behind the desk.

Troy opened and closed his mouth, his eyes darting between the two of them. "I—yeah, sure. Are you okay, Brynn?"

Aaron took a deep inhale before letting it out, his patience wearing thin.

Brynn must have sensed his need because she spoke up. "I'm fine, but something important came up. Would you mind?"

"No, not if you're sure." Troy turned a wary glance towards Aaron.

Brynn picked up her coat from behind the desk along with her bag. "Thanks."

Aaron waited for her to get her coat on before he slipped his arm around her and led her towards the door.

Once they were outside, Brynn asked, "Aaron? Where are we going?"

"Home."

"But . . . don't you have to work? And why did I need to take the afternoon off? What's going on?"

He spun around, pulling her into an alley between Shattered Cove Records and a boutique. Her lips parted in a gasp. The fog of their shared breaths mingled between them. Droplets of melting snow dripped from the eaves above, pitter-pattering on the ground. The hum of cars driving by became background noise as the thundering of Aaron's heart grew louder.

"Are you sure you can handle another one of my truths?"

She swallowed and jerked her head into a nod. "Yes."

"We're going home because I can't wait another second to taste you." He caressed her face with his hand, his thumb tugging her lip down. "What kind of husband would I be if I didn't take care of my wife's needs?"

Her brows scrunched together. "My needs?"

His eyes dipped before they locked on to hers again. "You think I'm going to leave you wet and aching?"

Her gaze flared and her mouth slackened. And fuck him, he couldn't help imagining how those plump bare lips would look around his cock. But that wasn't what today was about. His needs would come later. But her pleasure? Damn. He was salivating at the opportunity to bring her to heaven.

"I don't expect anything in return. But can I take care of you, sunshine?" He held his breath, waiting. Hoping.

After what felt like an eternity, Brynn replied, "Yes."

That was all he needed to hear before he picked her up and carried her the rest of the way to the car.

BRYNN

Brynn's body vibrated as a flood of emotions tumbled through her. Nerves twisted her belly. This new side of Aaron did something to her that made the pieces of her hidden in shadow come to life. Something about the way he took charge and got possessive of her made her panties wet and her heart race. But why? She'd lived her whole life with men controlling her, and it had never felt like anything other than oppression. With Aaron, it freed a part inside her that she didn't know was caged.

The car turned down his driveway, and it became harder to take a full breath. Sweat beaded on her forehead. Could he hear how fast her heart was thundering in her chest? Aaron's firm grip stayed on her thigh, kneading the sensitive flesh, making the fire spread from her pussy down her limbs. She had no idea what was going to happen next. Uncertainty added another level to her lust because, deep down, she knew she was safe with Aaron.

He flung the car into park outside the garage, then darted

out of the car, his door shutting with a little more force than usual as he raced to her side. Her thigh tingled in the shape of a handprint where his had been.

Crisp wintery air shocked her lungs as her door opened. He held out his hand to her and she took it without hesitation. Anticipation slicked around her, soaking into every molecule. He wordlessly wove his fingers in between hers as he led her inside.

Aaron shut the door and pressed her against it. His mouth crashed onto hers. She looped her arms around his neck. His hands dug into her hips, lifting her before she hooked her legs behind him. Wildfire erupted, spreading through her limbs tangled around him, seeking devastation.

He gripped the side of her throat, his thumb brushing against the front with just a hint of pressure that had her core squeezing. "Are you ready?"

She blinked up at him in a haze of lust like she'd never felt. A feeling she'd been taught was the devil's work. If what she shared with Aaron was evil, she was walking into hell.

She nodded.

Aaron licked his lips, his jaw tensing, as if it were taking the last of his self-control to hold back. "Need you to use your words, sunshine. Tell me you want this. Want me to make you feel so good you see heaven."

She gasped. "Yes."

"You tell me if it's too much. Tell me if you change your mind and I'll stop right away. Just say stop, okay, baby?" Aaron's serious gaze locked on to hers.

"Okay."

He slipped his hand around hers and led her through the house, up the stairs, towards his room. The sound of the door shutting was amplified as the tension thickened.

She stood in the center of the space, her back to Aaron. Her mouth dry, her mind raced as she stared at the blue comforter on the bed. She was alone in a bedroom with a man for the first time in years.

The last time—

No, she wouldn't let Paul take this from her too.

"Turn around," Aaron's firm voice commanded, like a buoy in the raging sea.

She obeyed without hesitation, her knees wobbling and unsteady. Her gaze wandered up his broad chest, snagging on the hollow of his throat. His Adam's apple bobbed. God, that was sexy. His chin peppered in dark scruff from his five o'clock shadow had her thighs clenching. What would that feel like on her skin? And God, those lips. So full and plump. What dirty promises would he whisper between kisses? Finally, her gaze flicked over the slope of his nose to those dark fathomless eyes. Aaron walked forward, towering over her. She swallowed as her belly flipped and twisted.

"Take your clothes off."

Panic streaked through her, and her eyes widened as her body stiffened.

Aaron must have sensed her distress because his expression softened. "I want to see you bare so that I can worship every inch of you. Do you want that too?"

She nodded.

"Words, sunshine."

"Y-yes. I want that."

Whore.

Slut.

Temptress.

Deviant.

"Do you want me to take them off you? Or do you want

to do it?" He rolled up his sleeves, showing off his veiny forearms.

"I-I'll do it." She tucked her fingers under the hem of her shirt and slowly pulled it over her head. Cool air rushed over her exposed skin as her sweater fell to the floor. Aaron's gaze raked over her, scorching her bare flesh.

"Now your bra."

His instructions made it easier to comply because she could tune out the voices in her head, condemning her for the emotions Aaron stirred within her. How did he know she needed it like this?

Brynn reached around to her back, her hands skimming the mottled flesh as she unclasped the plain cotton bra and let it fall, joining the growing pile of clothes on the floor. *He's going to see my scars.*

"Fuck, baby. You're gorgeous." Aaron's tone deepened, coming out raw and gruff. His hands fisted at his sides, as if it was taking everything he had to hold back.

A surge of heady power crashed over her, boosting her confidence. She went to her jeans, undoing the button. The whiz of the zipper was the only sound in the room other than the heavy breaths coming from Aaron's heaving chest. His eyes locked on her movements, as if trapped in a spell. Maybe she was evil, a deviant like the prophet had said. All she knew was she felt like she was the most powerful woman in the world with Aaron's attention locked on her, as if he was enraptured by her every move.

She tugged the pants down her hips, over her thighs, and along her legs, taking her pale pink panties with it.

Stepping out of her bottoms, she stood bare and vulnerable, awaiting his instructions.

"Christ. You're . . . breathtaking." Aaron stepped closer.

Her eyes darted to the floor.

But his finger pressed under her chin, tilting her face towards his. "Don't hide from me. I need to see you want this. Are you ready for me to taste you?"

She nodded. Did he mean to kiss her? Or perhaps taste her skin? *Does he want to lick my pussy like the heroes in the books?* Did men really do that? Would he be grossed out by her smell? She hadn't shaved—

"Stay with me, sunshine. Get out of that head of yours."

Again, how did he know?

Aaron cupped her face, kissing her tenderly as he backed her up towards the bed. Her knees hit the mattress and she gripped his shirt. Somehow, the difference of having him fully clothed and her naked only made this moment hotter. His palms wrapped around her, one grabbing a handful of her ass, the other applying pressure to her shoulder.

He kissed her again, his mouth slanting over hers. She opened for him as his hand kneaded her butt. Swirls of arousal wove patterns of overwhelming need inside her. His sweet tongue delved between her lips, seeking hers. She kissed him back, her arms winding over his neck as he lowered her to the bed, crawling over her until her head rested on the pillow. His weight settled on top of her. Brynn's skin flamed hot and icy cold at the same time.

His hand skimmed up her hip to cup her breast, and a surprised whimper left her mouth.

"That's it, baby. Let me hear you."

He liked her sounds?

"Let's see how many of those sweet sounds I can draw from you." Aaron kissed her neck, trailing his mouth to her painfully hard nipple as he pinched and kneaded the other. Her back arched as his hot tongue licked the peak before he sucked the bud into his mouth.

"Aaron!"

"Hmmm," he hummed, the vibration sending a shock of arousal shooting through her.

His rough palm skimmed down her belly towards her sex.

Yes. Yes. Yes.

His teeth raked over her nipple as his finger slipped inside her pussy lips. Her hips rocked off the bed. "Oh, God!"

"You like that?"

She nodded, then remembered he wanted her words. "Yes."

"Good girl."

A rush of liquid heat doused her body in white-hot flames with the praise.

"God, I want to kiss you everywhere." His lips sent a cascade of shivers through her body as he kissed the sensitive flesh behind her ear and sucked. "Sound good to you?"

She moaned, his words causing something low inside her belly to pulse and tighten.

"Need the word, baby."

"Yes."

He took his time to kiss down her breasts, and her belly. He paid extra attention to the dip in her hips and her inner thighs.

"Now spread those sexy legs wide. Let me see your gorgeous pink pussy," Aaron instructed.

Brynn inched them open a little bit.

"More. Hook them over my shoulders."

She obeyed, her stomach tumbling with a sudden burst of self-consciousness. *Will I smell? Should I have shaved? The women in the books are always shaved. Will Aaron be grossed out?*

The first lap of his tongue swallowed up the voices in a gulf of pleasure. She hissed and then moaned. His tongue licked and flicked her bundle of nerves, making the tightening pressure increase in her belly. She needed something, but she didn't know what to ask for.

"Mm," he hummed against her clit as one finger entered her.

Her hips bucked at the building pressure. "Oh, Aaron, fuck!" She'd never in her life sworn before. But the way this man fluttered his tongue on her clit as he reached inside her, his finger hitting a spot that shot tingles down to her toes, had her speaking without thought or care. Out of control. Her body tensed and writhed. Her head shook back and forth. A rising tension swelled, want turning to need. She experienced a yearning like she'd never known.

"You taste so fucking good. That's it, baby. You're almost there. Want you to come. Just let go and come."

Come? Orgasm? But she'd never—was she even capable? *If I don't, will he be disappointed?* The worry drew her farther away from that invisible line. Should she fake it? Would he know?

He sucked her clit, drawing pleasure from her, but something held her back. Aaron worked her body, his finger driving in and out, building a hollow ache.

"I need . . ."

Aaron sat up, his chin glistening with her juices. "What do you need, baby?"

"More."

His gaze searched her face hesitantly. "Like what? Tell me and I'll make it happen."

She bit her lip.

He crawled over her. Resting by her side, he tugged her lip from her mouth. "Hey, you have nothing to be worried about. Nothing would make me see you as any less. Tell me what you want."

"I . . ." She blew out a breath. "It's not comfortable when all the attention is on me. I feel like I should be doing something for you."

He stroked the side of her face, tucking her hair behind her ear. "But this is about you, sunshine. I won't lie, this is for me too. It brings me joy to bring you pleasure."

"It does?"

He leaned down and kissed her lips, her essence on his mouth. It wasn't as bad as she'd thought. Musky and a little sweet.

"If you want me to make love to you, I will, but only if you think you're ready. If this is all we do today, I'm perfectly happy with that."

She studied his face, honesty shining through those deep brown eyes she wanted to get lost in. His warm chest pressed against hers, nothing but his shirt separating them.

"I want to see you naked too. And I want—I *need* you to make love to me."

"I've never heard a sexier fucking sentence." Aaron leaned over and kissed her chastely on the mouth once more before he climbed out of bed.

He unbuttoned his shirt, shucking it off. Her eyes landed on his defined pectoral muscles, down his flexing abs as he pulled off his slacks. Her gaze stayed glued to the elastic of the boxer briefs as he tugged them down. His long, thick cock curved up slightly, towards his belly with a neat patch of trimmed hair around the base. Memories of him fisting himself in the shower came back with a vengeance.

"Keep looking at me like that and I might come," he warned.

Her eyes darted to his. He smiled and then reached into the bedside table, pulling out a foil packet. He ripped it open.

"May I?" she asked, curious.

He handed her the latex.

"Can you show me?" She shyly flicked her gaze to his.

"Pinch the tip, and then you roll it on, like this." Aaron's hand engulfed hers, showing her how to roll the condom over his dick. "Perfect."

He crawled back over her, lining the tip of his erection at her entrance. She spread her legs wider to accommodate his large body over hers.

"You sure you want this?" Aaron checked again.

"Yes." She met his eyes, hooking her hand behind his head and pulling him in for a kiss. She hadn't been surer of anything before. Partly because she wanted to see if she could do this. And partly because she'd be more relaxed knowing he was also getting pleasure from their experience.

"If you change your mind, just say stop and I will. Promise?" he asked.

"Promise."

He slid inside her, slow and controlled. She gasped as his cock stretched her, filling her more than she thought possible.

His expression strained. "You doing okay?"

"Yes. More."

He rocked her, face to face, hovering above her as his weight rested on his arms, pinning either side of her to the mattress. Her breaths came in pants as he hit the spot that he'd touched before with his fingers. That pressure returned. She dug her nails into his shoulders, holding on as he drove inside her, harder and faster.

Thump.

Thump.

Thump.

The bed frame knocked the wall and Brynn froze. All sensation left her body as numbness leaked through her bones like poison until she felt nothing at all except violated and terror.

She stared at the ceiling.

Paul's wrinkled red face, covered in sweat, huffed over her. Brynn lay limp beneath him, unable to escape. She was trapped yet again by his greedy fingers and artificial-cherry-tainted breath. She lay frozen, as still as a corpse. It was always worse when she fought him. She closed her eyes, trying to hold back the tears that wanted to fall, because it only made him smile and go harder.

"Brynn!" Aaron shouted.

She gasped. Opening her eyes, she was no longer on her back, but in her husband's arms. *Oh my God!*

Her body trembled, numb, as if she'd fallen in an icy lake. She was so cold. The chill gnawed at the marrow of her bones, iced deep within her soul.

"You're safe. I got you. No one will hurt you again. You're not alone, Brynn," Aaron said, his hand rubbing soothing circles over the raised scars on her back. She held her breath as his head moved, most likely to take a better look.

She slammed her eyes closed again, hugged herself tighter against his chest, and cried harder.

He pulled back, his palm sliding up her nape to cradle her head. "Brynn, open your eyes and look at me."

She hesitated.

"Please, sunshine." The plea in his voice snapped something inside her chest.

She opened her eyes, now blurry with tears. *This is where he realizes I'm not worth it. I'm too broken.*

Aaron's soft gaze locked with hers. "We're gonna get through this together. You hear me?"

A sob tore through her, releasing an avalanche of grief. It crashed over her, threatening to suffocate.

He held her as she cried. He was calm, steady, despite the

storm raging inside her. She released the pent-up anger and overwhelming grief, all while two strong arms held her, wrapped in a cocoon of protection as she fell apart.

Would she ever get put back together again? Or was she shattered beyond hope?

33

___

AARON

Aaron clicked open his browser in his home office. It had been a few days since things had escalated with Brynn. *I should have known she wasn't ready.*

He'd unintentionally hurt her. After she'd calmed down, and her sobs had subsided, he'd drawn a bath for her, offering to wash her body. She'd turned him away and locked herself in the bathroom for an hour. He'd left her alone, and she hadn't even come out of her room for dinner when Dani got home from school.

Aaron typed in his search and surveyed the results that came up. How could he help Brynn? He didn't have much experience being with a partner who'd had sexual trauma. The scars across Brynn's back flashed in his mind. Rage heated his body, much like when he'd first seen them. He punched the keys harder than necessary on his laptop. He shook his head and ground his teeth. *If I ever get my hands on that motherfucker . . .*

Aaron forced a calming breath into his lungs before releasing it. Brynn didn't need his anger; she needed his patience. He'd been scouring the internet for any advice, compiling a list of ideas to bring up to Brynn when they had the chance to talk again. He'd given her space these past few days, but not too much, as he didn't want her to think he'd rejected her because of her trauma.

His eyes landed on a thread—victims of sexual assault sharing how kink helped them work through their past abuse. The power exchange was vital to many of their healing. Some of them wanted to replace the memory of the trauma with memories of a similar experience with someone they loved and trusted. A mind trick that worked for some.

Aaron's stomach churned at the thought of recreating a scene where Brynn had been violated. He wasn't sure he could do that if she asked.

He scrolled on, trying to keep an open mind, reading story after story of mostly women who found freedom in being restrained.

User TieMeUp69: *It was so hard to be there in the moment and enjoy what my partner was doing because I was always stuck in my head. The pressure to orgasm and wondering if I should be doing something for him took me out of the moment and made it impossible for me to enjoy the experience.*

He was given a pair of handcuffs as a gag gift one birthday and joked around that we should try them out. We did and it was like I was set free. With my hands immobile I didn't have to think about anything else because he was in control and I couldn't have done anything else, even if I'd wanted to. Of course, I knew he'd stop or let me out if I asked. That made me feel safe and free enough to come several times that night. After that, we invested in some light bondage equipment. He found a real love for shibari—a type of intricate rope bondage.

Aaron reread the comment twice. That was similar to what Brynn had expressed to him, wasn't it? He'd tuck this idea away for the future. Right now, he couldn't even think about bringing something like that up to her when he didn't know what had triggered her. Was it the sex? She'd seemed to be enjoying herself until he'd gone a little harder. Was that it? Had he been too rough?

A knock at his office door interrupted his thoughts.

"Come in." He shut the laptop as Dani walked in. "Hey, sweetheart. What's up?"

"I, uh, was thinking about what we could do to surprise Mom for her birthday tomorrow." Dani leaned her hip against the desk.

"Oh yeah?"

She had brought up her mom's birthday over their dinner that Brynn had stayed in bed for.

"She doesn't like a lot of attention. But whenever we do something special, it always revolves around food and stories."

Aaron scratched the stubble on his chin. "Hm, we'll have to see how we can use that. Speaking of celebrations, what do you guys normally do for Christmas?"

Dani shrugged. "Well, we didn't celebrate until after we came to Shattered Cove."

"You didn't celebrate the holidays?"

Dani shook her head. "No, it wasn't allowed. I actually didn't even know what it was until we left. Mom neither, I don't think. She was born on the compound like me."

What the fuck kind of place was this, and why was it still allowed to exist?

"Betty-Lou and Fred invited us to share their dinner the first year. They gave me my first ever present." Dani smiled, her eyes shiny. "We've spent it with them every year since. They don't have any kids, so they said I could be their granddaughter if I wanted."

"They sound like wonderful people."

Dani nodded. "They are. Fred told me he'd teach me how

to run the kitchen when I get a little older if I want. Said I could start washing dishes when I turn sixteen."

"That was nice of him. Do you like cooking?"

Dani shrugged. "I don't know. I prefer drawing, but I'm sure we could use the cash."

Aaron's heart tugged. If he had it his way, neither Dani nor Brynn would ever have to worry about money again. "I'm sure your mom wants you to enjoy being a kid for now."

Dani chuckled. "So she reminds me. My therapist at Hope told me it's probably because Mom never had that, and she knows how important it is."

Aaron cleared his throat. "I think she's right. I'm glad you have someone you can talk to about everything. You know my door is always open, too, right?"

Dani nodded. "Yeah. And thank you."

"Of course. Now, about your mom's birthday—"

His phone rang from his pocket, so he fished it out. "Hold on a sec." His mother's name flashed on the screen, but it was too late to ignore; his finger had already accidentally swiped the answer icon. Aaron held the cell up to his ear. "Hello?"

"Oh, thank goodness I caught you." His mother sounded out of breath while a murmur of voices blended into the background.

"What is it?"

"I need you to pick me up from the airport in Boston."

"What? Why—"

"I left your father."

A swoosh of air escaped Aaron as his mind spun. *What?*

"And I hoped I could stay with you. I know we didn't leave on the best of terms, but I want to fix that."

Aaron glanced at Dani. "Now's not a good time, Mom."

"Part of the reason I went was we don't agree. On big things. Things I know you care about."

He ran a hand over his face and shook his head. "I'll be there as soon as I can."

Aaron hung up the phone and stared at it as he tried to make sense of it all. His mother had left his father and was coming to stay with him. Stay . . . in his guest room . . . that Brynn was currently using. *Shit!*

His mother's visit was the absolute last thing he needed to deal with. But she was his mother, and if she'd done the impossible and wanted to make things right . . . well, he'd hear her out. Aaron stood to ask Brynn, but then stopped. She wasn't home. She'd gone Christmas shopping with Charli to the city.

He raked a hand over his face.

"Is everything alright?" Dani asked.

"Yeah. My mom is apparently coming for a visit."

Dani straightened, worry flashing in her blue eyes.

"She said she wants to make things right, and she's coming here without my father. If she makes you uncomfortable, I'll put her up in a hotel. But I'd like to hear her out and have her stay at least tonight. Are you okay with that?"

Dani hesitated, then shrugged. "Sure."

"Thanks. I just need to get a hold of your mom now." He picked up his phone and dialed Brynn. He hoped she would understand.

Like he didn't have enough to deal with without his mother coming into town. When it rained, it poured.

34

BRYNN

Brynn sipped her peppermint latte and eyed the collection of shopping bags in the chair next to her at the cute little café in the city not far from Shattered Cove.

"Do you think Aaron will like the gift you picked out?" Charli asked, picking up her own holiday-themed cardboard cup to take a drink.

Brynn shrugged, her eyes scanning the crowd around them in the small but busy café. "I hope so."

Charli waved her hand and set her coffee down. "Men are easy. Just get them some underwear and socks, maybe some beard oil. Doesn't matter as long as you give it to them naked." Her friend giggled.

Brynn's breath stuttered. She looked away, her attention stuck on a couple sitting parallel to them. The two men had their arms around each other as they sat side by side, hunched over a phone, their eyes lighting up as they laughed at whatever was on the screen.

"You okay?"

Brynn returned her gaze to Charli's forehead rather than looking in her eyes. She forced a smile and nodded. "Yeah, of course."

Concern lines appeared between Charli's eyebrows. "Is everything okay with you and Aaron?"

Brynn took another sip of her latte to buy herself some time. Charli was always inviting her to do things, like shopping today for the holidays. Maybe it was time Brynn tried opening up outside of the group meetings.

"Sometimes it's just hard with my past . . ."

Charli's expression softened. "I hear you on that. I'm not sure you know this about me, but my home life was no picnic while growing up. My mom was part of a really strict religion. Well, more like a cult."

Brynn's eyes widened. "She was?"

Charli nodded, her green eyes clouding over as if remembering. "Yeah, even though I got away and I had Finn those last couple years to help me through it, that shit doesn't leave you. It stays with you and pops up when you least expect it."

"It does." Brynn opened her mouth, then closed it. She couldn't ask for more information. What if it was too personal? What if Charli asked her for information in return?

"Just ask." Charli smiled. "I can tell you want to. Not many people can say they grew up in a cult and survived. I'm sure you have questions."

Brynn cleared her throat. "Actually, I did too."

Charli's forehead furrowed before she nodded and leaned in. "Wow. I want to say I'm so sorry for you to go through that, but at the same time, it's also comforting to know there is someone else who gets what it's like to experience what I have."

Brynn nodded. "It is. I guess I was just wondering if . . .

how did you let it go and not let it affect your relationship with Finn?"

Charli sat back, pulling her sweater closer together before she crossed her arms. "Honestly, it took a lot of talking and communicating. It didn't happen all at once. More like pieces that were relevant at the time. When he did or said something that reminded me of things I'd rather forget, I told him, and he made sure not to do it again. It's been a long road for both of us. We've both made a lot of mistakes along the way, but we kept moving forward."

"You guys seem so happy."

Charli's smile was incandescent. "We are, but it wasn't smooth sailing as you know. But I kept fighting for me, and for our marriage, and he did the same. It wouldn't have worked if only one of us gave our all. Trust me, I learned that from experience too."

"I'm glad it all worked out for you two."

Charli tucked a strand of her black hair behind her ear. "Me too. And I know you and Aaron will get through this together too. That man worships the ground you walk on."

Brynn's attention darted down to the cup in front of her. She wanted that to be true. She wanted to be worthy of such love. But she couldn't be intimate with her husband. There was no way they would work long term. Aaron deserved better.

Charli's hand rested on hers, making her look up.

"That man is a born fighter, an activist. Let him be your warrior too."

"I'm terrified," Brynn admitted. "If I let him all the way in, if I rely on him, he could . . ." Emotion choked her, wedging in her throat so that she couldn't even finish her sentence.

"He could love the pieces of you that you haven't shown

anyone. And you could have someone to lean on when things get tough." Charli's thumb swiped the top of Brynn's hand comfortingly. "I won't lie and tell you love is full of rainbows and butterflies. Because real, true love, takes work. It's raw, and vulnerable, and messy. Being loved so wholly and unconditionally means we're also at risk of being hurt. You just have to ask yourself, is he worth it?"

Brynn took a deep breath, filled with the scent of roasted coffee beans, cinnamon, and notes of peppermint. Holiday music tinkled in the background, melding with the noise of the patrons in the café, conversing and laughing, sharing the holiday joy.

She was surrounded by mirth and yet Brynn still carried a heavy weight on her shoulders. She wanted to try, for Aaron, for herself. She wished she could be a wife in every sense of the word, that she could have sex with her husband without it ending in a panic attack and flashbacks. But that wasn't her reality.

"I—" Brynn's phone rang, interrupting her reply to Charli.

She tugged it from her pocket. Aaron's name flashed on the screen. She looked up at Charli. "I have to get this really quick."

Charli waved. "No problem. I'm gonna call Finn and check in with him and Jamison."

Brynn swiped to answer. "Hello?"

"Hey, uh, how's shopping?"

"Good." She cast her eyes over to the bakery case of pastries.

"Awesome. I uh . . ." Aaron blew out a breath, almost as if he was nervous. They hadn't really said much since she'd left his bedroom in a towel, her face red and splotchy from crying, not even able to look at him.

"Is something wrong?"

"No. Well. Here's the thing. My mother called and she's in Boston. She wants me to pick her up. She said she left my father. I don't know what the hell is going on. She mentioned something about wanting to make things right and wanting to stay with us for a little while. I don't want to do anything to make you uncomfortable. I can put her up in a hotel."

Brynn shook her head even though he couldn't see her. She'd caused Aaron enough stress and complications in his life; she wouldn't get between him and his mother, especially if there was a possibility the woman wanted to mend things between them.

"No, it's fine. You should hear her out and bring her home."

"Are you sure?" he asked.

"I'm positive."

He exhaled on the other end of the line. "Okay, and you're okay with her staying in the house? You realize that means you need to move your stuff into my room, right?"

Brynn closed her eyes, her throat tightening. *I hadn't thought of that. Of course the woman thinks we're a regular happy married couple. Oh, God, this is going to be harder than I thought.*

But Aaron had already gone above and beyond for her and Danielle. It was time she returned the favor. "I'll take care of it."

"Okay, I'm leaving now. Should take me an hour and a half if traffic is decent to get there. I'm thinking I should be home around five. I'll give you an update from the road in case I need to take the scenic route. I'll have Dani start emptying the closet."

"Okay." Brynn's stomach flipped as nerves ratcheted up her spine. *I can do this. For Aaron.*

"Thank you, sunshine." Aaron's deep voice sunk into her

bones, warming her from the inside out like the nickname he'd bestowed on her.

He had it all wrong—he was the shining light, not her.

"It's the least I could do."

"See you tonight. And don't worry about dinner. All set in the crock pot," Aaron added.

She blinked back the emotion that welled in her eyes every time he did these seemingly little things that made all the difference to her. So many stark reminders that he wasn't anything like the man from her past. "Thank you."

"Drive safe."

"You too." She pulled the phone from her ear and ended the call.

"Everything okay?" Charli asked, standing, then grabbing her coat.

Brynn did the same. "Yeah. Aaron's mother just dropped in for an unexpected visit and I need to get home before they do."

"Ahh, the cleaning rush before the mother-in-law comes." Charli chuckled.

"Something like that." Brynn mused and grabbed her bags.

"Should we grab some of their desserts before we go?" Charli asked.

Brynn nodded. "I think that sounds like a great idea."

Maybe a few slices of cake would be the perfect icebreaker for a guaranteed awkward evening. The upside was maybe Aaron would be so distracted with his parents' situation that they wouldn't have to focus on what had happened between them.

I'm a terrible person. It wasn't that she wanted Aaron to have more stress in his life, but a distraction would be welcome, even if it only delayed the inevitable.

35

AARON

Aaron shifted his SUV into gear and pulled away from the airport into traffic heading back to New Hampshire. His mother's perfume filled the car as holiday music drifted quietly through the speakers.

"You look good. Marriage seems to be agreeing with you," his mother said, turning towards him slightly as he navigated through the city traffic.

Aaron nodded. "Yup . . . so you want to tell me what's going on?"

She straightened and rested her hands on her lap. "You never did beat around the bush. Always straight to the meat of things."

"Don't see a point in pussyfooting around the issues."

She sighed. "I left your father."

"So you said."

"We . . . had a lot to talk about after our visit with you and your lovely family."

"I bet you did." Aaron merged onto the highway as tiny balls of snow drifted down from the grey skies.

"I hated how things ended."

"So did I. And as much as I love you, Ma, if you make Dani or Brynn uncomfortable, I'm gonna have to take you to a hotel."

She was silent a moment before she responded, "I know. And I understand."

"Do you?"

"Your father and I got into a huge argument over this. You know how much I hate when we're in a disagreement . . . but I can't lose another child." Her voice broke with emotion.

Aaron's hand darted out to hers, and he squeezed tight. He wished he could pull the car over for this conversation, but they were in bumper-to-bumper traffic inching down the highway.

"You haven't lost me yet, Ma."

She sniffled. "I thought about what you said to us. I couldn't let it go."

"What did I say?"

"About how I could worship a god who would send the people I love to everlasting torture."

"Oh."

"The greatest commandment in the Bible is to love. Love others as you love yourself, as Christ loved us—the golden rule. And you're right. I can't follow a religion that would have me reject my children because how is that love? I did it, and thought I was doing what was right, and look what happened! My baby is dead." She pulled a Kleenex from her purse and wiped her eyes. "I won't lose you too. There has to be a way to have both. My belief in God, and my son."

"There is, Ma. I'm not asking you to give up your faith."

She squeezed his hand. "I know. And these last couple weeks, I've done a lot of soul searching and research, and a whole lot of praying. I know I have so much more to learn, but I want to. I want to be in your life and get to know your family."

Aaron fought the emotion welling in his own eyes at his mother's confession. How many years had he wanted this, and thought it impossible? "That's all I ever wanted, Ma. For you to try."

She reached across the console and hugged the side of him before settling back in her seat. She cleared her throat and patted her eyes dry again. "As for your father . . . He'll come around. I left him with a lot to think about."

"I can't believe you left him."

"You're worth it. And I know he loves us. Deep down he knows this is the right thing to do—he just needs to push his pride out of the way long enough to listen. Being on his own should light a fire under his britches."

Aaron pulled his mother's hand to his mouth and kissed it. "I hope so."

She breathed out. "Me too. Now, tell me what's new with you."

He chuckled. "Well, I'm trying to surprise Brynn for her birthday tomorrow. Any ideas?"

His mother smiled with glee, her eyes lighting up as she rubbed her hands together. "You know I do. We'll give her a birthday she won't soon forget."

He smiled and eased the car over the border to New Hampshire. "Sounds perfect."

Now if only he could find a way to get through to his wife that he wasn't going anywhere, and they'd figure things out between them. Because he wasn't letting her go without a fight.

36

BRYNN

Brynn shoved the last of her clothes into Aaron's dresser as Dani ran into the room.

"They're here!"

Brynn shut the drawer with her hip as her eyes wildly scanned the room for anything amiss. Dani had already transferred most of her things to a pile on Aaron's bed by the time Brynn returned home, so all she'd had to do was put them away.

"Are there fresh sheets on the bed in the guest room?"

Dani nodded. "Yes. Everything looks good there."

Brynn walked out of the room and down the hall, taking a quick peek inside. Everything was spotless. She breathed a sigh of relief and swiped a hand over her head. *Oh my God, I must look a mess.*

Brynn ran to the bathroom across the hall as Aaron's voice filtered up the stairs.

"Honey, I'm home."

"Be right there!" She glanced at herself in the mirror and

winced. Her cheeks were flushed and her hair a wild mess. She grabbed the brush and pulled it through her hair quickly.

"You look beautiful, Mom," Dani said, leaning against the door.

Brynn put the brush back and turned to her daughter. "If his mom makes you uncomfortable, we can leave. Okay?"

"Aaron told me he would take her to the inn if I felt uncomfortable at any time."

Brynn's shoulders relaxed and her heart quickened. *He cares that much for Dani?* Of course, he did. He married her so that her daughter could get lifesaving medical treatment. *So why did I doubt him?* "Ready?"

"Yup."

Brynn slipped her hand in Dani's and led the way downstairs where Aaron waited with his mother and her belongings.

Iris looked up to them, a warm smile tilting her lips that looked so much like the man's next to her. "Hello, ladies."

Brynn forced a polite smile as she stepped off the last stair. "Hello."

Dani leaned against her. Brynn wrapped her arm around her daughter's waist.

Iris's gaze volleyed between them. "I think I'll take a note from my son's book and get straight to the uncomfortableness. Last time I was here, I know I hurt the two of you. I've done a lot of soul searching since then, and I realize I have a lot to learn about love and kindness. I was hoping you'd be kind enough to give me the opportunity to do so?"

Brynn's gaze flicked to Aaron. His hands were in his pockets as he met her eyes. Patience exuded from him as they waited for her answer. Brynn turned to Dani. Her daughter offered her a smile and a nod.

Brynn faced Iris again, her throat tight. It was still so hard to speak up. "I understand it's a lot to wrap your head around. As long as you're respectful of my daughter, I'll give you the same courtesy. I would never want to come between you and your son. And I know we all need a second chance in life." Brynn reached out her hand to shake her mother-in-law's. "I'm Brynn, and this is my daughter, Danielle."

Iris slipped her hand into Brynn's, her eyes growing glassy. "A fresh start?"

Brynn nodded.

"In that case, I'm Iris, and I'd love for Dani to call me Yaya if you're both comfortable with that. I truly am excited to get to know my new daughter and granddaughter. Can I give you both a hug? I'm a hugger." Iris opened her arms to them.

Dani walked into the woman's embrace first, her child more trusting. At least their past hadn't taken all her innocence away. Iris released Dani and gave Brynn a quick squeeze.

"I'll take your things to your room, Ma. Why don't you guys get dinner plated? It should be ready by now." Aaron picked up the bags by his feet.

Brynn headed towards the kitchen, her steps a little lighter. One confrontation down, one to go.

A couple hours later they were still at the table. Dinner had started out a little awkward, but Aaron had been the buffer they all needed. He told more of his corny jokes, and Iris had shared stories of past holidays with Aaron as a child. It was the first time she'd gotten a glimpse into Aaron's life before he was a man.

"He had kids lined up around the block with cans of food

from their parents' pantries." Iris laughed, wiping away tears of joy.

Aaron shrugged, a smile playing on his handsome face. "The church pantry was filled to the brim, wasn't it?"

Pride shone in Iris's eyes as she looked at her son. "Sure was. A lot of people didn't go hungry that winter because of those donations. My little warrior."

Aaron shifted in his seat before he cleared his throat and waved his hand, as if it was no big deal.

"So, he was always this way?" Brynn asked.

"Oh, yes. My boy is a giver and a protector, as I'm sure you've witnessed." Iris placed a hand over Aaron's. "And I couldn't be prouder."

"Thanks, Mom."

Brynn had to fight back her tears. She knew what it would have done to her to hear those words from her mother. Aaron had to be much more affected than he was letting on.

"Well, I better get to bed. It's been a long day. Tomorrow, I promised to teach Dani how to make grits." Iris stood.

"Me too." Dani got to her feet, giving her mother a quick embrace before she did the same for Aaron.

Brynn's stomach flipped. She'd been hoping to put this part of the night off for as long as possible. "There's fresh towels in the bathroom closet upstairs if you need them."

"Perfect. You two sleep well." Her mother-in-law hugged Aaron tight.

Aaron's eyes closed for the briefest moment before he let his mother go. She opened her arms for Brynn. This was something Brynn would have to get used to, she supposed.

After Iris had disappeared up the stairs, Aaron turned to her. "Ready for bed?"

She nodded curtly and led the way. Anticipation thrummed in her chest as her heart raced, and with a shaky hand, she reached for the doorknob, then entered Aaron's room.

Aaron shut the door with a click. "You guys really did amazing switching everything in here so quickly."

Brynn walked forward, heading to the dresser to grab her sleepwear. "Thanks for making room for my stuff." She retrieved an old, oversized T-shirt and pair of shorts. "I'll just be a minute." Brynn escaped to the en suite bathroom, locking herself inside. The last time she'd been in here she was sobbing after their failed attempt at sex. She clenched her eyes closed and shook her head before getting changed into her pajamas. She brushed her teeth and went to the bathroom. Washing her hands, she forced herself to look at her reflection in the mirror and took a deep breath.

"You can do this."

Brynn tossed her clothes into the basket in the corner and left the room. Aaron was already changed into a pair of cotton sleep pants and nothing else. She averted her eyes from his broad muscular chest to the turned-down bed. Her arms folded together as she hugged herself. Nerves twisted in her belly, and her skin itched and tingled with anxiety. Tension wound around her like a cloud of smoke, heavy and suffocating. Aaron stood, his palms up, as if trying to show her he wasn't a threat.

"Can we talk for a minute?"

"I . . . I'd rather not. I'm really tired. Can we . . . just sleep?" She couldn't even look him in the eyes, afraid of the hurt she'd see there, or the resignation. A part of her wanted him to fight for her, even though she didn't feel worth it. And another part of her just wanted to run away so she didn't have to face the torrent of conflicting emotions swirling inside her like a rogue tornado.

He sighed. "Sure. If that's what you need."

She nodded and walked past him, climbing into the far side of the extra-large bed, then covering herself up. She closed her eyes, holding back the tears that wanted to slip free. His footsteps padded into the bathroom before the door shut. Brynn let out the breath she'd been holding. *I'm just prolonging the inevitable.* Someday soon, he'd see she wasn't good for him. Maybe that day was today.

37

AARON

Aaron lay in bed in the dark room. The only light came from the moonbeams slipping through the blinds, gently illuminating Brynn's sleeping figure next to him. She'd clung to the edge of the mattress, as if she was trying to take as little space as possible in his bed. But she'd already taken up all the space in his heart.

A small whimper left her lips. His ears perked up, alert to her pain. She rolled onto her back, her eyebrows furrowed, her mouth frowning. Whatever she was dreaming about, it wasn't good. Should he wake her? Or would that scare her more?

Brynn's arm reached out, as if searching the bed for him. In her sleep she sought his comfort, but when the sun rose, would she climb back into the protective shell she constructed around her?

Aaron pulled her into his arms and snuggled closer. At least on some level she knew she could trust him to protect her. Her breathing evened out as she relaxed against his chest. His chest swelled with pride that he could make her feel safe, even if it was when she was unconscious. He'd have to take extra care with her, but he'd find a way to get through.

"I love you, sunshine. Won't let anything bad happen to you again." He kissed her crown to seal his promise, then closed his eyes. One day soon, maybe not tomorrow, but eventually, she'd be able to hear the words from his heart and believe them.

* * *

Aaron opened his eyes to the blinding light coming from the window before slamming them shut again. He groaned, tugging the sleeping form in his arms tighter against his body. Brynn tensed as her ass pressed into his erection. Aaron leaned down and kissed her cheek. Maybe it was best he pretended nothing had changed until they could really talk about the other night. *And her scars.*

"Good morning, sunshine."

"M-morning."

"How did you sleep?" He pulled away enough to look down at her.

Her cheeks were stained pink. "Good. You?"

"Never slept better." He leaned over and kissed her temple.

Her eyes met his, wary and surprised.

I've got you, baby.

"What's your plan for the day?"

"Um, I'm off from the diner and Pippa said she didn't need me either."

Because I told them it was your birthday and I've finally organized a plan. He smiled to himself. *Time for the birthday surprises to begin.*

If he had his way, it would start with his mouth on her

pussy, making her come, but this was not the birthday for that. Maybe next year—because there would be a next time.

"Stay here. I've got a surprise for you. Okay?" Aaron kissed her lips before rolling out of bed, immediately missing the feel of her in his arms.

"Okaaay." Suspicion laced her voice as one of her eyebrows quirked up.

He smirked and gave her a wink. "Be right back."

Aaron left the room and bounded down the hallway to the stairs. The smell of his mother's famous cinnamon buns wafted into the house as he made a beeline for the kitchen. His mom and Dani drizzled the frosting on top as he rounded the corner.

"They smell divine, Ma."

She smiled. "I'm just so happy I had an excuse to make them again. Your dad's been having to watch his cholesterol."

"I can't wait to eat them." Dani clapped her hands excitedly. "Here's the candle." She held it up.

His mom transferred two rolls to two different plates and placed them on a wooden tray next to steaming cups of coffee.

Dani pushed the candle into one of the buns. "Mom's gonna love it."

"You two ready for the next part of the surprise?" Aaron asked, lighting the candle before lifting the tray.

"Almost," Iris answered, hooking her arm with Dani's. "We'll enjoy our breakfast down here and then finish getting ready, right, darlin'?"

Dani nodded. "Sounds good to me."

Aaron cast an appreciative glance towards his mother before he carried the tray back up the stairs to his bedroom.

Brynn exited the bathroom as he walked in, her hand covering her blushing cheeks. "What is this?"

"I thought I told you to wait in bed?"

"I had to use the bathroom."

"Well, get that fine ass back under the covers. You're ruining your birthday surprise."

She blinked and then obeyed, climbing back onto the mattress. "How did you know it was my birthday?"

"Shouldn't I know my wife's birthday?" He sat next to her, placing the wooden tray over her lap, extending the legs so that it balanced on the bed on either side of her. "A little bird told me."

"Dani." Brynn shook her head. Her eyes stayed glued to the tray, the flames of the candle flickering against the soft planes of her face.

"Make a wish and blow it out."

She peeked up at him, then closed her eyes before filling her lungs with air and blowing out the candle. Smoke danced where the flames used to be.

"This is my ma's special recipe. One of my favorites. I know I promised Dani birthday pancakes with sprinkles, I thought maybe you'd like these better."

Brynn remained quiet, still staring at the tray in front of her.

"Brynn?"

A single tear tracked down her cheek and he'd bet it was the same for the other side. His heart lurched. He wrapped his arm around her, pulling her against his chest. "What did I do? Are you okay?"

She nodded against his pecs, then pulled back, wiping the evidence away. "Nothing. You didn't do anything. This—" She motioned to the array in front of her. "—it's all so perfect. I've never really done much to celebrate my birthday before. I just . . . Thank you."

She'd never celebrated her birthday before? Surprise slammed into him, then anger heated his veins.

He placed his hand on her cheek, drawing her face up to his. "You deserve to be celebrated. Seems like we have a lot of birthdays to make up for. From this one on, I promise to make each better than the last."

Her gaze shuttered. "Aaron, you can't promise me things like that."

"I can if I mean it."

She stared at him, searching his eyes, as if she could see to the depths of his soul. He'd gladly let her, because all she would find there was a fierce love like he'd never known rising for her.

"About the other day—"

"Shh, there'll be plenty of time to talk about that later. Today is about you. Celebrating your existence and kick-starting a new year on this planet. We're beginning with breakfast and then you have to get ready to go out."

"Out?"

"Yup."

Her lips tipped up at the corners. "No hints?"

He shook his head. "Nope."

"You spoil me so much I may never want to leave." She chuckled.

"That's the idea, sunshine." He slanted his mouth over hers, lingering this time before he nuzzled her nose with his. *That's the whole idea.*

38

BRYNN

Brynn sipped her hot tea, reclining on the plush chair. The soft bathrobe around her was smooth as butter on her oiled-up skin. Her muscles were more relaxed than she'd thought possible after an extensive massage. Quiet flute music filtered into the rectangular room lined with pedicure chairs. Dani sat in one to her left and Iris on her right.

"There is nothing like a good spa day to reset, is there, dear?" Iris asked, taking a drink of her own herbal tea.

"This is my first time, and I have to say, I would agree." This experience was over the top, once in a lifetime. It was too much, not that Aaron would agree.

"I think I'll do a classic red for the holidays. What do you think, ladies?" Iris asked as the nail tech at her feet offered her an array of colors.

"Oh, me too." Agreed Dani. "Let's all match, Mom."

Brynn eyed the bold colors. The instinct to avoid things that made her stand out was strong. But today was her birthday, and it was time she did something because she wanted to. "Sounds good to me."

The nail tech pulled one of her feet from the water, drying it off before applying a foot scrub. As she worked, Brynn sipped her tea.

Iris leaned a little closer while Dani chatted with the woman working on her toes. "Thank you for letting me come along. I know my visit was unexpected and not so desired."

Brynn turned to her mother-in-law. "I'm happy you came, truly. And I know you being here means a lot to Aaron."

Iris's eyes crinkled at the edges. "Would you mind sharing a little with me about how you knew Danielle was . . . trans, is that the right word?"

Brynn nodded. "Yes. She's always been interested in things that are stereotypically feminine." *It's why we had to leave the compound.* "When we arrived here, it was the first time she could explore those interests. We discovered Hope Facility through a friend and Dani just, blossomed. I can't believe I hadn't seen how much of herself she'd been hiding before. It took a little while, but she actually told Aaron, and then me."

"She told my son first?" Iris's eyebrows rose.

"She trusts him. All the kids do. He's really an amazing person. He'd do anything for those teens, and eventually they figure that out."

Iris's smile was bittersweet. "I wish I could say I had some part in that, but he did all that on his own."

Brynn reached out, laying her hand on Iris's arm. "I think you taught him more than you realize. The fact that you're here proves how much you love him. And I understand what it's like to be a mother who made mistakes I'll regret for the rest of my life. The important thing is we work hard to make those changes and become the best version of ourselves we can be for our children."

Iris's eyes had a sheen to them. Her head tipped to the

side, as if seeing Brynn in a new light. "I appreciate you saying that, sweetheart."

Brynn nodded and faced forward, taking a drink of her tea as the tech moved on to painting her toenails.

"So, tell me, what do you want for Christmas, Danielle?" Iris asked.

Dani perked up. "Makeup, clothes, or some new art supplies."

Iris chuckled. "You've already thought about this, haven't you?"

"Yes. Usually Betty-Lou and Fred get me books, so I know they'll get me the new series I really want."

Iris's brows drew together. "They were at the wedding, weren't they?"

"Yes. They own the High Tide diner in town," Brynn said.

"Friendly couple. Are they family?"

"They are now."

"This is going to be the best Christmas ever!" Dani beamed.

"Are there any specific traditions you celebrate with your family?" Iris asked.

Brynn's stomach flipped.

"No. We weren't allowed to celebrate at the compound. Or do a lot of other stuff there," Dani answered before Brynn had the chance.

Iris cast her a questioning glance. "The compound?"

Brynn needed to change the subject back to a safer topic. "I know Aaron usually puts on a dinner for everyone at Hope."

Iris studied her a moment before she nodded. "He does?"

"Yes."

"My son doesn't ever do things halfway, does he?" Iris laughed.

Brynn shook her head, an amused smile playing on her lips. "Kind of like this birthday."

"Oh, just you wait. The surprises are not done yet."

"What could he possibly do next?" She turned to Dani. "Were you in on this?"

Dani smirked. "Yes. And I'm not saying a word. You'll just have to wait and see."

"You tell her, Danielle. Patience is a virtue," Iris teased.

Brynn's gaze focused on her sparkling red toenails as discomfort made way for excitement. She never knew what to expect from her husband, and she felt spoiled with all this attention he gave her—even after everything that happened between them. The way he'd held her this morning and kissed her—that wasn't for show. Was he still holding out hope that she could give more to him?

"I knew once my son fell for someone, he'd fall hard. I'm just glad he found a woman worthy enough of his love," Iris said.

Brynn looked up, her eyes wide. She really thought that? Wow. Gratitude that this woman thought her worthy of her son swelled in her chest. But could Aaron love Brynn? Denial crept its way up her spine, strangling her rib cage. Sure, he'd said this was real, but that didn't mean he loved her. No. He cared for her, that was obvious, but was it possible to love someone you didn't even truly know? He hadn't seen all the darkest broken parts of her. He didn't know what she'd been through, what she'd done. Therefore, he could never really love her. She wouldn't dare hope. Leaving the compound meant she was done believing in myths.

39

AARON

Aaron stared at his phone and the text his mother sent.

Mom: *She loved the spa. Made it home and found your note. I wish I had thought to take a picture of her face when she saw the dress you laid out for her on the bed. We're almost there.*

He tucked the cell in his pocket and looked out the restaurant doors of Atlantis. Two headlights appeared through the fog, slowing down and pulling into the parking lot.

Aaron turned to the small crowd of people behind him, huddled together. "They're here."

"Shh, everybody quiet," Charli ordered.

Aaron exited the restaurant and walked out to Brynn's car as they parked. He opened his wife's door first. She took his hand, gracefully standing, the red lace cocktail dress he'd bought her peeking out from under her coat. He couldn't wait to see it on her inside.

Brynn started to argue. "Aaron, this is too much."

He placed a finger over her matching red lips. Fuck, that color was hot on her. As soon as the woman at the boutique mentioned she had it to match the dress, he'd wondered what it would be like to see her full mouth painted crimson. His cock hardened uncomfortably.

"Aaron?" Brynn's voice drew him back to the moment.

"It's not too much. Remember what I said." He tapped the world necklace hanging from her neck as Dani and his mother climbed out of the car.

Brynn's gaze searched his under the setting sun. Speckles of gold glinted in her soft emerald eyes as she looked up at him. He leaned in and pressed a chaste kiss to her lips, needing to connect with her in some small way to ground him.

He hooked his arm through hers. "Ready, sunshine?"

"Aren't they closed on Mondays?"

"Not for birthday girls." He winked.

She swallowed and bit her lip.

"Ma?"

His mother grabbed his other arm, leaning on him as he led them towards the door, taking care on the salted driveway. Dani walked ahead, seemingly eager to get inside to the other part of the surprise and greet her friends no doubt.

Aaron released his hold and grabbed the door, ushering the women in his life inside before he followed them as a loud unified, "Surprise!" came from the gathered guests.

Brynn jumped. His hand immediately went to her waist, tugging her body against his, assuring her she was safe and he was there. Her hands clapped over her mouth, and her eyes rounded as a few delayed shouts of, *"Surprise!"* came from the toddlers and little ones running around with birthday hats on.

Brynn turned to him, then back to the friends she'd made in Shattered Cove, and his as well. "I . . . I don't know what to say."

"Happy birthday, Brynn!" Charli yelled.

Several *"happy birthdays"* were echoed by the other guests.

Brynn spun to Aaron and wrapped her arms around his neck. He held her as she hugged him, running his nose down her slender neck, exposed thanks to the hairstylist he'd lined up this afternoon to touch up her dye and style her hair.

"Thank you," she mumbled against his chest.

"Wanted to show you have family here. People who care about you, beyond just me. We're all here for you, Brynn."

She pulled back, her eyes glistening with something akin to awe, but it was the tiny ember of hope sparking to life in her gaze that warmed his heart and fed his own belief.

She lifted on tiptoes, and he leaned the rest of the way to kiss her, cradling the back of her head with his hand.

"Wooo!" Finn cheered.

"Remember there are kids present. Save those types of birthday celebrations until later," teased Bently.

Brynn tensed in his arms. He pulled away, then hugged her closer to him, giving her back a rub as he tried to comfort her. "Now that the birthday girl is here, we can have dinner."

"Yay!" shouted a few of the kids.

"What about cake?" asked Lyra, Remy and Mikel's eldest daughter.

"That's for after dinner," Remy reminded her.

"And we have a feast prepared," Atlas announced, motioning to the bar where there were several platters on warmers lined up buffet style. He'd been kind enough to prepare the food last minute and let Aaron rent the whole place.

Remy had insisted on supplying the cake as a gift.

Betty-Lou and Fred walked up to greet Brynn as Dani bounded over to Aspen. Aaron tugged the coat from his wife's shoulders, exposing the dress he'd picked out that hugged her slender body just right. It reached the top of her knees, showing off a tease of her toned calves in the red-bottomed black heels.

"This turned out lovely," his mother said as Brynn made her way through the room, smiling and thanking everyone for coming. Kids ran around as a few parents made their way to the food, fixing plates for their little ones.

"It did, didn't it?"

She handed him her coat, which he hung on the rack. "I'm going to say hi to Betty-Lou and get some dinner."

"Do you want me to get you a drink?"

She shook her head. "I can take care of myself. You go mingle with your wife." His mother placed her hand on his arm, looking into his eyes. "She's special. I can see why you chose her."

Getting his mother's seal of approval shouldn't have meant as much as it did, but he was glad to have it. "She is."

She patted his arm and headed towards the older couple in line for food. Aaron took a deep breath and made his way towards the gorgeous woman in the room, needing to touch her. Brynn's eyes sparkled as she smiled and laughed at something Pippa said, her chin held high, her posture confident. Nothing like the shell of a woman he'd first met. Every day she grew stronger. Even after her setbacks, the woman had clawed her way out. A true survivor. A warrior of her own making. And he'd be damned if he let her go.

He slipped his palm to her lower back. She glanced at him, a warm smile spreading her gorgeous red lips. Gratitude emanating from her like rays of sunshine as she leaned into his touch. The world could be burning down around them and he wouldn't notice, not when he was enraptured by her soft gaze and electric touch.

The party passed with laughter and stories, food and family. Everyone gathered around the large makeshift table where Brynn sat at the head on one end as Mikel carried the cake, with dozens of lit candles, then set it in front of her. Flames danced on her fair skin, flickering in the reflection of her eyes as everyone sang Happy Birthday to her.

"Make a wish!" Zoey, Jasmine's five-year-old daughter, shouted.

Brynn giggled. "Okay, I will." She cast a lingering glance towards Aaron. "This is the best birthday ever."

He smiled. He'd set out to make her feel loved and special, and it seemed he'd done just that. "Make your wish."

She stared at him a moment longer before turning towards the cake and blowing out every last candle.

He couldn't help but hope they wished for the same thing.

40

BRYNN

Brynn walked into the dark bedroom. The light switched on a moment later as Aaron's masculine scent wrapped around her. Her spirit was light and free. Joy poured from her soul after such a memorable day. Her birthday usually passed with nothing more than a home-made card from Dani and a cupcake from Fred and Betty-Lou. Her gaze flicked to Aaron as he unbuttoned his shirt and headed for the bathroom.

"Your mom didn't have to stay at Jasmine's inn."

He stopped in the doorway with his back to her. The room illuminated as he flicked the light on, his face turning to the side. He shrugged and pulled the shirt over his muscular shoulders before dropping it into the laundry basket.

"She wanted to give us privacy tonight."

Because she thinks this is real.

"I can just sleep in Dani's room since she's at Aspen's."

Aaron spun around, stalking towards her. The energy in the room shifted. Brynn's skin prickled as those dark eyes focused on her, intent and needy.

"I want you here, in my bed, where you belong." His voice had taken on a possessive edge much like the day in the bookstore.

She shivered.

"Besides, I have another gift for you."

"Another one? Aaron, this whole day has been more than . . ." She struggled finding a word that fit the magnitude of her gratefulness.

He took her hand, leading her over to the bed. He sat, tugging her arm so that she joined him on the mattress. "Told you it makes me happy to do things like this for you." He reached into the side table by the bed, pulling out a box from the bottom drawer and handing it to her.

Brynn accepted the package, her gaze wandering over the silver wrapping paper and blue ribbon.

Aaron's palm skidded up her back, rubbing up and down, soothingly. "Open it."

Her hands trembled. She pulled at the ribbon tentatively.

"You're killing me, baby. Just rip it open." He chuckled, stealing some of her nerves.

She bit back a smile and tore the paper, revealing a cardboard box. Brynn pulled the flap open and stared inside at the bowl with glittery designs running through it.

Aaron took it from her, pulling out the beautiful pottery piece. "Do you know what this is?"

"A bowl?"

The corners of his mouth turned up. "Not just any bowl. This is made using kintsugi, the Japanese art of putting broken pottery back together with gold."

Her eyes widened. This was real gold?

"The idea is that broken pieces can be turned into something even stronger and more beautiful than their original composition by embracing the flaws." Aaron handed the bowl to her. She carefully wrapped her hands around it.

Her eyes met his, emotion gathering in her throat, imprisoning her voice.

"I saw this and thought of you. I know you think that because of what happened, you're not whole." His voice softened.

She blinked, trying to keep the tears at bay.

His knuckles glided over her cheekbone before he cupped her face, tilting her head towards him. "But I wanted you to have a visual representation of what I see when I look at you. I see a woman who's been through hell. Someone who's faced more evil than any person should."

She sucked in a sharp breath, her chest painfully tight. He saw all that? And yet still he was here beside her?

"I also witness your strength, unlike any other. The fight you have. It takes a fucking warrior to break the cycle. You're not to be underestimated. And I hope you know just how amazing you are."

Tears ran down her cheeks, her reflection captured in his eyes. Aaron saw her as beautiful amidst her scars—at least the ones he knew about. "But I come from so much darkness. The things I've seen, and done . . ." *Or didn't do.*

"Don't you see what I'm saying, sunshine? Dark can be beautiful." Aaron leaned in, melding his lips with hers. "You're enough."

She set the bowl on the bed and collapsed against him. Strong arms held her as she clung to Aaron, finding solace in her husband. His heart beat a steady thud against her ear. His protective hold giving her a sense of peace she'd never known. She wept for the little girl inside who never got to run to the safety of arms that loved her. For the woman she was now who felt shattered. Aaron just gripped her tighter, as if he could be the gold that held her together, his soft lips kissing her temple and whispering soothing words of what she deserved, and how strong she was.

Sometime later, her sobs subsided. She pulled away from him and wiped her eyes. He handed her a tissue from the side table, and she wiped her face and sniffed.

"Brynn?"

"Yeah?"

"I hope you know I'm here for you. I mean, I'm in this. And we'll get through this together. You don't have to do it alone anymore." Aaron's voice was rough.

She looked up, meeting his red watery eyes. His own grief was a punch to her stomach. "How can you be real?"

He shook his head. "I've got my own broken pieces too. We all do. Some just have more than others."

A humble answer from a humble man. Had she expected something else?

Aaron cleared his throat. "Can I ask you something?"

She nodded.

"Was it something I did the other night that triggered you?"

She slammed her eyes closed and released the oxygen in her lungs.

His warm palm returned to her back, rubbing circles. "You don't have to answer, but I'd like to know so that I don't hurt you again in the future."

He thought he'd hurt her? Her heart ached. She could do this—for Aaron. She took a deep breath and faced him. "It wasn't you. I really liked you touching me . . . But, the sound of the headboard on the wall . . . It just . . . sent me back to a place I'd rather forget."

His body tensed next to hers. "It was the bed? Not me?"

Brynn nodded. "You were perfect."

He breathed out, as if relieved. "I don't want to push you more than you can handle. I hope that you know that."

"I do. I know you would never hurt me intentionally." She did—down to her bones.

"How about you take a bath, and then we can relax in bed?"

Both her heart and her body rejected the idea of leaving his embrace. Something had unlocked deep inside her tonight. Emotionally drained, she needed him to anchor her. It was her birthday after all.

"I'd love a bath."

"I'll be right back." Aaron kissed her head and got off the bed, disappearing into the bathroom a moment before the sound of water running started.

Brynn picked up the bowl, tracing the gold gluing the pieces together. Maybe it was the fact she was too emotionally wrecked to be anxious. Perhaps it was that she was still high on birthday wishes and Aaron's steady presence. But for once, she didn't care about anything else except capturing his full attention like she'd done once before. The memory of that empowerment intoxicated her, strengthening her resolve as she set the pottery down on the side table and made her way to the bathroom.

Aaron had lit candles on the counter. Steam filled the room, along with the scent of lavender no doubt from the special salts he kept under the sink for her. He turned, his naked chest shining with a sheen of mist.

"All set. I'll shower in the other bathroom and meet you in bed."

She spun around, pulling her hair out of the way of her dress. "Can you unzip me?"

"Sure." His fingers brushed the sensitive skin at her nape

before the steady tug of the zipper sent a rush of steam-filled air over her back. "There you go."

She turned around. "Thank you."

"Of course." He moved to pass her, but she stepped to her right to block his path.

His questioning glance spurred her on, so she tugged the straps of her dress down her arms. His eyes widened, feeding the rush of endorphins shooting through her veins. She needed this. This escape. This exchange. Drawing on his strength, she pushed her dress down, baring her underwear to him.

He swallowed, his throat bobbing, hands fisting at his sides as if trying to maintain control and not touch her. She reveled in his reaction, drunk on the power to capture Aaron's full attention—his lust.

"Brynn—"

She dropped the dress to the floor and stepped out in nothing but the red lace bralette, barely there panties, and stilettos he'd picked out to go with her dress. "Didn't you want to see the rest of your gift on me?"

He nodded. "Yes. But I don't want to push you for more than you're willing to give."

"You're not." She stepped forward, her heart thundering. A part of her felt like this was wrong, but how could it be when it felt so right?

"Tell me what you need from me, sunshine," he commanded, making her pussy clench.

"I need you to take a bath with me. To hold me, to touch me." Heat blazed in her cheeks. She'd never been this forward.

"Better get naked, then." His voice was gruff, as if he was barely holding on.

She stepped out of the heels, kicking them to the side, but she left her panties on. She flicked the light off, the only light in the room coming from the half a dozen candles he'd lit around the dim space. She reached to unclasp her bra, but he grabbed her arm.

"Wait. It may be your birthday, but I want to unwrap this gift." His words brought an electric thrill to her.

Her pussy wet and aching for his touch, she spun around.

Aaron wrapped his arm around her, tugging her so she stood facing the mirror, his front to her back. "Look at yourself. I want you to see what I see when I look at this gorgeous body."

She obeyed, her thighs pressing together at yet another order from him. It set something free inside her. The need to think—to choose. She didn't have to do anything but follow his soft commands.

He unclasped her bra, pulling it down her arms, baring her breasts. His hands cupped each peak, massaging gently. Her focus dropped to his ministrations, to the contrast of his warm brown skin tone against her white flesh. Tingles raced. Arousal gathered as he plucked at her nipples, his touch firm, as if he wanted her so much he couldn't hold back. He couldn't be gentle. Another rush of heady power crashed over her. She wanted to see him lose control. What would he be like? What would bring him pleasure? What would it take to make him so completely lost to his desire for her?

His chest heaved against her back as he pressed Brynn against the counter. His erection poking her lower back. She whimpered, her gaze meeting his. The lust burning in those brown eyes stole her breath.

He licked her neck before lowering his mouth to suck on the same spot. A moan left her as her eyes rolled from the delicious sensations rippling through her body. Gooseflesh erupted over her limbs. One hand dipped down, cupping her ass before gripping the edge of the scrap of lace that covered her sex from him.

"I can see how needy you are, sunshine. Don't worry. I'm gonna give you what you need." His voice was low and deep. "I told you to get naked." He yanked the edge of her panties, and she gasped as her body jerked from the wild possession in his actions.

"Don't worry, I'll buy you more." He spun her around. Flickering candlelight danced across the hard features of his face. "Need you to tell me if any of this is too much for you. Promise?"

She nodded.

"Need the word, baby."

"Promise."

"Good girl."

The praise sent a shock of pleasure spiraling through her. She whimpered.

Aaron gripped her ass and picked her up, Brynn's arms wrapping around his neck as his mouth crashed to hers, hungry and feverish. His tongue delved into her mouth, and she sucked on it, earning a groan that rumbled up his chest. His hand pressed against her neck like a collar, her body immediately relaxing—pliant and ready to do his bidding.

He squeezed the edges of her neck as his other hand slipped between her thighs. One finger entered her already slick pussy.

She dug her nails into his back, clutching him closer, holding on to the last thread of her sanity. Pleasure wound in her pussy, tension gathering in her womb.

"So beautiful." Aaron tugged on her bottom lip, grazing

her with his teeth, increasing the steady thrum of need building inside her. "This pussy was made for me. So fucking sweet, and wet." He added another finger, fucking her with his hands.

Whimpers and moans left her as she did all she could and held on for dear life.

"You like that, baby?"

She nodded.

He pulled his fingers out of her and she whined in complaint.

"You know the rules. Give me those words, pretty girl."

Brynn wanted to please him. She was greedy for more of the praise that fell from his lips. "Yes. I like that. I love what you do to me."

He slammed two fingers back inside her as she gasped. "Such a good girl."

Her chest filled with warmth as her arousal leaked down her thigh.

"You know what good girls get, don't you?"

"No."

He curled his fingers inside her, hitting that spot within that made her toes curl, bringing her to the brink of *something*.

"They get rewarded." He kept hitting that spot as his mouth tangled with hers.

Pleasure mingled with an ache for release. Tension drew tight, ready to snap. Rising pressure filled her to the edge of exploding.

Is this an orgasm?

"Tell me what you need," Aaron said.

Her mind spun. His question pulled her from the peak. She struggled to find the words. "I . . . just need . . . more." But what?

"Not until you come."

Her stomach clenched, anxiety swirling in her belly, pulling her further from the illusive finish line. *What if I can't?* She closed her eyes, trying to grasp on to her pleasure, but it was like grasping handfuls of sand. The harder she tried, the farther away it got.

"Do you want me to lick your pussy?" he asked, no longer commanding, but questioning her, making her nervous energy return.

Does he want to? Or is he just doing this to try and make me come? "You don't have to."

Aaron pulled back, his hands resting on her thighs as his brows drew together. "You okay?"

She forced a smile. "Yes."

"You seem like you're stuck in your head."

She hesitated and then nodded. "I'm sorry."

"Hey, it's okay. Did you enjoy what I did?"

"Yes," she answered honestly.

His shoulders lowered, as if in relief. "Come on." He picked her up off the counter and set her in the bath. The hot water eased over her sore feet and up her calves.

"You don't want me to . . . I mean we can still have sex."

He shook his head and undid his belt. The clang of metal drew her eyes down as he unzipped his pants.

"No, we're not." His fingers dipped into the waist of his elastic before he tugged his boxers down with his pants, leaving them in a pile on the floor. He stepped out of them and into the bath. He sat down, leaning against the back of the tub before he tugged her hand. "Sit down."

She did, the water rushing up her lap to the line under her breasts.

"Lean back against me." He wrapped his arms over hers, cradling her in his warmth, his cheek to hers.

Naked and slippery, their bodies fit together. She breathed out, relaxing into his hold.

"We're gonna take this nice and slow. We'll move at your pace. And we'll figure out what works for you, and what doesn't." His voice rumbled in his chest as he spoke.

"But this is at no point about needing to get me off. Do you understand? This is about you."

Her mouth dropped open. "Why can't it be about you too?"

He hesitated. "Bringing you pleasure is satisfaction enough for me. But I don't want to use your body for me to get off if you're not right there with me. If I just need a physical release, I can take care of myself." He kissed her temple.

"That's a lot of pressure," she confessed.

"What is?"

"I don't know if my body is capable of an orgasm. I don't think we should push for it. I enjoy what you do—a lot. Can't we just be content with that?"

He was silent a moment. "Was that why you got stuck in your head? Because I brought up you coming?"

She thought back to what happened. "I think so."

"Okay. Maybe from here on out, we don't stress over the end goal. We enjoy experimenting with different sensations and touches. The goal will be to learn what feels good for you."

"And you," she argued. This couldn't all be about her, or that would make her feel guilty.

"And me." He kissed her cheek. "We have all the time in the world, baby. We're in no rush, okay? Let's just have fun with this."

"Sounds good to me." Actually, it sounded like more than she would've thought possible. But maybe it was time she raised her expectations. And perhaps this once, she'd let go and enjoy the moment without worrying what tomorrow would bring. Because she'd spent enough of her life worrying over the future while being stuck in her past. All the ugliness of her trauma had left scars and done irreparable damage. But maybe she could try and find some beauty in what was left.

41

AARON

Aaron walked into the rec room of Hope Facility from his office. His eyes scanned the space, making sure everything was in order. Teens congregated around TVs and game tables. A few competitive cheers came from the foosball game in the corner. Laughter and friendly teasing filtered through the cinnamon-and-pine-scented room. The gas fireplace brought a cozy warmth to the large space. A few kids reclined in front of it with books or comics.

Aaron made his way past a serious game of chess as he veered towards the woman who'd occupied all his thoughts of late. Brynn sat with a small group of mothers whose kids attended the center. She passed out cookies and hot chocolate as she smiled and chatted. She fit here, in this little world he'd created. She complemented him and made him slow down. For once in his life, he couldn't wait to get home after his day of work. Before Brynn, he'd stayed at the center from morning to bedtime curfew. But he clocked out much earlier these days, all to be there to share dinner with his wife.

Her eyes lit up as he approached, her mouth tilting in a warm smile, something that seemed to come much easier to her these days. *That's partially my doing.*

"Hello," she greeted.

Aaron leaned down and pecked her on the lips, unable to control the need to show everyone in the room she was his. "Hey, beautiful."

Her cheeks took on a rosy hue as they always did when he showed her physical affection in front of others. "Macy, here, was just asking when the festivities will start on Christmas."

Aaron turned towards the small circle of women, sliding behind Brynn, his hands resting on her shoulders and gently massaging. "Usually, the kids are all up to open gifts around nine. Then we do a big breakfast at ten. There will be vans ready to take the kids sledding with hot chocolate until the big dinner at five."

The blond woman's smile widened. "Oh, that sounds wonderful. I'll make sure we're here by nine, then. I know Owen has some gifts he wanted to pass out to his friends."

"Perfect. Now, if you ladies don't mind, I need to steal my wife for a moment."

Brynn turned to him as she stood. He dropped his hand to hers, leading her towards his office as she waved goodbye. He needed to feel those soft lips against his before he lost his sanity.

He knew how to get on the same level as the teens, but the moms that stuck around were another story. After a few too many flirted with him or asked him out and he had to turn them down, their kids suffered from the awkwardness. He usually avoided them or had Leslie deal with them. But Brynn fit right into his life and work. Aaron needed to make her his in every sense of the word.

"Where are we going?" she asked.

"To my office." He opened the door and pulled her inside the room. He shut the door behind them, pushing her up against it before his mouth descended on hers. She let out a squeak of surprise before her mouth opened for him and her arms looped around his neck.

His tongue tangled with hers, sparks and shimmers of lust igniting a blazing need deep within him.

"You're so fucking beautiful. Couldn't resist touching you."

Her chest heaved against him as her nails dug into the skin on the back of his neck.

"I can't get enough of you." He trailed kisses down her neck and locked the door. "What do you need, baby?" He pulled back, her eyes taking on a hazy sheen of lust.

"What? Here in your office?"

"I just need a moment to touch you before I go back out there and have to avoid kissing you like I want to. Tell me you want this too?"

"I . . ." She bit her lip and dropped her focus to his chest.

The other night she was the boldest he'd seen her, and then she'd climbed back into her head.

"Tell me."

Her mouth parted and her green gaze flicked to his. "I don't want to choose."

"You want me to take control?"

She nodded shyly.

Aaron placed his finger under her chin, forcing her to face him. "Say it."

"Yes."

His stomach tumbled at her eager response. "Good girl."

The way her eyes darkened made his cock pulse with need. It seemed his wife liked to be praised. He stored that little bit of information away.

"Get on my desk, facing my chair."

Her throat bobbed before she did as he said. He walked around his desk and trailed his finger over her collarbone, making her shiver.

It was time to put his theory to the test. "Spread those pretty legs for me, gorgeous."

Her gaze snapped to the door, scarlet staining her cheeks. "But what if—"

"The door is locked. And we don't have much time before someone comes knocking. So be a good girl and do what I said."

Was this too much? Should he slow down? He was naturally commanding in the bedroom, but was it too much for Brynn?

His wife's thighs parted a few inches. He smiled, skimming his hands under the hem of the flowy skirt to her bare legs, bunching the fabric around her hips to expose the light-blue panties she wore underneath.

"Need you to do something for me, darlin'."

"What?" Her voice was nothing but breath sending another wave of desire thrumming through his veins. The scent of her arousal clung to the air, intoxicating him.

"Want you to sit back and let me taste you. Can you do that for me?"

She hesitated and then nodded, resting her palms onto the desk. Aaron dipped his finger into the edge of her panties and pulled them aside before he got on his knees. Dipping his head to the juncture of her thighs, he inhaled. Her legs tensed by his ears. He reached around to grab her hip with his other hand, holding her in place as he licked up her slit. Her sweet musk exploded onto his taste buds, feeding his hunger. He lapped as she clenched around him.

"God, you taste so fucking good. Best thing I've ever had on my tongue."

A tiny moan lifted from her mouth.

"Got to be quiet for me today, baby. Don't make a sound." Aaron flicked her clit with his tongue, up and down, side to side, around and around. Over and over again, until he found a rhythm that kept her legs clenching tighter and tighter around his head.

"Aaron," Brynn hissed through gritted teeth, her eyes glazed and wild. She trapped her bottom lip with her teeth, as if holding back a scream. He wanted to see it, the moment she let go, the exact second she saw heaven.

He thrust his finger inside her and continued to lick and lave. Her hips bucked. She was almost there—

Knock. Knock. "Mr. Ridley?"

Brynn tensed, her fingernails digging into his shoulders.

"It's okay," he whispered, pulling his finger out of her before putting her panties back into place. He spoke louder this time. "I'll be right out. Give me five."

"Okay," the boy's voice from the hallway answered.

Aaron stood, licking his finger clean while maintaining eye contact with Brynn. Her legs closed and she forced her dress back down. "I can't believe we just did that."

"Did you like it?"

Her gaze darted around the room before she nodded. Guilt clouded her vision.

"Hey." His tone changed from gentle to authoritative.

Brynn locked eyes with him once again.

"This is nothing to feel ashamed about. You did amazing."

Some of those clouds cleared in her green spheres.

"You were perfect." He kissed her lips and backed away. "Now, let's go." He held out his arm for her to take.

She did, then climbed to her feet.

Aaron leaned over and kissed her temple. "We'll finish what we started later."

A shy smile lifted the corner of her mouth.

He couldn't get enough of this woman, and from the way she'd trusted him like this, it seemed he was winning her over too. But something was still holding her back. He was determined to claim all of her, and he'd do it—one day at a time.

42

BRYNN

Brynn carried in the basket of freshly laundered clothing in need of folding and set it on the floor of Aaron's bedroom. Water splashed against the shower floor as Aaron bathed after a long day at work. Her phone beeped in her pocket. She pulled it out to find a photo of Aspen and Dani decorating cookies at Pippa's house.

Pippa: *I think I made too many cookies. I'll be sending a couple dozen home with Dani. Don't hate me!*

She'd just dropped her daughter off and it looked like they were already hard at work.

Brynn: *That's not a problem. Whatever we don't eat we can bring to Hope.*

"Brynn?" Aaron called from the bathroom.

She set her phone on the nightstand, her eyes catching on the wall behind the bed. She sucked in a sharp breath. The headboard was gone. She backed up a step. The mattress was set on a simple box spring.

He did this for me? He must have removed it to make sure

the thump of the headboard never happened again. Her eyes burned.

"Brynn?" he repeated.

"Coming." She made her way to the bathroom, his gorgeous naked form glistening through the glass as water rained down over him.

"Join me?" He smiled.

Her focus roamed over the hard planes of his chest and down his abs, which flexed under his movements to the deep V of his hips. Her breath caught. She'd never once known a more perfect man. Dark hair trailed from his belly button down to his long, thick cock.

"No one's home but us. Mom went shopping for gifts," he assured her.

She pulled off her clothes and tossed them into the basket in the corner of the bathroom. She was surprised at how quickly she'd gotten used to being naked in front of Aaron.

She'd never thought she could trust someone like this, nor expose her scars. But he hadn't even asked about them. Maybe he understood she wasn't ready to talk about them yet. *Maybe he understands me.*

She stepped into the shower, her feet landing on warm slate. She wouldn't get used to the luxury of Aaron's life. Heated floors, giant bathrooms, Egyptian cotton sheets. The man owned a freaking lake.

Brynn shouldn't have felt like she fit in, but the moment his strong arms wrapped around hers, everything made sense. Water cascaded down his body and onto hers, warding off the chill. He turned so that she was under the spray, his front to her back, and that eager cock of his standing to attention like it did every time she pressed against him.

She spun around, her gaze falling once again to his erection.

"You can touch me, you know. If you want," Aaron said.

Did she want to? Yes, she absolutely did. The missing headboard in the bedroom flashed in her mind. Aaron had done one thing after another just to make her feel more comfortable. His attention was always focused on her needs. But who took care of his?

Her skin prickled as nerves twisted her belly into intricate knots. She'd only read about blow jobs—thankfully, she'd never been forced by Paul since it had been against their beliefs. Surely, she could figure it out.

Brynn dropped to her knees, the hard slate pressing into her skin, grounding her while her heart raced.

"Brynn?" Aaron's gaze darkened.

She licked her lips, looking up at him. "Tell me what to do."

"Like explain, or order you around?" His voice was like gravel.

"The second one."

"You don't have to do this."

"I want to."

He nodded. "Lick me. Just the tip. Taste what you do to me."

Brynn leaned in, her tongue darting out to the salty release mixed with water dripping from the crown of his dick. It wasn't bad. She did it again, eyes on him.

Aaron's head tipped up as he released a groan of approval that made her pussy quiver.

"That's it, baby. Now take my cock into your mouth and suck." He gripped the back of her head, his attention focused on her.

The urge to please him roared inside her like a hungry lioness. Her lips parted, sliding him in slowly. His eyelids drooped halfway closed, lazy with lust as his abs clenched. His fingers tightened in her hair, the finest sensations of pain prickling her skull, but it only made her body hotter.

She guided him in as far as she could take him. Sucking gentle and then harder, testing out which sensation he reacted to more as he fucked her mouth. She swirled her tongue on the tip when she pulled him out and then slid him in even farther.

"Fuck, baby. Yes, just like that. Take my cock in that pretty mouth."

Aaron's dirty talk had her pussy dripping and her veins burning with need. The need to make him come. To bring him pleasure. There, on her knees, she wielded the most power she'd ever felt. Every groan slipping through his lips, every sigh of pleasure raking from his chest, all belonged to her. She was doing this.

She did as she'd read about, gripping the base of his penis with her hand, working him in tandem with her mouth while her other hand rolled his balls.

"Fuuuck. Brynn, I'm gonna come, baby."

A burst of pride shot through her as she kept the same pace, clenching her thighs together. Should she finish him with her hands? Let him come on her? Or let him come in her mouth and taste him?

She sucked harder.

"Brynn!" he shouted as he came, his body tensing and shuddering.

His face contorted with pleasure while hot spurts of cum shot out of his cock, filling the back of her throat. She pulled him out enough to swallow, then lick her lips, savoring every last drop.

Aaron heaved above her, his hands braced against the tile, his lazy focus remaining on her.

Had she done it right?

He shut off the shower, taking her hand and guiding her to stand. Her knees ached from kneeling so long on the hard floor. She winced, so he picked her up and carried her out of the shower, depositing her onto the bed.

"But I'm soaking wet," she argued.

"Do you trust me, Brynn?" Aaron's words were dark and low.

Her belly quivered at his tone. "Yes."

"I want to try something. You say the word and it ends."

"Okay."

He moved to the top of the mattress, reaching back and pulling out a black strap with a soft cuff attached to the end. He took her hand and placed it in the opening, pausing to search her face. "Can I tie you up?"

Her breaths came quicker as fresh arousal leaked from her pussy.

"We don't have to. I just thought maybe it would help get you out of your head enough to relax and enjoy me touching you. I read that it can help free your mind when you have no choice but to submit—not that you wouldn't have a choice. You say the word and it stops immediately."

Was this man in her head? How did he know this was a fantasy of hers? "Yes."

His eyes widened. "Yes, you want to be restrained?"

"By you," she confirmed.

Something a lot like triumph glowed in his eyes. He cinched the first strap closed around her wrist. "Too tight?"

She shook her head.

"Gonna need your words now more than ever, sunshine."

"It's perfect." *Like you.*

He repeated the actions with the second hand. "Say stop, and I let you go and this ends. I have no expectations other than to make you feel good. If something gets uncomfortable, tell me to slow down, okay?"

"Yes."

Aaron climbed over her, melding his mouth to hers. She tried to wrap her arms around his neck, but the restraints held her in place. Relief and arousal spiraled through her. She was at his mercy, completely vulnerable to his muscular frame as he settled over her. The man was powerful, capable of taking whatever he wanted. But rather than using his strength for his own selfishness, he was using his body to bring her pleasure— to fulfill her fantasies.

She was already wet and needy from the blow job in the shower. Her pussy throbbed. Aaron kissed down her body, leaving a blaze of pulsing lust as he went. His gaze didn't leave her face for long, attentive and assessing, as if ready to end this the moment he sensed it was the slightest bit too much for her.

"I didn't think anything could top the sight of you on your knees for me. But you like this, tied up, unable to do anything but take what I give you, fucking steals my breath away."

Her legs clenched around his hips as he cupped her breasts and kneaded the soft flesh.

"You like that, baby?"

"Yes."

"Right now, you belong to me. Your pleasure is mine. Your body, too, isn't it?" He licked her nipple, then pinched it, sending a zing of pain through her. That familiar tightening sensation doubled in her womb. Anticipation wound tight, making it harder to breathe. Her body hummed alive at Aaron's electric touch.

Two fingers dipped into her pussy, making her gasp.

"So wet already. Is this from sucking my cock?"

He curved his fingers, stealing her voice.

"Answer me." He used his other hand to pinch her nipple.

"Yes!"

"Say it. Tell me you loved sucking my cock."

"I loved it." Her eyes rolled up as he dropped his mouth to her clit.

His expert tongue brought her to the brink of pleasure, winding her closer and closer to the edge.

She tugged at her restraints, unable to do anything but experience the pleasure rippling through every cell as his fingers and tongue spun her higher and higher.

"Tell me who this pussy belongs to. Tell me you're mine."

"Yours—I'm yours."

Aaron sat, grabbing a condom from the drawer. He ripped it open with his teeth and slid it over his already hard cock before lining the tip at her entrance. Hooking one leg over his shoulder, he lifted her hips, and she wrapped the other around him. "Are you ready for me to fuck you?"

"Yes."

He drove his hips forward. His pubic bone hit her clit at the same time his dick filled her, making her cry out.

His assessing gaze locked on to her face as she gripped the strap holding her hands in place. "Look at me. Want you to know who's fucking you."

"More."

"That's it, baby. Take it. Take all of me." He thrust slow and hard.

It was ecstasy. Her mind was fuzzy, and she was unable to focus on anything but the pleasure hammering into her with every drive of his hips and his cock stretching her, sending delicious tingles racing through every cell with an avalanche of sensation. She moaned and whimpered, pulling at the restraints.

Every time he thrust, it hit that spot deep inside her. Her

body locked up, clenching. It was too much; she'd never felt so many strong sensations at one time before.

Dirty promises fell from his lips. This was a whole new shadow side of Aaron that matched her fantasies, as if he was one of the heroes from her dark romances come to life in this bedroom. If she submitted to him, it stripped her of guilt and expectation. She could just revel in the pleasure coursing through her, let him take control, and not obsess over what she should be doing.

"You're gonna make me come again."

And that's all it took. His words were like a detonator as the knowledge she was pleasing him sent her shooting off like a rocket. Her eyes widened and her back arched. A keening cry escaped her lips as her womb clenched and pure euphoria saturated her every cell. *Yes! Bliss. Oh, God.*

Aaron continued the same rhythm, his finger dropping to her clit, prolonging her first orgasm and sending a ripple coursing through her body. His mouth descended on hers, drinking in her cries before he deepened the kiss. His body tensed and shuddered around her as his cock pulsed deep within.

He pulled back, settling his weight on his elbows while scanning her face. She looked up at him through half-closed lids as the deepest relaxation she'd ever known settled into her bones.

"I . . . I came."

He smiled, pride shining in his eyes. "I knew you could do it. So fucking proud I got to witness it." He kissed her again, then untied her wrists, rubbing them and placing a chaste kiss to each one. "Thank you, sunshine." He pulled her into his arms, resting her head on his chest.

"Shouldn't I be thanking you?" She gave a dopey half smile.

"No." He kissed the top of her head. "Thank you for trusting me so completely. It's a gift I won't ever take for granted."

His words touched her heart, burrowing deep. She wasn't sure how, or when, but this man had become part of her. And for the first time in her life, she believed she could count on someone else to be there and not betray her. He'd done everything in his power to make her feel safe, to meet her needs, and so much more.

His hands grazed over the scars on her back, hesitating before he resumed his soothing rhythm. Maybe it was time she told him everything. Her lids drifted closed, safe and warm. She was naked in his arms, and yet she'd never felt more protected.

43

BRYNN

Brynn awoke cocooned in warmth the next morning. Aaron's hot breath tickled her shoulder and his steady heartbeat thrummed against her ear. His fingers traced lazily from her shoulder to her lower back, grazing the raised scars. He held her so completely, as if he cherished her. And the gift he'd given her last night went beyond pleasure but showed his true dedication to her happiness. She'd never had anyone besides her sister care about her joy. *I love him.* The words stuck in her throat. She couldn't say it without knowing if he felt the same way. But she could give him one gift.

"Can I tell you something about my past?"

He kissed her jaw. "Of course."

"When my sister tried to leave and they found her, they dragged her into the center of the compound and called everyone out of their homes. The sun was just coming up and it was so cold." Brynn closed her eyes, seeing the horrible memory, as if it happened just yesterday.

Aaron's hand stilled, as if he was too scared to move in case it caused her to shut down.

"Her name was Brynna."

"That's why you chose Brynn?"

She opened her eyes and nodded. "I'll never forget the complete and utter terror on her face when the prophet had Brynna's husband beat her in front of everyone."

Brynn's body tensed, and she slammed her eyes closed again, fighting off the tears. Her stomach roiled.

Aaron's strong arms tightened around her as he recommenced the soothing circles with his hand on her back.

"They stripped her naked and whipped her. That was the first time I stood up and said anything. She was always the one protecting me—my little sister. But it was my job, and I failed her. She'd asked me to run with her, but I had David—I mean Danielle. I was so scared they would take him from me. I didn't have any skills, or proper schooling. No money. If it had been just me to worry about, I would have gone with her."

"That sounds like an impossible choice," Aaron said, his voice free of blame.

"Because I spoke up, my husband, the prophet's son, dragged me to her. They accused me of conspiring with her, and not telling them—which was true. They whipped us." Brynn snuggled closer into his chest, holding on to her one sense of calm.

Aaron's grip was like iron, his muscles tense as a low growl rumbled in his chest. She could still smell the scent of blood in the air, hear her sister's screams. She could still taste her own salty tears, and feel the blinding burn of the whip as it split her flesh.

"We were separated after that. I didn't see her for two months, and when I did, she was a shell of the person she'd been.

Her bruises fresh, and her body nearly a skeleton. She didn't even look up at me when I called her name. She was . . . a ghost. Not the defiant, free spirit who I knew and loved. They broke her."

Aaron pulled in a ragged breath. "I'm so sorry, baby."

"I still stayed." The confession left her, the weight of her shame bearing down.

"It doesn't sound like you had a choice."

"You don't understand. I stayed for years after that. My sister . . . I found her . . . She'd hung herself in the tree we used to play at when we were kids." Pain lanced Brynn's heart, but her voice was emotionless, her body numb at the memory.

Aaron rolled over, cupping her face as he looked into her eyes. "It wasn't your fault."

"How can you say that?"

"You and your sister were victims in a horrible situation. You were brainwashed and abused. They used fear to control you. That's on them. Not you."

"But—"

"Do you blame Brynna?"

Her eyes narrowed. "No. Of course not."

"Why?"

She struggled. "I see what you're trying to do, but Brynna tried to leave. I didn't."

"But you *did*. You're here now. You got you and Dani out of that place."

Tears streamed silently down her cheeks. "Only after I knew I couldn't protect her anymore, after the thought of staying there was worse than the hell they swore awaited us on the outside. After Paul—"

A protective fury like she'd never known glinted in Aaron's usually soft brown eyes. Her breath stuttered.

"What did he do?" Contrary to his hard assessing gaze, Aaron's voice was even and gentle, but no less deadly. She'd never seen this side of him. A frisson of fear sparked in her belly. But he would never hurt her.

"Dani—David at the time, tried on my dress. Paul came in looking for another one of the wives and found him. Luckily, I was nearby, and heard Dani's screams."

Anger and vehemence radiated off Aaron in waves strong enough to rattle her to her core, much like when she found Paul with his fist cocked ready to deliver a blow to her child with his other hand clamped around Dani's neck. But Aaron's fury was different. His was protective—a righteous anger.

"I ran in screaming at him to stop. Women were not supposed to raise their voice, or go against a man, especially her husband. But something that day snapped in me."

"Your mama bear came out."

"I told him I asked David to put the dress on so I could mend it. That way . . ."

"That way what?" Aaron's voice had cooled a few degrees, as if he knew where this was going.

"That way he'd punish me instead."

Aaron sat, his body vibrating with barely contained chaos. He leaned against the wall and pulled her into his lap, facing her. "I need to hold you and look at you, so I know you're okay and in my arms. I want to know, if you're willing to tell me. But I won't lie. I want to murder the piece of shit that hurt you and Dani."

She gripped the back of his neck. "You can't. He's untouchable. The Livingston clan has people in government and the police force. They have their own banks, and complete control."

"No one is untouchable."

"Aaron, would you seriously take a life?" She searched his face.

"If it meant protecting you, absolutely." He hadn't even blinked.

Mixed feelings of anxiety and awe swirled through her. This man would keep her safe no matter what.

"Don't mistake me for the white knight, sunshine. Not when it comes to people I love."

Her eyes widened. He loved her?

"I knew it would scare you, that's why I waited to tell you."

She was utterly speechless.

His thumb brushed against her cheek. "What are you thinking?"

"I . . . I didn't think anyone could love me, and here you come knocking down all my walls."

He smiled, joy diffusing some of the dark emotions in his gaze. "Look at you. How could I not fall for you?" He kissed her, soft and sweet, stirring up feelings in her that both scared her and gave her life.

"You can't go after him. Please promise me you won't do anything to jeopardize your safety." *Or our future.*

"I won't seek revenge. But if he tries to come after you or Dani, I will do whatever it takes to keep you safe." His deep voice made the butterflies in her belly flutter and hot arousal stir in her core.

"Okay. Thank you."

"How did you get away?"

She looked down at his bare chest. "That same evening, I snuck into the room where they made the boys sleep. I woke Dani and we snuck out in the middle of the night. I took the money my sister had left for me in the tree. I hadn't told anyone, but she'd left a note for me. Told me to use it to escape with David. So, I bought us a bus fare to the farthest place and kept going. I'd read about the ocean in one of my textbooks, and I'd always wondered what it was like. So, we came to Shattered Cove. We stopped at the hospital—"

Aaron's grip tightened around her again. She met his eyes.

"Is that what was in the file Belle has with your name on it?"

"You know about the file?" She held her breath.

"She left her bag in my office, and when I picked it up, the file fell out."

"Did you read it?" she asked, pulling away enough to face him.

His grip tightened on her. "No. I didn't. I saw your name on it, and Shattered Cove hospital records. I wouldn't betray your trust like that."

She let out the breath she'd been holding. Of course he wouldn't betray her trust like that—not Aaron. "Thank you."

"I get it, sunshine. Everyone in your life who you were supposed to be able to trust let you down and betrayed you. I promise I won't be one of them."

"I . . . I believe you."

The corners of his lips quirked as happiness reflected in his gaze. He reached up and grasped a lock of her hair, twirling it in his fingers.

After a beat of silence, she asked, "Do you want to know the rest?"

"I want to know everything about you, but only when you're ready to share it."

That right there was the reason she wanted to give this man every part of her. "Belle was the nurse they brought in to help me in the emergency room. I wouldn't have gone except . . . I had a dislocated shoulder, a sprained ankle, cracked rib, and my face was so swollen I could barely see."

Aaron's chest heaved again, brushing against her breasts. "I want to kill that fucker."

"Aaron," she pleaded, fear streaking through her that he'd do something stupid and put everything they had in jeopardy. "I shouldn't have told you."

"No." He cupped her jaw. "I'm glad you did. I'm sorry. It's hard to imagine you hurting so much and knowing I wasn't there to help you."

"You're here now." And that meant everything.

"No one will ever hurt you again. Do you hear me? I promise you, if anyone tries, it will be the last thing they do." His deep voice sent a shiver through her.

"I believe you."

"You better, because I'm never letting you go. You're my wife. Mine to protect. Mine to cherish. And mine to love."

She swallowed the emotion that clogged her throat. "I love you too. I tried not to; I swear."

His warm chuckle met her ears. "You were resisting this, and I was fighting for you. That should tell you just how determined I was to earn every part of you. And just how much you mean to me."

"But why? I'm nobody special. And I swear I'm not just looking for compliments. I'm not gorgeous; I'm plain. And I come with so many walls and baggage it's not funny. Why pick someone who was worth so much work?"

She squeaked out a gasp of surprise as Aaron spun her around so that she was on her back and he on top of her, pinning her to the bed.

His gaze roamed over her face, nothing but lust and awe in his expression. "Let's get something straight. You are not only the most beautiful woman I've ever laid eyes on, Brynn, but you're fucking *it* for me. You have a past of horror and darkness, yet still you rose out of the ashes, burning bright like the fucking sunshine you are. You're the strongest person I know.

You don't need me. But I'm the lucky bastard that gets to call you mine. Because you chose me. You know I'm safe. You know I'm going to treat you like the queen you are. Just like I know you're the best fucking thing to ever happen to me."

Wow. When he put it like that . . .

Brynn leaned her head forward, capturing his mouth in a kiss full of promise. Aaron's lips parted, deepening the kiss and winding her up as he kept her hands pinned down, her body caged in, giving her the freedom to just be and experience the pure, raw love and devotion his every touch transferred to her as he worshipped her body. He only separated from her long enough to grab a condom.

Slow and languid, and without preamble, he slid inside her, taking everything she had to give. His cock thrust deep, blurring everything until her body felt warm and bright like she truly was sunshine. Aaron's gaze didn't falter from hers as he crossed her wrists above her head and pinned them down with one hand, using his other to palm her breast. She whimpered as pleasure radiated from her core, unfurling into her limbs with the buzz of electric arousal.

He kissed her again and everything fell away until they were no longer a tangle of body and limbs, but one of two souls connecting in every way imaginable. And when he sent her soaring over the edge into an orgasm, she didn't even try to hold on. Because there was no falling with Aaron—only flying.

Minutes later, he pulled out of her, lying beside her, and pressed her shoulder until she faced away from him. But instead of snuggling up behind her like she expected, his fingers traced the lines of her scars before his soft lips pressed against each mark embedded into her skin. Tears leaked from her eyes.

His lips brushed against the raised flesh sending a jolt of energy pulsing through her.

"We all have scars. Some just carry them on the inside."

Another kiss.

"Marks of life, brands of survival, experiences marked into our skin like a tattoo."

His nose skimmed her spine.

"But that's what they are. Reminders of what you've been through and survived. Not predictions of where you're going."

He tucked her back against his chest, nuzzling his chin into the crook of her neck. "Your scars are a part of you, like your freckles."

"They're ugly," she argued.

"They show you've walked through the fires of hell and survived. It's pretty badass if you ask me. It shows your strength. And that is beautiful." He kissed her shoulder, sending chills racing through her body.

Her heart drummed. Joy burst like a giant water balloon in her chest, releasing a gush of warm elation sinking into every cell. Hope glowed within her. Potent and powerful. Her family had promised her leaving would mean hell when, instead, it had brought her to heaven. Life truly couldn't get better than this.

44

BRYNN

Brynn scanned the photographs of tattoos on the wall in the small room at Squid Ink as the tattooist and professional piercer, Cleo, finished up with Dani's ears.

"Any fun plans for the holidays?" Cleo asked, adding the back to Dani's last earring.

"We're celebrating tonight with my stepdad and Yaya," Dani informed her.

"I always preferred celebrating on Christmas Eve myself too." Cleo smiled warmly. Her arms were covered in intricate tattoos with bursts of colors. Her fingers had little designs inked into her flesh. Her earlobes were stretched over large round pink discs. Dani had asked her about them, and she'd explained they were gauged. She had several other piercings in her ears, one in her nose, and every time she spoke, a glint of metal sparkled from her tongue.

Brynn was utterly fascinated by the woman with bright turquoise hair. To her, Cleo embodied a sense of freedom and confidence Brynn could only hope to possess one day. Being different than the norm was sure to garner looks and comments, or prejudgment from people. And to see someone embrace the truest expression of themselves bolstered Brynn's spirit and fed her determination.

"I noticed you've done some work over scars." Brynn pointed to the before and after photo on the wall of someone's arm with several thin white lines.

Cleo's eyes flicked from the picture to Brynn. "Yes. A lot of scar work depends on how fresh they are, or how deep the scar tissue goes."

Dani's eyes darted to the mirror Cleo held out to her. "I love them! It's perfect. Thank you so much."

"You're welcome, sweetheart." Cleo cleaned up her workspace as Dani slid off the chair.

Brynn looked closer at her daughter's new piercings. "They look gorgeous."

Dani hugged her. "I can't wait to show Yaya. I'll be in the waiting room with her, okay, Mom?"

"Alright."

Dani darted out of the room towards the black leather couches where they'd first walked in.

"Did you have something you wanted covered up?" Cleo asked.

Brynn hesitated. A tattoo was permanent. And it would probably hurt. But if she could take her scars and make them into something that reminded her of how she'd survived rather than the traumatic event itself, to help her see the positive, then it would be worth it. The fact that a tattoo was one more *"fuck you"* to the Livingston clan was just a bonus.

She turned to Cleo, her shoulders straight and her chin held high. "Actually, yes."

* * *

Later that evening, Brynn curled next to the fireplace with a cup of hot mulled cider with a dash of apple pie moonshine splashed in that Iris had insisted she try. Her belly warmed with each sip. Christmas music played softly through the speakers as the scent of their dinner wafted in the air, mixed with a hint of pine and the cinnamon and sugar cookies they'd baked earlier. Fat snowflakes flew down from the cloudy sky so thick it was like peering into a snow globe. Sparkling lights flickered from the tree they'd decorated together weeks ago with many presents stacked underneath it.

Would Aaron like his gift?

He sat beside her, his back to the couch before he wrapped his arm around her and tugged her closer, kissing her cheek. "Hey, beautiful. How are you doing?"

Dani and Iris's laughter filtered in from the kitchen.

"I'm doing great. Looks like we're getting a lot of snow. Do you think we'll be able to get out of here in the morning?"

"Yeah. I have someone coming first thing to plow the driveway. It's supposed to stop falling by midnight. The fresh powder will be great for sledding."

"I've never been."

"Well, we'll remedy that tomorrow."

His hand rubbed up and down her arm as she leaned against him. "You sure you're okay spending Christmas at Hope? I know I asked, but if it's important for you to stay here—"

She laid her hand on his thigh and gently squeezed. "It's more than okay." She pulled back to face him. "That place gave Dani exactly what she needed when we had nowhere else to go. Just like it gives all those teens a safe place. It's more than a facility. It's a family. It's *our* family. I wouldn't want to spend Christmas anywhere else."

He leaned in and kissed her gently. "I love how much you get me."

"I could say the same."

"Is it time for gifts now?" Dani walked into the room, hot cocoa with whipped cream in hand, Iris trailing behind her.

Brynn needed to talk to Dani about her and Aaron's relationship. She'd made it clear from the start this was just pretend, but then it had evolved into more. She had her daughter's feelings to consider when making major life decisions. Not that she worried Dani would be upset, especially if she saw Aaron as her stepdad and not a temporary roommate.

"It's alright with me." Aaron gave her daughter an affectionate smile.

"Aaron, you have to open the gift from me and Mom first." Dani grabbed for the package under the tree and Brynn's stomach flipped as nerves tangled in her belly.

He was so good at giving such meaningful gifts. She hoped he liked what she got him.

He pulled his arm from her shoulders so he could accept the gift from Dani.

"What could it be, I wonder?" He shook the box gently.

"Aaron was terrible as a boy with gifts. He'd guess what I got him every single year. I don't know how he did it." Iris let out an exasperated sigh and shook her head as she smiled.

Aaron grinned. "I knew where you hid them, Ma."

Her eyes widened. "You little stinker!"

He chuckled and tore the wrapping paper open to reveal the cardboard box. "And the intrigue continues." His deft fingers made quick work of opening the package, and he pulled out the T-shirt that Dani had chosen which read, *"Best*

Step Dad" only *"Step"* was crossed out and underneath was printed, *"Like a dad, only better."*

Aaron's eyes grew glassy as they switched from the shirt to Dani. He dropped it in his lap and opened his arms to her. She moved closer and gave him a hug. Seeing the two of them together like that unlocked the last of her reservations. Here was a man who accepted her and her child from another man, and all the baggage that came with them. Aaron was truly perfect.

Perfection isn't real.

She pushed away the thought. She wouldn't have believed it either if she hadn't seen it herself.

Because love is used to control and manipulate. No. That wasn't true. Real love was honest. The affection Aaron had for them wasn't about power, but joy.

"Okay, now see what Mom got you." Dani pointed to the box in his lap.

"Alright." Aaron reached in and pulled out the latest copy of the series he'd been reading in bed each night by his favorite author. Only this one wasn't for sale yet.

His eyes widened. "How did you get this?"

"Pippa has connections. She helped me get a signed advanced copy for you."

"I love it, and I love you." He pulled her into a kiss.

"Okay, you two." Iris sniffled. "You're gonna make me cry."

Brynn pulled away and beamed. "There's one other gift in there."

Reaching in, he pulled out the small silver heart keychain and cradled it in his hand, his eyes roaming over the inscription.

All of me.

His eyes met hers as she leaned in and whispered, "You

have my friendship, my trust, and now my heart." *All of me.* A symbol that he now held her heart in his capable hands.

He brushed her cheek with his hand and tucked her hair behind her ear, dragging his fingers over the sensitive spot there, sending a shiver through her—a promise of more later.

"I've never had a better gift. I promise to cherish it." He hugged her and turned his head to whisper back, "And I hope you know you have all of me, too."

She pulled back.

"Thank you, sunshine." His eyes said so much more than his words, conscious of their audience.

"You're—"

The doorbell chime interrupted her.

"Who could that be?" Iris asked.

"I wasn't expecting anyone." Aaron stood, setting his gifts carefully back in the box before he walked out of the living room towards the front door.

"Go ahead and grab my gifts for you, Dani," Iris instructed.

Dani moved towards the tree as Aaron returned, his father at his side with a handful of gifts in his arms.

Iris's eyes widened a fraction. The corners of her mouth quirked up only a second before the smile disappeared, her expression unreadable.

"Dad has something he wants to say," Aaron said, his arms folded.

Samuel cleared his throat, and Brynn stood, facing the men who looked so much alike.

"I came to . . . I came to say I've done a lot of reflecting since I was last here." His gaze wandered to his wife and stayed there.

It was clear the man wasn't used to being in the wrong. He

was struggling, but the fact he put his pride aside for his wife and son's benefit stirred compassion in Brynn.

"I don't want to lose you." Samuel turned to Aaron. "Don't want my family to suffer for a lack of understanding." Samuel's focus flicked to Dani and then to Brynn. "I don't understand why someone would be trans or gay, but I realized it doesn't matter because it isn't my life it's affecting . . . I want to try to understand. I want to get to know you all." Samuel took a deep breath and let it out. He scanned the room, meeting everyone's eyes settling on his wife. "I'm here to apologize for the things I said and ask if I could have another chance . . . And I brought gifts." He held up the boxes in his hands.

Iris stood and walked up to Brynn, wrapping her arm around her. "What do you think? Should we give him another chance?"

The fact the woman consulted her showed that Iris cared for her feelings, that she respected her. It was clear Iris loved her husband. And Brynn couldn't help but wonder if her mother-in-law suspected this would be the outcome the whole time—her husband showing up with his pride stripped and a new outlook on what matters most.

"I can only speak for me and my daughter." Brynn glanced at Dani who gave her a slight nod. "And I'd say we all need a fresh start sometimes."

Some of the tension left Samuel's shoulders as he walked forward, setting the packages on the couch before he stood in front of his wife. "Will you forgive me?"

Iris shrugged. "I suppose I can be persuaded. As long as you do the dishes from dinner. Every night. For the rest of our lives."

"Whatever it takes," Samuel promised before he pulled his wife into his embrace and kissed her.

"Everyone is kissing way too much tonight." Dani shook her head and blushed.

Iris pulled away, laughing. "Someday you'll know what all the fuss is about—but not anytime soon."

Dani mumbled something and grabbed a candy cane off the tree.

"Can I get you something to drink, Dad?" Aaron asked.

"I'll take some of that cider I smell."

"Go ahead and open your gifts from me, Dani." Iris nudged a package closer to Dani, who gratefully accepted it and got to work, ripping the gift paper.

Samuel edged closer to Brynn, speaking quietly, his voice muffled by the Christmas music still playing. "I'm sorry we got off on the wrong foot. But I appreciate you being willing to give me another chance."

"I want what's best for my daughter and my husband. You're his father and he loves you. I know he doesn't need you in his life, but he wants you there."

"I want to be here too. And I do want to get to know you and Danielle."

"I would like that."

"He's really something, my boy. I know I can't take credit. He's always been someone who needed to save people. Even as a kid, he'd find injured animals and nurse them back to health. Or sneak his lunch money to the homeless man on the street corner. I shouldn't have been surprised when he wanted to start a whole facility for people like his sister—or I guess I should say brother." Samuel sighed. "I've made a lot of mistakes as a father. That was made clear these last few weeks, and I finally had to face my choices."

"It isn't too late to build something with Aaron," Brynn encouraged.

"I'm glad he found someone as strong as you, Brynn. He

needs a partner by his side who can match his strength and keep him in line, much like I have in Iris."

Brynn didn't feel so strong most of the time. More like a shaky leaf amid a storm, clinging to the branch for dear life.

"Aaron needed someone who would be able to give to him for once, and I see he's found that in you. Even a savior needs saving sometimes." He winked and walked over to his wife, slipping his arm around her as they watched Dani open her gifts.

Brynn should have been enjoying the moment, but something niggled in the back of her mind at what Samuel had said. Had she given anything to Aaron? Or had she just taken? Was he drawn to her because he'd seen the brokenness in her and wanted to save her? Or did he truly see her as his equal?

Aaron walked in with a smile, handing his dad a drink before he walked towards Brynn. He kissed her cheek and tucked her close to his side, his hand resting on her hip. She turned to him, searching his eyes. Doubt crept up her spine like a dark shadow. Because if Samuel was right, and Aaron was only interested in her because he saw her as some sort of project—someone he could save—it would destroy her. But he'd given her no cause to doubt him. He'd always been blunt and honest.

He focused on her with a grin. "I can't wait to see you open my gift."

"I already have." She touched the earrings dangling from her ears.

"I have something else for you too."

"Oh?"

"But it's not down here. You definitely want to open this one in private." His eyebrows moved up and down suggestively.

A smile tugged the corners of her mouth up. "What did you do?"

"You'll have to wait and see, sunshine. Wait and see." He chuckled.

She'd wait, and she'd watch. And she'd hope she was enough.

45

BRYNN

Brynn closed Dani's door and made her way to Aaron's bedroom. She entered the dim room, her gaze snagging on his as he looked up from the book she'd been reading this week. The glow of the low lamplight beside the bed highlighted his naked chest.

"Interesting book." He closed the novel and set it on the nightstand beside him, next to two wrapped boxes. *My gifts?*

"Yeah."

"Come sit here." He patted the spot on the bed next to his side as he scooted towards the middle.

She sat, bending one leg higher and resting her knee on his thigh so she could face him.

"I get that romance novels are all about the fantasy, and sometimes it's nice to read things that you wouldn't ever do in real life but can experience through the safety of the written word."

That's one of the things I love about them.

"But, if you ever come across a scene you'd like to reenact

for real, I hope you know you can pass it on. I can make that happen for you."

She swallowed, searching his face. Those brown eyes had a way of seeing every part of her. "It's hard for me to talk about . . ."

"Sex?" he said, as if it was any other word of no consequence.

She nodded.

"Do you like the intimate scenes in this book?" He motioned towards the novel he'd been reading.

If she said yes, would it freak him out? The hero in that book was a possessive mafia leader who commanded the heroine's full submission. He degraded her with his words while he pleasured her, and then complimented her. And sometimes, he tied her in intricate rope patterns and even hung her from the ceiling while he had his way with her.

Her face burned hot.

Aaron dragged his knuckles over her cheek. "This is a safe place, sunshine. You tell me what you like, or what you're curious about. I'll let you know if I feel comfortable trying it, and then we can if you want. I want to learn how to be the best lover for you. By telling me what you like and what you don't, you're helping me."

She took a deep breath, letting it out before she nodded. "I like those scenes."

"You like the tying-up part?"

"Yes."

"And you like that he takes control?"

She nodded.

"You like when I call you a good girl."

Her eyes darted away as her face flamed once again.

"There's nothing to be ashamed of. How about I tell you

something I'm into and then you answer one of my questions?"

"Okay."

He smiled. "I love eating you out."

Now her ears were burning. "You do?"

"Love your taste and smell. I'd do it every day if I could." His eyes darkened with lust, as if imagining doing just that.

Brynn's pussy clenched.

"Now, my turn for a question. Did you like how the hero called her names?" Aaron's face tipped to the side, but his expression remained neutral.

She swallowed. "Yes."

His palm landed on her thigh, gripping, then relaxing, then squeezing again. Aaron's touch added gasoline to the spark of arousal already ignited from this conversation, turning her desire into a wildfire. "Which ones?"

"W-what?"

He straightened and leaned forward a fraction. "Which names did you like?"

Her jaw clenched, her throat dry. Nerves twisted in her stomach.

"If I called you my little slut?" he asked, digging his fingers a little deeper into her thigh.

A ripple of need spread through her, and her lips parted.

"Or fuck toy?" His thumb grazed her bottom lip before cupping her face. "You like those?"

"I-I think so."

"Are there any names you don't want to be called in bed?"

"Bitch, and whore." She'd been called a whore by Paul and the prophets. She didn't want anything to remind her of back then, especially not when she was intimate with Aaron.

"I can do that. At any time you don't like something I say or do, tell me immediately, okay?"

"Alright."

"Now, open your gifts." He plucked the smaller box from the nightstand and handed it to her.

She accepted the present. "But the earrings you gifted me were more than enough."

Aaron leaned in and kissed her lips. "You know I like giving you things. Now open these so I can move on to my other favorite thing." He nuzzled her neck.

She giggled and pulled at the wrapping paper, her core clenching in anticipation of his wicked mouth.

She opened the white box, revealing a large silicone ring with an attachment with what looked like a miniature rabbit on top, its little bunny ears curving towards the ring.

She held it up. "What is it?"

"It's a cock ring."

Her eyes widened. "A what?"

He chuckled and clicked a button. It buzzed in her hand. "And it vibrates."

"I can see that. But what's it for?"

"I put it on, and then when I'm inside you, these little pieces here—" He pointed to the ears that most definitely did not belong to a rabbit. "—they vibrate against your clit, making everything more intense."

"Oh." She swallowed.

He took it from her hands and put it back in the box. "We don't have to try anything until you want to. I just thought it might be a fun way to help you relax and get you multiple orgasms."

"You think it's possible for me?"

"Why wouldn't it be?"

After a beat of silence, he handed her the next gift.

She smiled. "Does this one vibrate too?"

He smirked. "You'll have to open it and see."

She tore the paper and her stomach flipped.

"This is a vibrator. It's curved so it will hit your G-spot, and this part will flutter against your clit."

"This goes inside me?" she squeaked, looking at the rather large toy. It was all a bit overwhelming.

"This is for you to explore your body on your own, learn what you like, and it's nice and quiet, so no one can hear it from outside the room."

"I'm supposed to use this?"

Aaron wanted her to touch herself? To give herself an orgasm? It was the polar opposite of everything she'd been taught.

"I can use it on you too. I'll show you how it works. But this is first and foremost for you. I know you like to do things for yourself, and I thought, as much as I love giving you an orgasm—and fuck it's my favorite thing in the world, don't get me wrong—I just thought that . . ."

She met his gaze, realization dawning. "You gave me this so that even for my pleasure I wasn't dependent on someone else?"

"Yeah."

Gratitude and awe clogged her throat. Who would have thought a sex toy would illicit this kind of emotion from her?

"Aaron?"

"Yeah, sunshine?"

"Make love to me."

He took the box from her hands and set it on the nightstand, brushing the wrapping paper to the floor. "Get up."

Brynn stood, and he followed. She backed up to make room for him. At his full height, he towered over her. She shivered at the dark look in his gaze.

"Strip."

Brynn hesitated, eyeing his defined chest and those chiseled abs highlighted in the dim light.

His hand collared her throat, adding pressure to the sides of her neck, sending a heady dose of lust shooting through her.

"In this room, I'm in control. Everywhere else, you have power—except here. In these four walls, you're my fuck toy, aren't you?" Aaron's voice was dark as midnight and as deep as the ocean. "Answer me."

Electric desire shocked her system at his rough command.

He was playing the part she'd wanted. And she trusted that if she protested in any way, this possessive, deliciously dominant Aaron would disappear, and the man who held her when she broke apart would take his place. She was safe with Aaron. "Yes."

"Good girl."

Oh, holy hotness. He was making her fantasy a reality.

"Now strip so I can see the fucking smoking body that is mine." He released her throat, sitting on the bed, legs spread wide like he owned the fucking world. His gaze remained on her face, ever watchful and perceptive.

The intoxicating rush of adrenaline coursed through her veins at the knowledge she held the power to captivate such a powerful man. She pulled her blouse over her head, revealing the black lace, demi-cup bra she'd picked out just for him. His Adam's apple bobbed as his gaze dropped, following her hands at work, as if he was entranced. She slipped her skinny jeans down her hips, revealing the matching panties, then kicked them off to the side.

"Fuck, you're beautiful. Turn around."

She spun, slowly.

"Have I told you how much I love this ass?" he asked, grabbing a handful of her flesh.

"No."

"Face me and take the rest off."

She turned back to him, unhooking the bra from the front and letting it fall as cool air rushed over her breasts, making her nipples harden.

"Come closer."

Brynn stepped forward on shaky legs. Aaron slipped his finger around the flimsy lace, his touch searing her skin. He yanked, jolting her body forward. She gasped as the shredded remnants of her underwear fell to the ground. That dominant display stirred something warm and dark inside her. She wasn't going to have any underwear left if he kept this up.

"Touch yourself."

Her eyes widened as a sliver of anxiety shot through her.

"Don't make me ask twice, sunshine. Stick those fingers of yours in that pussy and play with your clit."

"I-I don't . . ."

"Disobedience gets you a punishment."

"P-punishment?"

"Unless you tell me to stop, I'll spank that sweet ass of yours," he informed her.

He would spank her? Sure, she'd read about it, but would she want to experience that in real life? Brynn wasn't sure, so she slid her fingers into her already slick folds, finding the little bundle of nerves, and slammed her eyes closed.

"Be a good girl and open your eyes," Aaron instructed.

Brynn reluctantly obeyed, not ready to test his punishments.

"That's it, make yourself good and wet for me." He slid his pants off, taking his underwear with them. Her attention dropped to his cock, springing free, her mouth salivating.

"Is my pussy wet for me?"

"Yes." Her voice was all breath.

"Use your other hand and play with your nipple."

She dragged her hand up, squeezing and pinching.

"That's it, pretend it's my hand doing it to you, and my finger swirling around that clit."

Brynn whimpered at his dirty words, her skin tingling and flashing hot.

"Come closer."

She stepped towards him as he sat up straighter, grabbing her wrist and pulling her hand from her pussy. His gaze met hers as he slipped her finger into his mouth, sucking her arousal.

Her thighs clenched.

He hummed around her digit, sending vibrations up her arm that burst into all-encompassing need.

Only this man could unravel her so completely. Only Aaron could plow over her defenses and convince her to show her wildness. And only he could illicit such compliance from her. Not because he told her to, but because she trusted him. And she wanted to please him. He would return the pleasure tenfold; she'd learned that from experience. Out of everyone in the world, Aaron had earned her submission.

"Get on the bed, legs apart, arms up," Aaron ordered.

Brynn crawled up the mattress, spreading out like a starfish.

He moved around the bed, this time securing her hands and feet to the leather cuffs and straps tucked under the mattress. He opened the box with the bigger vibrator, clicking a button until a little light flashed on. Brynn tugged on the restraints as nerves twisted with anticipation into a swirling tornado of want within her.

"First, I'm gonna eat this pussy, and then I'm gonna drain every last drop of pleasure out of your body until you beg me to fuck you. Those are the words I want to hear. When you're ready, I want you to say, *'Please fuck me, Aaron.'* Understand, sunshine?" He dug his fingers into her thighs, fueling the ache deep within.

"Yes."

He lowered his head to her mound and licked up her center, humming his approval. Brynn closed her eyes from the tease of pleasure. She was too turned on, already on the verge of bursting.

He licked and swirled her clit as the vibrating silicone wand slipped the first inch inside her sex. Brynn's legs pulled on the restraints. Aaron used his left hand to press her hips to the bed as his tongue lapped and laved, taking his time to spin her higher and higher towards the heavens. The vibrator pulled out and then pushed in even farther. He slowly fucked her with it, going deeper each time. Her legs shook from the onslaught of sensations slamming into her. The wand hit the magic spot inside, and Brynn's back arched off the bed. He sucked her clit into his mouth, and she exploded.

White spots appeared in her vision as she clamped her mouth shut, locking in the screams that wanted to escape.

Ecstasy more intense than she'd ever felt splintered through her with a brutal force as her orgasm decimated what was left of her control. She whimpered as he withdrew the wand, sliding it through her folds and around her clit as he pulled his face back. She panted, her hands clenching as tight as her toes while he wound that wicked toy around and around her clit.

"Aaron."

"Yeah, baby?"

She ached. Needed him inside her.

And then he dipped the toy just below her clit and a new sensation tumbled through her. She arched off the bed, the restraints pulling her back down.

"Oh, oh, ohhh!"

Aaron's hand clamped over her mouth.

"Shh, gotta be quiet. Take what I give you like a good little slut. But those screams are for my ears only."

Her eyes rolled to the back of her head as he drew the vibrator down lower to her perineum and back up. The urge to push hit her hard, almost like she had to pee. She clenched her inner walls, tight, holding it back.

Aaron released her mouth and stuck two fingers inside her, hitting her G-spot while he used the vibrator up and down, over and over the area that made her want to bear down.

He finger-fucked her harder, right as it hit that—

"Fuck!"

Liquid squirted out of her, and she slammed her eyes shut as a rush of pleasure encompassed her body with warm euphoria.

Aaron sat up, a proud smile parting his lips, eyes shining with lust. "You squirted."

"I'm sorry."

"For what? That's the hottest fucking thing I've ever seen."

"Me peeing?"

He chuckled. "No, Brynn, that wasn't pee. You ejaculated. It means I'm doing something right down here."

"Women can ejaculate?"

"Yes." He thrust the vibrator back inside her, stealing her breath. It was too much, her body more sensitive to every touch as he pinched her nipple.

"Please?"

"Please what, baby?"

"Need you."

"You know the magic words." He moved the vibrator to her clit and her ears rang.

She shot up from the bed as far as the restraints would

allow. Aaron's hand clamped over her mouth as she struggled. It was too much. Too much pleasure it bordered on pain.

"Please fuck me, Aaron," she said against his hand, the words muffled.

The vibrator turned off as he sat up. She took a deep breath, her body boneless and limp. The straps against her ankles loosened, setting her legs free. Goose bumps covered her flesh as he kissed up her body, sucking on her neck. She arched again, pressing her breasts into his hard chest. His mouth slanted against hers. Tasting her essence, she deepened the illicit kiss. Her tongue tangled with his as his cock nudged her entrance. She pulled her knees up, digging her heels above his ass, giving him access.

"I want to take you raw. Can I do that?"

Brynn's eyes widened. "I'm not on birth control."

"I had a vasectomy."

She blinked.

"It's totally reversible. But it means I can't get you pregnant. I just didn't want the responsibility to be soley on my partners for birth control—I've read those side effects. And I'm clean."

"Then take me bare."

He kissed her again as he slid inside her, inch by inch, stretching her. The sensation was a little different this time, maybe because she had already orgasmed and every cell was electrified, magnifying each brush of his skin against hers. But connecting without anything between them sent a new surge of all-encompassing urgency barreling through her. She clenched around him as another orgasm shuddered through her body. She wouldn't have believed it was possible if she hadn't experienced it for herself. The toys had helped her climax quicker and left her body a thousand times more sensitive. Every nerve ending was alert, all synapses firing with wanton desire.

"Look at me, sunshine."

Her eyes met his as he rocked into her, slow and steady. Liquid heat warmed her from the inside out. Her limbs floated as if she was riding on a cloud. Her body synced with his as he rocked her higher and higher on their little puff of bliss.

As she stared into his soft gaze, she connected with him in a way that was spiritual. They shared bated breaths. The only sounds were the slap of skin against skin as he thrust into her harder. Muted groans of pleasure. Everything else ceased to exist but the live connection they shared. She floated out of her body, but this time she wasn't numb. No, this time she was warm, and safe, and filled with complete and utter rapture. Brynn flew, as Aaron held her body, propelling her into delirium encompassed in a deeper intimacy than she knew existed between lovers.

And then he burst like a star, exploding inside her. Fathomless affection shone in his amber spheres eclipsing all else as they burst into their orgasms together.

Aaron trailed tender kisses over her neck, to her jaw, and then her mouth as his movements stilled, their bodies slick with sweat. "I love you, Brynn. I fucking love you and I'm never letting you go."

"I love you too."

And she wouldn't let him go either. Nothing could tear them apart.

46

BRYNN

Sometime later, Aaron moved, waking her from her peaceful slumber.

"Sorry, baby. I gotta change the sheets. You stay here and I'll take care of it and bring you a washcloth," Aaron whispered.

She blinked her eyes open. Her heavy limbs protested her movement as she sat up and rubbed her eyes. "No, it's okay. I need to get a drink before bed."

Brynn stood while he stripped the mattress. She grabbed his robe, tying it around herself. She went to the bathroom and relieved herself, cleaning up the semen dripping down her thighs. She flushed and washed her hands.

On her way out of the room, he grabbed fresh linens from the closet. Lifting the dirty ones, she carried them down to the laundry room. She started the washer before heading towards the kitchen, but then stopped. Aaron's office light was on. She walked inside, reaching for the switch when her gaze snagged on the blue velvet box on his desk. She must have accidentally left her gift from him in there when she grabbed a deck of cards.

Brynn grabbed it and turned to go as a flutter of paper had her stopping. She spun back around and picked up the item that had fallen. Her eyes caught on the name of the bridal boutique she'd gotten her and Dani's dresses from. She brought it closer and studied the letterhead. It was a credit card statement. There was no way his suit cost seven thousand dollars, was there? Not when they were having such a big sale there—

Brynn scanned the other charges. Sure enough, the car dealership had also issued a charge for ten thousand dollars.

She dug through the pile of papers, finding a receipt for the bridal store. Her wedding dress and Dani's hadn't been quite the deal she'd been led to believe. Her hands trembled as her eyes raced over the two papers. But how?

Charli had mentioned to the boutique owner that she was the future Mrs. Ridley, and they'd shared a look. Was Charli in on this too? And the car—another sale—another lie. He'd gone and made the extra effort to let her think she was paying the full price for the car, but it turned out it was all a ruse. Aaron, the same man who'd had the opportunity to read evidence of her past in a file but didn't, wouldn't possibly lie to her. Would he? This had to be a mistake. Surely there was an explanation for this. But what? The record was in her hands in black and white. He'd promised she would be able to pay for the dresses, and then he'd gone behind her back and included one of her few friends in on the deceit.

Her stomach clenched and turned to stone as tears burned her eyes. Aaron had lied to her. She'd told him she wanted to do these things on her own and he'd agreed to let her. Only he'd manipulated her.

Bile rose in her throat as her knees gave out. Her back

thudded against the desk as she clamped a hand over her mouth to quiet the sob that was wrenched from her body.

He lied to me. Over something as trivial as a dress and a car. Was his dad right? Did Aaron see me as a project? He barely knew me when he proposed, but he was willing to spend thousands of dollars on a wedding dress for a fake event. He kept buying me clothes after too—did I escape one controlling man for another? The glint of her ring caught her eye. *He's been manipulating me from the beginning. No. That didn't add up with the man he was. He'd been so patient, so giving. He respected her boundaries . . . except when it came to money.*

She shook her head. She'd been naive enough to believe in happily ever afters. Brynn should have known better than to trust someone who seemed so perfect. No one is perfect.

His betrayal cut deep. She closed her eyes, curling her body and clenching her muscles tight as confusion and hurt raged within her.

Brynn's eyes shot open, determination rising. She swiped her tears away. She needed to go back upstairs and go to bed, pretending for a little longer that everything was okay. And when his parents left, she'd confront him.

Maybe this doesn't have to be the end. She clung to the ember of hope like a life raft.

47

—————

AARON

Aaron waved goodbye as his parents backed out of the driveway in his dad's rental car. He turned and went back in the house. Dani lay on the sofa, flipping through one of her comics.

"Where's your mom?"

"I think she's upstairs."

Aaron jogged up the steps, heading to their bedroom. Brynn had been quiet the last few days, and she'd kept her distance from him. He needed to check in with her. Having his parents there might have been too much for her. Or maybe she'd been triggered somehow?

He cracked the door open and froze. Brynn sat on the bed, her hands clasped in front of her with her head bowed.

"Are you okay?" he asked.

She didn't even bother looking up, her mouth set in a grim line. "Did you lie to me?"

Her words were a direct shot to his chest. "What?"

Her chin tipped up as she squared her shoulders. "You heard me."

"No, Brynn." He clenched his fists, his head spinning. "I haven't lied to you. Do you want to tell me what this is about?"

"You promised me you'd respect my boundaries."

He nodded, his mind searching for any clue as to what was going on.

"You said you'd be honest with me. And when we agreed on things, I believed you when you said you would let me do things my way."

Aaron squeezed the back of his neck. "Did I cross a boundary? Was having my parents here too much?"

Her gaze turned sad as she stood, pulled a folded piece of paper from underneath her, then handed it to him.

Aaron reached out, opening the document, his gaze scanning the bank statement. His breath caught in his throat, realization dawning. "You mean the dresses."

"Let's not forget the car." She crossed her arms over her chest.

"I want to clarify, you're upset because I paid for these things?"

She scoffed. "I'm hurt because you promised me I could, but you tricked me. You used my friend to do it. And what's worse, I was proud I could do something like buy a car on my own. You took that from me."

Aaron sat down on the bed and ran a hand over his face. "Brynn, I knew you couldn't afford the dresses. I wanted you and Dani to have something special. The owner of the boutique is a friend, so I called in a favor. It wasn't meant in malice."

She sat next to him. "But do you know how that makes me feel? How I can feel betrayed by that?"

He sighed. "I didn't think it was that big of a deal. I was only trying to help."

"I understand that. But we agreed, and then you went behind my back after I trusted you. And I can understand that we didn't really know each other well then, but just recently we got the car."

"You needed something safe and reliable and there was no way you could afford it on your own." He grit his teeth.

She couldn't be mad at him for protecting her. "So tell me that. Talk to me. Don't trick me and go behind my back," she argued.

"You wouldn't have listened. You want to do everything yourself—and I respect that. But when it comes to safety, I just . . . I knew I could fix this, so I did."

"Can you see how I feel betrayed by this? I trusted you and you lied to me. But what's worse is you manipulated me."

"That's not fair. I put a few grand down on a car; it was a gift. How can that be manipulation?" He stood, pacing the room. "No, this is bullshit."

Brynn sniffled and his gaze shot to her. "I'm sorry I hurt you. But I don't think what I did for you . . . that my intentions were wrong."

She shook her head, wiping tears from her eyes before they could fall. "Your intentions were not wrong. But the way you went about it was. We agreed on something and you went behind my back to do what you wanted to get your own results. You treated me like a child. And I . . . I've lost trust in you."

He sucked in a breath, her words spearing through his chest.

She stood, then walked over to the dresser, opening her drawers. Was she going to run? She couldn't. It wasn't safe. The dilapidated garage they'd lived in before flashed in his mind. They couldn't go back there. Brynn pulled out another drawer, then filled her arms with clothing. Was she leaving him for good? No. Danielle still needed his help. She couldn't end up like Emmanuel. If Brynn shut him out, Dani wouldn't get the help she needed. And fuck, this woman owned his heart. No. This wasn't the end. He just had to make her see reason.

"What are you doing? You can't leave."

"I think it's for the best. I'll move this stuff—"

"Think of what this will mean for Dani. She needs to be somewhere stable, where she can get professional and medical help. If you leave, she'll suffer. You can't just run away from this—from me. You can't do this on your own. You need me, Brynn. And fuck . . . I want you."

Brynn froze before she turned to him, eyes shining with hurt and rage. "I was going to move back into the guest bedroom so we could have some time to calm down and see if we could work past this . . . but you . . . you're just like *them*."

He blinked, his body trembling with barely contained anger at the accusation.

"You telling me I can't make it without you, after you spent so much time verbalizing how much I'm capable . . . was it all a lie?"

He ground his teeth. "I didn't mean it like that."

"And worst of all, you are using my love for my daughter to try and manipulate me yet again into staying . . . because you want me." She swallowed. "That's what my family, what Paul said. *'You're nothing without me, Miriam. You need me. You can't take care of David by yourself. You can't just run away, Brynna proved that, didn't she?'"* Brynn choked out the words as she shook her head and darted to the closet for a suitcase.

Aaron had fucked up. That wasn't what he'd meant at all. How had his good intentions spiraled into this mess?

She sniffed. "I guess your dad was right." She grabbed more clothes from the drawers, taking armfuls to the suitcase.

He frowned. "About what?"

She zipped up the suitcase. "He said you had a savior complex. I don't know why I didn't see it before. That's what this is, isn't it? You saw a broken bird and wanted to fix its wing."

"Are you the bird in this analogy?" Aaron stepped forward, placing his hand on her arm.

"Don't touch me." She jerked away from his touch, and it stabbed him in the heart.

"Brynn." He softened his tone and held his palms up. "Can we just talk about this? This is one big misunderstanding. I love you. You know that."

Her rage- and hurt-filled eyes met his as she tipped her chin. "Do I? I thought I knew a lot of things about you, and it seems I was wrong."

Aaron growled in frustration, panic rising with every breath. "I started falling in love with you the moment you walked down that aisle." He stepped into her space, needing to get close to her—to convince her this was all a mistake.

Brynn shook her head and crossed her arms over her heaving chest as she stood before him. Pain reflected in her shiny emerald gaze.

"I fucked up by not telling you, okay?" His shoulders slumped in defeat. "I'm not your ex. Haven't I proved that yet?"

She swallowed. "I can't do this anymore." She tugged the ring from her finger and set it on the nightstand.

The blood drained from Aaron's face. "You're really leaving me?"

She straightened her spine. "Yes."

"Don't do this, Brynn. Take some time to cool off and we can talk about it more."

"I would have, but . . . you sounded just like him and I..." She tilted her head up and closed her eyes, taking a deep breath before she focused back on him. "I can't be here right now." She picked up her suitcase and set it on the ground. Grabbing the handle, she then moved to pass him.

"Sunshine, please?" He stepped in her way.

"Let me go, Aaron."

He shook his head, everything inside him roiling at the thought of watching her walk out his door. His heart raced, every beat agony. "Don't do this, Brynn. Give me a chance to make this right. I didn't mean it the way it came out. I love you. I'll fight for you, for us. Just—" He ran his hands over his head. "I won't let you go."

Her face paled.

"Jesus. I don't mean it like that. God dammit! I keep fucking this up," Aaron yelled and walked away from her, pacing the floor. He stopped, staring at Brynn as the floor squeaked from the hall. Dani had heard the shouting and came to investigate.

"Is there nothing I can say to convince you to stay and give this more time?"

Brynn dragged the suitcase as she walked past him and towards the door. She turned her head at the last moment, not even looking at him, but her voice broke. "Let me go."

Aaron's ears rang as his blood thumped wildly in his chest. How had everything gone to hell so quickly?

"Fuck!" he screamed, punching his hand into the mattress.

He was losing the most important people in his life. Why? He'd only meant to help, and somehow, he'd ended up hurting the woman he loved most.

Let me go.

Aaron's chest felt like someone had slammed a battering ram through it. Devastating loss encompassed him as he fell to his knees, his face falling into his hands as tears tracked down his cheeks. Now he was the broken one.

48

———

BRYNN

Brynn slipped two pieces of bread into the toaster for Dani's breakfast. Her gaze roamed the cute apartment Pippa had let her and Dani rent above the bookstore until she found something else. It was much nicer than the one she'd rented before, and despite Pippa's urging, Brynn paid rent. Because of her savings, she could afford it, at least for a little while. It only had one bedroom, but she and Dani would make do.

She placed the plate of eggs in front of a solemn Dani at the table. "The toast will be ready soon."

Dani picked up her fork and silently shoveled a bite into her mouth.

"Do you have all your homework done?"

Dani nodded, her mouth still set in a grim line.

"Are you excited about the science fair coming up?"

Another dismal shake of her head. Worry slithered around Brynn's rib cage, squeezing tight. Brynn sat across from her at the small table.

She set her hand atop Dani's. "Are you doing okay?"

Her daughter still wouldn't meet her gaze.

"You haven't been yourself lately."

Finally, Dani looked up, angry defiance in her eyes. "I miss Aaron and my friends at Hope."

It had only been a week, but Brynn, too, had felt the loss. "You knew it was temporary. It was all supposed to be pretend." *Supposed* to, but in the end she'd developed real feelings for the man. "I won't let us be trapped again."

The toast popped up.

Dani dropped her fork. "How were we trapped?"

Brynn sighed and stood, checking on the toast.

"In the compound, you couldn't use cars. Aaron gave you the keys and taught you how to drive."

"Danielle—"

"I heard him on the phone with the dealership before you went for your test. He asked them about safety; he wanted you to have the best."

Brynn slashed the butter knife over the bread, accidentally tearing a hole in it due to her anger. "He lied to me."

"Or he knew you wouldn't be able to afford it and he saved your pride by arranging it all."

Brynn gasped and spun around. "My pride?" Her brows drew together. Was she a prideful person?

"Aaron married you so I could get the treatment I needed, Mom. He *married* you. He actually listens and spends time with me. No one but you has ever done that. And he did it even before you guys were married. He never changed. Aaron only got better as we got to know him."

"Yes, he did something amazing for us, and I will be forever grateful. But he . . ." Some of the steam left her. He had done all those things. And what had he asked her for in return? "But he lied to me."

"You lied to people too. You let everyone believe your marriage was real from the start," Dani pointed out.

Brynn carried the rest of her daughter's breakfast over to her and set it on her plate before sitting across from her once again. "That was for a good reason." For Dani.

"How is that different than why he didn't tell you about the car?"

It's not. "How did you grow up so fast?" Here she was getting admonished—by her fourteen-year-old.

"Aaron loves you."

Brynn's heart tore at her daughter's words. *I love him too.* And maybe that's what this was really about. Maybe she'd blown this out of proportion because he'd hurt her, and loving him meant leaving her vulnerable. The longer they were together and the stronger her feelings grew for him, the more power he'd have to cause her irreparable hurt. So, instead, she ran, destroying them in the process.

Her eyes slammed closed. *I can't believe I told him he was like Paul.* Aaron was nothing like her ex. Nothing like the men of her past. *So why did I lump him in with them?*

I won't let you go. Aaron's promise whispered in her mind. This past week he'd shown up to the diner and the bookstore three times trying to get her to talk. She'd ignored him and walked to her apartment, not taking the keys to her car when he offered. She'd had Pippa follow her there to leave it while Aaron was at work. She left it at his house, along with all the jewelry and clothes he'd bought her. *I am prideful.*

Each time he'd looked more defeated. He hadn't been back in four days. *Because he's finally given up.*

Tears tracked down her cheeks. She wiped them away, but more kept coming.

"Mom?" Dani's voice brought her back to the present.

Brynn sniffed and forced a smile. "I'll be okay. You've

given me a lot to think about. You should go before you're late for the bus."

"I can skip a day and stay with you," Dani offered.

Brynn shook her head. "No, I've got to get to work soon anyways. You go to school. I'll be fine."

Dani finished her breakfast while Brynn got busy making herself some tea that would no doubt be as tasteless as everything else had been this week. She kissed her daughter goodbye and watched from the window as Dani boarded the bus to school. Only then did she let herself break down, a sob tearing from her gut.

"What is wrong with me?" she demanded. "Why did I push him away when he's the best thing that ever happened to me?" Tears streamed down her face. "Why am I so messed up? He loved me despite everything. And I hurt him."

She lay on the bed, curling into a ball, her regret leaking from her eyes. She hadn't saved her sister. She'd stayed long enough to inflict lasting scars on Dani; her daughter would have trauma from the childhood she'd endured at the compound. A good man had come into their life, given more than anyone else may have in their situation, and what had Brynn done but thrown it in his face?

Was it even possible to fix the mess she'd made? Or had she ruined her chance at happily ever after for good?

49

AARON

Aaron hunched over his shot of whiskey at The Shipwreck. Charlie had tried to talk to him, but she must have read his misery because she'd nodded towards Mason across the room and left him alone.

Mason leaned his back against the wooden bar, on the stool next to him. Aaron had just finished explaining the truth to his friend.

"Wow. I wondered, with how quick everything happened."

"Pippa didn't tell you?" Aaron asked.

"She knew?" Mason's eyes widened.

"Brynn told her in the beginning."

"That little . . . I can't believe she didn't say anything to me."

"I know Brynn swore her to secrecy." Aaron hoped he didn't just start something for the happy couple. They'd dealt with enough issues between them.

Mason waved his hand. "That figures, then . . . So, was she a project for you to fix?"

Aaron's jaw clenched as he straightened. "Absolutely not."

One of Mason's eyebrows rose as he scrutinized Aaron.

Aaron sighed. "I wanted to help her, yes. I knew I could save Dani from possible terrible outcomes. But everything between Brynn and I was because I cared about her. Yes, I wanted to help her work through her shit, but isn't that true for anyone who loves their partner?"

Mason nodded. "Yeah, it is. But we can't always save them. Some people have dragons only they can slay. Other times, you just have to get used to having those demons around because they aren't going anywhere. Sure, they may slink into the shadows, but they're still there, waiting for the opportunity to sneak back out when it's least convenient."

"Speaking from experience?" Aaron asked.

"Unfortunately."

"I can't let her go. I love her like—" He clutched his chest at the blooming ache that never seemed to ease since she'd told him she was leaving.

"Like she's a part of your soul," Mason finished for him.

"Yeah." Aaron ran a hand over his overgrown stubble. He hadn't shaved in days. He hadn't been home either. The house just seemed so empty and lifeless without Dani and Brynn. So, he'd poured himself into working at Hope and sleeping on the couch there.

"I can speak from experience. A marriage won't work unless you're both fighting for it. If she isn't willing to forgive you and try to move on, then . . ." Mason cast a sympathetic gaze his way.

"Then I'm fucked."

"Is there anything else she needs from you that you haven't given her yet?"

Aaron tipped back his shot glass, letting the alcohol burn his throat. He set it on the bar and shook his head. "I've given her time and space even though it's killed me. She won't let me give her the car back; she's so fucking stubborn and independent. She won't let me take care of her at all."

"You can be too independent. The trick is learning to be interdependent—each being able to stand alone at some times, and then lean on each other when needed." Mason crossed his arms over his chest. "Maybe you should give her what she wants."

"Let her go?" Aaron's voice broke. How could he let someone he loved so fiercely go?

"Maybe she needs to see you'll do whatever she needs, despite how much it will destroy you. That makes you the opposite of her ex."

Aaron's stomach churned, bile rising in his throat. Chaos erupted in his body at the thought of divorcing Brynn. Everything inside him rejected the idea. But maybe Mason was right. He couldn't make this marriage work without Brynn. And if she really wanted him to leave her alone, even if it went against everything his heart told him, he'd let her go.

He breathed out in defeat, every last bit of hope draining with it.

50

BRYNN

Brynn wiped the table down and glanced out the window of the High Tide diner and froze. She gasped. Her eyes widened; her heart raced. It had been just a flash, but she'd thought for sure she'd seen Paul across the street in the passing crowd of people heading towards Hope Facility's Winter Wonderland fundraiser in Green Park.

She searched the spot where she'd seen him, but no one was there.

It's just my imagination. I'm safe. Paul has no idea where I am.

"Can I go to the park now, Mom? I finished my homework. Aspen said she's at the bookstore waiting for me, so we can go together with Pippa," Dani asked, shouldering her backpack over her winter coat.

"Sure. Have fun." Brynn opened her arms for a hug.

"Can you meet me there after your shift ends?"

Ugh. *And risk running into Aaron, and with an audience?* "Oh, I actually have some errands to run. I'll see you at six for dinner, okay?"

Dani gave her a quick squeeze and then bounded out the door. Brynn finished wiping the table down and went to refill coffees for the few patrons left in the diner. Once she'd done that, she went to the table in the corner, getting to work wrapping silverware in napkins.

"Brynn?"

"Hmm?" She turned towards Betty-Lou's curious expression.

"Are you okay, dear?"

Brynn straightened. "Yeah. Why wouldn't I be?"

"I've called your name three times."

"Oh, I'm sorry. Did you need something?"

Betty-Lou studied her. "You've been very distracted this week. Is everything okay with Dani and Aaron?"

Hearing his name was like a knife to Brynn's gut. She forced a smile. "We're fine."

She squeezed Brynn's arm before smoothing her hands down her blue checkered apron. "Now, your shift is over, but I was going to run to the storage shed out back for some more deli containers. Can you watch the front for me?" Betty-Lou wiped her hands on a dish towel.

"No problem."

Betty-Lou gently laid a hand on Brynn's. "If you need anything, Fred and I are here for you."

Brynn pressed her palm to the kind woman's touch. "I know. And I don't know if I've ever really told you how grateful I am for all you've done for us."

Betty-Lou winked. "Just about every other day." She laughed. "Jasmine is coming in for a to-go order of pies. They're all boxed up with the invoice on the counter."

"Okay."

Betty-Lou patted her hand and waved to the few Pirate MC members at a booth across the diner before she went out the back doors. The one with the scar on his face looked Brynn's way. Her attention darted to the silverware and napkins in front of her. She got to work, rolling them together.

The door opened, bringing in a gust of crisp wintery air with it. Brynn looked up in time to meet Aaron's tired gaze. Her body tensed as a cacophony of emotions clamored to the surface. Nerves flipped in her belly as he approached her, a yellow folder in his hands.

"Can we talk for a second . . . please? I promise I'll leave you alone after. I just want to say one thing." He sounded like he'd swallowed gravel. His shoulders hunched forward. Gone was the usual lively spark in his expression, replaced only with defeat.

She nodded, unable to speak, and gestured to the seat across from her. She didn't have it in her today to ignore him like she had been, and a large part of her was still so confused about everything that had happened between them. If he was an honest man, then why did he lie to her? Why did he say those things to her if he truly believed in her?

Aaron slipped into the booth and set the envelope on the table. Dark circles rimmed his eyes. His beard was growing out, and his normally pressed and ironed dress shirt was wrinkled. He looked as bad as she felt.

Aaron took a deep breath, as if preparing himself while he loosened the grey scarf around his neck. "I only ever wanted to bring you happiness and help you feel safe. I'm sorry I hurt you in any way. It truly was unintentional. I should have been honest with you."

I overreacted. The words were on the tip of her tongue, but she held them back. She wanted to hear what he had to say.

He continued, "I only ever wanted to give you the space to spread your wings and fly." Aaron's gaze dropped to the table, then flicked back to her, sincerity shining in his eyes. "I do love you . . . And I want to take care of you the way a husband should—and to protect you at all costs. If that makes me wrong for you, I don't know what else to do."

But will I be just one more person you're trying to save?

"I never wanted to fix you, Brynn, or save you, however you put it."

"You didn't?"

"Not once. Yes, I wanted to give you the world. I wanted you to heal, but I know most of that has to come from within you. My goals were to provide you with a safe environment to do so and the support I thought you needed. But it wasn't to save you for my ego. It was because I cared about you, and that affection turned into love. And when you love somebody, you want the best for them . . . even at your own expense."

Tears welled in her eyes. He deserved so much better than her.

"Despite everything inside telling me not to, I'm giving you what you asked for." He slid the envelope to the center of the table. "I'm letting you go." Aaron's voice cracked, and the force of what he was saying hit her full force, sucking the air from her lungs.

"But I'll never stop loving you." He stood abruptly. "And if you change your mind and want to work this out, I'll be waiting."

Brynn wanted to grab his hand and tell him to stay, but that fear inside wrapped around her like thick ropes, keeping her firmly planted in the seat, and her mouth closed.

He left the diner, his head bowed and his shoulders slumped as he headed towards Green Park. Brynn's heart hammered in her chest. She grabbed the envelope and opened it. Divorce papers slid out with something shiny clinking to the table—the necklace he'd gifted her with the globe pendant, his subtle reminder that she deserved the world. She picked it up and stared at the stack of paperwork, her gaze snagging on the sticky note attached in Aaron's bulky masculine script.

Sunshine, you were never broken to me—only beautiful.

He'd given her everything and never expected anything in return that she wasn't ready to give. And now he'd served her the divorce papers. *Because I asked him.* He'd let her go.

When you love somebody, you want the best for them . . . even at your own expense. He'd given up what he wanted most for her. In the process, he'd relinquished any control over her. She was free.

She waited for the rush of relief, but only emptiness and loss filled her. *Because I'd never been under his thumb.* Aaron had been the one to set her free. He'd literally given her the keys to her cage. *Then why did I push him away?* Had it all been her way of testing him? She'd needed to know how much he loved her. She'd known the love in his heart for her was true. And she'd forced his hand to see if he'd free her. Her final test of love. Yes, it was fucked up, but it was the last thing that held her back from giving herself so fully to him.

"Brynn?"

Jasmine walked over, a tentative smile on her face.

Brynn slid the papers and necklace back into the envelope and stood. "Hey. You're here for your pies."

"Yes. There should be four."

Brynn made her way behind the counter before grabbing Jasmine's order, her hands shaking. Mind racing. Adrenaline coursed through her veins as panic seized her chest.

"Hey, are you okay?" Jasmine asked, her brows drawn together.

"I'm . . ." Brynn exhaled. "How did you know Atlas was the one? How did you know you could trust him after everything with your past?"

Jasmine's eyes widened a fraction before she cast a glance

around the diner. The Pirates all stood, giving them a friendly wave before they left. Only an older gentleman at the counter a few seats away, and a family with a young boy remained.

Jasmine leaned closer to Brynn and lowered her voice. "It took time. And his actions matched his words. He wasn't perfect, obviously—no one is. But he tried, and he keeps aiming to do better. That's all I can ask. He put my needs first, and he just . . ." Jasmine sighed dreamily. "He's there for me through life's ups and downs. When I have my difficult times and it's hard for me to get out of bed, or when I get triggered when we're intimate, he's always patient and understanding. He makes me feel loved and cherished."

Brynn nodded. That's how it was with Aaron. The man gave her what she needed so many times before she even knew she needed it. He's been more patient than a saint. Loving him didn't mean oppression, but freedom like she'd never known.

"Oh, hello, dear." Betty-Lou greeted Jasmine with an armful of supplies.

"I have to go." Brynn rushed by her friend, turning around to her as she headed for the back of the diner. "Thank you."

Brynn raced to the locker room, switching out her apron for her coat and bag. She fumbled with the zipper as she darted back out to the front of the restaurant.

"Where are you going in such a hurry?" Betty-Lou asked as Brynn grabbed the envelope from the counter, sliding the necklace out and clasping it on her neck.

"To get my husband back."

Hopefully it wasn't too late.

51

BRYNN

Brynn ran down empty Main Street as fast as she could without slipping on the icy sidewalk. *Everyone must be at the winter carnival.* The nippy wind cut through her half-zipped coat. The sign for Green Park was surrounded by twinkling holiday lights. Music from the live band at the gazebo grew louder the closer she got. Hundreds of people congregated around the park designed to look like a winter wonderland for Hope's annual winter fundraiser. *Where is Aaron?*

She searched the faces, moving slowly through the pathway, weaving between bodies. Laughter filled the air with the scent of hot chocolate, kettle corn, and spiced cider.

A flash up ahead drew her attention to the giant tree the town had decorated for the holidays. The same photographer who took her wedding photos aimed the camera at Aaron. He was surrounded by Leslie, his other staff, and several of the kids from Hope, Dani included. Leslie turned towards him, and Aaron leaned down so she could speak into his ear. A smile appeared on his face, but it didn't reach his eyes.

Brynn stepped forward, only to have something hard press into her spine as a hand snaked around her arm, squeezing hard.

She sucked in a startled breath and turned. "Paul!"

His cold blue eyes narrowed on her. Stress lines marred the loose weathered skin around his face. His cheeks sagged, looking more like jowls. His grey hair stuck out of his wool hat at odd angles. He looked so much older than the last time she'd seen him—right before he'd kicked her prone body in the ribs.

"If you scream, I'll pull this trigger. And then I start taking out these heathens one by one."

Panic slashed through her. Brynn's heart pounded. She cast one quick glance towards Aaron and then Dani by his side, giving him a hug. Aaron held her daughter like she'd always dreamed a father would hold her. *And I pushed him away.*

"Where is my son, Miriam?" Paul demanded, his hand squeezing the soft spot under her arm harder, making her wince.

"Dead."

Paul spun her around. He moved to her right side, still clamping her arm with one hand and keeping the gun pointed at her spine with the other. "You think I don't know you've allowed him to wear women's clothing? You think I haven't been watching you?"

He'd been watching her?

"Do you see what leaving the compound did? It corrupted my son. And you brought shame onto my household."

Brynn stumbled forward as he forced her towards the park exit. Was this the last time she'd ever see Dani again? Or Aaron? *He doesn't even know how I feel. He thinks I hate him.*

"You will pay for your deceit and treachery. For your disobedience." Paul yanked her arm.

Brynn searched the crowd, everyone seemingly ignoring her as they wrangled small children, or eyed the tables with games and food.

Green stormy eyes caught hers. The biker with the scar.

Brynn mouthed the words, *"Help me."*

The Pirate's gaze cut to Paul, then he walked straight ahead, brushing against her.

Her stomach hardened to stone. *He's not going to rescue me.* Tears burned her eyes. If she struggled, Paul would shoot. She couldn't risk these people's innocent lives. The man had been unhinged when she'd known him at the compound. Now that he'd found her . . . *I'm going to die.*

"You will go before the council and admit all you've done. Tell them you were possessed by a demon, then you will be punished accordingly. Then they will have to grant me my rightful place by their side once again."

"You mean you got demoted when I escaped?" Brynn couldn't hold back the mockery in her tone.

"You little whore." Paul shoved her down an alley, head-first into the brick building. Pain burst as the porous stone scratched the tender skin of her face. Her cheek burned.

Paul's hand pressed her head against the hard brick, until her jaw ached. She bit back her whimper, knowing from experience he got off on her pain.

"You left and they accused me of not being able to control my household. Your parents were publicly shamed and stripped of everything. Two daughters who were too weak to withstand temptation. Two disgraces."

"Don't you dare talk about my sister like that. She was ten times the person you will ever be!" Brynn yelled, shoving against the wall with all her might.

"Be silent!" Paul spun her around, his fingers digging into

her neck, choking her. She tugged his hands away, nails scraping his exposed hands, drawing blood.

He leaned in, an evil glint in his eyes and a violent smile on his mouth. "You have so much more fight in you this time. That's gonna be real fun to break, just like I did with your sister."

Brynn's eyes widened. Rage burned her veins with white-hot fire. She brought her knee up hard, hitting him between the legs.

Paul grunted and released her throat. Brynn fell to the ground, coughing and gasping for oxygen.

"You're gonna pay for that!" Paul roared, his fist connecting with her cheek.

Brynn landed on her back from the force of his hit, her vision darkening as pain split though her skull.

He bound her hands in front of her with heavy-duty zip ties, then aimed the gun at her. Even if anyone passed by them, would they see in the overcast afternoon as snow drifted from the grey heavens?

"Now, get up," Paul ordered.

Brynn didn't move, instead lying on the cold hard ground, icy wetness seeping into her clothes as the first few snowflakes drifted down. If she got in the car with him, her life would be over. There was no way she would be able to escape a second time. But if she fought him, he'd shoot her here and kill her.

Tears dripped down the sides of her cheeks: grief for not getting to tell Dani one more time how much she loved her, and how proud she was of her. *What were my last words to her?* Regret for how she'd left things with Aaron spilled down her face, stinging her wounds.

"Either you get up and get into the car, or I start your punishment here by tearing off those horrendous pants you are not supposed to be wearing and taking what is rightfully mine with my gun in your mouth."

Brynn clamped her legs closed, immediately rolling to her side, then stumbling to her feet. She straightened her spine and returned his empty glare. "You won't ever touch me like that again."

Paul laughed and shoved her around the corner towards a parked Mercedes. He opened the door to the back seat and motioned for her to get inside behind the tinted windows. "You're mine. I think you've forgotten that. You will always be mine to do with as I please. And as soon as we get somewhere more private, I'm going to remind you of who you belonged to first and always," he seethed, pushing her inside and slamming the door.

She scrambled for the other side, trying to open the door, but it was child-locked, and she was trapped.

And no one will even know I'm gone for hours.

He climbed in and started the engine. "Get on the floor and lie there until I say so, or so help me I'll use the crowbar in the trunk to knock you out."

Brynn slid to the floor, wincing in the tight space.

Her face throbbed and her throat burned. Terror encompassed her as he drove, the stops becoming less frequent; she guessed they were out of the center of town. Each second took her farther from the ones she loved—and her safety.

Her hope for escaping dwindled with each passing second until all that remained was a small ember, barely alive. She'd lived most of her life in fear. Fear of her father's beatings. Fear of her forced child marriage. Of Paul's summons to his bedroom. Of losing her pregnancy and getting blamed for it. Of carrying a pregnancy to term and having her children be vulnerable just like she had been. Of leaving. Of staying. She'd carried that terror with her, even into her relationship with Aaron. That uncertainty and wariness had really been what controlled her, warping a good thing in her mind until she'd believed Aaron caused her harm.

She should be concerned of dying. But as her mind settled into this realization, a calmness entered her body. Brynn might die today, but it would be on her terms. She wouldn't submit like she had in the past. She wouldn't let them control her with fear anymore.

I'm not going down without a fight.

Brynn crawled onto the seat behind Paul's, quickly grabbing the seatbelt with bound hands and notching it into place.

"Get back on the ground!"

"Fuck you!" She wound her zip-tied hands over his head and pulled as hard as she could, looping her arms against his throat.

Paul's hand slapped against hers as the car veered off the road. They spun and twisted. The crunch of metal groaned as everything went upside down, the car rolling and spinning to a stop.

Pain lanced up her leg, and her arms felt like they'd been torn from her sockets. White particles floated in the air, no doubt from the powder of the airbags. She blinked, trying to see better. Brynn slipped her arms from under Paul. He didn't stir. *Is he dead?*

She hung, suspended in the air from her seat belt. Wincing, she brought her arms up and undid it. Her stomach dipped as she crashed to the roof of the car, which was now below her and covered in shards of glass.

She ignored the stinging in her hands and knees as she crawled out through the shattered window. Her breath turned into white puffs of smoke.

A moan came from inside the car.

He's alive!

She scrambled to her feet, her ankle screaming at her in pain. She limped as fast as she could down the road, heading back towards town. Hopefully someone would drive along soon.

Bang!

Brynn flinched, then fell to the ground. She turned back. Paul was leaning against the car, face bloody with a gun in his hand aimed at Brynn.

"You bitch! You're going to pay for this," he yelled.

She pressed her bare hands into the icy asphalt and stood on shaky legs, straightening her spine, her chin held up. "You'll have to kill me. Because I'm not going to let you have any more control over me."

Bang!

She jumped.

Paul laughed. "When I get a hold of you, you're gonna wish you were dead."

Brynn's gaze searched left and right. Evergreen trees lined either side of the deserted road. A thin sheet of snow covered the asphalt, with no tire tracks on the other side. She was truly alone. A crow cawed somewhere above. An omen. Snowflakes fell on her overheated skin as adrenaline coursed through her. Chest heaving, a sense of knowing settled into her bones. This was where it would end.

"No one gets away with embarrassing me like you have. Since you ran off, the prophet wouldn't even let me have another wife. You ruined everything!" His steps came closer, the sound of the slush beneath his shoes like a countdown to her death. But she wouldn't run anymore. No, she'd face him head-on. Brynn wasn't the obedient victim she once was. And she wasn't going down without a fight.

"Good. It means you can't abuse any more children."

"You little—" He aimed the gun at her chest, the metal pressing through her thin shirt exposed by the open coat.

She ground her jaw, her gaze dropping from his like she'd been taught. Only this time it wasn't out of obedience, but survival. "You're right."

He hesitated, the gun moving slightly to the right, away from her heart. "You think you can fool me with this act? You believe I'll be lenient with you because you change your tune now?" A dark laugh escaped him as he leaned closer and taunted her. "No one is coming to save you, Miriam."

"Then I guess I'll have to save myself." She grabbed the gun and shoved it away from her as she threw all her weight into him.

Bang!

Searing pain lit up her shoulder as they both crashed to the ground. Paul cried out, one hand reaching towards the back of his head on the asphalt. She clung on to the gun, as if her life depended on it—because it did. She took advantage of his pain and leveraged her weight on top of him to twist the gun from his hand.

Scrambling off him, she aimed the gun at his chest as he clutched his head with one hand and rolled to his side.

"Don't move!" she screamed.

"You're not going to shoot me." He stumbled upright, his hand coming away from his skull, his own blood gleaming on his fingers.

"Are you sure?" Her voice was colder than the winter air around them.

Paul froze, his eyes widening a fraction. "What are you going to do? You attacked me when I came to town, trying to find my child who you kidnapped."

"Liar!"

He shrugged. "That's the story the cops will believe when they get a phone call from my cousin in the FBI."

"You bastard! Why couldn't you just leave us alone?"

Paul smirked. "I told you, Miriam. You're mine. We took vows that bound you to me for all of eternity. You will be punished for what you've put me through in this life and the next."

"What I've put you through? You raped me when I was fifteen, and hundreds of times after that. You beat me. You humiliated me. Because of you I lost my sister." Brynn shook her head, tears blurring her eyes as her head spun with dizziness. "You tricked me into believing I was too weak . . . but you were wrong. I'm not broken. I'm fucking unbreakable."

Brynn pulled the trigger.

52

———

AARON

Aaron shook Ryan's hand.

"I'll get the digital copy of these photos to you later this week for the website," he informed him.

"Thank you very much." Aaron nodded, then turned around, searching for Dani. He wanted a minute alone with the girl to let her know no matter what happened between Brynn and him, he'd be there for her. Hopefully Brynn wouldn't fight the one stipulation he'd added to their divorce papers—that Dani be kept on his health insurance plan.

"Aaron."

Aaron turned toward the brisk deep voice of Blade, the leader of the local Pirates MC, who nodded towards the side of the tree, away from the few festivalgoers glancing curiously at them.

Aaron followed him, his gaze snagging on the scar that ran from his forehead, down his cheek.

Blade ran a hand over his beard. "We got a problem."

"What is it?" Aaron had worked with the Pirates several

times before. His group had been there for a lot of the kids when they needed protection.

"Your wife."

Panic streaked through Aaron. "What do you mean?"

"Brynn left here with a man, and it didn't look voluntary. She mouthed help me to me. When I looked back, it was clear he was holding a weapon on her."

The blood drained from Aaron's face. "You didn't follow her? We have to go!" Aaron stepped around Blade, but his friend held up his hands. "My men are already en route. I slipped my phone in her pocket to track them. He had a weapon, and if he's crazy enough to kidnap a woman like that, he's unstable enough to start shooting up the park. There was nothing I could do while she was in a public place. I had to get my guys on the other side of the park. Without my phone it took a few minutes."

Aaron's chest heaved. *Brynn is in danger! I must get to her.* "Take me to her!"

Blade ran with him to the street where Aaron had parked. "Give me your keys."

Aaron handed them to his friend and jumped into his car. Blade started the ignition and peeled out of the parking spot. Aaron grabbed his phone, shooting Mason a quick text, telling him to take Dani home with him and not let her out of his sight.

Aaron's shoulders inched up towards his ears. Adrenaline thrummed in his veins. Brynn was in danger, and he wasn't there to protect her. He'd just spoken to her God damnit! *I shouldn't have let her go. But who would have taken her?* His gut flipped. There was one man she'd worried would find her. One man wicked enough to take a woman away at gunpoint.

"I'm going to fucking kill him," Aaron growled as they raced out of town.

"You need to keep your hands clean. You're doing a lot of good work for this town. The kids need you. The last thing you want is to get your hands dirty and have it fall back on you. The boys and I will handle this. Understand? I can't have you going out half-cocked."

Trees whipped by as anxiety churned in Aaron's gut. "If he's hurt her, I can't make any promises."

Blade nodded. "Wouldn't expect anything less."

Two big trucks blocked both lanes ahead. Blade pulled over onto the shoulder of the road. Aaron's eyes widened as he shoved his door open, then raced towards the scene in front of him.

Steam rose from a wrecked car, upside down in the ditch on the side of the road. Four armed men in leather cuts surrounded a bleeding older man who looked vaguely familiar. He was the man Aaron had seen outside the bookstore. One of them stood by a shaking Brynn, speaking softly to her.

Aaron's heart stuttered. *Brynn.*

"She shot me!" the pale man being held by one of The Pirates said as Aaron and Blade approached.

"She got the drop on you with her hands bound? Sounds like a warrior to me." Blade's voice was deadly.

Aaron's gaze dropped to Brynn's zipped hands as rage lit his veins on fire. He raced towards her. The glint of metal in her hands made him freeze. Brynn trembled, her eyes vacant and glassy, as if she was in shock.

"You don't understand. She's my wife. She took everything from me. I need to bring her back. She must be punished for what she's done."

His wife? This was Paul, her ex. He'd known where she was. He'd been watching her. *And I missed it. Fuck!*

Aaron stepped closer, holding out his hand to Brynn.

"Brynn? Honey? It's me. You're safe. You can put the gun down."

She blinked and turned to face him. The swollen bruise below her eye and the cuts on her fair skin made him clench his teeth. But it was the blood on her shoulder that had him seething.

"Aaron?" Her eyes searched his face, confusion shining in them.

He offered her what he hoped was a comforting smile. "Yeah, sunshine, it's me. Give me the gun, baby." Aaron held out his palm.

Brynn looked down at her hand, as if she was surprised she still had it, then she handed it over to him. Aaron slipped it to one of Blade's men by his side.

"Do you know what we do to men who hurt women?" Blade asked.

"I-I . . ." Paul's voice trembled. "You don't understand. She's mine. My wife—I can do whatever the hell I want to her. And there isn't anything you can do to stop me."

Aaron dove towards Paul, grabbing him by the throat and sending a punch to the patch of blood on his rib cage. Paul howled in pain.

"You fucking piece of shit. You think it makes you a man to hurt someone smaller than you? To take what doesn't belong to you?"

Paul struggled against him, his face turning red as he struggled for a breath.

"Aaron." Brynn's sweet voice brought his attention back to her.

He dropped Paul like a sack of potatoes, the man yelping as he hit the hard asphalt. Aaron reached out to Brynn and wrapped her in his arms, taking care to be mindful of her injury. She wobbled, unbalanced, but he was there to support her.

"I'm so sorry," he said. *Sorry I wasn't here to protect you. Sorry I lied. Sorry to have caused you pain for even one second.*

Brynn relaxed into his embrace, leaning her head against his chest. She turned away from him, lifting her chin to face the man who'd abused her and stolen so much from her, and then she took her power back like the fucking queen she was.

"You will pay for everything you've done to me and so many others. I won't stop until the truth of what happens at the compound and in that town are shown to the world. You should have left me alone. Should have forgotten I existed, just like I'll forget you."

"You'll never forget me. You were mine first!" Paul sneered, scrambling to his feet.

Blade walked around, shoving him to his knees once again and pushing the barrel of his gun into Paul's temple. Paul flinched.

Brynn shook her head. "I was never yours. I belong to no one." She took a deep breath. "Did you know the body regenerates itself every seven years? That means, seven years from today, you will have never touched a single hair on my head. I will erase every trace of you . . . You have no power over me anymore."

Aaron's chest expanded with warmth. This woman who'd showed up in Shattered Cove as timid as a little mouse was standing up to the man who abused her. He'd tried to drag her back into hell and still she'd fought back.

"You two better get out of here. It's only a matter of time before another car comes along. We have a tow on the way for the wreck, so no one will know what happened," Blade said.

Aaron met the man's eyes—they promised retribution. As

much as Aaron wished he could be the one to dish it out, Brynn needed him more. He nodded.

"Are you taking him to the sheriff?" Brynn asked.

Blade shook his head. "You said yourself there's a lot to expose at this compound place. I think in a few hours, probably less, he'll be mighty talkative, don't you, Ares?"

The man next to Blade smiled. "Definitely. And then Casanova here can use his special skills to take down the whole lot of them."

"You can't take us down. We own the town. The police station. The bank. We have people in government. You can take me in, but I won't tell you a thing. And you'll get a call to let me go. I want my lawyer!" Paul demanded.

The men around them laughed, as if he'd just said the funniest thing in the world.

Ares stepped forward, shoving his gun in Paul's mouth. "You are going to pay for everything you've done to her tenfold. And you're gonna sing like a canary. I suppose there will definitely be some lawyers where you're going. Probably a lot of cops as well, now that I think of it." Ares withdrew his gun and tucked it into his pocket.

Paul's eyes widened as he looked around wildly. "Where are you taking me?"

"To hell," Blade said, stepping forward. He pulled out a knife from his pocket and lowered it to Brynn's wrists, freeing her from the restraints. Blade cast a serious gaze towards Aaron and then to Brynn. "We were never here. You never saw this scumbag. And when you go to the hospital to get checked out, ask for Dr. Burton. He'll treat you without question. Just tell him Blade sent you."

"But I should report this. I didn't last time," Brynn argued.

Blade focused on her. "You could. You can go through the legal system and submit to the process of being photographed and give your statement, hire lawyers. Or . . . you let us handle it. And I *promise* you, he'll never bother anyone ever again. And we'll take down the whole compound you spoke about in exchange for your silence. We'll get the FBI what they need to dismantle the entire thing and bring all those motherfuckers to justice."

"He has a cousin in the FBI," she warned.

Blade nodded. "We'll keep that in mind when we take out the trash."

"Are you going to kill him?" Brynn asked.

Blade's expression was unreadable. "Don't ask me questions you don't want to know the answer to. The less you know, the better."

Brynn wavered on her feet, casting a glance towards Paul. "For Brynna."

Blade didn't even bat an eye at Brynn's words. *Does he know more about Brynn than I thought?*

Blade waved his hand and his men hog-tied Paul, stuffing his mouth and duct-taping it to muffle his screams.

Brynn turned to Aaron. "Am I a horrible person for saying yes to this and not feeling guilty?"

Aaron shook his head. "No, sunshine. You're human." He focused on the men piling into their cars and tossing Paul into the trunk. Blade pulled out his phone and walked towards the crashed Mercedes. Sometimes justice was bloody and outside the law. But Aaron was a big believer that the punishment should fit the crime—especially when it came to people who preyed on children and women.

Brynn melted into his arms, and he held her close, savoring the moment as long as it lasted. Because any moment now, Brynn would send him away again. And it just might kill him this time.

53

BRYNN

Brynn held on to Aaron's arm as he helped her back into his SUV from the hospital. She hadn't let him go since she'd called him away from enacting his revenge. Luckily, she didn't have any serious injuries. The bullet had only grazed her shoulder.

Brynn hadn't said much since the accident site—still in shock of all that had happened. But she wasn't wasting any more time on Paul. She'd forget him, just like she'd promised —or she'd do her very darnedest.

"Mason texted to say Dani wanted to stay the night with them. I thought you'd be fine with that since you don't want her seeing you like this, I'm sure. You need time to come to terms with things on your own I would guess."

Here he was again, taking care of her needs before she could even voice them. "She doesn't know, right?"

He shook his head. "No, and we can't tell her what really happened."

"I was in a car accident. That much is true."

He nodded and closed her door. Her gaze stayed glued to him as he walked around to his side and started the engine.

He drove them out of the parking lot of the hospital, heading back into town. The tension was so thick in the car, she could taste it. How should she start this conversation? Should she just blurt out that she loved him and apologize? No. There was something more important she had to say first.

"Thank you." Her voice came out as a whisper.

He didn't even turn towards her. He'd barely looked at her since they left the crash site. She'd hurt him, deeply, that much was evident. *Have I done too much damage to fix us?*

"I failed you. You have nothing to thank me for." He turned onto Main Street, then pulled into the parking spot in front of the bookstore. He climbed out of the car as soon as the engine cut off, going around to her door. She stumbled out of the SUV, her mind reeling. Her aches had settled into a dull throb thanks to the medication from the doctor.

He pressed his hand to her lower back, guiding her up the stairs on shaky legs and her still-sore ankle. He took the keys from her hand and unlocked the door, ushering her inside. "I know you don't want me here, but I can't leave you alone, not after everything. I'll be down in the car if you need anything. Make sure to set the alarm after me," Aaron instructed, turning to go.

"You didn't fail me," Brynn blurted.

He shook his head, turning back to her. "I should have been there."

"I pushed you away. I told you to go. That wasn't your fault."

"But if I'd told you the truth—"

"I overreacted."

He spun to face her this time.

"You scared me because you made me trust you. That

meant you had the most power to hurt me. I ran away to protect myself," she confessed.

He blinked, as if in disbelief. "I went back on my word to let you pay for the dress. And I omitted the facts about the car sale."

"That was wrong. But I know you had good intentions. You can't do that again in the future. And I can't run or shut down when I get scared. But I'm done letting fear rule my life."

"Future?" His eyes lit up with hope, a complete contrast to the man who'd walked out of the diner hours before. "As in, I'll have another opportunity to fuck up?"

She smiled. "I'm so sorry I said those things to you. You're nothing like Paul. I let my own insecurities and past cloud my judgment . . . Aaron Ridley, I love you with all my heart. And I trust you would never hurt me of your own volition."

"You do?"

She nodded and pulled the globe necklace from under the scrubs the nurses had given her, as her clothes were too stained and wet to save. "You want my truth?"

He nodded. "Yeah."

"You said I deserved the world, but to me, you're my world. You and Dani. Aaron, I love you more than I thought possible. And I trust you with my life. With my child. With my heart. Will you be my husband for real?"

Aaron stepped forward, lifting his hand to cup the uninjured side of her face. "My truth—It's always been real to me, sunshine." His lips gently brushed hers, soft and stirring.

Brynn reached for his coat, shrugging it down his shoulders as she kicked the door closed behind her.

"I love you, too, Brynn. So fucking much," he said as his coat fell to the floor. She shrugged out of her coat and walked forward, grasping his shirt over his heart and kissing him with more force. He backed up as she maneuvered him to the couch. She pushed him gently until he got the hint and sat.

Brynn backed up, crossing her arm to try and pull the hem of her shirt up.

"Brynn? You're hurt. We don't have to—"

"Shh." She winced as she pulled the hem over her head and let the top fall to the ground. "I need to feel you. Need you to take away his touch."

Aaron's gaze fell to the bruise over her cheek, to the fingerprint purple marks on her neck. His jaw clenched.

She reached out her hand to his tense arm, the muscles flexing under her touch. "Hey, I'm safe now."

"I should have taken care of him myself," Aaron gritted.

She tugged her pants down, leaving her naked before him, then straddled his lap. "No, you shouldn't have. You're right where you should be. I need you, here with me. Inside me. Loving me."

His gaze darkened. "I'm going to erase him."

She shook her head. "No more thinking about Paul. He doesn't get to steal anything else from me, including my time with you." Brynn tugged Aaron's shirt. He helped her, pulling it over his head and tossing it on the floor with her clothes.

"I don't have anything to tie you with," Aaron rasped.

"That's okay. I want to try something else. Take your pants off."

She moved to the side so he could take off his bottoms, leaving him naked on the couch. She straddled him once again, rubbing herself on his hard cock as she kissed him.

"I don't want to hurt you." His palm skidded down her spine, grasping her ass to tug her harder over his erection.

She shook her head, her gaze meeting his. "You won't." She believed it with all her heart.

Aaron leaned in, sucking one tight bud into his mouth,

swirling his tongue over her nipple, then sucking as his fingers dove into her pussy. She kissed him, her body already alive and sensitive to his touch.

"I just want you. Need you inside me." Sitting up on her knees, she slipped her hand around his cock and lined it up with her already slick hole.

Aaron groaned. "I need you too."

And maybe that's what a relationship was supposed to look like. Two people who needed each other, but who could also stand on their own two feet. They went to each other because they wanted to, because they could depend on their partner. Because life was better with one another. Not because they couldn't survive without them—a mutual dependence on the other out of choice and trust.

Brynn lowered to her knees, his dick sliding in, as if it was made for her—and perhaps it was. Because Aaron was everything she needed and more. Her imagination couldn't have conjured up a better man.

He rocked his hips gently as she ground down on him. Their bodies moved as one, slick with sweat. Urgency roared. She needed to connect with him, make up for their time apart. The hurt, and the fear. She rode him, holding on to his shoulders while he kissed her. His hands rested firmly on her hips. Even in this position, he was in control. She sucked on his tongue as her pussy crashed down on him. His cock stretched her, reaching deeper the harder she fucked him. Tension coiled, winding her higher and higher with each grind of his hips.

"I love you, sunshine." His voice was harsh and raw against her lips. His exhale became her inhale until even their breaths synced.

"Love you too."

"Look at me, beautiful. Want to see you come." Aaron

dipped his finger to her clit, lighting her up with an explosion of technicolor. She tensed around him, edging onto that cliff.

"Come with me." She kissed him, squeezing tight and fucking him harder and faster.

His thumb swirled over her clit. His other hand cupped her face, smoky amber spheres locked on hers. Everything else slipped away except the sound of skin slapping against skin, panting breaths, and merging moans. The scent of her arousal permeating the room. Pleasure roared as her orgasm charged through her with a force she'd never known. A keening cry left her mouth as stars blasted through her vision.

Aaron's eyes flared, his expression serious as his pupils dilated. His cock pulsed inside her, his arms flexing tight. She was encased in his warmth. His cum filled her. Aftershocks rocked through her trembling limbs. Ecstasy pooled in her womb, curling out into warm wisps of pleasure saturating every cell. Nothing separated them anymore.

"You saved me, sunshine."

Brynn's brows drew together.

Aaron gently grazed his finger down her cheek. "Without you, my life was nice, but now, I'm happier than I ever knew possible. Together, we can do anything."

"We saved each other." She leaned forward and kissed him.

"You're so fucking strong and amazing. I feel so lucky I get to be your husband."

She smiled dreamily. "And I'm happy I get to be your wife."

"Do you want to get married again? Have another ceremony?"

She shook her head and climbed off him, snuggling into his arm as she faced him. "I meant every word I said at our wedding."

"I did too."

"I'd like to add to it though. Aaron Ridley?"

"Yes?"

"I promise to love you with all my heart. To put your needs as my priority. To communicate with you even when I don't want to. To honor and cherish every moment we have. And I vow to obey and submit to you—"

His eyes widened.

She smiled. "But only in the bedroom."

His deep chuckle rumbled in his chest. "I can get behind that."

"What about you? Do you have anything to add?" Her hand rested against his heart.

His thumb traced her jaw. "All that I am is yours. I will be your protector, your lover, your friend, and the best damn husband I can. And I promise to give you all my truths."

He kissed her slowly, taking his time, as if he had all the hours in the world. Sensual brushes of his tongue released an electric sensation cascading through her body, igniting the need within her again.

Aaron pulled back, adding a chaste kiss to her nose and then forehead. "You're my forever."

The dam in Brynn's heart exploded with warm gratitude and glowing joy. As her husband rolled on top of her, she parted her thighs, welcoming him in. He slid inside her, rocking as he whispered his vows over and over again. It was impossible to get enough of this feeling. Unbound bliss. All-encompassing love. Transcendental euphoria. Not in a million years would she believe this could be hers to experience. But it was. And she was never letting go.

EPILOGUE - BRYNN
SIX MONTHS LATER

Brynn walked into the heart of Shattered Cove—Green Park. A warm summer breeze blew over her skin, making her green backless sundress billow in the wind. Aaron's palm rested on her lower waist, right over her healed tattoo. Branches adorned her back covering her scars with empty cocoons hanging from them. Three vibrant butterflies flitted above them: one for her sister, Dani, and herself, signifying her freedom. Cleo had done an amazing job that far exceeded Brynn's expectations, and now she proudly carried not only a piece of her sister wherever she went, but every time she looked at her reflection, she'd be reminded that all the pain she'd been through had brought her to this place where she was loved, safe, and free.

Aaron ushered her forward past the giant rainbow flags and underneath the red, black, and green Juneteenth banner and a few Loving Day signs. There was so much to celebrate in the month of June. The scent of grilled meat, fried foods, and summer filled her nose.

Dani skipped ahead of them, waving towards Aspen who

sat on a picnic blanket with Pippa, Mason, and their twins, eagerly pulling on their parents' shirts to stand on their wobbly little legs.

"I'm gonna go say hi to Aspen," Dani announced as she widened the gap between them.

"What about you, sunshine? Do you want to set up our picnic blanket and rest while I make my rounds, or come with?" Aaron asked, lifting the basket in his hand.

"Let's put this down somewhere and I'll go with you."

He leaned in and kissed her softly on the lips. "Thank you."

"For what?"

"For just being you. And for being patient. I know mingling with people isn't your favorite thing." They walked towards the gazebo where a local band were finishing setting up their instruments.

"No, it isn't. But you have an important reason to do it—keeping Hope a part of the community, garnering support, and giving these kids a chosen family." Brynn motioned to the teens decked out in rainbow shirts with Hope Facility printed on them.

His hand moved from her lower back to her shoulder, pulling her tighter against his side. "And now I don't have to do it alone."

"Look, there's your parents." Brynn pointed to the red checkered blanket underneath a giant maple tree and waved.

Iris beamed and tapped her husband's shoulder, and they both stood, clad in T-shirts that read, *"I love my transgender granddaughter."* Brynn's eyes stung as a wave of gratitude washed over her.

"Hey, sweetie." Iris held out her arms and hugged Brynn and then Aaron. Samuel shook hands with Aaron and nodded hello to Brynn.

"I figured you'd be by a little later," Aaron said.

His dad shrugged. "We were up early anyways. Thought we'd come and lend a hand setting up and make sure these Northerners know how to properly throw a Juneteenth barbecue."

Brynn didn't miss the surprise that filtered into Aaron's gaze before he smiled. He and his parents' relationship was getting better.

"I love your shirts." Brynn grinned.

Iris's eyes sparkled. "Well, we wanted Danielle to know we support her, and what better time to do it than for Pride month?"

"Thank you."

"Hey, do you mind watching our basket while we make our rounds?" Aaron handed the picnic ensemble to his father.

Samuel took it. "No problem."

"We'll be back," Aaron announced, slipping his hand in Brynn's and leading her towards the gazebo.

Emma, lead singer of The Siren's, greeted them with a smile. Her red lipstick matched her red-tipped blond hair. Link, the mechanic of Shattered Cove, had his arm draped around her.

"Hey, man." Link reached out and bumped fists with Aaron.

"Hey, how's it going?" Aaron asked.

"Perfect now that I got my wife home for a couple months." Link smiled over at Emma, looking at her like she hung the moon.

Emma laughed. "It's good to be back."

"We're gonna have a cookout on the beach two weekends from now," Aaron said. "You guys up for it?"

Link turned to Emma. "What do you think, little bird?"

Emma's eyes brightened. "I think that sounds like fun."

"We're ready, Em," one of her bandmates called.

"Guess that's our cue. Nice to see you again, Brynn. I'm sure we'll catch up at book club."

"That sounds wonderful. Pippa is hosting this month," Brynn answered.

"See you Friday." Emma waved, and Link gave Aaron a nod before they climbed the stairs to the gazebo, taking care over the black cords to all manner of instruments on the ground.

"I think I should start a book club for the guys. What do you think?" Aaron asked, sliding his fingers between hers as he led her towards the picnic tables.

"You mean to read romance novels?"

Aaron shrugged. "Yeah, why not? I mean it doesn't always have to be, but there are some pretty awesome things a man can learn between the pages of a book written by a woman about women's wants, needs, desires, and thoughts."

She grinned. "I would agree with you there."

"Hey, I read that chapter you marked for me." He lowered his voice, leaning in to her ear. "Give me a few days to get the supplies we need, and we can try out that fantasy of yours, okay?"

She shivered, her belly doing a summersault. "I can't wait."

"And I signed us up for that class about BDSM. We now have access to the videos. We can start watching tonight if you're up for it?"

She flicked her gaze towards her husband, the man who loved her so unconditionally. Aaron was the perfect lover, her partner in all aspects, and she couldn't be happier. "Absolutely."

"What the hell do you think you're doing?" a loud voice boomed from behind them.

Brynn spun around. Local fisherman, Nash Emerson, was staring daggers at a woman Brynn didn't recognize sitting in the dunk tank.

The woman crossed her arms and leveled him with an equally hard glare. "What I do is none of your business."

"The hell it isn't!" Nash yanked open the door to the back of the booth before he wrapped a burly arm around the woman and pulled her out. The woman's face flushed as anger burned in her brown eyes.

"*Bájame, cabrón!*" she cried.

"Shouldn't we do something?" Brynn asked Aaron. Would Nash hurt her?

"Why can't you just listen to me?" Nash growled.

The woman stood straight, shoving him away, tipping her chin in defiance. "Why can't you stay away from me?"

"Pretty hard to do when you're living with my sister and carrying my goddamned baby!" Nash's chest heaved, his nostrils flaring before he cast a glance around him, as if just realizing they'd garnered an audience.

"Well, that explains a lot," Nova Emerson said, appearing at Brynn's side. She marched forward, took the woman's arm that her brother had been yelling at, then disappeared around the corner. Nash wiped a hand over his face and shook his head, as if lost.

"And I thought the fireworks tonight were going to be the highlight of entertainment." Aaron chuckled. "I better check on Nash. Give me a sec?"

Brynn nodded. "Of course."

Aaron kissed her cheek, then walked across the path to his acquaintance.

Brynn spun around, looking for something to occupy her time with. Blade and his men sat around an airbrush tattoo table offering free artwork for the kids. He caught her gaze and gave her a nod.

Brynn smiled and waved. She'd never asked what became of Paul. But two months after everything happened, the FBI raided the compound she'd grown up in. It was all over the news. The leaders were charged with everything from embezzlement and insider trading to child neglect and abuse. The Pirates had kept their promise, and she had every intention of doing the same.

Aaron's warm palm slid to her waist. "Ready to keep going?"

She leaned into him. "Yeah. Is Nash okay?"

Aaron shrugged. "He's not really a talker. I let him know if he needs anything, I'm here."

"You're a good man—the best."

Aaron led her towards the picnic area and kissed her temple. "I do what I can, but my wife? She's the real heroine of this story."

"I don't know about that."

"Why?" They walked under the shade of a few oak trees.

"Because she wouldn't be where she is without the patience, love, and understanding of her amazing husband." A giggle slipped free.

"I think you would have found your way. You just needed a safe place to land, and someone who listened and ordered you to take up space and disagree with them."

She laughed again, and this time Aaron joined her.

"Hey, you two newlyweds!" Mikel called out, standing from the picnic table next to his seven-year-old son, Phoenix, who was busy reading a book out loud while his cousin Zoey drew pictures next to him.

Remy spun around, then set a plate in front of their daughter, Lyra. "Brynn! How are you?"

"I'm great. And you?" Brynn gave her a hug as the rest of their friends got up from their seats around the two picnic tables pushed together. Their family was so big now that they even had a few blankets set out where Bently and Belle's foster teens sat, happily chatting and snacking.

Remy pushed her braids behind her shoulder. "I'm just trying to come to terms with the fact that next month I'll officially have a teenager." She motioned to Lyra on the blanket with Bently and Belle's adopted daughter, Amara, with her friend, Lyric. The boy couldn't keep his eyes off her, suggesting he might have more than friendly feelings towards her.

"Honestly, I take it one day at a time," Brynn replied.

"Everything all set for the fireworks later?" Aaron asked Bently.

Bently wound his arm around Belle's shoulders. "Yup. Fire department will start setting up in a couple hours."

Atlas, and Finn joined them, their conversation droning in the background as their wives greeted Brynn.

Mia and Andre, two more of their friends, joined them, their three-year-old daughter and five-year-old son charging ahead.

"*Buenas tardes!*" Mia cried. "You guys have done a wonderful job this year with the Juneteenth event."

"I barely had anything to do with it." Brynn shrugged as Andre picked up his son and threw him high into the air before catching the giggling boy.

"We both know that isn't true." Jasmine smirked, brushing a crumb off her toddler son Hart's cheek before he snuggled shyly into Atlas's arms.

"You and Aaron make a great team," Belle added.

"I like to think so." Brynn cast a quick glance at her husband, his broad shoulders showing off his salmon-colored

T-shirt that stretched over his muscular torso. The bright color contrasted with his warm brown complexion.

"I know that look," Charli teased, drawing Brynn's attention away from her handsome husband.

"What look?" Brynn asked.

The ladies laughed together.

"The same look that got me pregnant again." Charli sipped her cup of lemonade.

"You're pregnant?" Brynn asked.

"Congratulations!" Remy said, the other ladies joining in.

"About time you caught up." Mikel clapped Finn on the shoulder.

Finn beamed. "Yeah, now that Jamison is three, we figured we were ready for one more. The doctor cleared Charli, so we decided to give it a go."

"If only my husband would let me out of his sight for more than five minutes now." Charli's mouth turned up into a teasing smile.

Finn shook his head. "Not gonna happen, Charli baby. Not after what happened last time."

Charli pressed her hand over her husband's heart before she stood on tiptoes and kissed him. "I'll be much less stressed this go around, and no one is trying to kill me, so I think we'll be okay."

A low growl came from Finn. "You bet your pretty ass you will. Because I'm not leaving you alone."

Brynn stifled a giggle as she turned towards her in-laws across the park. Sometimes blood family caused hurt. Especially when they only loved and accepted a version of you that didn't even exist. Love with control wasn't real love. The truest love came with acceptance and the freedom to be your true self.

Dani approached her grandparents, motioning to their

shirts, a bright smile on her face. Sometimes those people could learn and do better. It wasn't always the family you were born into that would love you the hardest, but the family you chose.

She returned her attention to the circle of friends around her. This was Brynn's family.

Each couple balanced each other out. The men all looked upon their wives with the same worshipping look Aaron pointed at her. And Brynn knew from the book club meetings that their wives were more than satisfied in every area of their marriages.

None of them had had it easy, but they'd all gotten their happily ever afters.

Some people thought that the end of a story was when the couple said *"I do"* and then they rode off into the sunset. But really, the moment when Brynn stood before Aaron and made her vows wasn't the end, but the beginning of a story they'd write every single day by choosing each other, by connecting and sharing experiences. Chapter by chapter, they'd weave a story unique to them. When the tough times came, they'd thread their fingers together and hold on as they faced the challenges together. Their lives would mingle as their souls had until nothing lay between them but hope for a brighter tomorrow.

The Beginning . . .

Thank you! We hope you enjoyed reading *Hope Between Us*.

Do you want more of Aaron and Brynn? Visit the website

below to join our newsletter and get an exclusive bonus steamy scene 5 years into their future.

WWW.AMKUSI.COM/HBUBONUS

You can also turn the page for a sneak peek of Chapter One for Book 1 of The Emerson Family of Shattered Cove series, ***Stepping Into Tomorrow*** (featuring Nash and Isabella's story).

Or visit the website below to order Book 1 in The Emerson Family of Shattered Cove Series right now.

WWW.AMKUSI.COM/ STEPPINGINTOTOMORROW

SNEAK PEEK OF STEPPING INTO TOMORROW

CHAPTER 1

Isabella

Inhaling a shaky breath, Isabella cupped some of the cool water from under the tap and splashed it to the back of her neck. The icy water grounded her. She would have put it on her cheeks, but for the first time in years she'd actually done her makeup and dressed up—except for Robert's funeral. But that was six months ago.

Isabella dried her hands quickly and left the bathroom, her gaze sweeping over the tent bustling with wedding activity under the soft Edison bulb lighting.

"Whiskey, double," a deep bass voice said over the upbeat music playing through the venue to her right. His shoulders hunched over as he sat at the bar, so only one side was visible to her.

Tingles spiraled over her skull. Her lungs seized. Tufts of wild curls stuck out of the top of his hair, like the wild break of a crashing wave. Sharp cheekbones slanted towards a wide, strong nose. Serious thick, eyebrows slanted together with a permanent crease between them as if he perpetually frowned.

He ran a massive hand over his neatly trimmed beard. His wide shoulders flexed as he moved to accept the drink the bartender slid across to him. Two long, thick umber fingers wrapped around the glass before he tipped it to his full brown lips, his pink tongue darting out as if savoring every drop. The move shouldn't have been sexy, but Isabella's blood turned molten just the same.

Her gaze roamed up his veined forearms to the white dress shirt rolled up at his elbows and farther to the material stretched taut across his broad shoulders, tapering in at his waist. Black dress pants wrapped around his thick thighs. The man looked as if Poseidon himself had crafted him from the depths of the sea in his image.

Isabella tried to swallow, but her mouth had gone dry. *Wow.*

Someone bumped into her, drawing her out of her-lust induced daze.

"Sorry," they apologized.

She shook her head, forcing herself towards the table with her waiting friends. She'd never been affected that way by someone—had her very breath stolen and held captive.

Isabella weaved around a few people, grabbing a fresh glass of champagne from a passing server, eyes zoned in on the table she'd been assigned with her close friend, Tessa.

"Did you get cake yet?" She flopped into the seat next to Tessa before taking a gulp of the bubbly beverage.

"Not yet."

"*Dios*, there was a long line to use the restroom."

Tessa chuckled. "Isn't there always?"

"True."

"How is it being back in your hometown?" Tessa asked, picking up her glass and taking a sip.

Isabella sighed. "Honestly, it's good to be back. I feel like I've made the right decision. Eli is having a blast with his grandparents. I think it will be good for him—for us."

Tessa's eyes flashed with sympathy. "So you're gonna go with one of the apartments we looked at this weekend?"

Isabella shook her head. "No, I'll move back in with Mom and Dad and see what I can find later. I think they need more help at the marina than they're letting on, and it's not like I have much to occupy my time with right now anyways."

Tessa gasped. "Now? I thought you weren't leaving me until the end of May. I'm supposed to get another month with you at the shop."

Isabella pulled her into a hug, not sure how she'd be able to start over without her one constant—her best friend. "I don't mean right now. I'm sticking around for a little while. Same plan. I still have to finish going through Robert's things." Her eyes stung with the reminder.

Tessa took Isabella's hand in hers. "Do you need help?"

Isabella shook her head. "No. We had most of it done before things got too bad—as he insisted. But it's the second last thing on his list for me to do."

A list Robert had compiled before his ALS got too bad for her to complete after he passed. Even in death, he was trying to take care of her.

"What's the last item?"

Isabella's cheeks flushed. "To move on with someone new . . . actually, he specifically said a one-night stand."

Tessa's eyes widened. "Seriously? That sounds like Robert. He wanted you to be happy."

Isabella nodded, a soft smile turning her lips up as memories of the man who was once her best friend flitted through her mind.

"Do you think you're ready for that?" Tessa asked, her voice soft and free of judgment. If anyone knew how to seize the day, it was Tessa.

Her reaction to the stranger at the bar was still thrumming through her veins. "I . . . do. For something fun—definitely not something serious. A one-night stand . . . well, that has potential." *Not that I've ever had one.* But maybe the new Isabella could do it. The Isabella who was moving half way across the country. She lifted her drink to her lips.

"A wedding is the perfect place to find that." Tessa scanned the room. "Anyone caught your eye?"

Isabella pressed a cool hand to one of her flushed cheeks. "I did see a man by the bar when I went to the bathrooms. He was alone and . . . I don't know, he looked . . . well, hotter than Hades, actually." *And just as mysterious too.*

Tessa's attention focused on the bar. "Him?"

Bella turned to look in the same direction, her attention catching on the man in question. *What made him so withdrawn at a wedding?* "Yeah. There's just something about him . . ." The people around him gave him a wide berth, as if afraid whatever weight he carried on those broad shoulders would rub off on them.

"Go for it," Tessa encouraged.

Isabella spun back to her, chewing on her bottom lip. "I don't know. It's been so long since I had to do something like this."

"You don't have to have sex with the guy if you don't want. But at least try and talk to him. Ease yourself into it," Tessa pushed.

Am I really ready for this? It's just a conversation, right? Just one small step into the new me. And the new Isabella is confident. Fake it 'til you make it, right? "If I do, will you finally ask Roy about doing that tattoo you've wanted?"

Panic flashed through her friend's gaze before she turned her attention to the very man they were speaking of. He wasn't hard to find with his blue-tipped hair and several face piercings. He was down on bent knee speaking to a little boy —Joshua, the bride's son.

"I—"

"Come on. What are you so worried about?" Tessa and Roy had been dancing around each other for so long. One of her last best friend duties would be giving her friend the little push she needed to reveal her secret to the perfect man for her.

"You ask him for the tattoo and I'll go talk to the man at the bar. Deal?" Bella asked, holding out her pinky finger, trying to act like the idea didn't terrify her.

"Deal." Tessa hooked her pinky finger in Bella's.

"What are you two trouble-makers up to now?" Roy's voice lilted with his Irish accent. Isabella smiled to herself as her best friend tried to act like she wasn't effected by the man, but her shiver gave her away.

"Cold?" he asked Tessa.

"A little." She reached for her sweater, but he'd already picked it up off the chair and held it out for her arms, anticipating her needs.

Isabella wanted someone to do that for her. To have a man look at her like she was the sun and moon as Roy did to Tessa. She hadn't found it with Robert, but maybe someday she would.

But she'd learned her lesson. Though Robert was a great man, and best friend, he was not her person. She'd never settle for less again. The next time she agreed to marry a man, it would be because she'd found the kind of love that she'd only read about in books or witnessed in a few lucky friends.

"Well, wish me luck." Bella stood, smoothing her glittering gold dress over her plentiful curves. "I'm so nervous."

"'Bout what?" Roy asked.

"Stepping into tomorrow." Isabella sighed. Using the phrase her and Robert had shared bolstered her confidence.

"Do I look okay?" Bella plucked the fabric from her belly and rolled her shoulders back.

"You look grand," Roy assured her.

Bella smiled and turned to Tessa, nodding towards Roy. "Well?"

"Well, what?" Roy asked.

Isabella cut her friend a warning look. They'd made a deal, after all.

Tessa stood abruptly. "I wanted to know if you'd dance with me?"

"Of course. That'd make me right delira."

Tessa's eyebrows drew together. "Delira?"

He smiled. "Deliriously happy, as you Americans say."

Isabella laughed.

Tessa slipped her hand in Roy's before focusing on Isabella. "A deal's a deal. Get your cute ass over there and say hello."

Nerves swirled in Isabella's stomach. She bit her lip and nodded. Her chest rose as she took one last deep breath. "Don't wait up for me." She spun round and walked towards the bar with her head held high.

Legs trembling, Isabella moved to the empty seat next to the intimidating man. The energy around him shifted as she got closer like he was a black hole, ready to swallow up anything and anyone around him. A slow song drifted through the speakers as the bartender moved to the opposite end of the drinks station, filling orders. *I should have downed my champagne before coming over.*

She turned to her right, putting on her friendliest smile. "So, are you here for the groom or the bride?"

It wasn't the best ice-breaker, but she thought she'd at least get a response. Instead, awkward silence pressed between them like stagnant air.

Her belly squeezed. His only reaction was a small tightening of his shoulders as if he could make himself smaller and stay invisible. The thought was ludicrous, not just because of his sheer size, but because he was so handsome. Something about him made her want to crack him open and see what laid inside.

"What can I get you?" the bartender asked, wiping down the space in front of her.

"Tequila please."

He got to work, filling a shot glass and plating a lime for her before setting the salt shaker beside her drink in front of her.

"Are you from here?" the bartender asked. At least someone was talking to her.

She sipped the tequila, savoring the flavor on her tongue. " I flew in from Colorado."

His eyes widened with interest. "That's cool. Always wanted to go skiing there."

"You should do it then."

"Someday." He smiled before moving to the other end to help another guest.

Isabella took another sip of her drink before picking up the salt and shaking it over the lime wedge. She set down the shaker and retrieved her drink, savoring another small sip before sucking on the end of the salty fruit. A burst of citrus flooded her mouth, the tang mixed with the salt and liquor warming her.

"I believe the salt is supposed to come before the liquor, then the lime." The mystery man's voice was as deep and rich as the whiskey he drank.

She turned to him, her breath stuttering. "So he speaks."

The corner of his lips twitched before they flattened back into a thin line. He grunted.

"You here for the groom or the bride?"

A small puff of air left his nose, a subtle scoff. "Not too many here for the bride. She has a history with the town. The fact that you don't know that makes me think you're a plus one."

"Subtle."

"Hmm?"

"Trying to see if I'm here alone and single?" she added, just a little bit hopeful.

"Was I right?" He fingered his glass, swirling the last sip of amber liquor.

"My friend Roy is Maddy's cousin. I came with him and my best friend, Tessa." She turned, focusing on the very couple mentioned on the dance floor dancing close.

Roy solely focused on Tessa. She gave them a quick wave and smiled, hoping to encourage her friend.

"Third wheel, huh?" the man asked.

She shrugged. "I'm used to it."

Isabella turned away from the couples moving on the dance floor to the man next to her and gasped. Two dark eyes stared at her, fathomless and magnetic. Something akin to sympathy flashed in his gaze before it was gone, hiding behind the shadows of secrets kept in those eclipsed orbs. She recognized the pain though—this man was grieving. That was the weight he carried.

Her lungs strained with the need to breathe. Isabella sucked in a ragged breath, her heart racing.

"I made a deal with my friend that she would do something she'd been too scared to do, and so would I."

His eyes flashed as he leaned in closer. The whiskey scent on his breath wrapped around her like silk ties binding her in place.

"What is it you had to do?" He cocked his head to the side.

"I had to come talk to you."

He grunted, but still, his attention burned her flesh. His focus lazily roamed over her figure before returning to her face. His expression was stoic, but those eyes gave him away. Lust flickered like a flame as his pupils dilated.

"Why do I scare you?" he asked.

"You don't. Not like that. Just talking to a man, putting myself out there for the first time." Heat burned her skin. *Good Lord. Would he think I mean I'm a virgin?* The liquor loosening her tongue. "First time in a long time, I mean."

"So why do it at all?" he pressed.

She sighed. "Because sometimes, to move forward you have to do something scary and uncomfortable. And I need to do something different. Because what I've been doing has led me to a place I don't want to be anymore."

He blinked as if she'd surprised him. Silence passed as the wedding guests laughed and spoke around them. It was as if they were in their own little bubble, separate from everyone else. She was held in the trance of his perceptive gaze.

Maybe it was the mixture of champagne and tequila. Or maybe it was the fact that after today, she'd most likely never see this man again. But for once, her inhibitions were lowered. What did she have to lose?

"I'm ready to get out of here." She left the invitation hanging in the air, hoping he'd make a move.

His jaw tensed, his eyes clouding over as if fighting a war with himself—to accept her invitation or not.

She was already committed to this—what was one more step? One last try? If she'd learned anything in the last twelve years, it was that her pride could take a hit and she'd survive. Still, her stomach tipped and her hands grew clammy with sweat as she readied herself to ask the question. *Here goes nothing.* "You want to join me?"

To continue reading Nash and Isabella's story, visit the website below to get your copy of *Stepping Into Tomorrow* today.

**WWW.AMKUSI.COM/
STEPPINGINTOTOMORROW**

ACKNOWLEDGMENTS

Putting together this book—this whole series, really—has taken a team. From the inception of Shattered Cove, we knew we wanted to dive deeper into how trauma affects people differently. And how finding a happy, healthy, and healing future with the right loving person is possible. How survivors can carve out a future not dependent of repeating the same cycle as their past. Why? Because it happened for us. And we believe others like us deserve hope too.

We want to extend a special thank-you to Cindy Madsen, for your help and insight into what it is like to be a parent of a trans teenager, and what that process looked like for you. Thank you for sharing some insight into your beautiful journey with us.

To our sensitivity editors Renita and Curtis, proofreader Judy, and every beta reader we've had that shared your culture, your disability, and honest feedback to help bring The Shattered Cove Series to life, thank you!

Our ARC readers, you guys rock! We enjoy our release week chats and hearing your feedback, and just how much YOU love our characters as much as we do.

To our cover designer Regina, thank you for your artistic designs and help bringing our vision to life.

To our readers. You are the reason we're able to do what we do and provide you with steamy, diverse, and emotional stories that rip your heart out and put it back together just a little different than before. Thank you for your support buying our books and leaving reviews.

To Dani and everyone at Wildfire Marketing, thank you for all you do to get the word out about The Shattered Cove Series.

To Lauren and her team at CREATING ink, thank you for making these stories amazing.

And finally, to our daughters, Ellyson and Emelynn, thank you for being so patient when Mama has to meet deadlines and locks herself into the office all day.

JOIN OUR NEWSLETTER

The best way to get updates about new releases, sneak peeks, pre-orders, giveaways, and more is by joining our newsletter.

You'll also receive a FREE short novel that's not available on any retailer to read.

Visit the website below to join now.

WWW.AMKUSI.COM/NEWSLETTER

Inn Romance Series, make sure you get your copy so you don't miss out on three wonderful love stories.

Thank you again for reading *Hope Between Us!*

Cheers,

Ash & Marcus

ABOUT A. M. KUSI

A. M. Kusi is the pen name of a wife-and-husband team, Ash and Marcus Kusi. We enjoy writing emotional romance novels that are inspired by our experiences as an interracial/multicultural couple.

Our novels are about strong women and the sexy heroes they fall in love with, are emotionally satisfying, and always have a happy ending.

Discover more about us at:

WWW.AMKUSI.COM

To receive updates about new releases, preorders, giveaways, and more, visit the website below to join our newsletter today:

WWW.AMKUSI.COM/NEWSLETTER

After you join the newsletter, we will send you a FREE story to read.

To contact us, use this email address: amkusinovels@gmail.com

Happy reading!

Ash and Marcus

tiktok.com/@amkusi.romanceauthor

instagram.com/amkusinovels

facebook.com/amkusi

pinterest.com/amkusinovels

ALSO BY A. M. KUSI

Choose your next read from these series and standalone novels today.

A Fallen Star (eBook FREE on all retailers)

(Book 1 in The Shattered Cove Series)

Glass Secrets

(Book 2 in The Shattered Cove Series)

Defying Gravity

(Book 3 in The Shattered Cove Series)

The Lighthouse Inn

(Book 4 in The Shattered Cove series)

His True North

(Book 5 in The Shattered Cove series)

In The Grey

(Book 6 in The Shattered Cove series)

Brave Love

(Book 7 in The Shattered Cove series)

Beautiful Collision

(A Shattered Cove Novel)

One Holiday Kiss (eBook FREE on all retailers)

(A Shattered Cove Short Story)

The Orchard Inn

(Book 1 in The Orchard Inn Romance Series)

Conflict of Interest

(Book 2 in The Orchard Inn Romance Series)

Her Perfect Storm

(Book 3 in The Orchard Inn Romance Series)

For a complete list of all our books, visit:

WWW.AMKUSI.COM/BOOKS